The North Doesn't Speak

Clifton Wilcox

Fredericksburg, Virginia

Print ISBN: 978-1-969770-51-7

EBook ISBN: 978-1-969770-50-0

Published by Windward Publishing LLC., Fredericksburg, Virginia.

The characters and events in this book are fictitious. Any similarity to real persons, living or dead, is coincidental and not intended by the author.

Wilcox, Clifton

The North Doesn't Speak

Windward Publishing, LLC

2026

Dedication

"They taught me silence to keep me small.
They taught me obedience so I would forget how to choose.

I learned both well enough to survive—
and just poorly enough to remember.

This is for those who were watched, measured, and underestimated...
for those who learned to speak without moving their lips,
to plan without leaving a trace,
to wait without surrendering.

They believed we were quiet.

They never asked what we were learning in it."

—Lila Carter

March 30, 1861

Table of Contents

Books by Clifton Wilcox

Fiction

Cool's Last Stand

Where Despair Comes to Play

The Monuments Must Bleed

Keeper of the Fallen Ages

I, Monster

Harvest of Eyes

The Case Against Jasper

Crimson Plume: The Song of Corvus

Framed in Love

Echoes of the Forgotten

Blacktop Harvest

The Plagiarist Game

The Black Forest Protocol

Outcome without Appeal

Deliberation

The Lore Hunter: Brown Mountain

Pact of Shadows: The Black Orchard

The Black Ledger of Salem

The Four That Bind

The Last Star

The Lore Hunter: Devils Highway

Every Cough Was a Crime

Chapter 1

Prologue – The Mark

He did not remember deciding to run. He remembered the moment before it, the way his breath had already changed as if his body had reached a conclusion without him. The decision was a door that had opened in the dark, and once it opened, it did not close again.

The night offered no light worth trusting. The moon was there, he thought, because the air held a pale suggestion of silver, but it did not lay itself across the earth the way it was supposed to. It stayed behind something, veiled and stingy, turning the world into a smear of blacks and charcoals. He could see only in pieces: the flash of a branch's pale underside as it whipped past, the sudden white eye of a stone in the path, the faint glimmer of water when he crossed a shallow run.

He ran anyway. He ran like the ground might take him back if he stopped.

Leaves snagged his ankles. Vines grabbed at his calves with a patience that felt deliberate. His feet found roots and holes, each misstep threatening to twist bone or tear skin, but pain had become a small thing beside the larger terror of being caught. Pain was familiar. It could be endured. The other thing could not.

Behind him, there had been dogs.

At first, when he crossed the last fence line and the last strip of tended land gave way to the wild, he had heard them plainly. Their voices were a chorus that rose and fell like a single animal breathing. The sound carried in the night, too clean to be mistaken for anything else. He knew those dogs. He had fed them scraps when the men in charge were too busy to notice. He had watched them strain at their chains, eager for the work they were trained to love.

He had not thought his heart could beat harder than it did when the first bark cut through the air.

Now the barking was farther back, swallowed and blurred by trees. It came and went depending on how the wind shifted. When it faded, it left a worse kind of quiet behind it, a quiet that made room for thoughts.

North, he told himself.

The word had never been given to him as a promise. It was not spoken the way people spoke of heaven. It was spoken like a direction whispered over a shoulder, quick as a breath, as if the very sound might be overheard by something listening. North. Sometimes it came dressed in other words: up, away, beyond. Sometimes it came in gestures, a tilt of a chin toward the horizon, a look held a second too long. North was not a place so much as a refusal.

He did not know where it was. He did not know who lived there. He did not know what waited if he reached it. He only knew that the word existed, and the existence of the word meant someone had gone far enough to need it.

He had taken it into his mouth in the last week, turning it silently the way a man might turn a coin he did not yet own. He had felt it on his tongue when he lifted sacks of feed, when he dragged water, when he stood in line and listened to the night insects sing their endless song. North. The word became a small heat in the center of him, dangerous and stubborn.

That heat was what moved him now, driving him through briars that tore at his shirt, leaving threads behind like evidence. His lungs burned. His throat was raw from breathing so hard. Every time his foot struck the earth, the sound felt like a shout. He tried to place his steps the way he had been taught to work quietly in the master's house when he was younger, back when he was loaned out sometimes to carry trays and keep his eyes down. That skill did not belong to him tonight. Tonight he was a pounding thing, a frightened animal.

The woods thickened. The trees crowded closer, trunks like pillars holding up a roof that blocked what little moon there was. The smell changed. The air tasted damp, heavy with rot and sap. He tasted iron, too, though he did not know if it came from blood in his mouth where he'd bitten his tongue, or from fear itself.

He had planned nothing beyond movement. There had been no map, no mark on a page, no sign carved into a fencepost. Planning required time and tools and the kind of calm that was never allowed to last. He had only stolen small things, not items that would be missed quickly. A strip of cloth. A crust of bread hidden in his sleeve until it turned warm and soft. A piece of twine. Not enough to live, only enough to pretend he could.

He had told no one.

He could not bear the thought of seeing another face change when he whispered what he meant to do. Some people would have begged him not to go. Some would have asked to come. Some would have looked at him as if he'd already died. All of them would have carried the knowledge, and knowledge was never safe. It traveled in bodies, in flinches, in the ways eyes avoided certain directions. It traveled to the wrong ears. It traveled to men who had learned how to listen without seeming to.

He ran with his secret sealed behind his teeth until his jaw ached from the pressure of holding it.

A low branch struck his cheek, hard enough to make his eyes water. He did not stop. Tears ran into the corner of his mouth, tasting of salt and dirt. The world tilted for a moment as his foot slid on wet leaves, and his shoulder slammed into a tree. Stars burst behind his eyes, bright as sparks off a forge. He thought of the blacksmith on the plantation, the way metal screamed when it met the hammer. He wondered, absurdly, if his own bones would sound like that if he hit the ground wrong.

Keep moving, he told himself. Keep moving north.

But how did you move north when the sky refused to guide you? He lifted his gaze, searching for the dipper he'd heard about, the one that supposedly pointed the way. The clouds were thick. The stars were stingy, blinking through gaps like eyes that did not want to watch. He tried to feel direction in his skin, the way some animals could.

All he felt was his sweat cooling on his back and the itch of bites blooming along his neck.

He changed course anyway, trusting his instincts as if they were a compass. He angled toward higher ground, thinking distance would help, thinking the dogs would struggle in thicker brush. He thought the farther he ran, the thinner the world behind him would become, like smoke unraveling.

For a few minutes, he let himself believe it.

The barking vanished entirely. In its place there was only the sound of his own passage: the rasp of his breath, the slap of his feet, the frantic whisper of leaves against his legs. The silence that followed was so complete it made him slow despite himself. The quiet felt staged, as if the night were holding its breath.

He stopped for the first time since leaving the fields. Not fully, not safely, but enough to crouch behind the wide base of a pine and press his palm to his mouth. His chest heaved. His heart thudded against his ribs as if trying to break out and run without him. He listened.

Nothing. No dogs. No shouting. No crack of branches announcing men pushing through the undergrowth. Only the distant, constant sound of insects and the faraway murmur of water.

He closed his eyes. In the darkness behind his lids, he saw the yard as it would look at dawn. The fence line. The empty spot where he'd been assigned to stand. The overseer's face when the count came up short. He imagined the calm before anger. He imagined how quickly calm could turn.

He forced the images away.

North, he thought again, and this time it was not a direction. It was a prayer.

He moved on, slower now, placing his feet with care. He tried to keep to low ground where his silhouette would not break against the skyline, but the terrain fought him. The woods had their own rules. The path that seemed easy was often the one that led into brambles or mud. He found himself skirting a patch of standing water, the smell rising foul and sweet. Mosquitoes swarmed around his ears. He slapped at them and kept going.

He realized he was shaking. Not from cold, though the sweat on him chilled when the wind slipped through the trees, but from the strain of holding himself together. Running had been simple. Running had been one demand. Now there was thinking. Now there were choices. Choices were dangerous.

He passed a fallen log and stepped over it, then paused when he saw what lay on the other side: a scrap of cloth caught on a thorn, fluttering slightly in the breeze. It might have been there for days, left by any traveler, but his mind seized it as a sign, because the mind loved signs when it was desperate. He reached out and touched it with two fingers. The cloth was damp. Cold. Ordinary.

He left it and kept moving.

After a time, he could not measure, his breath began to settle into a rhythm. His legs still burned, but the pain dulled into something steady, something he could carry. He began to think again in fragments. He wondered if there would be a road ahead, and if roads were worse than woods. Roads meant people. People meant questions. He wondered if the North had woods like these, or if it was all open land and cities the way some talked about in hushed, disbelieving tones.

He wondered if the North was quiet.

He had heard it said that freedom was loud, that it rang like a bell, that once you had it you could not stop yourself from speaking. But he did not trust that. He had lived long enough to know that silence was not the absence of sound. Silence was something forced into you. It was a shape you learned to fit.

The forest shifted again, thinning for a few yards before tightening. The ground rose. He climbed, hands grabbing at exposed roots to pull himself up. At the top he paused, crouched low, and peered through the branches. Beyond the trees the land dipped into a darker hollow, and for an instant he felt as if he were standing on the edge of an enormous bowl.

He listened again. He expected, irrationally, to hear the dogs return in a rush, to hear men calling out, to hear the whole world behind him surge forward and close around his ankles.

Instead, something else cut through the night.

Not a bark. Not a shout. Not the crack of a whip.

A single note, thin and sharp, like a blade drawn slowly from its sheath.

A whistle.

It came from ahead. Close enough that the sound did not have to fight the trees to reach him. Close enough that it felt placed, deliberate, as if someone had stepped into the darkness and chosen that exact moment to announce they were there.

His body went still. The breath that had finally found rhythm caught in his throat. The woods held its quiet, and in that quiet the whistle sounded again, clearer this time, unhurried.

He had believed distance would mean safety. He had believed the dark would hide him.

In the moonless night, the North did not answer. The woods did not offer guidance. And whatever lay ahead did not need to chase him to catch him.

It only needed to wait.

The whistle hung in the air after it ended, as if the sound had weight and the trees were holding it up.

He stayed crouched on the rise, one hand sunk into the pine needles for balance, the other pressed hard against his own ribs as though he could keep his heart from making noise. His eyes scanned the hollow below, but darkness turned everything into suggestion. The trees down there were packed close, their trunks almost touching. The undergrowth looked like a single black mass. If someone stood among it, they could be a shadow inside a shadow.

He listened for the dogs again, for the familiar panic of pursuit. Nothing came but the insects and the faint, steady murmur of water somewhere out of sight. The quiet was wrong. It felt arranged.

The whistle sounded a third time, nearer than before, not louder so much as cleaner. Whoever made it did not do it to locate him. It was not a question tossed into the night. It was a statement.

His mouth went dry. He had heard men whistle to each other on the plantation, short little patterns when they thought no one was listening, when words might carry too far. The overseer had his own signals, sharp as a snapped twig. The field hands had softer ones sometimes, a thread of melody to pull work along. This whistle was neither. It was too measured, too bare. It held no tune, only intention.

He forced himself to move, to climb down the far side of the rise and put distance between himself and the sound. His legs wanted to run. His mind warned him not to. Running made noise. Running was a flare in the dark. He eased his weight forward and lowered a foot into the slope, trying to find ground that would not betray him with a crack or a slide.

A twig snapped anyway, crisp as bone.

He froze. The snap seemed enormous. He waited for an answering shout, a bark, a rush of feet. None came. For a few seconds he convinced himself the sound was swallowed, lost. Then a different noise arrived from the hollow, faint but unmistakable: the soft shift of bodies moving through brush, slow and confident, as if they did not care whether he heard them.

His skin tightened along his arms. He tried to breathe through his nose, but the air smelled of wet leaves and old rot, and the smell made him think of cellars, of the kind of darkness that stays even at noon.

North, he told himself, but it sounded ridiculous now, like a child trying to say a word that belonged to adults. North was a direction when you could choose your path. This was something else. This was a door closing.

He stepped again, then again, inching down. The slope leveled out. He moved into thicker trees, forcing himself to keep low. He could not see far. He could only see what was directly in front of him: the pale underside of a leaf, a slick patch of moss, the faint line of a fallen branch.

The whistle came again, almost lazily, from his left.

He turned his head too fast, and his shoulder brushed a cluster of leaves. They hissed against his shirt. That small sound seemed to carry, and in the instant after it, he understood with an awful clarity that whoever was out there did not need to spot him. They only needed to let him make his own mistakes. The woods would announce him.

He tried to change direction, angling right, but the ground dipped into a shallow ravine choked with ferns. He stepped down into it, sinking ankle-deep in mud, and the cold grip around his foot nearly made him cry out. He yanked free, leaving his shoe behind for a heartbeat before it slurped loose. His breath came faster. Panic rose like bile.

Then he saw them.

Not all at once, not clearly. First, he saw a pale oval between two trunks, like a face turned toward him. Then another, lower, half-hidden by brush. The darkness shifted, and what he had taken for a stump became a crouched man. They were positioned ahead of him, across the mouth of the ravine, spaced just far enough apart to cover the path without needing to move.

His mind tried to make them belong to something he understood. Hunters. Travelers. Men lost like him.

But they were too still. Too ready.

He stopped, and the moment he stopped, a shape behind him rose from the ferns as if it had been part of the earth.

A hand clamped over his mouth.

The grip was hard enough to grind his lips against his teeth. The palm smelled of smoke and something sour, a living smell. His breath turned hot inside his own mouth. His hands flew up, grabbing the wrist, trying to pry it away, but the arm was locked like a bar of iron.

A second hand caught his shoulder and wrenched him backward. His feet scrabbled for purchase in the mud. He made a sound that was meant to be a shout and came out as a muffled groan.

"Easy," a voice said near his ear, low and close. Not kind. Not angry. Controlled, as if the speaker was addressing a tool that might break if mishandled. "Don't waste yourself."

The man holding him shifted his stance, bracing. Another figure stepped into his line of sight, close enough now that the faint light caught the whites of his eyes. He was white. His face was narrow, the bones sharp under skin stretched tight. He did not look excited. He looked attentive, as if he were watching an animal to see where it would bolt.

The whistle came again, farther away this time, answered by a second whistle with a slightly different pitch. Call and response. A net tightening.

More bodies emerged from the trees. Two, then three, then more. They moved with the quiet practice of men who had done this before and would do it again. One carried a lantern with a shutter over it, the light barely a slit, enough to guide their feet without throwing their presence into the woods. Another held a length of rope coiled over his forearm, already prepared.

The man behind him pressed harder. “Thought you could go north,” he murmured, and the word north sounded like mockery in his mouth, a sweet he could crush. “You ain’t the first.”

The running man tried to bite, tried to twist his head, but the hand on his mouth shifted, forcing his jaw shut. The taste of sweat filled his throat. He thrashed, and the men did not shout, did not hurry. They simply adjusted. A knee drove into the back of his leg. His balance broke. He went down in the mud, and the impact knocked air from his lungs. Before he could draw it back, a boot landed on his shoulder, pinning him. The rope came out.

He felt it slide around his wrists, rough and wet from the night air. The fiber bit into skin already torn by briars. He bucked, and the boot pressed down harder, grinding him into the earth. Someone laughed softly, as if at a private joke.

“Keep him quiet,” another voice said. This one was older, tired, the voice of a man who had seen enough suffering that it no longer surprised him. “We got a walk to make.”

They hauled him up. The rope around his wrists was tied to another length around his neck like a leash. He gagged when it tightened, the coarse line scraping his throat. He stumbled forward, dragged rather than led. He tried to look at their faces, to find some crack of human uncertainty, something he could speak to. He found only blank focus.

He wanted to ask who they were, but he knew. He had always known in the back of his mind. There were men whose work was to grow things from the soil, and there were men whose work was to keep other men from leaving it. Sometimes those jobs belonged to the same hands.

The whistle sounded again, no longer ahead but somewhere to the side. It guided the group through the trees, a simple signal that said this way, this way, as if they were cattle being moved along a familiar route.

As they walked, he tried to mark the direction, tried to count turns, tried to fix landmarks in his mind, but the woods offered nothing that would hold. One dark trunk looked like another. The ravine he had stumbled into could have been any ravine. The hollow could have been any hollow. He realized with a cold, sinking dread that the men escorting him did not need a map. They owned these woods the way they owned the fields. Every path belonged to them.

At some point the ground leveled and the trees thinned. A strip of moonlight finally fell through a break in the clouds, and he saw his own hands in front of him, wrists bound, knuckles smeared with mud and blood. The sight made something break open inside him. Not hope. Hope was gone. Something closer to grief. A sharp awareness of how brief his running had been, how small.

He tried again, a desperate sound in his throat. “Please,” he managed, the word shredded by the rope’s pressure. “Please.”

No one answered.

The silence they gave him was worse than any insult. It was as if his pleading did not qualify as language. As if the only speech that mattered was a whistle, a signal, a command.

They walked until the night began to thin at the edges. Not sunrise yet, but the world shifted, the darkness losing some of its density. The insects changed their rhythm. The air cooled. He could smell smoke ahead, and then he saw it: the faint orange pulse of a fire beyond the tree line.

He tried to dig his heels in. He tried to pull back, but the rope snapped tight and yanked him forward. A man behind him jabbed something into his ribs, hard enough to bruise. He stumbled on.

The woods ended abruptly, and the open land beyond made him feel exposed, like a wound uncovered. He recognized the shape of the outbuildings in the dim. He recognized the fence line. He recognized the space where the yard spread wide and bare, designed for work in daylight and spectacle when needed.

There were already people gathered, more than he expected at this hour. They stood in a loose line near the main yard, heads lowered, bodies too still. He knew some of them by shape, by the way they held their shoulders, by the limp of a man who had been hurt last harvest. He saw faces turned away as if looking was dangerous.

They brought him into the center of that open space.

He understood then why the whistle had sounded ahead of him, not behind. It was never meant to guide him away. It was meant to lead him back, straight into the place where everyone would be forced to watch him fail.

The rope tightened again, and his breath hitched. He lifted his head, and in the growing gray of dawn he saw the men who owned the morning waiting near a low fire. He saw metal laid out on a table, dark shapes that would soon glow. He saw an iron resting close enough to the heat that its tip was already beginning to take on a dull, hungry red.

He had thought the worst thing in the night was being caught.

He was learning what dawn was for.

They stood him close enough to the fire that he could feel it pulling at the sweat on his skin. It was not warmth. It was a dry, greedy heat that made the air taste of ash.

The yard had a shape he knew too well, even in this thin gray light. Packed earth, trampled flat by years of boots and bare feet. The long stretch between the quarters and the main house where nothing grew, where nothing was meant to grow. A place kept empty on purpose. Empty made it easier to see what was happening.

The people gathered there did not gather like people at a celebration. They gathered like fence posts. A line of bodies, shoulders close but not touching, eyes trained on the ground as if the earth might open and offer something better to look at. He recognized the stillness. It was the stillness of being counted. Of being watched for any sign that you might be thinking your own thoughts.

The men who brought him in loosened the rope from his neck but did not untie his wrists. One kept a hand on his arm as though he were a wagon that might roll away. The other stood behind him with the rope still looped, slack in it only because they wanted slack, because they were choosing how much air he could have.

He looked for the overseer first, because the overseer was always where punishment lived. He found him near the fire, a little apart from the others, posture straight, face unreadable. A man built from rules. The kind of man who did not need to raise his voice because everyone knew what his silence meant. He did not hold the iron. He did not need to. Power did not always touch the tools it used.

There was a table set up near the fire. Rough planks laid across barrels. On it lay metal, dark and heavy, shapes that made his stomach clench. A pair of tongs. A hammer. An iron, its handle long enough to keep a man's hands away from the heat. The head of it was stamped into a shape, a mark that was hard to see in the low light, but he knew what it was meant to do. It was not meant to cut. It was meant to announce.

A man crouched at the fire, feeding it with split wood. As he pushed a log in, sparks lifted, tiny orange insects that died almost as soon as they were born. The iron lay close to the coals, its tip beginning to darken to a different kind of darkness, the kind that promised red beneath.

The man who had whispered in his ear in the woods stepped to his side. His hand pressed the back of his neck, forcing his head down. The running man fought it at first out of instinct, but his muscles were already failing him, trembling with exhaustion and shock. He was aware of how he smelled: mud, sweat, fear. He was aware of the blood drying along his cheek where the branch had struck him, pulling his skin tight.

A voice carried across the yard, calm as a reading from a book. "Look up."

It was not shouted. It did not need to be. The sound of it moved through the gathered people, and heads lifted in a wave, not all at once, but with the inevitability of a tide. Some looked at him with wide, empty eyes. Some stared past him. Some turned their faces slightly, as if to obey without truly seeing. He recognized an older woman in the second row, her mouth set hard, her gaze fixed on the ground even as her chin rose. There was a boy near her hip, too young to understand why dawn felt like this, his eyes flicking between the fire and the men, searching for a cue.

The running man swallowed. His throat was scraped raw from the rope. "Please," he said, and the word came out wrong, thin and cracked. He tried again, louder. "Please."

No one answered him. Not a comforting murmur, not a soft shake of a head, not even a curse thrown his way. The silence of the line was complete, and he understood why. Speech could be counted as agreement. A glance could be counted as sympathy. Sympathy could be punished.

The iron was moved with the tongs, lifted from where it had been resting. It was not fully red yet, but it was changing, a dull glow beginning to breathe through the metal like a living thing waking up.

The smell reached him before the sound did. Not the smell of burning wood, but a sharper scent of heated metal. The air around the iron shimmered, bending slightly as if the world itself did not want to be near it.

He jerked against the rope around his wrists. The men holding him did not tighten their grip in panic. They tightened it as routine. One of them pushed him forward and down, forcing him toward a post set in the yard for this purpose. It stood weathered and dark, the wood polished smooth in places by bodies pressed against it. He had seen it before from a distance, always trying not to notice it. Now he could see the old stains in its grain, the scratches where nails had dug in.

They turned him so his left shoulder faced the fire. His shirt was already torn from the run, but not enough. A hand fisted the fabric and yanked it down, exposing skin slick with sweat. The morning air hit him there, cool and then instantly stolen by the heat rolling off the fire.

He strained his neck, trying to look back at the crowd. The line of faces blurred. He wanted one face to hold his gaze and hold him back, as if recognition might be a rope thrown across water.

"Don't," someone hissed, but the sound was not meant for the men with the iron. It came from the line, a warning to him, not a plea. Don't make them do more. Don't make them notice me. Don't make this worse.

He tried to speak to the silence anyway, because what else was left. "Remember," he said hoarsely, not sure who he was talking to. "Somebody… remember."

A low murmur moved through the gathered people, not words, just a shift in breath. A small ripple of fear at the audacity of the request. Memory was dangerous. Memory made a thing last.

The overseer stepped closer. He did not raise his voice. He did not need to. "You," he said to the man with the iron, and nodded once.

The iron came toward him.

Time did not slow the way stories said it would. It sharpened. Each second became a thin slice. He could hear details with painful clarity: the faint crackle from the coals, the scrape of boots on packed earth, the soft grunt of a man adjusting his grip on the rope.

The heat hit his skin an instant before the iron did, like the opening of an oven. His body flinched away on instinct. The man holding him slammed him back against the post, forearm across his chest like a bar.

Then the iron touched.

It was not a clean pain. It was an invasion. A sudden, total sensation that crowded out everything else. The world became white for a blink, and in that blink, he thought he would die from the sheer force of it.

The sound that came out of him did not feel like his own. It was not a shout so much as something ripped from deep inside, a scream torn loose and made into air. His knees buckled. The men held him up, because they did not want him to faint. Fainting was a mercy. They wanted him awake. They wanted the line to hear him.

The smell arrived immediately, sickening and thick. Flesh burning. Hair searing. A sweet, terrible odor that made the back of his throat convulse. He gagged, but there was nowhere for the gag to go. His stomach was empty from the run. The gag became a dry heave and then another scream.

Someone in the line sobbed once, a single broken sound, and then swallowed it down so fast it was almost imaginary. A hand snapped out and pressed into the sobber's side, a reminder to stay still.

The iron lifted away. Air rushed onto the wound, and the rush felt like another form of pain, cold and stinging, as if the skin had been peeled back to something rawer than raw.

He sagged against the post, panting, saliva hanging at the corner of his mouth. His eyes searched wildly for the mark, as if he could see it without a mirror, as if knowing its shape would let him fight it. He could not see it, but he could feel it. The mark pulsed with its own heartbeat.

The man with the iron did not look at the wound. He turned the iron toward the fire again, as if the work was not finished, as if there were always more marks to make. His face was flat. This was a task, no different from branding livestock.

The overseer's gaze swept the line. Not a glare. A measurement. He was counting reactions. He was watching for a head that lifted too high, for a jaw that tightened, for a hand that curled into a fist. The punishment was not only for the one against the post. It was for the idea that had carried him into the woods.

The running man sucked air through his teeth. It hurt to breathe. It hurt not to breathe. He shook, not with cold but with a trembling that came from his bones.

He found a face in the crowd at last, a man he had worked beside in the fields. The man's eyes met his for the briefest moment. In them, the running man saw something like apology and something like fear, and beneath both, something else: a thin, stubborn spark that could not afford to show itself.

The spark vanished as quickly as it came. The man's gaze dropped away.

The iron clinked softly against the tongs as it was set down. Someone poured water into a bucket nearby, and the sound was ordinary, almost obscene in its normality. Life continuing. A morning beginning.

They did not give him time to steady himself. Hands hauled him away from the post. His feet dragged lines in the dirt. He tried to twist his head again toward the trees at the edge of the yard, toward the direction he had run, toward the darkness that had seemed like a hiding place. It was daylight now, thin and pale. The woods stood there pretending to be innocent.

North, he thought, and the word no longer felt like heat. It felt like a wound that had been opened and left uncovered.

As they pulled him past the line, he saw the people's faces more clearly. Some were blank with practiced emptiness. Some were wet-eyed but unmoving. Some carried a hatred so deep it had turned into stillness. Every face held the same lesson: this is what happens when you try to leave. This is what happens when you think distance can protect you. This is what happens when you put a word in your mouth that does not belong to you.

He tried to speak again, but all that came out was a rasp.

The men dragged him toward the outbuildings; toward whatever came next. Behind him, the line began to loosen only when the overseer allowed it. Bodies shifted like a field after a wind passes through, slow and cautious, returning to the shapes they were required to hold.

The fire crackled as if satisfied. The iron cooled in the morning air, but the mark on his shoulder did not. It burned on, a private blaze made public, an announcement pressed into skin.

The yard swallowed his scream and kept its silence.

And somewhere beyond the trees, beyond the fences, beyond the place where the word north had been born in whispers, the world waited without answering, as if it had never promised anything at all.

Chapter 2

Borrowed Moments

The days after the branding moved in a strange way, like time had learned to limp.

Work resumed because it always did. The yard was swept. The post stood where it stood. The men who had held the iron returned to their routines with the same hands, the same mouths, the same calm. The mark did not disappear just because eyes stopped looking at it. It lived under cloth, under skin, in the way shoulders flinched when someone stepped too close.

Elijah Boone heard about the punishment the way most things were heard: not as a story told cleanly, but as fragments carried from mouth to mouth until they became part of the air. A boy delivering water to the forge had whispered, "They burned him," then shut his mouth so fast it was like biting down on a nail. An older man with joints ruined by years of labor had said nothing at all, only lifted his chin toward the yard when the smoke from that morning's fire still hung thin in the heat. Elijah had not asked questions. Questions were hooks. You kept your skin away from them.

But he saw the man later, briefly, being led toward the quarters with his shirt hanging loose over one shoulder. The cloth had stuck in places, and when it pulled away it did so reluctantly, as if it did not want to reveal what lay beneath. The man's face was the face of someone whose body had learned a new truth. His eyes did not settle on anything. They moved the way hunted animals' eyes moved, always measuring distance, always looking for an edge to run toward even when there was nowhere to go.

Elijah watched until the man disappeared into the crush of bodies and doorways, then turned back to the fire of his own work. At the forge, heat had purpose. Heat shaped tools. Heat made metal honest. In the yard, heat was a language with only one message.

It should have ended there, in the silence that followed such demonstrations. It should have been enough.

Then the word went around that there would be a gathering.

Not a celebration. Nothing that belonged to them. A controlled overlap, permitted because it pleased the men who owned the land to imagine themselves benevolent, to exchange goods and speak of neighbors the way farmers spoke of weather. Two plantations, close enough that their boundaries almost touched in the woods, arranged a day for trading and prayer, a day where enslaved hands would be useful in a different configuration, and where enslaved eyes would be reminded that the world was bigger than one set of fences and still belonged to the same people.

Elijah heard it from the master's son, who came into the blacksmith shed with a lazy grin and the smell of tobacco on his clothes. "You'll be mending harness at Carter's place tomorrow," the boy said, as if sending a man to another plantation was no more significant than moving a hammer from one peg to another. "Don't be slow about it. Their stock's in need."

Elijah nodded. "Yes, sir."

The boy lingered, picking up a horseshoe blank with two fingers and turning it like a curiosity. His nails were clean. "And keep your eyes where they belong. Folks'll be about."

"Yes, sir," Elijah said again, and the boy left with his warning satisfied.

That night, the quarters held their breath. The idea of leaving the familiar yard, even for a day, unsettled people in different ways. Some were afraid because they knew what the woods had done to the runaway, how quickly the night could close and how easily you could vanish into a punishment meant for everyone. Some were afraid because they had never stepped outside their assigned world at all. Fear took many shapes, but it always lived in the same place: behind the ribs, tight as wire.

Elijah lay awake listening to it. He did not plan to run. Not tomorrow. Not with men watching, with dogs trained to love the chase. But he did not sleep easily either. The image of the man at the post kept returning, not as a single moment but as a lesson that repeated itself until it felt like a sound. When sleep finally took him, it was thin and broken, full of heat and the scent of burning.

Morning arrived washed in pale light. The kind of day that looked harmless if you did not know what could happen in daylight. Elijah was marched with a small group down the road that cut between the properties. They walked in a line, a white man on horseback behind them and another ahead, making sure distance did not become opportunity. The road was rutted and bordered by trees that leaned inward as if listening. Birds called from branches, careless and free in a way that made Elijah's stomach tighten.

As they approached Carter's plantation, he saw the fields first, then the main house set back like a watchful eye. It looked different from his own plantation and still the same. Different paint. Different porch posts. The same shape of ownership.

The yard of Carter's place was busy. Wagons were arranged in a rough circle. Barrels of salt pork, sacks of meal, and bundles of fabric sat under the supervision of white men who moved with the lazy assurance of those who never feared being told no. A preacher had been invited, too, a thin man with a Bible held up like proof of something. A few white women stood together near the porch, their dresses pale in the sun, their laughter too bright for the place.

And scattered among all of it were the enslaved, brought out in numbers larger than usual, arranged in usefulness. Women carried water. Men unloaded goods. Children were told to stand still and keep quiet, which meant they fidgeted and were slapped for it. The air smelled of sweat and dust and horses. Underneath it all was the faint, constant scent of smoke, as if every plantation had the same fire burning somewhere, even when it wasn't visible.

Elijah was directed toward a cluster of tack and broken harness laid out near the stables. A white man he didn't know pointed and spoke without looking at his face. "Fix those. Need them ready by evening."

Elijah knelt among leather and buckles and set his hands to work. He was careful with the tools he had been allowed to bring, careful with his own body. On days like this, you did not invite attention. You became useful and small.

Still, there were moments when his gaze lifted without permission, pulled by movement in his periphery. It happened when a group of women passed with baskets, and his eyes followed them without thinking. Not because they were women, not like the crude noticing the white men did, but because he was measuring the new yard, mapping it the way an animal mapped unfamiliar terrain.

That was when he saw her.

She was near the edge of the porch where the shade fell in a wide band, carrying a tray held level with both hands. She was younger than some of the other house women but moved like she had learned to be older than her years. Her posture was straight, her steps measured. She did not rush, though the work demanded speed. It was not defiance. It was control, the kind that could look like calm if you did not know how much calm cost.

Her name, he would learn, was Lila Carter.

At first, he noticed her not because she was beautiful in any simple way, though there was beauty in her face, in the strong line of her jaw and the soft fullness of her mouth. He noticed her because her eyes were different from the eyes around her. They did not skitter. They did not plead. They did not try to disappear. They watched without being obvious about it, taking in the yard as if she understood every part of it and did not trust any of it.

A white woman on the porch spoke to her, gesturing with two fingers toward the table where food had been arranged. Lila shifted her path and did what she was told. Her face did not change. If there was anger, if there was fear, it stayed behind her eyes like something locked in a room.

Elijah looked down quickly, as if he'd been caught staring into a mirror.

He went back to the harness, threading leather through a buckle, pulling it tight. His hands were scarred from work, not just from the forge but from everything that came before it. Old cuts. Burns that had healed shiny and pale. The skin on his palms thickened into calluses that made sensation duller. Those hands were his only honest possession. He could not stop them from shaking sometimes, but he could make them work.

A shadow fell across his knees.

He kept his gaze down for a beat, then glanced up.

Lila stood a few feet away, the tray gone, her hands empty now. She was close enough that Elijah could see a faint mark on her wrist where a bracelet of labor had rubbed the skin raw. Close enough to see that her calm was not ease, but a practiced holding. Her eyes flicked briefly to the harness pieces spread around him, then back to his face.

He felt, in that small exchange, the dangerous thing that happened when two people recognized each other as fully human in a place built to prevent it.

"You fixin' that?" she asked quietly.

Her voice held no flirtation, no softness meant to coax. It was simply a question, as careful as stepping over a threshold.

Elijah swallowed. He could feel the presence of white eyes in the yard even when none were pointed directly at him. He could also feel other eyes watching for different reasons. "Yes," he said. One word. Safe.

Lila's gaze dropped to his hands as he pulled the leather taut. "You got a steady way," she said.

He didn't know how to answer that without saying too much. Compliments could be traps. Conversation could be evidence. Still, something in him reached toward the sound of her voice as if it were warmth. "It's what I do," he said.

Her mouth shifted slightly, not quite a smile. "They say your place got a forge."

Elijah's fingers paused on the strap. How did she know? The question was simple, but it carried threads. He glanced past her shoulder. People moved. A white man laughed near the wagons. A child cried and was hushed sharply. No one seemed to be listening. That did not mean no one was.

"They say a lot," Elijah replied, keeping his tone flat.

Lila's eyes met his again. In them, he saw a thought sharpen, then tucked away. She had asked and received a boundary. She respected it. That respect felt like a rare thing, as rare as clean water in August.

A moment stretched between them, thin as wire. In that moment, Elijah became aware of another presence, not close like Lila, but positioned. A man stood near the corner of the stable, half in shadow, his body angled as if he were waiting for an instruction that had not yet come. He was enslaved, like them, but there was something in his stillness that did not match the rest of the yard. Other people's stillness was enforced. His looked chosen.

His eyes were on them.

Elijah did not know his name yet. He only knew the sensation of being measured, the way the overseer measured faces in the yard after the branding. This gaze did not carry the same authority, but it carried attention, and attention was its own kind of danger.

Lila seemed to feel it too. Her chin lifted a fraction, and her shoulders drew in just slightly, not as fear but as adjustment. Her voice lowered further. "I got to go," she said, and the words were both true and a retreat.

Elijah nodded, forcing himself not to look like he wanted her to stay. "Go on," he said.

She stepped away, moving back toward the porch where she would become invisible again in plain sight, another body doing what was required. Elijah watched her for one heartbeat too long, then returned his eyes to the harness.

The man by the stable did not move. He continued to watch, not openly enough to be accused of anything, but steadily enough that Elijah could feel it like a pressure at the back of his neck. It was not jealousy, not yet. It was something quieter. Curiosity with teeth.

Elijah bent closer to his work and forced his hands to keep their rhythm. Leather through buckle. Pull tight. Check the stitching. Make it hold.

Around him, the unlikely gathering went on, full of ordinary sounds and staged kindness. White voices rose and fell. Horses stamped. The preacher began to speak about obedience and salvation as if those words belonged in the same mouth. Somewhere in the yard, laughter broke out, brief and nervous, then died.

Elijah listened to it all as if from a distance. The day had offered him only a handful of words with Lila Carter, words that were careful and small. Yet those words clung to him with an insistence that felt dangerous.

Not because they promised anything.

Because they proved something could still begin. Even here. Even under watch.

And in a world that branded hope into flesh, beginnings were not gentle things. They were sparks, and sparks were always being looked for.

Elijah kept his eyes on the leather as if the strap could punish him for looking up. He worked the buckle through its holes, tugged it snug, then tested it with a careful pull. The harness lay across his knees like a quiet animal, familiar in every part, but his hands had lost their ease. They moved correctly while his mind moved elsewhere.

He felt the gaze again from the stable corner. Not heavy enough to force him into a mistake, just present enough to make each movement feel recorded.

When he shifted to reach for an awl, the iron point clicked against another tool. The small sound made him flinch, and he hated himself for it. He forced his shoulders to settle. Fear was contagious; it leapt from one body to another faster than any whispered word. The man in the woods had taught them that. The brand in the yard had sealed it.

A pair of boots passed nearby, white leather, clean. The man wearing them spoke to someone out of Elijah's sight, and his voice floated down with the easy boredom of ownership. Elijah did not look up. He made himself smaller, useful and forgettable, the way you survived long days.

Then, from somewhere closer, he heard Lila's voice again. Not directed at him this time. Directed toward a white woman on the porch, soft and agreeable, the voice of someone who knew how to keep her face smooth while the inside of her stayed sharp.

"Yes, ma'am. Right away."

Elijah did not lift his head, but his attention tilted toward the sound. The yard held layers of speech, and you learned to listen for what mattered, the way you learned to listen for dogs in the night. Lila moved across the packed earth with another tray, the weight balanced, her steps measured. She did not hurry. She also did not linger. She moved like she had decided, long ago, that rushing belonged to people who thought they controlled time.

As she passed the wagons, a white man laughed too loudly at something another said, and the preacher's voice rose and fell about sin. Amid it, Elijah caught the faintest shift: Lila turned her head as if glancing toward the stables, then forward again. The glance lasted no longer than a breath. It was nothing anyone could accuse her of. It was also deliberate.

Elijah kept his hands working. If he looked up now, it would be too obvious, too eager. There were rules even for longing, and the first rule was never to let it show as want.

The tack pile beside him had been growing smaller, sorted into what could be fixed and what had to be replaced. He picked up a broken rein and began to stitch the split seam. His needle passed through leather with a steady push, the motion practiced. A stitch was a kind of patience. Pull. Tighten. Lay the next one close.

A shadow fell over him again, thinner than before, as if whoever cast it did not want to announce themselves.

He waited one count, then glanced up.

Lila had stopped near the edge of his work area, just outside the stable's deeper shade. The tray was gone again. Her hands were empty, fingers relaxed at her sides, but her posture remained composed, as though she carried something unseen. Her eyes did not go straight to his face. They flicked to the harness, then to the ground, then finally met his, and in that measured sequence he understood she was doing what he was doing: building the moment carefully, keeping it small enough to survive being witnessed.

"You done with that one?" she asked.

Elijah lowered his voice without thinking. "Near done."

Her gaze shifted past him, not to avoid him but to check the yard. A white man stood by the wagons, talking, his head turned away. The enslaved men from Elijah's group worked in a line farther down, watched by the rider who sat on his horse like a statue. Lila's eyes returned.

"They keep you busy," she said. The words were ordinary. Safe.

"They like to see hands moving," Elijah replied.

Her mouth tightened slightly at that, not a smile, not quite. Agreement, maybe. Or recognition. "Same at our place," she said. "Busy don't mean free."

The sentence landed between them with more weight than it should have carried. It was a simple truth, spoken plain. Elijah felt his chest go tight. Words like that were dangerous because they sounded like thinking. Thinking was what got marked.

He looked down at his stitches. "You best not say too much," he murmured.

Lila did not react like someone offended. She nodded, slow. "I know," she said. "I just—" She stopped herself. The rest of the sentence stayed in her throat.

Elijah let silence do some of the work. Silence could be a shield if you held it right. He finished the seam, tied off the thread, and ran his thumb along the stitches to check for weakness. The leather held. It did not matter. His mind did not.

Lila shifted her weight, subtle as a change in wind. “Your name?” she asked, and kept her tone light, as if asking for a tool.

He hesitated. Names made things real. Names could be carried away and used. Still, there was a hunger in him, not for risk, but for a point of connection that wasn’t just a glance in passing.

“Elijah,” he said quietly. “Elijah Boone.”

Lila’s eyes did something small at the sound of it, as if she tucked it away carefully. “Lila,” she answered. “Lila Carter.”

Elijah had already heard it in his mind since the moment he’d learned it. Hearing her say it made it different. Not sweeter. More serious.

He nodded once. “You work in the house.”

“I do,” she said. Then, with a careful glance toward the porch, she added, “Mostly. When they need me.”

Elijah understood that too. Need meant you were moved like a piece on a board. Need could put you close to things you weren’t meant to hear and also close to hands you weren’t meant to refuse.

He chose his next words like selecting metal from a pile. Wrong choice and you ruined the whole piece. “You got folks here?” he asked, keeping it casual, the kind of question that could belong to any gathering.

Lila's gaze steadied on his, and in it he saw calculation, not cold but precise. "Some," she said. "And some not mine. Just… people you see enough to know."

Elijah felt the presence at the stable corner sharpen, though he did not look. He could sense attention the way you sensed heat off a forge.

Lila continued, her voice still even. "You come over often?"

"No," Elijah said. "First time in a long while. They send me when something breaks."

She looked at his hands again, the scars and burns. "You make things that last," she said.

He almost laughed at the irony of it. He made things that lasted for people who wanted him not to. He kept their world running. He kept their horses shod, their hinges smooth, their chains repaired. He kept the structure tight around everyone's throats.

He said, instead, "Sometimes."

The space between them filled with the noise of the yard. A child called out and was hushed sharply. A barrel rolled and thumped into place.

The preacher spoke louder about obedience, as if volume could make the word holy.

Lila's eyes flicked to Elijah's shoulder, then to the ground. "They catch that man?" she asked, and the question was so softly placed it might have been mistaken for a sigh.

Elijah's throat closed. The runaway's scream had traveled beyond fences. That was the point. "Yeah," he said. "They caught him."

Lila's face did not change, but her fingers flexed once at her side, then went still. "We heard," she said. "Not the whole of it. Just… enough."

Elijah heard the unspoken: enough to be afraid. Enough to stop yourself from imagining. Enough to make the word north taste like blood.

He kept his gaze down and spoke without moving his lips much. "Don't listen to too much of it," he said. "They want it in your head."

Lila's voice came back, almost soundless. "It already is."

That was the truest thing said between them, and because it was true, it made Elijah's pulse quicken. He wanted to say something that could help. Help was another dangerous word. Help implied the possibility of change.

Before he could shape a response, a voice called from the porch. "Lila."

Lila turned her head smoothly, the movement controlled. "Yes, ma'am."

"Bring the water. And mind where you stand."

Lila's eyes returned to Elijah for a fraction of a second. In that second, a message passed that was not a plan, not a promise. Only this: I see you. I heard you. I know what we are both doing just by standing here.

"I got to go," she said again, but this time there was something else under it, a tension like a string drawn tight.

Elijah nodded. "Go on."

She stepped away, and the yard swallowed her back into her role. Tray. Water. Quiet. Useful. The kind of usefulness that let white people forget you had thoughts.

Elijah watched her only long enough to be sure she reached the porch without drawing extra attention. Then he forced his gaze back to the leather.

From the stable corner, the man who had been watching finally moved. He stepped out of shadow with the slow ease of someone who believed he belonged wherever he stood. He was about

Elijah's age, maybe a little older, lean and straight-backed. His shirt was clean for field wear, and his hair was kept close. His eyes were the unsettling part, bright with focus, not dulled by fatigue the way so many were. He looked at Elijah's hands, then at the half-mended tack, as if assessing quality.

"You do good work," the man said.

Elijah did not like the sound of praise from that mouth. Praise could be bait. "I do what I'm told," he replied.

The man's gaze slid past Elijah toward the porch, where Lila moved between white women like a shadow trained to carry. Something shifted in the watcher's face, too small to name, then smoothed away.

"You Elijah Boone?" he asked.

Elijah's shoulders tightened. "Who asking?"

The man's lips curved in something that wasn't friendly. "Name's Samuel," he said. He did not offer a last name, as if he didn't need one. "We got work needs doing here plenty. Harness, hinges, all manner of things. Maybe I'll tell Mr. Carter you worth borrowing more."

Elijah met Samuel's gaze and held it, careful not to show what he felt. "Tell who you want," he said. "Ain't my choosing."

Samuel watched him a moment longer, then nodded, like a man filing away a detail. "No," he agreed softly. "Ain't your choosing."

He turned and walked back toward the stables, unhurried, as if the conversation had been nothing at all.

Elijah kept stitching, but his hands had gone cold. Over the sounds of the yard and the preacher's droning, he could still hear Lila's voice saying the truth that mattered. It already is.

And now, threaded through that truth, was the awareness of Samuel's attention, measuring and patient. Elijah had known from the moment he saw those eyes on them that the day had offered more than a brief exchange. It had offered a witness.

He worked until the leather was whole again, until the straps looked as though they had never been split. The work would hold. That was what he was good at: making things hold.

It did not comfort him.

Not when he could still feel the weight of Lila's measured words, and Samuel's measured silence, settling into place like a lock.

By late afternoon the harness lay in a neat stack beside Elijah's knee, each strap repaired, each buckle tested twice. He kept his hands moving even after the last stitch was tied, fussing with ends that did not need fussing, rubbing a thumb over leather as if he could smooth the day itself flat.

The yard at Carter's place began to loosen from its morning stiffness. Barrels emptied. Wagons were reloaded. The preacher's voice finally thinned into nothing, the last "amen" swallowed by the ordinary sounds of work. White men drifted toward shade and drink, satisfied with the appearance of order. Enslaved bodies were redirected without explanation, herded into the next task as if a person could be poured from one purpose into another.

Elijah was called back with the others when the rider on horseback whistled, the sharp note familiar in its meaning. He stood, gathering the few tools he'd been allowed to bring, and felt grit in his knees from kneeling so long. His back ached with the slow burn of labor, but the ache was not what held his attention.

He looked for Lila without meaning to. He told himself it was a habit of assessment, the way you scanned a yard for danger, for the overseer's mood, for where you should not stand. But his gaze slid, quiet and hungry, toward the porch where she had moved all day like a careful shadow.

He caught a last glimpse of her near the doorway, hands full again, posture straight. She did not look toward him. If she did, she did it in a way he could not see. That; too, felt deliberate. A choice made in plain sight.

Samuel stood near the stable corner as if he had never left it, watching the line of men gather. When Elijah's eyes met his, Samuel's expression gave nothing. It was not a warning, not a threat. It was simply the knowledge that Samuel had seen what had passed between Elijah and Lila and had decided it belonged to him now, as information if nothing else.

The road home was quieter than the road there. Exhaustion weighed the group down, and with it came a deeper caution, the sense that talking was a waste of energy and also a risk. Elijah walked with his eyes down, boots sinking into ruts, the dust rising pale around his ankles. The trees on either side leaned inward as they had in the morning, listening without faces.

As they passed the boundary where one plantation's order blurred into another's, Elijah found himself thinking of the branded man again, not as a figure in a story but as a fact embedded in the land. Somewhere not far from this road there was a hollow in the woods where a whistle had sounded, where darkness had turned into hands. Somewhere on this earth there was a post polished smooth by bodies pressed against it. The day at Carter's had offered him something like a beginning, and the memory of that brand insisted on sitting beside it, a reminder of what beginnings could cost.

When they reached home, the yard was already dimming toward evening. The air carried the smell of cooking and sweat and damp earth cooling. Elijah went straight to the blacksmith shed as he'd been taught to do, returning tools, answering to the master's son with the same flat obedience that kept a man alive. He nodded when spoken to. He did not mention anything about Carter's place except the work, except the harness, except what could be said without leaving a trace of himself in the words.

Only when he finally stepped away toward the quarters did he feel the day's weight shift onto his shoulders properly, heavy as a sack of iron.

Inside his cabin, the light was low, the air close. The others inside spoke in murmurs, exchanging bits of the day that were safe to exchange: who had been sent where, what had been broken, what had been fixed. Elijah answered when needed. He ate what was given. His mouth accepted food without tasting it.

When the talk thinned and bodies began to settle, he lay down on his pallet and stared at the dark beams above him. The night sounds rose around the quarters like they always did: insects, a distant animal call, the occasional cough. A baby cried once and was soothed quickly. Beyond those sounds, another layer existed, one he could never fully separate from the rest: the quiet vigilance of men who listened for footsteps, for doors opening, for the particular rhythm of an overseer's patrol.

Elijah closed his eyes.

Lila's voice appeared immediately, as if his mind had been waiting all day to bring it forward cleanly.

"You got a steady way."

"You best not say too much."

"It already is."

He replayed the small exchange the way a tongue worried a sore tooth, returning to it even though it hurt. He could see her hands empty at her sides, the slight raw mark at her wrist. He could see the way her eyes had moved, not darting, not pleading, but measuring the yard the way he measured heat in a forge. He could feel, again, the dangerous relief of being looked at like a person.

He thought about saying her name. He did not. Names carried.

He tried to sleep and found that the moment on Carter's yard would not lie still. It changed each time he returned to it. In one replay, he noticed the way Lila's chin had lifted when the white woman called her, a small refusal to be bent even as her feet obeyed. In another, he noticed the way Samuel's gaze had sharpened when he stepped from shadow, how he had spoken Elijah's name like he'd already owned it.

Elijah rolled onto his side, the pallet creaking. He listened to the room for signs that someone was awake, that someone might be watching his thoughts on his face. He forced his breathing to slow, forced his body into stillness, but his mind kept moving as if it had been set loose.

He wondered what Lila would do now that the day was over. Would she lie awake the same way? Would she replay those measured words until they turned into something else?

He wondered, too, if Samuel was replaying it.

The thought brought a cold edge. Samuel did not look like a man who let things pass without collecting them. He looked like a man who stored moments away the way other men stored nails, sorted and ready for use. Elijah could not decide which was worse: that Samuel might want Lila, or that Samuel might simply want control over what passed between people.

At some point his exhaustion won, not with peace but with collapse. Sleep took him in uneven pieces.

In one of those pieces he dreamed he was back at Carter's place, kneeling among the tack. The leather was warm and alive under his fingers like skin. Each time he pushed the needle through, it came out red. Not just red, but glowing, like the tip of a branding iron. He tried to drop it and found his hands stuck, stitched into the leather as if he was being sewn into the plantation itself. He looked up and saw the branded man at the post in the yard, but the man's face was Lila's face, eyes steady, mouth set, as if she'd already decided not to scream.

Elijah woke with his heart pounding and his jaw clenched so hard it ached. The cabin was dark, quiet. No one else stirred. He lay back down and stared at the ceiling again, sweat cooling on his ribs.

Across the distance, at Carter's plantation, Lila's night held its own shape.

She finished the last of the evening work under the watch of the house, moving between rooms with practiced quiet. The white family's voices drifted through doorways and down hallways: talk of trade, of neighbors, of weather that mattered only to crops and comfort. Lila did not join those conversations. She carried water. She cleared plates. She kept her eyes lowered at the right times and lifted them only when asked.

When she was finally dismissed, she stepped out of the main house into the night air and felt the difference like a hand leaving her throat. The yard outside was dim, lit by a few lamps and the weak spill of light from windows. The quarters lay beyond, darker, clustered like a separate world.

She walked with her posture unchanged, because posture was habit, and habits kept you safe. But inside her, the day had not ended. It had folded itself into her the way smoke folded into cloth.

In the privacy of her small space, she sat down and let her shoulders drop only a fraction. Even alone, she did not let them drop fully. Privacy was never certain. Walls were thin. Ears were trained.

She thought of Elijah's hands. Scarred, capable, careful. The steadiness of them had unsettled her more than any pretty word could have. She had spent years watching hands that took, hands that struck, hands that held a Bible while they lied about mercy. Elijah's hands had done something else. They had made something broken hold again. That was a skill. That was also a kind of danger.

She replayed their conversation exactly as it had happened, then replayed it again with different emphasis, as if changing the weight on a word might change its meaning.

"You got folks here?"

"Some."

What had she meant by it? What had he heard? She had answered cautiously, but even caution felt like a confession in her chest. She had wanted to tell him more, not because she trusted him fully yet, but because she recognized the same tightness in him, she carried in herself. A mind that did not rest. A spirit that did not settle into obedience no matter how carefully the body pretended.

And then, threaded through her memory, Samuel's presence rose. She saw him the way she had seen him at other times: not loud, not crude, never openly forceful. Always placed. Always near enough to be unavoidable while pretending it was chance.

She remembered his eyes on Elijah. She remembered, too, the way Samuel had watched her move all day, his attention sliding over her like a hand you could not slap away. The proposal he would one day make was not spoken yet, but she felt its outline in the air around him, the slow insistence of a man who mistook politeness for invitation.

Lila lay down and stared into the dark. The sounds of the quarters rose around her, the soft shifting of bodies, quiet murmurs, a cough, a distant laugh that died quickly. She tried to let the day drain out of her.

Instead, it replayed.

Elijah's voice, low: "You best not say too much."

Her own voice, smaller than she remembered: "It already is."

She thought of the branded man, the smell that had traveled, the lesson pressed into everyone's morning. She thought of the word north, whispered like it had teeth.

Then she thought, uninvited, of Elijah looking at her that last time, careful not to look too long. It was not a promise. It was not even hope, not yet.

It was recognition.

And recognition, in a place built on erasing, was its own kind of haunting. It followed you into the night. It waited behind your eyelids. It replayed itself until you could not tell whether it was comfort or a warning.

In the dark, on both plantations, the same silence settled over sleeping bodies. The insects sang. The air cooled. Somewhere a man walked a patrol with a lantern held low, the light cutting thin slices through the night.

And in the quiet where speech was dangerous, thoughts kept moving, circling the same moments again and again, wearing grooves into the mind.

Borrowed moments did not end when the day ended.

They returned in the dark, over and over, until they felt less like memory and more like something alive, something watching from inside.

Chapter 3

The Shape of Want

The days after the gathering did not return to normal so much as they settled into a new arrangement, the way ash settled after a fire. Nothing looked different at first glance. Work still began before the sun decided what color it wanted to be. Orders still came down like weather. Feet still moved because stopping invited attention. But Lila felt the shift in the small spaces, in the moments between tasks when a person's mind might have wandered if it were allowed to.

Samuel began to be present in those spaces.

The first time, she told herself it was coincidence. She was carrying linens from the washhouse toward the back steps of the main house, arms full, the cloth warm from sun and labor, when Samuel appeared at the edge of her path as if he'd been standing there all along.

"Let me take some," he said.

It was not a demand. That was the problem. He spoke the way a helpful man spoke, the way the decent ones sometimes tried to sound when decency was a luxury no one could afford. His hands were already half-raised, palms open, waiting for her to allow it.

Lila tightened her grip on the linens. "I got it," she replied.

Samuel did not withdraw. He stepped closer, smiling faintly like a person being patient with a child. "Ain't no need to strain yourself. Missus don't like drops in the dirt."

He reached anyway, not to grab, not to fight her, but to slide his fingers under the edge of the top sheet as if the work belonged to him too. The movement was practiced, careful, meant to look like service. Lila could not shove him away without making it a scene and making it a scene would make her a problem. Problems were handled.

So, she let the top portion shift into his hands.

The cloth left her arms with a soft exhale of weight. It should have been relief. Instead, it felt like a concession she hadn't agreed to give.

Samuel walked beside her toward the steps. He kept his pace matched to hers, close enough to be conversation, far enough to be proper. Proper was a mask everyone used.

"You been in the house since you was little, right?" he asked, tone casual.

Lila kept her gaze forward. "Since I can remember."

"Makes you different," Samuel said. "You see things."

She heard the question hidden inside the statement. What do you see? What do you know? Who do you hear? She answered the way survival had taught her to answer. "I see what they tell me to see."

Samuel chuckled softly, not mocking, not quite. "You always talking careful."

"I always breathing careful," she said before she could stop herself.

Samuel's smile flickered, then returned, smoother. "Careful keeps you living."

They reached the steps. Samuel handed the linens back at the door, one corner at a time, as if he were returning something borrowed. Lila took them and stepped inside. When she looked back, he was already turning away, unhurried, as if he had never intended to stay.

All day she caught glimpses of him at the edges. Near the smokehouse when she fetched meat. By the garden path when she carried scraps to the kitchen. At the well when she lifted water and felt the rope burn her palms. Always there at the moment she had to move through, never quite in her way, never quite absent.

By the third day she stopped calling it coincidence.

It became a pattern the way the overseer's patrol was a pattern, the way punishment always came with an audience, the way the house's demands arrived just when you thought you might have a breath to yourself. Samuel's presence did not shout like those patterns did. It slid in quietly, like dampness under a door.

He did not ask again about linens. Instead, he found other ways to be useful.

"I told the cook that flour barrel's near empty," he said one morning as she passed the kitchen doorway. "She ain't like it. But she need to know before missus get mad."

Lila paused only long enough to keep from seeming rude. "All right," she said.

"And the little one," he continued, meaning the master's youngest boy, "he been slipping out back to the stables. You don't want to get blamed for him tracking mud."

"I don't watch him," Lila answered.

Samuel tilted his head, still mild. "No. But they'll say you was supposed to."

That was the cruel skill of his approach. He never sounded like he wanted anything from her. He sounded like he was protecting her from things she already understood. It was a kind of help that assumed closeness, assumed the right to speak into her day.

Sometimes he brought information; sometimes he brought objects.

A length of twine, offered with a shrug. "Thought you might need it, tying bundles."

A scrap of soap, small and worn thin. "House gets plenty. Ain't nobody counting pieces."

A needle, tucked inside a folded rag. "You keep yours sharp? This one's better."

Each offering forced Lila into a choice. Refusing made her look ungrateful, and gratitude was expected from her like obedience. Accepting placed something invisible between them, a thread he could pull later if he decided it was his.

She learned to accept with her face blank and her words spare. "Thank you." Not warm. Not cold enough to be noticed. The safest temperature.

Samuel seemed satisfied by any response at all.

At night, when she could finally sit on the edge of her pallet and let her hands rest, Lila replayed his words the way she had replayed Elijah's. But where Elijah's voice had carried caution like a shared secret, Samuel's carried an interest that felt like a hand hovering just above skin.

She told herself to ignore it. Plenty of men watched women. Plenty of men tried to carve out small pleasures in a world that offered none. Want had nowhere clean to go on a plantation. It twisted. It found corners.

Still, Samuel's want did not look like hunger. It looked like planning.

She started noticing how he placed himself. How he always appeared near a doorway she had to pass through, near a task she had to finish, near a person she had to speak with. How he rarely spoke when white people were within earshot, and when he did, his words were harmless as dust. He waited until her work pulled her into spaces with fewer eyes.

He did it so smoothly she almost respected it, and that almost made her angry.

One afternoon, she was sent to carry a tray to the side parlor where the master entertained a guest. The room smelled of tobacco and polished wood, and the men's voices floated out with their laughter, soft and dangerous. Lila kept her eyes down as she set the glasses and stepped back.

When she exited into the hall, Samuel was there, leaning near the back stairwell like he belonged to the house's shadows. He straightened as soon as he saw her, attentive.

"You in there with them?" he asked, voice low.

"I carried a tray," she said.

Samuel's brows lifted slightly, as if he already knew and wanted her to confirm it. "They talking business?"

Lila stopped walking. That was too close to a question he had no right to ask her. She kept her face calm, but inside something hardened. "They always talking business," she replied. "Ain't my place to listen."

Samuel stepped aside so she could pass, but he moved with her, matching her pace down the hall. "You got a way of being near things," he said. "Some folks don't even notice what they hear. You do."

"Don't," Lila said quietly.

It was not loud. It was not an argument. It was a line drawn in a whisper.

Samuel's eyes held on her face. For a moment, the mildness slipped. Something sharper looked out from behind it, measuring her refusal the way a man measured a gate latch that didn't open on the first try.

Then the mildness returned, quick as a blink. "All right," he said. "I'm only saying, you don't got to carry everything by yourself."

She kept walking. She did not look back. She could feel him fall half a step behind, then stop entirely, letting the distance appear like choice.

That night, as she lay listening to the quarters settle, she tried to convince herself that her "don't" would be enough. She had said it with restraint, the way you said things when you needed them to land without echo. She had not embarrassed him. She had not challenged him in front of anyone. She had given him an exit that preserved his pride.

But Lila had seen men like Samuel before. Men who turned every kindness into a test and every boundary into an invitation to negotiate. She could not afford to treat his attention like the harmless interest of a lonely man. It sat on her skin too long. It followed her into places it should not.

Across the property, in the smaller male quarters nearer the fields, Samuel lay awake with his hands behind his head, staring at the dark rafters as if he could see through them. The night around him was full of ordinary sounds: breathing, a cough, the distant bark of a dog that was not hunting tonight. He listened anyway, because listening was habit and advantage.

He replayed the gathering at Boone's neighbor plantation the way he had replayed it since that day. He saw the blacksmith, Elijah Boone, with his scarred hands and his careful eyes. He saw Lila near the porch, her posture controlled, her face giving away nothing, and he remembered how she had angled her body toward Elijah for those few measured words.

It had not been much. That was what made it important. People didn't risk even small things unless the want underneath was strong.

Samuel told himself he did not want trouble. Trouble brought whips. Trouble brought chains. Trouble brought heat in the yard and the smell that never left your memory. He had seen the branded man brought back not long ago, and he had watched the way everyone's eyes went dead on command. Samuel had watched, too, the overseer's calm, the precision of the lesson. He understood lessons.

He did not want to be the one taught.

But he wanted Lila. Not in the simple way men spoke about women when they thought no one could hear. He wanted her attention, her acknowledgement, the sense that when she moved through the day she would have to account for him. He wanted the part of her that stayed quiet, because quiet meant there were thoughts kept behind it. Thoughts had value.

And if Elijah Boone thought he could take up space in Lila's mind, Samuel decided, then Elijah Boone would learn what it meant to be seen.

Want took different shapes depending on the man holding it. Some men begged. Some men grabbed. Samuel planned.

So he would insert himself where he could, softly at first, like a wedge tapped into wood. Not enough to split anything yet. Just enough to change the shape of what could fit.

Tomorrow he would find another moment to be useful. Another reason to be near. Another thread to lay down between himself and Lila, thin as twine, easy to overlook until there were too many to step over.

In the dark, Samuel smiled to himself without showing teeth.

Lila, staring at the ceiling of her own cramped space, felt the day's weight still pressed into her. Samuel's voice, mild and persistent, ran along the inside of her skull like a finger tracing a seam.

Careful keeps you living.

She understood the truth of it. She also understood the warning hidden there, whether he meant it as warning or promise.

Careful kept you living, yes.

But careful also kept you trapped.

And Samuel, she realized, was learning exactly where her carefulness made room for him.

Lila learned quickly that refusing Samuel outright did not make him vanish. It only changed the way he approached her, the way water changed shape when a hand tried to cup it.

After she told him "don't" in the hall, he stopped speaking to her for a day. Not as punishment, not openly. He simply removed his voice from her path and replaced it with looks that were easier to deny. When she passed the smokehouse, she felt him watching from a distance that could be called coincidence. When she carried dishwater out back, she saw him near the fence line, hands busy with a task that did not need doing at that hour. When she stepped off the kitchen stoop into the yard, he was never directly in front of her. Always slightly to the side, positioned so that if she looked his way, she would have to admit she'd been looking.

It was a quiet game, and Lila hated how well it fit into the plantation's larger rules. The place was built on what could not be said. You could be surrounded all day and still have no witness, because witness required a person's willingness to see what was happening.

The following morning, the mistress sent Lila to the garden for herbs the cook claimed she needed. It was still early, the light thin and colorless, and dew clung to the leaves like a second skin. The garden sat behind the house in a fenced square, neat rows meant to look like gentleness. But Lila had learned that a garden could be another kind of cage: pretty, controlled, watched from a window.

She knelt at the edge of the mint, fingers working carefully to pinch and pull without bruising. The smell rose sharp and clean, almost foreign in a world where most scents were sweat, smoke, and livestock. For a moment, the mint made her think of the gathering at Boone's neighbor plantation, of that brief, strange overlap where the air had carried too many voices at once. She did not let herself think the name Elijah. She did not let herself replay the sound of his voice. Those were indulgences, and indulgences could become needs.

A shadow fell across the row.

Lila kept her hand steady. She did not look up right away. She adjusted her grip on the small basket beside her and continued picking, as if the shadow was just a cloud.

"You always up before the sun," Samuel said.

His voice was low enough that it belonged to the garden. Not the house. Not the yard. Not anywhere that required permission.

Lila did not answer at first. Silence, she had learned, could be a boundary. Silence could also be interpreted as acceptance if the wrong person was listening.

Samuel crouched at the other side of the mint, careful not to step on the plants. He wore the same calm he always wore, the expression of a man offering help. His hands reached out and began to pick too, as if the work was what had brought him here.

"You don't have to do that," Lila said finally, keeping her voice flat.

Samuel smiled faintly, eyes on the leaves. "Ain't a burden."

"It's not your task."

He plucked a sprig and laid it in her basket as though he had the right. "You in the house. You got more eyes on you than I do. I'm just making it easier."

There it was again, the way he framed himself as protection. The way he spoke as if her life was an equation he understood better than she did. Lila kept her gaze on her hands. "I don't need it easier," she said. "I need it quiet."

Samuel's fingers paused. For a breath his face tightened, then he resumed picking, slower. "Quiet is what I'm giving," he said. "I could talk loud if I wanted."

The words were simple. The meaning behind them was not.

Lila sat back on her heels and finally looked at him. His eyes were fixed on the mint, but they flicked up to meet hers the moment she moved, as if he had been waiting for it. His attention felt trained. Not like a man stumbling into desire, but like a man practicing a skill.

"You keep finding me," she said.

Samuel shrugged, a small movement meant to look harmless. "This place ain't big. Folks cross paths."

"You make sure," Lila said, and hated that even that much felt like a risk. Calling a thing what it was could make it real enough for someone else to punish you for it.

Samuel's mouth tilted. "If I was making sure, you'd know."

Lila's stomach tightened. She reached for the basket and stood, brushing dirt from her knees. She turned toward the house. Samuel rose too, not rushing, not crowding, but matching her pace as if it were natural.

They walked along the fence line where the vines climbed, green and obedient. Behind them the garden held its perfect rows. Ahead, the back steps waited, and beyond them the house with its doors and its rules.

Lila stopped before the steps. "Don't come up here," she said quietly. "Not with me."

Samuel halted half a step behind her, as if she had guided him there. He looked past her at the door, then back at her face. His voice softened, and that softness was another tool. "You think I'm trying to get you in trouble."

"I think you don't care if I do," Lila answered.

Something in Samuel's expression flickered, quick as a struck match. Then it steadied again.

"I'm trying to keep you from it," he said. "You got a way about you that makes folks look twice. You don't even see it."

Lila's throat went tight. She wanted to tell him he was wrong. She wanted to tell him she had spent her whole life watching where eyes went, what they lingered on, what they took. She did see it. She saw too much.

Samuel continued, as if encouraged by her silence. "At that gathering, you and that blacksmith… you was careful. You did it smart." He said smart as if it were praise. "But I saw it. Others can see it too."

The mint scent clung to her fingers. She curled her hand into a fist around it to keep herself from shaking. "I didn't do anything," she said.

Samuel's gaze traveled over her face as if searching for cracks. "That's the thing," he said softly. "You didn't. You kept it clean. You kept it polite. That's how I know it meant something."

Lila stared at him. For a moment she could not find words, because what he was saying was so twisted it made her feel as if she'd stepped into a hole covered with leaves. Her restraint, her caution, her refusal to show anything that might be used against her, had become proof in his mind.

Samuel leaned closer by a fraction, not close enough to touch, close enough to make the air feel smaller. "You don't laugh at my words," he said. "You don't spit at my feet. You don't tell me to get lost. You just… move careful." He paused, and his eyes sharpened. "That ain't how a woman acts when she wants a man gone."

Lila felt heat rise behind her eyes, not tears but anger that had nowhere safe to go. "How a woman acts?" she repeated, keeping her voice low because the house behind them had windows. "You think I got choices like that?"

Samuel's face held steady, but his jaw tightened. "Everybody got choices."

"Not the ones you mean," Lila said. The words came out before she could swallow them, and she felt their danger as soon as they existed.

Samuel's gaze slid toward the yard, checking for watchers, then returned. "You can choose who you stand near," he said. "You can choose who you speak to when you got a moment. And you can choose who might help you when things turn."

Lila's mind flashed, uninvited, to dawn in the yard on Elijah's plantation: the fire, the iron, the line of faces forced to look. She had not been there, but she had smelled the story on other people's mouths. She had heard the way the word branding made voices thin.

"When things turn," she echoed.

Samuel nodded as if they were discussing weather. "You know they always turning. One wrong look from missus. One bad day for the master. One rumor. And you in that house, you catch the blame quick."

Lila forced herself to breathe evenly. Samuel spoke as if he was the only person who understood the plantation's cruelty, as if she had not lived inside it since childhood. That was part of the misreading too. He mistook his observations for wisdom and her silence for ignorance.

"I don't need a man to tell me the house is dangerous," she said.

Samuel's lips parted as if to reply, then closed again. He watched her a moment longer, and in his eyes she saw the shape of his want more clearly than before. It was not the hungry, careless want that made men grab in the dark. It was the want that wanted to be agreed with. The want that wanted to be owed.

He exhaled slowly, as if calming himself. "I'm offering you something," he said. "Not everybody gets offered."

“What?”

“Somebody looking out,” Samuel replied. “Somebody who can hear things. Somebody who can speak when it matters.”

Lila almost laughed, but she did not. Laughter would have been a gift to him, proof that he could move her. “You mean somebody who can trade,” she said, the word slipping out before she could soften it.

Samuel’s eyes narrowed. For the first time, the mildness in his face struggled to stay in place. “You don’t know what you talking about,” he said.

Lila held his gaze. She did not blink. “I know what it feels like when someone keeps showing up,” she said. “I know what it feels like when a person says they helping but they really counting what you owe.”

Samuel’s nostrils flared. His voice dropped another notch, almost intimate, almost gentle. “Ain’t nobody counting,” he said. “You make it hard. That’s your trouble. You take kindness and you turn it into something else.”

Lila felt her pulse in her throat. She thought of Elijah’s caution, of the way he had warned her not to say too much because words could become evidence. She thought of Samuel watching them, collecting the moment as if it belonged to him.

"I'm going inside," she said.

Samuel stepped aside, finally giving her the space she had asked for, but he did it like a man demonstrating that he could. Like the space was his to grant. "Go on," he said. "I ain't stopping you."

Lila opened the door and stepped into the dim back hall. The air changed immediately, cooler and heavy with cooked grease and polished wood. Behind her, the door remained open just long enough for her to hear Samuel speak again, not loud, not for anyone else.

"You ever need something," he said, "you know where I be."

Lila did not turn around. She closed the door with careful pressure, making sure it did not slam. Even the sound of a door could be interpreted.

She carried the herbs to the kitchen and handed them to the cook, who grunted without looking up. Then she moved through the day as she always did, a body in motion, a face arranged into the right kind of emptiness. But inside her, Samuel's words kept scraping.

You was careful. That's how I know it meant something.

He had taken her restraint and turned it into invitation. He had taken her politeness, the forced politeness of survival, and treated it like encouragement. It was a kind of theft that left no bruise to point at, no mark anyone else would recognize.

And that was what frightened her most. Not that Samuel wanted her. Want was common. Want rotted everywhere here.

What frightened her was the certainty beneath his want, the way he believed her boundaries were simply part of a larger conversation that would end where he decided it ended.

By afternoon, when she was sent to the parlor again to refill glasses, she felt his presence without seeing him. A pressure at the edge of her awareness, as real as heat off a fire. In the room, the master's voice rose in laughter, and the guest's voice answered. Lila kept her eyes down, hands steady.

In the doorway, she caught a glimpse of her reflection in the dark glass of a framed picture: a young woman with a straight back and a calm face, carrying a tray as if carrying nothing at all.

Samuel, she realized, did not see that calm as armor.

He saw it as surrender waiting to happen.

After the garden, Lila moved through the rest of the day as if nothing had happened. She carried trays. She wiped counters. She stood in doorways waiting for permission to cross them. Her face did what it had been trained to do, smoothed itself into a harmless shape.

But something had changed, and it was not in Samuel. It was in the space around her, as if the air had learned his outline and kept it even when he wasn't there.

In the late afternoon, the mistress sent her to the linen closet off the back hall, the narrow one that smelled of starch and cedar. Lila walked there with the measured pace expected of her, opened the door, and stepped inside.

The closet was dim. Light slipped through a high vent in a thin blade, catching the edges of folded sheets like pale bones. She reached for the stack she needed and paused without knowing why, hands hovering.

She listened.

No footsteps in the hall. No voice calling her name. No sound but the faint settling of the house and, farther away, the kitchen's clatter. Still, her spine tightened as if someone had just breathed against it.

Samuel wasn't there. He couldn't be. The back hall belonged to the house, and he had been careful not to follow her into it.

And yet her body held him anyway.

She took the sheets and left the closet, closing the door with the same careful pressure she'd used earlier, as if the sound of wood meeting wood might invite a consequence. As she turned, she saw the hallway empty, long and straight, with the back door at one end and the stairs at the other.

She told herself she was imagining things.

It did not matter. Imagination and danger often felt the same at first. You didn't get to wait until proof arrived. Proof was what they punished you with.

When she reached the kitchen, the cook snapped, "You late with that."

"I'm here," Lila said, voice even.

The cook took the sheets and muttered something under her breath that did not count as speech because no one had asked to hear it. Lila stayed long enough to be assigned the next task, then moved again, always moving. Work was the safest place to hide because it made you look like you belonged to your body instead of your thoughts.

By dusk the house shifted into its evening rhythm. Lamps were lit. Water was carried. The master's boots sounded on the floorboards like punctuation. His children ran through rooms until someone shouted at them to be still. The mistress's voice rose once in irritation, then fell back into the controlled tone of someone who believed irritation itself was a kind of authority.

Lila served supper and kept her eyes lowered at the right moments, lifting them only when necessary. Still, she felt the day's earlier conversation crawling under her skin.

You ever need something; you know where I be.

It was offered like comfort. It sat like a trap.

When the mistress finally dismissed her, the order came with the usual lack of ceremony, as if the woman were flicking a crumb from her skirt. Lila nodded. "Yes, ma'am," and retreated down the back hall.

Outside, the air had cooled. The yard was darker now, lit only by a few lamps and the weak spill of light from windows. The world beyond the house spread out in deeper shadow, with the quarters clustered in their familiar shapes. The smell of smoke and damp earth lay heavy, the scent of a day closing.

She started toward the quarters and kept her posture straight. Even now, even with fewer eyes, she did not allow herself to hurry.

Halfway across the yard she sensed it again, the pressure at the edge of her awareness. Not a sound. Not a movement. Something quieter than that, something that made her want to turn her head and then warned her not to.

She forced her gaze to remain forward.

A voice came from the side, low. "Evening."

Lila stopped so abruptly she hated herself for it. Her heart kicked hard once, then resumed its steady beat as if it had not betrayed her. She turned her head slowly.

Samuel stood near the edge of the smokehouse, half in shadow, hands loose at his sides. He had placed himself where he could speak to her without seeming to approach her. He looked like a man who happened to be there.

"Evening," she answered.

He nodded toward the path. "You heading back?"

"You can see that," Lila said.

Samuel's mouth tightened, then smoothed. "Just talking."

Lila kept her face blank. "Talking gets people in trouble."

"Only if they talk wrong," Samuel said.

The yard around them felt too open. Even with darkness, the space carried sound. The house windows were lit. The kitchen door was still active with bodies going in and out. Somewhere, a dog barked once, a bored sound, not the hunting bark of that other night that had been turned into a story and forced into everyone's mouth.

Lila shifted her weight. "I'm tired," she said.

Samuel did not move closer. He didn't need to. "I been thinking," he said, and the words landed like a hand on her shoulder, familiar in a way that did not belong. "About what I said. About you being careful."

Lila's jaw tightened. "Don't."

Samuel's eyes held hers. In the dark, they looked lighter, sharper. "That's what I mean," he said softly. "You always telling me don't. Like I'm a child. Like I'm trying to harm you."

"Aren't you?" Lila asked before she could stop herself.

For a moment, the night seemed to still. Samuel's expression did not break, but something in it cooled, as if a thin layer of warmth had been peeled away. Then he exhaled and nodded once, slow.

"You scared," he said, as if naming it made him generous. "I get that."

Lila did not answer.

Samuel continued. "You think I'm like them." He tilted his head slightly toward the house, not pointing directly, but the direction was clear. "You think I want to take something."

Lila felt anger rise again, hot and useless. "You already taking," she said. "My quiet."

Samuel's lips pressed together. He looked past her briefly, toward the quarters, toward the dark shapes of cabins and the thin threads of smoke lifting from chimneys. When his gaze returned to her, his voice was calm again. Too calm.

"I ain't your enemy," he said.

Lila believed he believed it. That was part of what made him dangerous. Some men knew they were cruel and leaned into it. Samuel carried his want like a reason, like something that made him righteous.

"You don't get to decide that," she replied.

Samuel's eyes narrowed a fraction. "You keep talking like you got nobody."

Lila stared at him. "I got me."

Samuel's mouth twitched, almost a smile. "That's a lonely way to live."

"It's the way that keeps me alive," Lila said, and felt the truth of it settle in her chest like a stone.

Samuel studied her for a long moment. The silence stretched, thin but unbroken. Lila felt the urge to fill it, to say something that would make him step back, something that would end this. She did not. Ending things cleanly was a privilege.

Finally, Samuel spoke again, quieter. "You don't like being watched."

The words hit so close to the bone she almost flinched. Everyone here was watched. That was the structure. But Samuel said it like it was personal, like it belonged to her alone.

"I like being left alone," she said.

Samuel nodded slowly. "Then you should be careful who you let stand near you. Folks see things, and they talk. You know that."

The shape of the threat was soft, like a cloth held over a mouth. Not spoken outright. Not loud enough to be accused. But clear in its intention.

Lila's hands curled at her sides. She kept her voice even with effort. "What folks?"

Samuel shrugged, easy again. "Any folks. Like I said, I ain't the only one with eyes."

Lila understood then what his presence meant. It wasn't just wanting her. It wasn't even just wanting control. It was wanting her to live with him in her head, the way she now did. To make her choices bend around the possibility of him.

He had succeeded.

She lifted her chin slightly. "I'm going," she said.

Samuel stepped aside, granting space again like a man granting mercy. "Go on," he replied. "I ain't stopping you."

She walked away without hurrying, because hurrying would have been an admission. Each step felt deliberate, heavy with the effort of appearing unbothered. She did not look back.

Behind her, Samuel's voice followed, soft enough that it could be mistaken for the night itself. "You remember what I said."

She kept walking until the quarters swallowed her into their darker cluster, until the lamps from the house were farther away and the air smelled more like bodies and smoke than polished wood. Only then did she allow her breath to change, a small release that did not feel like relief.

Inside her cabin, the night's sounds closed around her: low murmurs, the rustle of straw, a distant cough. Lila sat on the edge of her pallet and pressed her fingertips into her palm hard enough to leave marks.

Samuel had not touched her. He had not raised his voice. He had not done anything a person could point to and say, There, that is the harm.

But his presence remained.

It remained in the way she listened for footsteps outside her door even when she knew she would hear none. It remained in the way she measured her own movements, not just for the white eyes she'd always feared, but for his attention, which was something else: not authority, but access. The knowledge that he could be anywhere he chose to be and could speak to her as if he had a right.

She lay back and stared at the ceiling. The dark above her held no answers. She tried to replay Elijah's voice instead, to replace Samuel's with something steadier.

You best not say too much.

Elijah's caution had felt like a warning offered as care. Samuel's caution felt like a leash.

Across the distance, on Boone's plantation, Elijah felt a shift he couldn't name. Days passed, work filled his hands, heat filled his shed, and still something kept tugging at the back of his thoughts. At the forge, he could read metal. He could tell when it was close to breaking by the way it resisted the hammer, by the sound it made when struck. People were harder. But the world had begun to sound different, as if something in it had been tightened.

He noticed small things. A pause in conversation when he walked near the quarters. A glance held too briefly by someone who usually didn't look up. A tool moved from where he'd left it, not stolen, just shifted, as if to remind him that even his space wasn't fully his.

And in the middle of those small wrongnesses was Samuel's face from the gathering, eyes bright, voice mild.

"Ain't your choosing."

Elijah had taken those words as truth. Now they felt like something else. Like prediction.

He worked late one night, finishing a hinge the master wanted fixed before morning. The forge glowed, coals breathing orange, the iron on the anvil ringing with each strike. The sound should have been familiar enough to calm him.

Instead, between hammer blows, he thought he heard a whistle.

Not the sharp, deliberate one from the woods, not the overseer's signal. Something softer, half-formed, like the memory of a sound more than the sound itself.

He froze, hammer held midair, listening.

Nothing but the crackle of coals and the distant night insects.

Still, his skin stayed tight.

Because that was how it started. Not with chains. Not with shouting. With the sense that something had noticed you. With the sense that even silence had become crowded.

Elijah lowered the hammer and forced himself to keep working. The hinge had to be finished. The metal had to be shaped. His hands had to stay steady.

But in his mind, Lila's face hovered, and Samuel's gaze hovered behind it, patient and unchanged.

Some kinds of presence did not need to be in the room to do their work.

They only had to remain.

Chapter 4

Whispered North

The word did not arrive as a declaration. It came the way smoke came under a door, faint at first, almost deniable, and then suddenly you realized it had been there long enough to settle into your clothes.

Elijah heard it in pieces.

It started with a man at the edge of the quarters, old enough that his back had taken on the permanent curve of work. He was mending a split board on the side of his cabin with a nail he'd straightened and reused, tapping carefully so the sound wouldn't carry. Elijah had paused nearby, waiting for his turn at the water barrel, listening the way people listened now, not for comfort but for changes.

The old man spoke without looking up. Not to Elijah exactly, but into the space between them.

"They say the river got a way," he muttered.

Elijah didn't answer. He watched the nail head sink into the wood with each tap.

"A way where the dogs lose it," the man went on, still quiet, still not lifting his eyes. "Where the scent don't hold."

Elijah's fingers tightened around his empty tin cup. The river they all knew about cut along the far edge of the property like a boundary that didn't need a fence. It was wide in places, shallow in others. It carried mud and branches and the occasional dead animal, and it carried sound. Sometimes, at night, you could hear it moving even from the quarters, steady as breath.

"Ain't no way," Elijah said finally, because denial was its own form of safety.

The old man's mouth twitched. Not a smile. Something closer to a grim habit. "Ain't no way," he agreed, and drove the last tap in.

Elijah took his water and walked away with the words clinging to him anyway.

The second piece came two nights later, after the last chores had been assigned and finished, when the quarters settled into their strained version of rest. Elijah sat outside his cabin with a bit of wire in his hands, working it into a hook he could hide in the blacksmith shed later. Small tools came from small steals. You didn't build a plan; you built the possibility of one.

Two men sat on a low log a short distance away, their bodies angled inward as if sharing warmth. Their voices were kept low, but the night had a way of carrying sound when it wanted to. Elijah wasn't trying to listen. Listening happened anyway.

"I'm telling you, my cousin—" one began, then stopped, swallowed, restarted. "My cousin gone two years back. They said he dead. But I heard different."

"You heard a ghost?" the other murmured.

"Hush," the first said, sharper. "I heard he made it. Up."

Up. They used it like a direction and like an answer.

The other man let out a breath that might have been a laugh if laughter still came easily. "Up where?"

The first man hesitated, and Elijah felt that hesitation like a weight. Then, so quietly it was almost a thought, the word was breathed into the dark.

"North."

Elijah's hands paused on the wire. The hook shape held halfway, unfinished. He kept his gaze down, kept his posture loose, forced his breathing not to change. Even a still body could look guilty if it went too still.

The second man didn't respond right away. Elijah imagined him staring at the dirt the way people did when they were trying not to show their hunger. Finally, the second man said, "Don't say that."

"I didn't say nothing," the first replied quickly, too quickly.

Silence fell over them. Not a comfortable silence. A silence that sounded like retreat.

Elijah waited, expecting the conversation to die. It did not die so much as fold inward.

The first man spoke again, softer. "They say there's folks. Not like here. Folks what help."

The second man's voice came out flat, as if trying to cut the idea down before it could grow. "Ain't no folks like that."

"Maybe," the first man whispered. "But they say it. They say if you get to the river and you follow it till it bends; there's a mark. Something carved. You see it and you know."

"You know what?" the second asked.

The first hesitated again. "You know you ain't alone."

The words landed like a stone dropped into still water. Elijah felt the ripples inside his own chest. You know you ain't alone. It was a sentence that could save you or kill you, depending on who heard it.

A door creaked somewhere, and both men fell instantly silent, their bodies returning to the shapes required of them. Elijah forced his hands to move again, bending the wire as if that was all he'd been thinking about.

The door that had creaked belonged to a cabin farther down. A woman stepped out, wrapped in a shawl, and spat into the dirt. No one called out. No one moved. The night resumed its careful stillness.

Elijah finished the hook, hid it under the edge of a loose plank, and went inside. He lay on his pallet with the word north moving behind his eyes like a shape he couldn't stop seeing. It was not comfort. It was not even hope. It was something restless that made the air in the cabin feel thinner.

By morning, the rumor had traveled without ever being spoken directly. Elijah could feel it in how people watched the tree line. In how a man paused a beat too long when the river's direction was mentioned during work. In how a woman's hand tightened around her child's wrist when a dog barked in the distance, as if the bark might carry more meaning now.

Rumors did not need volume. They needed need.

Even the master's yard seemed to sense it. The white men moved with a subtle shift in attention, their eyes sweeping the fields more often. The overseer lingered longer at the edge of the work line, hands on hips, head tilted as if listening for something beyond sound. Elijah watched him the way he watched a heated bar of iron, knowing that when it glowed it was already too late to touch.

At the forge, the day's work demanded focus. Elijah mended a cracked plowshare, the metal splitting along a seam like bone. He heated it until it softened and took it apart with a chisel, then welded it back, hammering the join until the ring of metal sounded whole again. The labor steadied him, but it couldn't drown the word. North sat at the edge of each hammer strike, patient.

Around midday, a boy was sent to fetch nails. He was small enough to be overlooked by the white men and old enough to know what kinds of speech could get you hurt. He hovered at the shed doorway, eyes darting.

"You heard?" the boy murmured, barely moving his lips.

Elijah did not look up from his work. "Heard what?"

The boy swallowed. "Somebody say there's a line. Like a road, but not a road. People say it's under the ground."

Elijah's hammer slowed. He set it down carefully. "Ain't no such thing," he said, because sometimes denial was the only prayer a man could afford.

The boy nodded too fast, terrified of having spoken at all. "Yes, sir. I mean yes. I ain't say nothing." He stepped inside, grabbed the nails, and fled as if the shed itself might accuse him.

Elijah stood alone with the fire and the sound of his own breath.

Under the ground. The phrase had a strange feel. It made Elijah think of graves. It made him think of the way the branded man's scream had been swallowed by the yard and then buried under routine as if it had never happened. If there was a road under the ground, it was a road built from silence, from people disappearing without leaving a trace.

That was what made the rumor both dangerous and irresistible. It suggested an escape that didn't require you to outrun dogs or fight men with ropes. It suggested a hidden structure inside the structure, an unseen passage that existed right alongside the one they were trapped in.

A way that belonged to someone else.

That night, Elijah didn't seek conversation, but he found himself closer to it, as if the rumor pulled bodies into new shapes. He sat on the step outside his cabin and watched the darkness between cabins. Not much happened. People spoke in low tones, then stopped when someone passed. A woman hummed a half-song without words, the melody broken and cautious, like she didn't trust music either.

Elijah sensed movement near the far corner of the quarters, a figure standing where shadow gathered thickest. For a moment his body tightened, expecting to see an overseer or a patrol light. But it was not white. It was one of their own.

Samuel.

He was far enough away that no one would call it hovering. He was also placed where he could see without being seen too clearly. Elijah could not make out Samuel's expression in the dark, but he could feel the attention. It came off Samuel the way heat came off coals, steady and deliberate.

Elijah looked away first, pretending not to notice. That was the rule. If you acknowledged the watcher, you gave him shape.

Still, Elijah's mind worked. Samuel had been at the gathering. Samuel had watched him and Lila. Samuel had stepped forward and spoken Elijah's name like it mattered. Now Samuel stood at the edge of this new whisper as if he'd been waiting for it to be born.

Rumors were alive, Elijah realized. Not like stories told for entertainment. Alive like a thing that fed and grew. Alive like something that could be trained.

He thought of the whistle in the woods from those that tried to escape, the sound that had not chased but guided. He thought of how quickly the runaway had been caught, how prepared the men had been, as if the woods belonged to them too. A rumor could become a whistle if the wrong person held it.

And Samuel was the kind of man who held things.

Across the distance, on Carter's plantation, the word arrived for Lila differently. Not through men by a log, not through boys with big eyes. It came through the house, through the white mouths that assumed she was furniture.

She was in the side hall with a basket of folded cloth when she heard the master speaking to a visitor, his voice irritated in that smooth way irritation took when it wore authority.

"Had another one try it," he said. "Not ours, over Boone's way. Caught him quick, though. Made an example."

The visitor made a sound of agreement. "They're getting ideas," he said. "Heard talk of a route. People helping them."

"People helping them," the master repeated with contempt. "There's always somebody eager to play hero, even if it costs them. We'll tighten patrols along the river. Put fear back where it belongs."

Lila kept her eyes down on the cloth, fingers moving. Her face remained arranged, empty and agreeable. Inside her, something cold moved.

A route. Along the river.

The rumor wasn't just in the quarters. It had reached the men who owned the land. That meant it was either true enough to worry them, or useful enough to punish.

Later, when she carried water to the back stoop, she caught two kitchen women speaking in the tight space between tasks. Their voices were low, their heads bent together, not in friendship but in shared risk.

"They say north got folks what hide you," one whispered.

"Don't," the other warned, glancing toward the yard.

"I'm just saying what I heard," the first insisted. "They say there's signs. A cloth on a fence. A mark on a tree."

The second woman's mouth tightened. "They say a lot of things. People who go chasing them things don't come back."

Lila stepped past them without reacting. She did not ask. She did not listen too openly. But the words threaded into her anyway, tangling with everything else already inside her: the brand's lesson, Samuel's presence, Elijah's steady hands.

That night, in her cabin, Lila sat with her knees drawn up and pressed her fingertips to the inside of her wrist, feeling her own pulse. The rumor of north felt like a door she had not allowed herself to see, and now that she'd seen its outline she could not unsee it.

It terrified her for the simplest reason.

It made her imagine.

And imagination, she knew, was what they punished first. Not the act of escape, not even the attempt. The thought that escape could exist was what they branded into flesh and forced everyone to watch.

Somewhere outside, a dog barked and then went quiet.

Lila listened until her breathing matched the darkness again.

On Boone's plantation, Samuel remained at the edge of the quarters longer than he needed to. He was not close enough for anyone to accuse him of eavesdropping. He didn't have to be. He understood something most people didn't dare to name: information moved even when bodies didn't. It slid under doors. It rode on the back of a warning. It hid inside a denial.

North. River. Mark. Route.

Each fragment found a place in Samuel's mind, not as hope, but as currency waiting to be spent.

When he finally turned away from the quarter's dim cluster of cabins, he did it without hurry. The night was thick, full of soft sounds and restless insects. Above him the sky offered a few stingy stars, blinking like eyes that did not want to witness.

Samuel walked with his hands at his sides and his face calm, and the rumor followed him as faithfully as a shadow.

Alive, and growing.

Two days after the rumor first took on a shape Elijah could feel in the air, the master's son came to the forge with a list folded in his fist and impatience written across his face.

"You're going back over to Carter's," he said, as if he were announcing the weather. "Fence latch on their east line busted, and Mr. Carter asked for you by name."

Elijah kept his eyes on the bar of iron cooling on the anvil. He counted his breaths before he answered. Being asked for by name was not a compliment. It was a hook. It meant someone had noticed the steadiness of his hands and decided to make use of it.

"Yes, sir," he said.

The master's son lingered, tapping the folded paper against his palm. "You don't need to talk while you're there. You just work. Understand?"

Elijah nodded once. "Yes, sir."

When the boy finally left, Elijah stood alone in the shed with the forge's heat pressing into his face. He could still smell smoke on the air from the coals, sharp and familiar. Somewhere outside, the day moved on with its usual cruelty, indifferent and efficient. But inside him, the word north moved with it, a quiet second heartbeat.

He was marched with two other men down the same road as before, a white rider behind them and another ahead. The road cut between trees that leaned inward like they were curious. Elijah watched the branches, the undergrowth, the places a man might step off and vanish if he were willing to die for the chance. He watched and kept walking, because watching did not change the chain of decisions that led a body from one place to another.

At Carter's plantation, the yard was less crowded than it had been during the gathering. No preacher. No wagons of trade goods. Just the ordinary motion of labor: men hauling boards, women moving water, children pushed into corners where they were told to be silent.

Elijah was directed toward the east fence line, where a section near the woods had sagged and the latch hung wrong, the metal bent as if it had been struck in anger. A white man in a sweat-darkened hat pointed without looking at Elijah's face.

"Make it hold," he said. "And don't take all day."

Elijah knelt in the dirt with his tools and examined the damage. The hinge pins were loose. The latch plate had warped. It wasn't a hard fix, but it would take care, and care was what he had. He set his hands to it and tried to keep his thoughts sealed behind his teeth.

Still, he listened.

Sound traveled differently near the woods. The house noises softened here, replaced by insects and the occasional birdcall. Farther down the fence, two enslaved men worked with axes, splitting fallen limbs for firewood. Their conversation was low, broken by the rhythm of chopping. Once, Elijah caught a word that snagged: river. Another time: patrol. Each word landed and then disappeared into the air as if the air itself was trained to swallow them.

Elijah kept his eyes on the hinge.

When he first saw Lila, she was not coming toward him. She was moving along the yard's edge with a basket balanced on her hip, headed away from the house toward a line of outbuildings. She walked with the same controlled pace he remembered, neither hurried nor slow enough to draw irritation. Her face was arranged into the quiet mask required of her.

He did not call out. Calling out was a flare.

He watched her pass behind a stack of boards and vanish for a moment. His hands tightened around the pliers until the metal bit his palm through callus. He forced himself to loosen his grip and return to the latch, bending it back into shape with measured pressure.

After some time, he sensed movement near him and did not look up immediately. He waited until his hands had a reason to pause, until he could lift his head as if he were only checking his work.

Lila stood a few feet away, the basket gone, her hands empty. She did not step closer. She did not stand too far. She placed herself at a distance that could be explained if anyone asked: close enough to speak about the fence, far enough not to look like she had come for him.

Her eyes flicked to the hinge, then to his hands, then to his face.

"You fixing that for them?" she asked, voice quiet.

Elijah kept his tone flat. "That's what they sent me for."

Lila nodded once, as if considering the obvious. Her gaze moved past him, toward the yard, checking the line of sight from the house. A white man crossed the open space carrying a bucket. He did not look their way. A dog lay in the shade near a post, head on its paws, watching nothing.

When Lila spoke again, her words were ordinary, shaped to be safe. "You got a long walk from your place."

Elijah bent closer to the hinge as he answered, as if focusing. "Ain't my choosing."

Her mouth tightened slightly at the echo of the phrase. She had heard it before, in his telling or in the way words traveled. Or maybe she simply recognized the truth of it the way anyone here recognized it.

Lila waited a beat. Then, in a voice so low it seemed meant only for the wood between them, she said, "They talking up here."

Elijah did not respond right away. He slid the hinge pin back into place and tested the swing of the gate, letting it move with a soft creak. He kept his head down, as if concentrating on the latch, and asked without lifting his eyes, "Talking what?"

Lila's fingers flexed once, then settled. "You know," she said. "That word."

Elijah's throat tightened. He could hear the old man's voice in his mind, muttering about the river having a way. He could hear the two men on the log, one of them too hungry to keep quiet. He kept his face still.

"People say lots of foolish things," he said, and the sentence was both denial and a warning. Don't make me repeat it. Don't make me own it in my mouth.

Lila's eyes held on him. She did not flinch from his caution. If anything, it steadied her.

"They say it's not foolish," she murmured. "They say there's marks."

Elijah felt the fence post under his palm, rough wood warmed by sun. Marks. He thought of a different mark, pressed into flesh, and the way the yard had been forced to witness it. He did not let that memory reach his face.

"What kind of marks?" he asked, careful. A question was dangerous, but sometimes not asking was worse. Not asking left you with only your own imagination, and imagination could run wild into death.

Lila glanced toward the woods, then back. "Like you wouldn't notice unless you already looking," she said. "A piece of cloth tied where it shouldn't be. A sign on a tree. They say you follow the river till it bends and there's something cut into the bark."

Elijah's hands continued working as she spoke. He tightened a bolt. He aligned the latch plate. He made his body look like a man doing his assignment, because bodies were always being read.

He said, "Who told you?"

Lila's eyes dropped to the hinge, then lifted again. "The house," she answered simply. Then, more carefully: "White men talking like I'm furniture. They mad. They saying they'll set patrols."

Elijah swallowed. The rumor had reached the men who owned the land. That meant the air was already tightening. It meant the river would no longer be just water. It would be watched like a mouth watched for forbidden words.

He kept his voice steady. "That ain't new," he said, but he knew it was. Not the patrols themselves. The reason. A reason made a difference. A reason made a man's eye sharper.

Lila hesitated, then said, "They mentioned your place."

Elijah's pulse jumped. He kept his head down, pretending to inspect the latch. "They always watching," he murmured. "They just like to pretend they ain't."

Lila looked past him again, checking angles. Her calm was practiced, but he could see the strain in it, the way her shoulders held themselves as if she were bracing for impact.

"There's another thing," she said.

Elijah forced himself not to look up too quickly. "What?"

Lila's voice thinned. "Samuel."

The name landed with weight. Elijah's hands went momentarily still, then resumed, slower. Samuel had been in his thoughts like a thorn he couldn't pull out clean. Hearing Lila say the name made the thorn turn.

"What about him?" Elijah asked and hated that he needed to ask.

Lila's eyes stayed on his face now, steady and direct in a way that felt like trust and fear braided together. "He been listening," she said. "Not just to me. To everybody. He shows up where talking happens. He offers things. He acts like he helping. But it don't feel like help."

Elijah felt the heat rise behind his ribs, a useless anger. "He bothering you," he said, keeping it low, making it a statement so she wouldn't have to say yes.

Lila's jaw tightened. "He don't touch," she said. "He don't do nothing you can point at. He just stays. He says too much like warnings."

Elijah understood the shape of that kind of threat. A leash made of words. A trap made of courtesy. Samuel didn't need to grab; he needed to position.

Elijah's voice came out rougher than he intended. "You stay away from him."

Lila's expression flickered, not amused, not offended. Something like tiredness. "I try," she said. "He makes trying into a game."

Elijah fitted the latch and tested it. The gate swung and caught cleanly now, clicking into place with a final sound that felt too decisive for the conversation happening beside it.

Lila watched his hands as he wiped dirt from them. She spoke again, quieter still. "At my place, they saying river. They saying bend. They saying they'll catch the next one and mark them same as that man."

Elijah's stomach turned. He could smell the branding again in his memory, sweet and terrible. He forced his face to remain calm.

He said, "At my place, folks saying the same things. But nobody know nothing for sure."

Lila let out a breath, small and controlled. "You think it's real?" she asked. Not loud enough to be a question the world could hear. Only enough to be a question he could answer.

Elijah hesitated. Truth could kill. Lying could kill too.

"I think," he said slowly, "that people don't risk saying it unless they need it bad."

Lila's eyes held on his. In that brief second, the yard around them felt farther away, as if the open space had blurred and only this small circle of careful speech existed.

Then a voice called from the direction of the house. "Lila!"

Her shoulders did not jump. She did not flinch. But something in her eyes closed, a door shutting quickly.

"Yes, ma'am," she called back, voice rising to the polite tone required.

She looked at Elijah one last time, and the look carried more than words could. It carried the exchange itself: pieces of rumor traded like contraband, handled with bare fingers because gloves didn't exist for this kind of risk.

"Be careful," she said, the sentence shaped so it could mean anything if someone overheard. Careful with the gate. Careful with the tools. Careful with your own mouth.

Elijah nodded once. "You too," he replied.

Lila turned and walked away at the same measured pace, becoming again what the house required her to be: a quiet body moving on command. Elijah watched her go only long enough to ensure she didn't look back.

Then he bent to gather his tools. As he did, he felt it, the subtle shift in air that came when someone else entered a space without announcing themselves.

He looked up.

Samuel stood near the fence line a short distance away, half in sun, half in shadow. He hadn't approached close enough to be accused of eavesdropping. He didn't need to. His eyes moved from Elijah to the direction Lila had gone, then back again. His face was calm, almost mild.

Elijah forced his posture loose, his expression empty. He lifted the repaired latch once more, testing it as if that was all that mattered, and called out in a tone meant to sound neutral, "Gate's fixed."

Samuel didn't answer the statement. He stepped a fraction closer, still not close. His voice was conversational. "Good," he said. "You always make things hold."

Elijah kept his gaze on the hinge. "That's the work."

Samuel's eyes stayed on him. Elijah could feel the attention like a hand at the back of his neck.

"A lot of talk these days," Samuel said lightly, as if discussing weather again. "Talk make folks restless."

Elijah's jaw tightened. He kept his voice flat. "Talk don't change nothing."

Samuel's mouth tilted, almost a smile. "Don't it?" he murmured, and the softness of the question was what made it sharp.

Elijah shouldered his tool bundle and stood. The fence behind him felt like a boundary he couldn't trust. The woods beyond it held the river somewhere, bending and moving, carrying both rumor and consequence.

Samuel watched him with the patience of a man collecting pieces. Elijah understood then what Lila meant. Samuel's harm wasn't in what he did. It was in what he noticed, and in the way noticing could be turned into power.

Elijah started toward the yard where the white rider would be waiting to march him back. As he walked, he kept his face arranged, his body obedient.

Inside his head, the cautious exchange replayed already, each phrase examined for weaknesses.

Marks. River. Patrols. Samuel listening.

And beneath it all, the word north, not spoken aloud between them, but present anyway, like a living thing that had learned their names.

Elijah did not speak on the walk back. The rider behind them seemed content with silence, the horse's hooves keeping time with their footsteps, the road unfolding like a sentence nobody wanted to finish.

He carried his tools the way he always did, bundled tight, weight familiar against his hip. Familiar weight was comforting because it asked nothing of him. But his mind had been given new weight, and it did not settle so neatly.

Marks. River. Bend.

Samuel listening.

He kept his eyes forward and let his face go slack, a mask made from long practice. Still, every so often, his gaze flicked toward the trees as if he might catch sight of something that would prove the rumor one way or the other. The woods gave him nothing. They stood there, indifferent, as if they hadn't swallowed a man and returned him as a lesson only days ago.

When they reached Boone's plantation, the yard already carried the late-day exhaustion of bodies pushed too hard. Men moved slow with sacks on their backs. Women leaned over wash tubs, wrists red from soap and scrubbing. A child stumbled under a pail and was snapped at to mind himself. Ordinary cruelty, ordinary rhythm.

Elijah was sent straight to report, to stand where he was told and answer with the right words. "Latch fixed," he said. "Gate holds." He did not mention the rumor. He did not mention Lila. He did not mention Samuel's eyes.

The master's son barely looked up. "Good. Get back to the shed. We got a plow waiting."

Yes, sir. Always yes.

At the forge, heat met him like a familiar hand. The coals were down from the day's earlier work, but a few stirred orange when he raked them. He fed the fire, pumped the bellows, watched the flame wake. In the growing glow, he could pretend his thoughts were only tools to be shaped and set aside.

But the rumor had already changed the shape of his attention. He found himself listening between hammer strikes, the way he had listened for a whistle in the night. Every small sound seemed to carry the possibility of meaning. The creak of the shed door. A footstep outside. A pause in voices beyond the wall.

When the plowshare finally sat on the anvil, heated to a workable red, Elijah lifted his hammer and began to strike. The iron rang clean, a sound that should have steadied him. Instead, it reminded him of another ring, the clink of tongs against a branding iron in morning air. His jaw clenched.

He worked until dusk made the shed's edges go dark and the fire's glow became the main light in the world. Then he banked the coals and stepped outside, his skin prickling with cooled sweat.

The quarters were settling. People moved in and out of cabins, quick and quiet. A low murmur of conversation rose and fell like wind through grass, never staying in one place long enough to be held.

Elijah walked toward his cabin and stopped when he saw the old man again, the one who'd spoken about the river. The man sat near his doorway, hands busy with a broken shoe, a nail held between his fingers like a secret.

Elijah approached as if he only meant to pass by. He didn't slow until he was close enough that speaking wouldn't require raising his voice.

The old man did not look up. "You been off," he said.

Elijah's throat tightened. "They sent me to Carter's."

The old man's nail paused. "Carter's got fences too," he muttered, and something in the way he said it implied fences could be more than fences.

Elijah kept his gaze on the man's hands. "They do," he agreed.

A moment stretched. The old man's eyes flicked up, quick and wary, then back down. "You hear the same talk we hear?" he asked, as if asking about weather again.

Elijah's pulse shifted. He could feel, faintly, how dangerous it was to answer wrong. Denial could be safety. Denial could also be a lie that left you blind.

"I hear folks restless," he said carefully.

The old man gave a sound that might have been agreement. "Restless get you killed."

Elijah didn't answer. He waited, letting silence act like a cover.

After a beat, the old man spoke again, quieter. "Restless also get you moving," he said.

Elijah's mouth went dry. He looked away, scanning the darkening yard without seeming to, making sure no one stood too close. The overseer was nowhere obvious. That didn't mean anything. Eyes didn't need a body attached to them.

"You ever see a mark?" Elijah asked and hated how the question sounded in his own mouth. Like he wanted it.

The old man's hands resumed their work, slow and careful. "Ain't seen," he said. "Heard."

Elijah let out a breath through his nose, controlled. "That don't help."

The old man's nail pressed into the sole. "Ain't supposed to," he murmured. "If it helped easy, they'd have it already."

Elijah felt a strange, sharp laugh try to rise and forced it down. The truth of the statement was a kind of cruelty. Everything that could save you had to be hidden well enough that it might never be found.

He started to step away, then stopped himself. "If a man did see something," he said, keeping his tone flat, almost bored, as if the thought didn't matter. "Where he supposed to look first?"

The old man finally looked up. His eyes were tired and hard; a face built from endurance. "Why you asking?" he said, not accusing, just measuring.

Elijah held his gaze for a fraction, then let his eyes drop. "Ain't asking for me," he lied.

The old man's mouth tightened. He studied Elijah the way Elijah studied metal, looking for weakness, for cracks. "That's what people always say," he replied.

Then, after a moment that felt like a decision, he spoke. "River," he said. One word. "Not where it loud. Not where folks fish. Where it run mean and shallow and you cut your feet if you ain't watching." He paused. "And you don't look with your eyes. You look with your sense. Things that don't belong."

Elijah nodded once, as if he'd been told nothing more than how to mend a shoe. "All right," he said.

The old man dropped his gaze back to his hands. "Don't bring that question back here," he muttered. "Questions got echoes."

Elijah walked away with the word question repeating in his head. He entered his cabin and sat among the bodies and the dim. People talked low, traded safe complaints, spoke of hunger and sore backs and the master's mood. Elijah listened and contributed only what was required.

But under the ordinary words, he felt the rumor moving like something alive, making the walls thinner.

Later, when most had settled and the night had grown quieter, Elijah lay on his pallet and stared into the dark. He thought of Lila's face, the controlled calm that had held even when fear pressed against it. He thought of her telling him about patrols, about Samuel's presence, about white men talking as if she were furniture. He thought of her asking, "You think it's real?"

He hadn't answered. Not fully.

Because real was not the right word. Real didn't mean safe. Real didn't mean possible. Real only meant it existed, somewhere, for someone else.

In Carter's quarters, Lila lay awake too.

Her day had ended with the same demands it always ended with, a list of tasks completed, a body put away like a tool. She'd carried water, cleared plates, folded cloth until her fingers ached. When the mistress finally dismissed her, Lila had nodded and walked out with her face smooth, the way you did when you wanted to leave no trace of your insides behind.

Outside, the yard had been busy with men finishing late work. She'd kept her eyes forward and felt, rather than saw, Samuel's attention at the edge of her path. She didn't know if he was there. She didn't need to. Her body had learned his outline the way it had learned the outline of every threat.

In her cabin, she sat with her knees drawn up and her hands clasped around them. The rumor had spread here too, but it carried different weight when you heard it through the house. White men spoke of tightening patrols with the same tone they used to speak of fixing a roof, as if freedom was a leak they could patch.

Elijah had told her, in the safest words he could manage, that people didn't risk saying it unless they needed it bad.

Need. That was the center of it.

Lila tried to tell herself she could live without asking the question. She had lived this long by keeping her thoughts measured, by swallowing every hunger that didn't serve survival. Want could make you careless. Careless got you hurt, got others hurt, got you marked.

But the rumor kept turning in her mind until it found its shape.

Not a plan. Not even hope.

A question.

If there really were marks, if there really were a bend in the river where something was carved or tied or left wrong on purpose, then someone had made it. Someone had risked leaving a sign for another person to find. Someone had looked at a world built to trap them and still believed a path could exist through it.

And if that was true, then another question followed, quieter and more dangerous.

Why not me?

She pressed her fingers to the inside of her wrist again and felt her pulse. It did not race. It stayed steady, stubborn. The same steadiness she'd noticed in Elijah's hands.

She pictured him kneeling by the fence latch, fixing what they told him to fix, making it hold. She pictured, too, the way his face had stayed blank while his eyes listened. A man trained to look harmless while his mind stayed sharp.

Lila knew what Samuel wanted from her. Attention, agreement, debt. A place in her life that he could claim. She also knew what the plantation wanted: her compliance, her quiet, her acceptance of the boundaries as if they were the edge of the world.

The rumor offered an edge beyond the edge. It offered a place the plantation's rules couldn't fully touch.

But she had seen what happened to men who ran with nothing but a word in their mouth. She had heard that scream carried on other people's tongues. She had smelled the fear of it in the way people went silent when an overseer passed.

The North, if it existed, would not come down here and announce itself. It would not speak loudly. It would not make the choice easy.

So, the question formed in her like a bruise you couldn't point to.

If the North doesn't speak, how do you know where to go?

And if you did know, if you found the mark, if you reached the bend, could you trust what you saw?

She closed her eyes and tried to sleep.

In the dark, Elijah's mind and Lila's mind moved in their separate cabins, shaped by distance but pressed by the same invisible hand. The rumor did not give them comfort. It did not promise them anything.

It only gave them a question they could not unthink.

Somewhere outside, a dog barked once and then went quiet, as if listening.

And somewhere else, not in either cabin, Samuel lay awake with his own kind of calm, the kind that came from collecting rather than longing. He did not need to speak the word north aloud. He had already stored its fragments away.

Marks. River. Bend. Patrols.

He understood, with the same cold clarity he'd felt watching the branding, that the idea of escape was more powerful than the act. A body could be caught. A body could be dragged back and marked and made into a warning.

But a question, once it formed, was harder to chain.

Samuel stared into the dark and listened to the plantation breathe.

He could not stop the question from spreading.

But he could decide where it led.

Chapter 5

First Trade

Samuel waited three days after the word began to thicken in the air.

Not because he was unsure. Because he was learning the new shape of the plantation's listening.

The rumor had done what rumors always did here: it made people careful in the wrong places and careless in the right ones. Men who had never spoken about anything beyond sore backs and hunger suddenly had too much silence in their mouths. Women who had learned to keep their eyes down began to glance toward the tree line as if the woods had started calling their names. Even the children, who didn't know the word north but knew the sound of adult fear, moved with a new clinginess, hands gripping skirts and sleeves tighter.

Samuel watched all of it the way he watched work lines and doorways. Not with excitement. With measurement.

He did not speak the word. He didn't need to. He listened for where it slipped out on its own, for who couldn't help themselves. He listened for the people who couldn't keep their need quiet.

And he listened for something else, too: the places where white men's attention shifted.

The master didn't say north. The overseer didn't say it either. But the patrols along the river began to lengthen. The dogs were fed earlier, riled sooner, as if they were being trained to want the chase before the chase even came. A rifle that usually stayed above the mantle in the main house was carried out one afternoon and leaned beside the porch, close enough to touch.

Fear, Samuel understood, was a currency on both sides. The difference was that on one side it was spent. On the other, it was collected.

He needed to know which side he could afford to be on.

The first time he tried, he chose something small. Not a plan. Not the word. Not anything that would draw blood quickly enough to stain him. He chose a loose thread and watched to see who pulled it.

The loose thread was a man named Isaiah, field hand, quiet, the kind of quiet that didn't ask to be seen. Isaiah wasn't a leader. He wasn't the sort the overseer watched out of habit. But Samuel had noticed two things about him: he lingered near the river line when he could, and he talked to people who were hungry for talk.

Samuel had heard him one night, voice low behind his cabin, telling another man about a bend in the water where the bank dipped and the reeds grew thick. He had spoken as if the river could hide you if you treated it right. He hadn't said north. He hadn't said marks. He hadn't named anything that could be held up as proof.

But he'd spoken like someone who had decided the river was more than water.

Samuel didn't hate Isaiah. That wasn't the feeling. Hatred took too much heat. Heat made you reckless. Samuel had survived by staying cool.

What he felt was simpler and sharper. He felt the instinct to test the fence before he tried to climb it.

On the fourth morning, Samuel made sure he was assigned near the main yard where the overseer's movements were easiest to predict. There were places the overseer liked to stand, places that gave him the widest view, and Samuel had watched him long enough to know how he preferred his control arranged. The overseer liked the angle by the feed shed, where he could see the work line and the quarters in the same sweep. He liked the shade near the stable when the sun got high, and he liked the open space by the toolshed when he wanted his presence to be felt like a hand on the back of a neck.

Samuel positioned himself to cross that open space with a bucket in each hand. The movement wasn't suspicious. Everyone carried things. Work was always being moved from one place to another, like bodies.

As he crossed, he saw the overseer exactly where he expected: near the toolshed, hat pushed back, a length of switch resting easy in his hand as if it were part of him. The overseer's eyes were lazy but not soft. They slid across the yard the way a blade slid across whetstone.

Samuel slowed just a fraction, enough to appear hesitant. Hesitation could be read as a reason. A reason could be used.

"Sir," Samuel said, keeping his tone respectful, small.

The overseer's eyes settled on him. "What."

Samuel shifted his grip on the buckets as if the weight was awkward. "Ain't nothing much," he said, then stopped as if reconsidering whether to speak. He let a little fear show, not enough to look guilty, enough to look loyal.

The overseer's gaze sharpened. "Spit it out."

Samuel glanced toward the quarters, then back. "I heard some talk," he said. He did not say where. He did not say when. He didn't offer a story, only the shape of one. "Just talk. Folks saying things about the river line."

The overseer's face didn't change, but Samuel saw the tiny shift in his stance. Interest, controlled.

"Who," the overseer said.

Samuel swallowed as if the name cost him. "Isaiah," he answered quietly. "He been pointing folks toward the reeds down past the east bend. Could be nothing. Could be just foolishness."

The overseer stared at him for a long moment. Samuel held still, letting his face carry a careful combination of worry and obedience. He did not look proud. Pride could make a man look like he wanted reward. Wanting reward could make you look like you had a habit.

The overseer finally spoke. "You go on."

Samuel nodded quickly. "Yes, sir."

He carried the buckets away and did not look back. He did not need to. He could feel the overseer's eyes on him for another beat, measuring whether this was true or a trap. Samuel kept walking with steady steps, the same pace he'd always had, as if nothing had happened.

Inside him, something tight loosened, not relief but anticipation. He had dropped a pebble into deep water. Now he would watch what surfaced.

He did not have to wait long.

By midmorning, the yard's usual noise had changed. A sharp whistle cut through the air, not the distant, deliberate whistle that had drawn a runaway into hands in the woods, but the overseer's call. Men flinched and shifted into readiness without thinking. Samuel kept his head down, hands busy, but his ears stayed open.

Two white men moved toward the field line, walking with purpose. One carried rope coiled at his hip as if it were another tool. A dog that had been lying in shade lifted its head and began to pant, alert, excited by the movement of authority.

Samuel didn't follow. Following would make him visible. Instead, he watched from the corner of his eye, catching pieces.

Isaiah was brought in just before noon.

They didn't drag him. Not at first. They walked him in with a hand clamped hard around his upper arm, fingers digging into muscle. Isaiah's face was pale under sweat, his eyes wide and unfocused like he couldn't decide where to land them. His feet stumbled once, then corrected. He tried to hold himself upright, as if posture could negotiate.

The overseer spoke to him in a voice that carried just far enough to be heard by the nearest workers. He didn't need to shout. Shouting was for spectacle. This was for something else: the quiet reminder that attention could fall at any moment.

"You like the river, Isaiah?" the overseer asked.

Isaiah's mouth opened, closed, opened again. "I don't know what you mean," he said, and his voice cracked on the last word.

The overseer nodded as if Isaiah had answered correctly. Then he turned and walked a slow circle around him, studying him like livestock.

"Funny thing," the overseer said. "I got folks telling me you been talking. Telling people where to go. What to look for."

Isaiah shook his head too quickly. "No, sir. I ain't—"

The overseer's hand moved fast, backhanding Isaiah across the mouth. The sound was sharp and clean. Isaiah's head snapped sideways. Blood appeared at the corner of his lip like a small, bright line.

The yard quieted. Not fully. People kept working, because stopping was a way to volunteer for notice. But bodies leaned inward without meaning to, ears straining while hands pretended not to.

Samuel kept his eyes on the ground. He could feel the moment settling into the air like ash.

Isaiah swallowed, eyes shining. "I ain't said nothing," he whispered.

The overseer crouched slightly to meet Isaiah's gaze, voice low enough that only the closest could hear, and that was on purpose. Secrets didn't stay secret here. They seeped.

"Somebody says you did," the overseer replied.

Isaiah's eyes darted, not toward Samuel, not directly, but toward the cluster of men near the edge of the yard. His gaze passed over Samuel's position without catching. Or maybe it caught and refused to acknowledge it. Samuel remained still.

The overseer straightened. "Take him," he said, and this time there was no quietness. It was an order that snapped.

They didn't take Isaiah to the post. Not today. The post was a lesson for the whole plantation, and the overseer didn't waste lessons when he didn't need them. They took Isaiah behind the toolshed where the sound could still carry but the sight wouldn't make the yard stop breathing. Punishment didn't always require an audience. Sometimes it required imagination.

The first cry came quickly, then cut off, replaced by a choking sound and the wet rhythm of blows.

Samuel worked through it. He kept his hands moving and his face arranged into the emptiness that passed for safety. But inside him, his mind counted.

One blow. Two. The pause. The next. The way the sound changed when Isaiah's body stopped resisting and simply took what was given.

Samuel didn't flinch. Flinching would be noticed. Noticed could become questioned. Questions had echoes.

When it was over, Isaiah was brought back out and released with a shove. He staggered, caught himself on one knee, then pushed up again. His shirt hung wrong at the shoulders. His lip was swollen, blood dried dark. He did not look at anyone. He moved through the yard like a man who had learned that air itself could hurt.

Nobody spoke to him. Not because they didn't care. Because care had to be hidden the way plans were hidden, deep enough that it didn't show.

Samuel watched Isaiah disappear toward the field line again, forced back into work as if pain was simply another task.

A hollow settled in Samuel's chest. Not guilt. Guilt was a luxury. The hollow was something closer to understanding.

The system responded.

It responded quickly, predictably, efficiently. A whisper could become a blow. A suspicion could become bruises. A name could become a body bent wrong.

And the man who delivered the name remained standing.

That evening, when the food was handed out, Samuel received something different.

Usually, portions were measured the same, thin and dull, enough to keep a body working and not enough to make a body strong. But when Samuel stepped forward, the woman distributing the bowls hesitated and then, without meeting his eyes, tipped her ladle again. A little more. Not much. A small extra weight in the bottom of his bowl.

Alongside it, a piece of salt pork that looked less boiled-down than usual landed with a soft, greasy thud.

No one said anything. No one looked at him too long. But Samuel felt the shift as clearly as if someone had placed a hand in the center of his back and pushed.

He carried the bowl away and sat where the light was low. He ate slowly, careful not to show hunger. Hunger was readable. Hunger made you look like you could be bought too easily.

Across from him, men chewed with tired jaws and blank faces, their eyes fixed on nothing. Isaiah sat farther away, alone, head bowed, hands shaking slightly as he lifted food to his mouth. Every movement looked like it hurt.

Samuel swallowed his own bite and let the salt sit on his tongue.

It wasn't the extra food that mattered most. It was what the extra food meant.

The overseer hadn't spoken to him again. The master hadn't called him up. There had been no open praise, no declaration of loyalty. The plantation didn't work that way. It worked in glances and small privileges, in silent acknowledgments that told you where you stood without ever saying it out loud.

Information had weight here. It could bend a man's spine. It could loosen a ladle.

Samuel finished eating and wiped his mouth with the back of his hand, then kept sitting as if nothing inside him had changed.

But something had.

He had tested the system with a thread, and the system had tightened exactly where he expected it to. He had given a name, and he had been paid in quiet.

Samuel looked out into the dim between cabins where the night gathered itself. Somewhere, beyond fences and trees, the river moved, bending and carrying secrets. Somewhere, in another cabin on another plantation, Elijah Boone lay with his own question pressing against his ribs. Somewhere, Lila Carter listened for footsteps that might or might not come.

None of them knew what Samuel had done.

That, Samuel thought, was part of the power too.

The best trades were the ones no one else recognized as a trade until it was too late to refuse the price.

The extra food sat in Samuel's stomach like something alive.

Salt did that. It didn't dissolve the way thin stew did. It stayed. It reminded you it had been given.

Samuel chewed slowly, eyes lowered, jaw working with the same steady rhythm he used when he listened. Around him, men scraped bowls clean and pretended not to notice the slight difference in his portion. Pretending was the first layer of survival. You pretended you hadn't seen a man get pulled behind the toolshed. You pretended you hadn't heard the wet cadence of blows. You pretended you didn't know why Isaiah's shoulders now sat at the wrong angle under his shirt.

Samuel swallowed, and with the swallow came the next thought, quiet and unavoidable.

A name had become pain.

He told himself, again, what he had told himself when he first decided to test it: he had not held the switch. He had not tied the rope. He had not dragged Isaiah anywhere. He had only spoken what he had heard. If it had not been him, it would have been someone else. The overseer was already listening. The rumor was already in the air. The plantation did not need Samuel to be cruel.

The reasoning had the clean shape of a tool, the kind Elijah Boone might have made in a forge: useful, sharp, made to do one job well.

It still felt heavy.

Later, when the bowls were taken and the night began to thicken, Samuel sat outside his cabin a while, letting the air cool his skin. The quarters had quieted into that careful hush people wore when they were too tired to talk and too afraid to say the wrong thing even if they weren't. A few murmurs drifted, then stopped as bodies shifted. Somewhere a woman hummed without words, the sound so soft it barely counted as music.

Isaiah did not come out.

Samuel didn't need to see him to know where he was. Behind a door, lying on a pallet, trying to breathe without moving the bruises. Trying to decide whether pain was safer endured in silence or shared with someone who might not know how to hold it.

Samuel leaned back against the cabin wall and stared at the dark between trees. The night was full of ordinary sounds: insects, a distant horse shifting in a stall, a dog settling with a sigh. The ordinary sounds did not erase what had happened. They simply showed how quickly the world continued.

That was the price, Samuel thought. Not the extra food. Not the salt pork that still lingered on his tongue.

The price was learning how little the world cared.

In the morning, Isaiah appeared in the work line again.

He moved slower than usual, but he moved. That was what they wanted. The plantation did not reward a man for breaking; it rewarded itself for making sure the break didn't interrupt labor. Isaiah's eyes stayed low. His mouth stayed shut. The skin at his lip had split again in the night and left a dark smear at one corner.

Samuel saw him as the line formed and forced himself not to look too long. Looking was a kind of claiming. Looking said, I did this, even if you never said it out loud. He kept his face arranged in the dull mask everyone wore and waited for the overseer's gaze to pass over them.

The overseer did not stop at Samuel. He didn't pause. He didn't acknowledge him with a nod.

That was deliberate.

Open gratitude would make Samuel visible. Visibility could turn him into a target for envy, for accusation, for the kind of desperate anger that made men take risks just to feel less powerless. The overseer understood people the way Samuel did. He would not hand Samuel a reward that came with a spotlight. He would hand him something quieter and more effective.

Security.

Not safety, not the kind that didn't exist here. A thin layer of protection, like an oiled hinge that didn't squeal. A sense that when the overseer's temper snapped, it might snap toward someone else first.

Samuel did not smile. Smiling would make him look fed.

As the work day unfolded, he felt the changes in small ways. A white man who normally shoved past him without a glance now pointed and said, "You. Bring that over." Not "boy," not "you there," but "you," like Samuel's body had gained shape in their eyes.

At midday, when the sun sat high and made everything smell hot and sour, the overseer walked the line and stopped near two men arguing in low voices. The argument was nothing, a tight exchange over whose turn it was to carry a heavier load, but the overseer's presence made it dangerous. One of the men tensed as if expecting a blow.

The overseer looked at them, then looked past them.

His eyes landed on Samuel for half a heartbeat.

Nothing was said. Nothing was done.

The overseer moved on.

But the glance was enough. It traveled faster than any spoken word. By evening, men watched

Samuel out of the corners of their eyes the way they watched a snake that hadn't struck yet but might. Women pulled their children a little closer when he passed. Not because Samuel had ever harmed a child. Because a man who could make harm happen without lifting a hand was a man you treated carefully.

Samuel had wanted power.

This was what it looked like.

It did not feel like triumph. It felt like standing in a doorway and realizing you could not go back into the room you'd left, because the room now knew what you were.

That night, Isaiah finally sat outside his cabin for a moment, shoulders hunched as if the air itself hit bruises. A woman, older, slipped out and handed him something in a cloth. Not much. A bit of lard, maybe, or a poultice. Care given in the smallest possible way.

Isaiah's eyes lifted once, scanning the yard. They passed over faces and did not settle on anyone. When they reached Samuel, they did not stop. Either Isaiah didn't know, or he did and refused to grant Samuel the dignity of acknowledgement. Samuel wasn't sure which would be worse.

The woman who had helped Isaiah went back inside quickly. The door shut. The yard reclaimed its hush.

Samuel waited until he was sure no one could accuse him of approaching, then stood and moved toward the common water barrel as if he needed a drink. He didn't. His mouth was dry for reasons water couldn't fix.

As he dipped the ladle and let the cool water run over his tongue, a man near him muttered, "They got him good."

Samuel kept his eyes down. "Who?"

The man looked at him the way you looked at someone who pretended not to know something everybody knew. "Isaiah," he said. "For talking."

Samuel nodded slowly, as if hearing it fresh. "Folks should keep their mouths shut."

The man gave a short laugh without humor. "Folks mouths been shut. They still get beat."

Samuel lifted the ladle again, buying himself time. The man leaned closer, voice lowered. "You know anything about it? Who told?"

It was asked casually, but the question had an edge. Not accusation, not yet. Testing. Like Samuel had tested the system, now someone else was testing him.

Samuel shrugged, a movement meant to look tired. "Overseer don't need nobody to tell," he said. "He hear things when he want."

The man studied him for a moment. Samuel kept his face empty. Finally, the man looked away and spat into the dirt. "Ain't right," he muttered, and walked off.

Samuel set the ladle down and stood there longer than he needed to, listening to the water barrel settle. The question who told hung in the air after the man walked away, as if it had weight.

That was another part of the price.

Once you traded information, you began to live inside other people's suspicion.

Not just fear of white men, which was constant and expected, but fear of your own. The wrong glance could mean someone had connected the dots. The wrong word could mean someone decided to make you pay, not for Isaiah's bruises exactly, but for what you represented. A man who could speak to power and be fed for it.

Samuel went back to his cabin and lay down. He listened to the quarters breathe. He listened for footsteps, for murmurs, for the subtle change in night sound that meant someone had moved closer than they should have.

No one came.

Still, his body stayed ready.

In the dark, he found himself thinking of the runaway from the woods, the one dragged back not as a man but as a warning. Samuel remembered the whistle that had cut through the trees ahead of him, sharp and deliberate. A signal. A guide. A sound that meant you were already caught even if no hands had grabbed you yet.

The plantation worked on signals. The overseer's whistle. The master's tone. The quiet instructions carried in glances.

Samuel had become one of those signals now.

He turned his head on the pallet and stared at the black rafters. The extra food, the glance from the overseer, the shift in the way people avoided his eyes, all of it formed a shape that felt like a collar settling into place.

He had thought information was a tool he could pick up and put down.

But tools changed the hand that used them. They left calluses. They left scars. They changed how the world responded to you.

At Carter's plantation, far enough away that Samuel couldn't see it, the consequences traveled anyway. That was the other truth about information: it didn't stay where it was spoken.

A man was punished on Boone's place. A whisper tightened. Patrols lengthened. Dogs were riled sooner.

Elijah Boone would feel it in the way conversations stopped when he stepped near. Lila Carter would feel it in the way the house spoke sharper about the river line, the way "example" rolled off white tongues like prayer. Neither of them would know Samuel's name belonged to the chain of events.

Samuel knew.

And because he knew, he could not fully return to the old kind of ignorance. Ignorance, he realized, was not stupidity. It was distance. It was the ability to tell yourself a thing happened without your hand in it.

Now his hand was in it, even if it never lifted a switch.

He closed his eyes and tried to sleep.

Sleep came in thin patches. In one patch he dreamed of the forge on Boone's plantation, the orange glow of coals. He saw Elijah's scarred hands holding a bar of iron with tongs, the metal hot enough to soften. Samuel stepped closer in the dream, not to touch the iron, but to whisper a name into it. The iron took the name the way flesh took a brand. It hissed. It smoked. When Elijah struck it with the hammer, the sound was not metal ringing, but a scream swallowed into shape.

Samuel woke with his heart steady, not racing, which frightened him more than a racing heart would have. He lay there listening to the night, to the ordinary sounds that proved nothing had changed.

But everything had.

The trade had been made. The payment had been received. The system had answered him with bruises on another man's body and extra salt in his own bowl.

And the price of information, Samuel understood as the dark held him, was never paid only once.

It kept charging interest. Quietly. Patiently.

Just like him.

The next morning, Samuel woke before the first full light and lay still on his pallet, listening the way he always did. Not for comfort. For information.

The quarters breathed around him: a cough muffled into a shoulder, straw shifting under a turning body, the soft exhale of a man who would rather not wake and still did. Outside, a dog barked once and then fell quiet, as if it had remembered what barking could lead to.

Samuel sat up slowly. The dream of the forge clung to him; the sound of that imagined scream stuck under his ribs. He rubbed his face with both hands and let the feeling pass without naming it. Naming was how things turned into burdens.

When he stepped outside, the air was damp and cool enough to make his skin pebble. Smoke from early fires lay low to the ground. A few figures moved already, shapes in gray light. Nobody greeted him. That was new. It wasn't hostility exactly. It was distance, measured and wary.

He understood it. A man who traded words for bruises became an object people had to walk around carefully.

Samuel walked toward the water barrel as if thirst had brought him, though what he wanted was to see who stood near it, who avoided it, who looked away too quickly. He dipped the ladle and drank, then let his gaze drift the way a tired man's gaze drifted.

Across the open space, Isaiah stepped out of his cabin and paused as if the simple act of standing upright required negotiation with pain. He moved stiffly toward the work line, shoulders held wrong, jaw clenched as though his teeth were keeping the rest of him from breaking apart. No one spoke to him. A few men shifted to make room without acknowledging why.

Samuel watched Isaiah without staring. Staring would be a confession. Still, he felt something tighten and then settle again in his chest. Not guilt. Not even fear.

Recognition.

The system did not care what Isaiah had actually said. It cared that it could make him pay. It cared that the payment would be witnessed, felt in the air, carried home in silence to every cabin. Isaiah's pain wasn't a response to truth. It was a response to the possibility of truth.

And Samuel, by handing over a name, had shown he could help the system move faster.

The overseer arrived later, boots cutting through the yard with the steady tempo of a man who liked being heard. He carried himself loose, as if nothing in the world could touch him. A switch hung in his hand like an extension of his arm. He did not need it most days. The sight of it did the work.

The work line formed. Heads lowered. Bodies arranged.

Samuel stood where he was assigned and kept his face empty. The overseer walked the line slowly. He stopped near Isaiah.

"You feeling better today?" the overseer asked, voice mild in a way that made it worse.

Isaiah's throat worked. "Yes, sir," he managed.

The overseer nodded as if approving of recovery, then leaned in slightly. "Good," he said. "Don't let me hear you got river talk again."

Isaiah's eyes stayed down. "No, sir."

The overseer straightened and moved on, satisfied. The lesson had been delivered without wasting time on another beating. That was how you knew it had worked. When fear continued the punishment on its own.

The line began to move toward the fields. Samuel's assignment was near the yard that morning, hauling feed sacks and stacking them by the stable. Work that kept him close to the overseer's orbit. Close enough to be useful. Close enough to be watched.

A white man by the stable, one of the younger ones who liked to show authority by making his voice loud, pointed at Samuel. "You," he said. "Get that saddle down and bring it here."

Samuel did as he was told without hesitation. He brought the saddle, held it steady while the man tightened a strap, and then stepped back. The man didn't curse him. That, too, was a change. Small, but it mattered. Cruelty was default. When cruelty softened, it meant someone had decided you were worth keeping in working order.

Near midday, the overseer called Samuel over with a short tilt of his head. Not a shout. A gesture. That was how the overseer marked differences between men. He didn't need to raise his voice for someone who was already paying attention.

Samuel approached at the right pace, not eager, not slow.

The overseer stood in the shade of the toolshed. From here, he could see the yard, the stable, and the start of the field line. He could see enough to feel in control.

"You been hearing anything else?" the overseer asked, as if asking about weather.

Samuel kept his eyes lowered. "Ain't heard nothing worth troubling you with, sir."

The overseer's mouth twitched, almost pleased. "That so?"

Samuel hesitated in a way that looked like reluctance. "Folks always talking," he said. "But talking don't mean doing."

The overseer studied him. Samuel held still. He let the overseer see a man trying to be careful, trying to be useful, trying not to invite trouble. That was the version of him that could be trusted.

The overseer nodded once. "If you do hear something worth troubling me with, you bring it."

"Yes, sir," Samuel replied.

The overseer leaned closer, voice dropping. "And you don't go spreading it around. You understand me? I don't need the whole place stirred up by a man who likes to hear himself talk."

Samuel's answer came quick and quiet. "Yes, sir. I understand."

The overseer straightened, satisfied. He reached into the pocket of his coat and pulled out a small plug of tobacco, pinched off a piece with his thumbnail. He held it out without ceremony.

Samuel did not reach for it too fast. He let a beat pass, as if unsure he was allowed. Then he took it with his fingertips. "Thank you, sir," he said.

The overseer turned away, conversation ended. Samuel stepped back and returned to his work, the tobacco hidden in his palm like a warm coin.

It wasn't the tobacco that made Samuel's thoughts sharpen. It was the gesture.

Extra food had been payment delivered through someone else's hands, quiet enough that it could be denied. This was direct. Not praise, but acknowledgment. Not a promise, but a positioning.

Samuel understood the language of it. The overseer had just told him where he could stand.

Not with the men who whispered. Not with the ones who looked toward the tree line with hunger in their eyes. Not with the ones who wanted the word north to mean something bigger than fear.

With power.

That afternoon, Samuel found himself watching the plantation differently. It was the same yard, the same fences, the same white men who moved like the land itself belonged to their bones. But now he could see the pathways that were invisible to most people because most people refused to believe they existed. How a word moved upward. How a suspicion became a tightening of rules. How punishment could be aimed like a tool and then put away until needed again.

He had always known the plantation ran on control. What he had not fully known was how much of that control depended on men like him, men who were willing to become the narrow channel information had to pass through.

There were others, of course. There were always informers, always the ones who tried to stand closer to the house to keep the whip from their own back. But Samuel sensed the difference between begging for favor and being invited into usefulness.

Begging made you disposable. Being useful made you necessary.

Later, while he stacked feed, two men nearby spoke in low voices, their heads bent as if their shoulders could hide their mouths. Samuel didn't move closer. He didn't need to. The words drifted anyway.

"They saying Carter's place got patrols now too," one murmured.

"Everybody got patrols," the other replied.

"Not like this," the first insisted. "They saying Mr. Carter asked Boone for that blacksmith again. Like they watching fences. Like they fixing things to keep folks in, not just keep stock."

Samuel kept his hands working. Elijah Boone's name landed in his mind with the calm weight of a tool added to a box. He remembered the blacksmith's scarred hands, the steadiness of them, the way he had looked at Lila Carter like recognition was a form of hunger. Samuel had watched that hunger from the stable shadows and filed it away.

Now the hunger had a direction. Now it had a rumor feeding it. Marks. River. Bend.

Samuel didn't need to know the truth of it to use it. He only needed to know who believed.

As the day wore down, he began to understand that alignment wasn't a single choice made once. It was a series of small permissions. A man in authority giving you a piece of tobacco. A ladle tipping a little extra. A glance that said, I see you. I know what you are. Keep being it.

The frightening part was how easy it started to feel.

Not easy like joy. Easy like habit.

When the evening meal was distributed, Samuel received a normal portion this time. No extra. No special piece of meat. The woman with the ladle did not hesitate when she served him. That should have unsettled him, but it didn't. He understood something new: payment did not have to be constant to be real. It only had to appear at the right times, enough to keep a man aware of what he could lose.

He ate with the others and listened. Men spoke less than before. The air held too many consequences now. Isaiah sat among them, chewing slowly, eyes fixed somewhere beyond the bowls and bodies. His silence was louder than speech.

When darkness fell and the quarters quieted, Samuel walked a short distance away from the cabins and stood where he could see the edge of the yard. The night was thick, but he could still make out movement near the main house. A lantern bobbed. A white figure crossed a porch.

Samuel thought of Lila Carter across the boundary, moving through a different house, carrying trays and silence, feeling his attention even when he wasn't there. He thought of Elijah Boone working in the glow of his forge, hearing whispers between hammer strikes, unable to unthink the question that had formed.

He could almost taste the shape of what was coming. Not because he could see the future, but because he could see how pressure changed people. He had watched it happen with Isaiah. He had watched it happen with the branded man who had been dragged back to make hope smell like burnt flesh.

Samuel pressed the tobacco into his cheek and let it sit there, bitter and strong. He told himself again that he was only surviving. That this was only a way to keep his own skin from being the lesson.

But survival was not neutral. Survival had direction. It leaned. It aligned.

The overseer had told him, bring it to me. Don't spread it. The words sounded like instruction. They were also an invitation.

To become a gate.

Samuel stood in the dark and listened to the plantation's night sounds. Somewhere, a dog shifted and sighed. Somewhere, a man coughed. Somewhere, a woman murmured a prayer that didn't dare ask for too much.

Samuel felt the familiar thrill of knowing something other people didn't know, and he recognized it for what it was.

Not hope.

Power's shadow.

He had stepped into it, and the shadow had adjusted around him as if it had been waiting.

Chapter 6

Forged Intentions

The next day the master brought a broken chain to the forge and stood in the doorway long enough to make the air feel owned.

Elijah didn't look up right away. He kept his hands steady on the tongs, holding a bar in the coals while it took on heat. The fire breathed orange, then brighter, and the iron began to change the way it looked, the dull surface turning slick as if sweat had risen from it.

The master cleared his throat.

Elijah lifted his gaze just enough. Not challenge. Not question. Just recognition.

"This came off the mule rig," the master said, tossing the chain so it landed with a loud, accusing clatter on the packed dirt. "Link snapped. I want it fixed before sundown."

"Yes, sir," Elijah replied.

The master watched him a moment longer, eyes traveling the forge the way a man's eyes traveled a field he intended to harvest. "And you keep your work clean," he added, as if Elijah had ever had the option not to.

"Yes, sir."

The master left. The doorway brightened with his absence, then shrank back to its usual shape. The forge was Elijah's only space that came close to privacy, and even that wasn't real. Privacy on a plantation was just a moment the eyes happened to be pointed somewhere else.

Elijah set the chain aside and turned his attention back to the bar of iron. He pulled it from the coals and laid it on the anvil, and the first hammer blow rang out, loud enough to announce to anyone listening that he was doing exactly what he was supposed to do.

He struck again. And again. The metal flattened, obeying the force. That was what always steadied him about iron. It resisted, but it did not lie. It changed when heat and pressure demanded it. People were different. People resisted in ways you couldn't see and broke in ways you didn't hear until it was too late.

Between hammer blows, his mind moved where his hands could not.

Marks. River. Bend.

And the other kind of mark, the one pressed into flesh, the smell of it living in stories and in the way people went quiet when they remembered. The plantation loved marks. It loved making a body carry evidence of what it had tried to become.

Elijah knew better than to think the rumor of north would save them by itself. A word didn't open a gate. A question didn't cut a shackle. A rumor didn't feed you when you were cold and lost in the woods. But rumors did one useful thing: they made a man start looking at the world like it had seams.

And seams could be pried.

He let the iron cool a fraction, then returned it to the coals and picked up the chain. The broken link was an easy fix. Heat, shape, close it clean. The kind of work he could do with his eyes half shut. That was why they valued him. That was why they watched him without appearing to. A blacksmith could make a plantation run smoother. A blacksmith could also make it fail in ways that looked like accident.

Elijah heated the link until it glowed. As he worked it back into shape, he listened to the world outside his shed.

Footsteps passed, slow and heavy. Voices, distant. A dog barked once and was silenced quick, as if even animals had learned the rules.

Then he heard the one sound that mattered most.

Not the sharp whistle from the woods in the story of the runaway. Not the overseer's call. A softer sound, a scrape, like a boot toe against wood, right outside the shed.

Elijah did not turn his head. He kept his hammer moving, kept the metal ringing. The sound was his cover and his camouflage. Anyone watching would see a man working, nothing else.

A shadow leaned into the doorway.

Elijah caught it in the corner of his eye and felt his body tighten anyway.

Samuel stood there, just inside the line where a man could claim he hadn't entered. His face was calm in that practiced way, his posture loose, as if he had no purpose beyond passing by.

"You got a lot of work," Samuel said.

Elijah didn't answer right away. He dipped the link back into the coals, then set the tongs down and reached for a different tool with deliberate slowness. He did not give Samuel the satisfaction of making him pause.

"They keep finding things to break," Elijah said at last.

Samuel's mouth tilted. "Things break when people want them to."

Elijah's eyes stayed on the chain. "Things break because they made cheap," he replied.

Samuel stepped another inch into the doorway, still not enough to be accused of coming in. He looked around the forge, at the tools hung on pegs, at the anvil worn smooth at the edges from years of use. He looked at it the way a man looked at something he might someday need.

"They sent you over to Carter's again?" Samuel asked, casual.

Elijah's hand stilled for half a heartbeat. He resumed, tightening his grip on the tongs until the metal bit into his palm through callus.

"No," he said. "Not this time."

Samuel nodded as if that answered more than it should have. "Fence work," he murmured. "They worried about fences now."

Elijah's jaw tightened. "They always worried. Just depends what they scared of today."

Samuel's eyes flicked up to Elijah's face, then back down, as if he were watching for the moment Elijah's expression gave him something. "Folks say you can fix any latch," Samuel said. "Make it hold."

Elijah kept his voice even. "That's the work."

Samuel didn't move. He didn't leave. He occupied the doorway like a thought you couldn't shake.

"You hear the talk?" Samuel asked.

Elijah didn't look at him. "I hear people talking about a lot of things."

Samuel's mildness deepened, as if he were amused by Elijah's caution. "You always careful with words," he said. "That's smart. Careful keeps you living."

The phrase hit Elijah like a hook because he'd heard it before, not from Samuel's mouth but through Lila's fear. He pictured her face in the dim of that fence line exchange, the controlled way she'd said Samuel's name as if speaking it too loudly might make it appear.

"You come in here to talk to me about living?" Elijah asked, voice flat.

Samuel lifted one shoulder in a shrug. "I come in here because it's hot," he said. "And because folks can't hear over your hammer."

Elijah struck the chain link hard, closing it with a clean seam. Sparks jumped and died. "Folks hear what they want," he said.

Samuel's gaze moved, slow, taking inventory. Not just of tools, but of possibility. "A man with your hands," Samuel murmured, "could do a lot."

Elijah finally turned his head enough to meet Samuel's eyes. He did not let anything show on his face. "A man with my hands does what he told," he said.

Samuel smiled without warmth. "Yes," he agreed. "That's what they like about you."

Elijah held Samuel's gaze. He understood then that Samuel wasn't here for idle talk. Samuel was here because Samuel had begun to see the forge the way Elijah did: as a place where the world could be altered in quiet, where metal could become something else and still look like itself.

Samuel stepped back from the doorway at last. "I won't keep you," he said, and the words sounded polite. They weren't. They sounded like a man reminding you he could return whenever he wanted.

Elijah nodded once and turned back to the fire. He waited until Samuel's footsteps faded into the yard before he allowed his breath to deepen.

The forge felt smaller after that. Not because Samuel had taken up space in it, but because Samuel's attention had. Attention was a kind of ownership on a plantation. The master owned your body. The overseer owned your time. A man like Samuel tried to own your choices.

Elijah finished the chain and set it aside. Then he did what he always did when his mind needed somewhere safe to go. He worked.

But he chose what to work on.

The day's official tasks were simple: mend a plowshare, straighten a bent nail, repair a hinge. Elijah did them all. He did them well, because doing them well bought him the only currency he had: being considered useful enough to be left alone for a few extra minutes.

In those minutes he made small changes that looked like nothing.

A nail, forged slightly thinner at the shank so it would snap under the wrong kind of weight. Not today. Not in a way that could be traced to him. Just a weak point introduced into the plantation's confidence.

A hinge pin, filed just enough that it would slide free if you knew which direction to lift. To anyone else it would still hold. To a hand that knew the trick, it would open like a secret.

A length of wire, drawn out long and straight, then coiled tight around a wooden dowel and hidden inside a hollowed handle of a tool. Wire could become many things. A hook. A snare. A way to lift a latch from the other side of a door.

He did not tell himself he was making escape tools. Naming it made it too real, and real things drew eyes. He told himself he was practicing. He told himself he was keeping his hands sharp. A blacksmith who didn't practice got sloppy. Sloppy work got punished.

Still, as he shaped each small piece, he thought of the river's bend. He thought of marks cut into bark. He thought of the way Lila had said cloth on a fence, something you wouldn't notice unless you were already looking.

He understood that if there was a path north, it wouldn't be a road you walked like a free man. It would be a series of small openings. A loose hinge. A latch that lifted. A nail that snapped at the right time. A tool hidden in plain sight.

He understood, too, that the plantation's power depended on things holding.

Fences. Chains. Habits. Fear.

So, he began to imagine the opposite, not as a dream but as a craft. What would it take for something to fail without announcing it had been tampered with? What would it take for a gate to open quietly? What would it take for a lock to believe it was still locked?

Late in the afternoon, as the light shifted and the heat in the forge became less punishing, Elijah heard footsteps again. He tensed, expecting Samuel.

But it was a boy, one of the smaller ones sent to fetch nails and carry messages. The boy hovered in the doorway like he was afraid of the fire.

"You got them spikes?" the boy asked, eyes wide, voice thin.

Elijah nodded and handed him the bundle. As the boy took them, his fingers trembled. He leaned in just a fraction and whispered, barely moving his lips.

"They beat Isaiah again?"

Elijah's hand froze on the edge of the anvil. "Who told you that?" he asked, careful.

The boy swallowed. "Ain't nobody told me. I just… folks saying his back look worse."

Elijah kept his face blank. "Folks say a lot," he murmured.

The boy nodded too fast, fearful of his own question. He turned and hurried away.

Elijah watched him go, then turned back to the coals. That boy's whisper was another seam. The consequences of talk spreading outward, touching even the ones who didn't have words for the rumor. Fear traveled through children faster than any direction word like north.

Elijah looked at the wire coil he'd hidden, at the filed hinge pin set aside among ordinary scrap. He thought of Samuel's eyes in his doorway, calm and measuring.

A blacksmith's edge wasn't just in the sharpness of his tools. It was in his ability to change the shape of the world and make it look unchanged.

Elijah fed the fire again, not because he needed more heat for the day's work, but because the glow gave his hands something to do while his mind tightened into resolve.

If the plantation wanted everything to hold, then he would learn how to make things fail.

Quietly.

Cleanly.

At the right moment.

And without leaving a mark that could be traced back to his hands.

Elijah carried the finished chain to the main yard just before sundown, holding it in both hands the way you held something that could become evidence if it swung wrong.

The master took it without thanks, glanced at the seam, and gave a short nod that meant approval and dismissal at the same time. "Go on," he said, already turning away, already done with Elijah's presence now that the work had been collected.

Elijah went back toward the quarters with his shoulders loose and his face arranged. Around him, the yard was thinning into evening. Tools were put away. Bodies shifted from one kind of labor to another, from work that was ordered to work that was necessary. The air cooled, but the heat of the forge stayed in his skin like a private brand.

As he walked, he let his eyes travel in the way he'd trained them to: not staring, not searching, just noticing. Noticing the places a fence post leaned. Noticing where the ground dipped near the edge of the yard, where rainwater collected and left a long soft patch that held footprints longer than it should. Noticing the way a gate near the smokehouse didn't catch clean unless you lifted it slightly, a flaw that most men cursed and compensated for without thinking.

He didn't call those things a route. He didn't call them a plan. But his mind began to hold them as parts.

A hinge that would slide free if you knew the trick.

A nail forged thin enough to fail under the right weight.

A latch that could be lifted from the outside with a hooked piece of wire.

All small. All deniable. All the kind of wrong that looked like wear and poor construction if anybody bothered to look.

That was the shape of a path here. Not a clear line north. Not a map. A series of failures you could make happen on purpose.

In the quarters, the night gathered slowly. Men sat outside their cabins, chewing on the last of the day's food, eyes half-lidded with exhaustion. Children drifted between doorways until someone pulled them inside. The sound of the river was too far away to hear, but Elijah thought of it anyway, bending in the dark beyond the far line like a thought you couldn't shove down.

He saw the old man again, the one who'd spoken about the river having a way. The man sat on his step with his hands busy, always mending something, always making use out of what should have been thrown away. Elijah approached and stopped close enough to be seen without making it look like a meeting.

The old man didn't look up. "You got that look again," he muttered.

Elijah kept his gaze on the dirt. "What look."

"The look like you got something in your head that don't want to stay there," the old man said.

Elijah let a breath out through his nose. "I got work in my hands," he replied.

The old man's fingers paused for a fraction, then resumed. "Work don't keep a man safe," he said, and it wasn't wisdom offered gentle. It was a warning stripped clean. "Work just keep him useful."

Elijah nodded once. Useful bought you a little time. Time was the only thing you could trade without asking permission.

"You said river," Elijah murmured, keeping his voice flat. "Mean and shallow. Things that don't belong."

The old man's hands kept moving. "That's what I said."

Elijah swallowed. "How a man know the difference between something that don't belong and something somebody put there to get him caught?"

That made the old man finally lift his eyes. They were tired eyes, sharp despite the tiredness. He studied Elijah like Elijah was a piece of iron held too long in the fire, close to losing its shape.

"You don't," the old man said simply.

Elijah felt the answer land heavy, because it was true. The plantation taught you that certainty was expensive and usually paid for with somebody else's pain.

The old man went on, quieter. "You want a sign that can't be lied about. Ain't such thing. White folks lie. Our folks lie too when they scared. River don't lie, but it don't care if you drown neither."

Elijah's jaw tightened. "So, what a man do."

The old man looked past him, scanning the dim yard the way you did when you talked about dangerous things. "A man do what he can check," he said. "He don't take one mark for truth. He look for two. Three. He listen for what match and what don't."

Elijah nodded, slow.

"And he keep his mouth shut," the old man added, as if the first lesson still needed saying.

Elijah started to step away.

The old man spoke again, low enough it barely counted as speech. "They say some folks leave a cloth. Like you heard."

Elijah's spine tightened. He kept his face neutral. "Folks say a lot."

The old man's mouth twitched, not amused. "Cloth can mean help. Cloth can mean trap. But you see cloth where cloth got no reason to be, you remember it. Don't go running. Just remember."

Elijah nodded once and walked away, his heart steady but heavy. Remember. That was all anyone could afford at first. Memory was the only map they were allowed to carry.

Across the boundary at Carter's plantation, Lila spent the next day moving through the house with her ears open and her face empty.

The mistress had her polishing silver in the front room while two white women sat nearby speaking as if Lila were a table. Their voices rose and fell, soft with gossip and sharp with complaint. Lila kept her cloth moving, kept her posture proper, and let the words slide into her without reacting.

"They've been bold lately," one woman said, tapping her teacup with a nail. "Bold and stupid."

The mistress sighed like the complaint was tiring her. "They get ideas from somewhere," she replied. "Mr. Carter says it's those preachers and busybodies up north, always meddling."

The other woman leaned in, voice lowering as if secrecy made cruelty more tasteful. "Do you believe there's truly a line? A route?"

The mistress made a small sound of contempt. "I believe there are fools who will die chasing rumors. And I believe we need to make the dying visible enough to stop the rest."

Lila's hand did not slow. Her breath did not change. Inside, something cold pressed against her ribs.

Make the dying visible. The phrase had the same shape as branding irons heating in morning light.

Later, when she carried laundry down the back hall, she heard Mr. Carter speaking to a man in his study. The door was cracked, not enough for her to be accused of listening, enough that the words slipped out anyway because white men assumed the walls belonged to them too.

"We've strengthened the patrol," Mr. Carter said. "And I sent word to Boone's overseer. If he's got any sense, he'll do the same on his side. The river's the problem."

A pause, then the visitor's voice. "You think they'll try again after what happened?"

Mr. Carter gave a short laugh. "Hope makes them stupid. Hunger makes them brave. Same thing, really."

Lila walked past with the laundry basket digging into her hip, her face blank as a plate.

In the kitchen, the cook's hands shook slightly as she kneaded dough. "They talking about tying bells to the dogs," she muttered when no white ears were close. "So, you hear them coming even if you asleep."

Another woman shook her head once, sharp. "Ain't no sleep when they on that talk."

Lila did not join in. Joining in was a way to be remembered.

But she stored it. Bells on dogs. Patrol strengthened. River watched. Boone's name in Mr. Carter's mouth.

Fragments.

That night, in her cabin, she sat with her back against the wall and let the day replay in pieces. The house did not speak of north as a place. It spoke of it as an infection. A rumor that needed cutting out. But the more they spoke, the more Lila understood something that felt like its own kind of terrible hope.

They were afraid of the river.

Not the way they were afraid of storms or sickness, things that came without permission. Afraid like men were afraid of a door they could not keep closed. If the river truly meant nothing, they would not waste attention on it. Attention was too valuable to give away for free.

The next morning, Samuel found Lila in the yard as she carried a bucket toward the wash area.

He did not step into her path. He positioned himself near enough to be spoken to without forcing it. His face wore that mildness again, the one that pretended not to know it was a mask.

"You keeping busy," he said.

Lila kept walking. "That's what they like."

Samuel fell into step beside her, not quite matching her pace, making it seem like coincidence rather than pursuit. "Heard Mr. Carter talking," he said, voice low. "They real stirred up."

Lila's fingers tightened around the bucket handle. "You hear a lot."

Samuel's mouth tilted. "Ears work fine," he replied. "Better than most."

She didn't answer.

Samuel continued, as if her silence invited him. "They saying Boone's place been having trouble too. Folks whispering over there."

Lila glanced at him, quick and controlled. "Why you telling me."

Samuel's eyes held hers with the same steady patience she'd come to hate. "Because trouble don't stay on one side of a fence," he said. "Because you don't got to be caught running to get punished for it."

Lila stopped at the wash area and set the bucket down with care. Water sloshed against the rim. She straightened slowly, meeting his gaze without flinching.

"You warning me," she said.

Samuel's voice softened. "I'm looking out."

"You keep saying that," Lila replied. "Like it make it true."

For a moment, something in Samuel's expression tightened, then smoothed back out. "It is true," he said. "You just don't like the way it sounds."

Lila stared at him. She thought of Elijah's hands and the way he could make something hold. She thought of the old man's words, about looking for two signs, three. She thought of the way a cloth could be help or a trap depending on who tied it.

Samuel shifted his weight, still calm. "If you hear something," he said, casual as dust, "something real, you ought to be careful who you share it with. Not everybody wants you safe."

Lila's stomach tightened. "You mean you," she said.

Samuel's mildness didn't break, but his eyes sharpened. "I mean me too," he answered, and there was honesty in it that made her skin crawl. "I mean anybody. You and that blacksmith, you got your heads full. I can see it."

Lila forced her face to remain empty. She bent and picked up the bar of soap beside the wash tub, pretending that was all she cared about. "You see wrong," she said.

Samuel leaned closer by a fraction, not touching. "Maybe," he murmured. "But seeing wrong can still get folks hurt."

He straightened and stepped back as another woman approached carrying linens. Samuel's face turned harmless again, the way it did when an audience appeared. He nodded politely, then walked away like he'd only stopped to speak about nothing at all.

Lila watched him go only long enough to know which direction he chose. Toward the main yard. Toward places where authority moved.

A gate, she thought.

That was what Samuel was becoming. Not a man chasing her. A man standing between whispers and consequences.

That night, Lila lay awake and let the fragments arrange themselves.

Bells on dogs.

River watched.

Boone's name in Carter's mouth.

Samuel's warning shaped like a threat.

And Elijah, on his side of the boundary, filing a hinge pin until it would slip free for a hand that knew how to lift it.

None of it was a plan. Not yet. It was too broken, too scattered, like pieces of a map torn into scraps and hidden in different pockets.

But Lila understood something she hadn't fully understood before.

A path wouldn't appear whole.

It would be assembled.

And assembling it would mean trusting what you could check, remembering what didn't belong, and learning to live with the fact that every fragment you collected could also be collected by someone else.

Somewhere out in the dark, beyond fences and patrol lines, the river kept moving, bending around the land like it had no master at all.

Lila listened to the night sounds and tried to imagine what silence would feel like if it wasn't crowded with watchers.

The thought was dangerous.

So, she didn't hold it like a dream.

She held it like a tool.

Two nights after Samuel spoke to her at the wash area, Lila was sent down to the root cellar with a lantern and a list that did not match what the shelves could offer.

The cook had pressed the paper into her hand without looking at her face. "Mistress says she wants pickled peaches for the table tomorrow," she muttered. "Like she don't know we ain't had peaches since last summer."

Lila read the list anyway, because reading was part of the performance. Obedience wasn't only in what you did. It was in how seriously you treated their nonsense.

The cellar door groaned when she pulled it open. Cool air breathed up from the steps, damp and sharp, smelling of earth and old brine. The lantern's flame shivered, then steadied. Lila went down carefully, one hand on the wall, the other holding the light far enough forward to keep the shadows from gathering too thick.

Shelves lined the cellar, jars and sacks arranged like order could stop time from rotting things. Lila moved along them with her face calm and her mind counting. Not peaches. Not enough beans. Plenty of salt. The usual imbalance of a place where their wants were stocked and hers were managed.

She reached the back shelf and paused. At first she thought it was a mouse, the faint scrape of something small shifting. Her shoulders tightened anyway. In the cellar, sound didn't travel out. That made it safer for certain kinds of talk and worse for certain kinds of trouble.

She lifted the lantern higher.

A folded cloth lay on the floor behind the last shelf, tucked into the corner where the dirt met the stone. It didn't belong there. Cloth was counted in the house. Cloth didn't end up in corners unless someone meant it to. Lila didn't touch it. She simply looked, letting her eyes register the shape and color.

Blue.

Not bright. Worn. But blue enough to hold the eye.

She thought of the old man's words Elijah had repeated in her head without meaning to. Cloth can mean help. Cloth can mean trap. But you see cloth where cloth got no reason to be, you remember it.

Lila lowered the lantern. She backed away without changing her breathing. She gathered what she could from the shelves and climbed the steps again, her hands steady on the jars as if her only worry was dropping glass.

When she came out, she closed the cellar door softly. She did not look around too quickly. She did not hurry back to the kitchen. She walked the way she always walked, like a woman with one task and no thoughts.

But inside her, the blue cloth stayed bright.

That same evening, Mr. Carter called her into the side hall and spoke to her as if he were offering a kindness.

"Tomorrow morning," he said, adjusting his coat cuffs, "you'll take a basket to Boone's. Some preserves for Mrs. Boone. It's neighborly."

Neighborly. Lila kept her eyes lowered so he wouldn't see the reaction flicker. Neighborly meant controlled. It meant they wanted eyes on fences, hands on latches, words carried back and forth in ways that benefitted them.

"Yes, sir," she said.

Mr. Carter nodded once, satisfied by her lack of questions. "You'll go with one of the boys. You'll do what you're told and come back. You understand?"

"Yes, sir."

He dismissed her with a wave. Lila stepped away and felt, not heard, the click of the decision behind her. She didn't belong to herself enough to refuse the errand. But an errand could be a seam if you knew where to press.

That night she lay on her pallet with her hands folded on her stomach, listening to the cabin's breathing and the distant plantation sounds that never fully went to sleep. She told herself she was only tired. That the cellar had made her jumpy. That the blue cloth was probably a rag dropped by someone careless.

Her mind refused the comfort. Careless didn't survive in this house.

By morning, the basket was heavier than it needed to be. A jar of preserves, a wrapped loaf, a small sack of coffee beans meant for Mrs. Boone, as if the Carters were generous rather than simply careful about appearances. Lila carried it at her hip. A white boy, one of Mr. Carter's, walked two paces behind her with a stick in his hand, tapping it against his leg like he was practicing being an overseer.

The road between plantations looked the same as it always had: dirt, ruts, trees leaning in. But now Lila saw the gaps differently. She saw where a person could step off if they were willing to vanish into underbrush. She saw where a horse's hoofprints held in softer patches. She saw, too, how the boy's gaze kept sliding toward the tree line as if he'd been instructed to watch it.

On Boone's side, the yard opened up, familiar and not. The same structure of control. Different faces. Different habits. Lila's body held itself tighter as they were directed toward the main house.

A woman she recognized as Mrs. Boone stepped onto the porch, smiling the thin smile of a white woman who believed civility made ownership polite. "Well," she said, "aren't you a neat one. Come up. Set it there."

Lila went up the steps, set the basket where she was told, and stepped back. Her eyes stayed down. Her ears stayed open.

Mrs. Boone fussed over the coffee beans, talking about how hard it was to get good supplies lately, how the roads were unreliable, how people were restless. She spoke of restlessness the way one spoke of weather, as if the bodies that carried the restlessness were not human enough to name.

While she talked, the white boy from Carter's drifted toward the porch rail, staring out at the yard as if bored. Boredom was his right. Lila envied it without allowing her face to show anything.

Then Mrs. Boone turned her head and called toward the yard. "Elijah! Come here a moment."

Lila's stomach tightened. She kept her posture still.

Elijah appeared from the direction of the forge, wiping his hands on a rag, his shoulders broad with labor. He stopped at the base of the porch, eyes lifting only enough to acknowledge the order. "Yes, ma'am," he said.

Mrs. Boone smiled down at him like he was a tool that had learned to speak. "Take this basket and carry it to the kitchen. And don't be clumsy with the jar."

"Yes, ma'am."

Elijah came up the steps. For a moment, he was close enough that Lila could smell the forge on him, that mix of smoke and iron and sweat. His eyes flicked to her face and held for half a heartbeat. Not longing. Not softness. A recognition made sharper by risk.

She did not speak his name. Names had weight.

Elijah lifted the basket carefully. His hands were steady, scarred, capable. When he turned toward the back hall, he did it without looking at her again. But his body angled in a way that made space for her to follow behind him without it looking like choice.

Mrs. Boone had already turned away, satisfied. The white boy from Carter's stayed on the porch, distracted by a dog gnawing at something near the steps.

Lila moved after Elijah, her steps quiet.

In the back hall, away from the porch's open sightline, Elijah didn't stop. He kept walking as if he belonged there, as if he was doing exactly what was required. Lila followed two paces behind, her face blank, her hands folded in front of her like she was waiting to be told what to do next.

They passed a doorway and the sound of a white voice drifted from inside, a man laughing. Elijah turned slightly into a narrow side passage, the kind used by servants, and Lila went with him without hesitation because hesitation drew attention.

He stopped near a stacked set of firewood, a place where their bodies could be close without looking like closeness. His voice was low. “You shouldn’t be back here.”

Lila kept her eyes on the basket. “Ain’t my choosing,” she said, and saw the slightest change in his expression, the brief tightening that meant he understood the trap of the phrase.

“Elijah,” she added quietly, because she couldn’t afford not to. “I saw something.”

His gaze sharpened. “Where.”

“Root cellar,” Lila said. “On my side. A cloth. Blue. Folded up like somebody placed it.”

Elijah’s jaw worked once, slow. “You touch it?”

“No,” she answered. “I just saw it. I remembered.”

He nodded once, almost to himself. “Good.”

Lila’s fingers curled, then uncurled. “What it mean?”

Elijah's eyes lifted toward the ceiling as if he could see through it to the yard, to the house, to the white boy waiting on the porch. "It mean somebody wants you to see it," he said. "That's all we can say for sure."

"A trap," Lila whispered.

"Or a sign," Elijah replied, and the fact that he allowed the possibility into the air at all made something in Lila's chest tighten painfully. Hope felt like a risk. Hope felt like stepping toward the river at night.

She swallowed. "Samuel been close," she said. "Closer than before. He talking like warnings again."

Elijah's shoulders stiffened, then eased back into stillness. "He's been in my forge," he said, and the words came out flat, controlled. "Standing in my doorway like he got a right."

Lila's throat went dry. "He watching you too."

Elijah looked at her then, fully, and the steadiness in his eyes didn't feel like comfort. It felt like agreement in a language neither of them wanted to speak too loudly. Shared danger wasn't romance. It was a recognition that the same shadow had touched both their backs.

"He ain't just watching," Elijah murmured. "He's counting."

Lila let out a slow breath. "Counting what."

Elijah's voice dropped even more. "Counting who talks. Who looks. Who thinks they got a path."

They stood in the narrow passage with the firewood stacked beside them like a wall. Beyond it, the house sounds continued, laughter and footsteps and the clink of dishes. The world that owned them went on without noticing the small, furious calculation happening between their breaths.

Lila's mind flashed to the blue cloth again. Folded. Placed. A mark that might be help or might be bait. She pictured Samuel's mild face, his eyes sharpening whenever she refused him, his calm certainty that he could arrange outcomes.

"We can't trust nothing," she whispered.

Elijah's gaze held hers. "We can't trust one thing," he corrected. "That's different."

Lila felt something inside her shift, not softening but aligning. He wasn't offering her a dream. He was offering her a method, the same method he used on metal: check the heat, test the seam, don't strike until you know where it will bend.

Footsteps sounded in the hall beyond the passage.

Elijah moved first, lifting the basket again as if they'd never stopped. He stepped out into the back hall with the same steady pace. Lila followed a half beat later; her face arranged again into harmlessness.

A white woman passed them, barely glancing, her attention already elsewhere. She did not see Lila's tightened hands. She did not see Elijah's eyes, sharpened by more than labor.

In the kitchen, Elijah set the basket down and turned away without looking at Lila again. That was the rule. You didn't give anyone a second look they could later describe.

Lila returned to the front, collected by Mrs. Boone's impatience, then escorted back toward the road by the Carter boy, who complained the whole way about mud on his boots.

On the walk home, Lila kept her gaze forward and her thoughts clenched tight so they wouldn't spill into her face. But inside, she replayed Elijah's words.

We can't trust one thing. That's different.

By the time Carter's house came into view, the day felt heavier. The yard looked the same. The fences looked the same. The air even smelled the same, smoke and sweat and damp earth.

But Lila saw the place as a set of seams now, and she felt, in her bones, that Elijah was doing the same on the other side.

The danger wasn't only in running. It was in noticing. Noticing made you a target for men like Samuel, men who listened for shifts and sold them upward.

And yet, as she stepped back into the yard and felt eyes slide over her, Lila understood something she hadn't allowed herself to understand before.

She was not carrying the danger alone.

It was shared now, whether they admitted it or not, braided between her memory and Elijah's craft, between the blue cloth in the cellar and the filed hinge pins hidden among ordinary scrap. Shared danger meant shared consequence.

It also meant, in the smallest and most dangerous way, shared purpose beginning to take shape.

Chapter 7

The Listening Circle

Samuel did not move quickly. Quick movement drew eyes, and eyes made stories. He moved the way a shadow moved when the light shifted: slow enough to seem natural, certain enough to be believed.

The morning after Lila's errand to Boone's, the quarters carried a new kind of tightness. Not louder fear, not the kind that made people run their mouths. A quieter fear, the kind that made people decide who they could stand beside without catching trouble.

Samuel watched that fear take shape.

He watched how Isaiah's bruises had become a warning people walked around. He watched how men stopped talking when Samuel came near, not because they knew what he'd done, but because they could feel the direction he leaned. That was the thing about power. You didn't have to see the whip to know where it would land. Sometimes you only needed to watch which way the air moved when a man entered a space.

Samuel's own work kept him near the yard that day, hauling feed and carrying water to places where white men expected it to appear without understanding how it got there. It suited him. The yard was a crossroads. People passed through it with reasons in their hands: buckets, boards, sacks, messages. Reasons were a cover, and Samuel had learned long ago that the safest way to collect anything was to look like you were simply doing what you'd been told.

He listened for names. He listened for hunger that didn't have food as its answer.

The first person he approached wasn't a man chasing north. Samuel didn't start there. Men with that kind of heat in them burned too bright; they could scorch you if you stood too close. He started with someone quieter. Someone who didn't want a route so much as she wanted one small thing: her child to stay where she could see him.

Her name was Ruth, and she worked laundry when the mistress needed it and field work when the overseer didn't care which hands got ruined. She was small-boned, with wrists like sticks, and she spoke little unless spoken to. But Samuel had noticed how she watched the main house when white men rode in. Not curiosity. Accounting.

Counting how many horses. Counting how many men. Counting whether any of those men might be the kind who came with papers and decisions.

Samuel waited until midday when the heat made people slow and the overseer's attention turned dull with satisfaction. Ruth was at the wash area with two other women, hands red, knuckles rough, lifting wet cloth and slapping it against the board with a rhythm that sounded like punishment given back in small, harmless pieces.

Samuel came close enough to be heard without being accused of hovering. He kept his voice low, ordinary.

"Ruth," he said, like he was just asking about work. "Your boy been keeping up?"

Ruth didn't look up right away. "He doing what he told," she replied, which wasn't an answer, but it was what you said when you didn't know why a question had found you.

Samuel nodded, watching the soap bubbles slide down the cloth like thin foam on river water. "He been seen near the stable," he said. "White men been moving around there more."

Ruth's hands paused for half a beat. Not long enough for anyone to accuse her of listening. Long enough for her body to betray her mind.

"My boy ain't done nothing," she said quickly.

Samuel lifted one shoulder, calm. "I ain't say he did. I'm saying eyes been on that side." He let the sentence settle, then added, soft as breath, "Eyes like to land on the young ones. Easier to move them. Easier to sell them. Easier to make a lesson out of them."

One of the other women made a small sound and turned her head, checking the yard. They were careful, but fear made people glance too sharply sometimes.

Ruth's fingers tightened on the cloth until water dripped faster. "Why you telling me this," she whispered, anger and terror braided together.

Samuel's tone stayed mild. "Because I seen a man get his family took once," he lied smoothly, and the lie worked because it sounded like the kind of truth everybody carried. "And because you don't got to find out after. Not if you paying attention now."

Ruth's eyes finally lifted to his face. They were tired eyes, but there was a blade in them. "And what you want for telling," she said. She didn't dress it up. She didn't pretend kindness existed here without hooks.

Samuel respected that. He kept his face soft anyway. "Ain't about what I want," he murmured.

"It's about who you trust to warn you when something shifts. Folks hear things. Folks see things. Most keep it to themselves because that's safer."

Ruth stared at him. The washboard creaked as another woman resumed scrubbing, louder now, as if sound could drown danger.

Samuel said, "If you hear talk that matters, not field talk, not hunger talk, but the kind that make white men sharpen up, you let me know. I can put it where it'll do you some good."

Ruth's mouth tightened. "You mean you tell them."

Samuel didn't deny it. Denial was the kind of thing a foolish man offered. Samuel wasn't foolish. "I mean I can make it so eyes turn away from your boy," he said. "I mean I can make it so trouble land somewhere else before it land on your doorstep."

Ruth's breath shook once. Samuel watched her swallow the taste of the choice he'd given her.

One of the women beside Ruth muttered, "This ain't right," but her hands didn't stop working. Nothing ever stopped, not here.

Ruth leaned closer, barely moving her lips. "You can't stop them if they want him."

Samuel met her gaze, steady. “I can’t stop the master from wanting,” he said. “But I can make the overseer busy with other things. I can make them think they already watched what need watching.”

He let the silence do its work. Ruth looked away first, not out of defeat but because looking too long at Samuel felt like agreeing.

When she spoke again, her voice was flat. “What kind of talk.”

Samuel kept it simple. “Anybody talking about river,” he said. “Anybody talking about marks. Anybody saying north out loud like it ain’t poison.”

Ruth’s shoulders rose and fell with a careful breath. She went back to scrubbing, harder now, as if she could scour the conversation away from her skin. She didn’t say yes. She didn’t say no.

Samuel didn’t need either. Not yet.

He walked away with the same unhurried steps he’d arrived with, and behind him Ruth scrubbed until her arms shook, as if the board under her hands might answer her with something clean.

By evening, Samuel had spoken to three more people, each approached by a different path.

To Joseph, a man whose leg had been damaged by a wagon wheel two seasons back and who now lived in the thin margin between being useful and being discarded. Samuel found him near the toolshed, struggling with a sack, jaw tight with humiliation.

"You don't need to tear yourself up," Samuel said.

Joseph's eyes flashed. "Ain't nobody asked you."

Samuel didn't flinch. "They looking for reasons," he replied, nodding toward the yard without pointing. "Reasons to send you off. Reasons to trade you. You know how they do."

Joseph's face went pale beneath the sunburn. "What you know."

Samuel offered him the smallest, cruelest kind of comfort. "I know how to keep your name out of their mouths," he said, and watched the words land.

To Mary, an older woman who helped in the kitchen and had learned how to hear white talk without appearing to hear it. Samuel didn't threaten her with punishment. He threatened her with the absence of small mercies. "You like getting the scraps before they sour," he said quietly as she worked near the back steps. "You like being allowed to carry a little bone home when they done chewing it."

Mary's eyes narrowed. "Who sent you."

Samuel shook his head. "Ain't nobody sent me," he said, which was true enough to pass. "But I can keep it coming, if you keep me informed."

Mary stared at him a long moment, then looked away toward the yard. "You building something," she murmured, and there was disgust in it, but there was also recognition. Everybody built something here. Some built hope. Some built protection. Some built traps.

Samuel's voice stayed calm. "I'm surviving," he said.

Mary snorted once, low. "Everybody say that when they cutting somebody else."

Samuel didn't answer. He didn't need to win Mary's approval. He needed her fear and her pragmatism to sit in the same room until they made a decision without calling it one.

And then there was Thomas, young enough to still believe in luck, reckless enough to flirt with it. Samuel found him behind the cabins after dark, speaking too close to another man, laughter too loose for a place like this.

Samuel didn't scold him. He didn't threaten him directly. He only stood in the dark long enough that Thomas's laughter faltered.

"You keep that mouth open," Samuel said, quiet, "and something going to crawl in it."

Thomas stiffened. "You spying now?"

Samuel tilted his head. "You want to call it spying," he replied. "Or you want to call it hearing what folks can't afford to say."

Thomas's eyes flicked toward the yard, toward the unseen line where white men might be. "What you want," he whispered.

Samuel leaned closer, not touching. "I want you to stay breathing," he said. "And I want you to tell me who else ain't learned to keep their breath quiet."

Thomas swallowed. "Why."

Samuel's mildness deepened into something colder. "Because the next time they make an example," he said, "it might be you. And I might be the only reason it ain't."

He left Thomas with that sentence and walked away, letting it hang in the air like a rope.

By the time the quarters settled, Samuel sat outside his cabin and listened to the new shape of silence.

It wasn't that people spoke more. They spoke less. But their eyes moved differently. They watched one another with an extra layer of calculation now, as if they could sense a line had been drawn across the dirt and they didn't know which side they were on.

That was the beginning of a network. Not a group that met in secret, not a circle that held hands and whispered oaths. Nothing so obvious, nothing so romantic.

It was a set of small agreements made under pressure.

A mother who would trade a name for a chance her boy stayed near.

A limping man who would offer overheard talk in exchange for being left useful.

An older woman who would feed information the way she fed scraps, carefully rationed, because she understood hunger in all its forms.

A young man who would learn to point away from himself if it meant his own skin stayed unmarked.

Samuel sat in the dark and let the night sounds move around him. Somewhere a dog shifted and sighed. Somewhere a man muttered in his sleep. Somewhere farther off, the river ran in its unseen bend, carrying the rumor like water carried everything, whether it was clean or not.

Samuel pressed his tongue against his teeth, tasting the memory of tobacco. He thought of Ruth's eyes, of Joseph's fear, of Mary's contempt, of Thomas's startled silence.

He thought, too, of Elijah Boone with his hinge pins and hidden wire, and of Lila Carter seeing a blue cloth folded where cloth had no reason to be.

They were building their own path out of scraps and seams.

Samuel was building his out of people.

And the thing about people, Samuel understood with a calm that felt like a sickness settling in, was that they were easier to shape than iron if you knew where they were already weak.

All you had to do was listen.

Then choose what to repeat, and what to keep.

Samuel learned quickly that information did not behave like food.

Food could be taken from your hands. Food could be counted, rationed, and withheld until your stomach stopped arguing and accepted whatever was poured into it. Information was different. It moved even when mouths were shut. It moved in the space between a pause and the next breath. It moved in the way a man's eyes slid toward the tree line and then away again, as if the trees had spoken his name.

And once it moved, you could not put it back.

The morning after he spoke to Ruth and Joseph and Mary and Thomas, Samuel did not go looking for more. He went looking for proof that what he'd started was taking hold.

He found it in the way Ruth's hands shook less when she saw Samuel pass, as if she had decided a thing without saying it out loud. He found it in Joseph's posture, straighter despite his bad leg, as if he had been handed a thread to hold onto. He found it in Mary's refusal to meet his eyes, a refusal that carried its own message: I see what you are, and I won't give you the comfort of pretending I don't.

He found it most clearly in the silence.

Not the usual silence, the one forced by white men and whips and the constant threat of being called out. This was a new kind. People were still quiet, but now their quietness had angles. It shifted depending on who was nearby. Conversations stopped not only when an overseer walked through, but when Samuel did. That wasn't fear of him exactly. It was recognition that sound could be carried, traded, spent.

Samuel kept his face dull and his steps steady. The worst mistake would be to look pleased.

Near midday, he was stacking feed near the stable when Ruth appeared with a bundle of linens on her hip. She moved like she always moved, quick and careful, eyes down. She did not approach him directly. She crossed the yard as if her path had always been this way. When she came within a few feet, she slowed just enough for her voice to slip out without lifting her head.

"They moving horses tonight," she murmured.

Samuel did not look at her. He shifted a sack into place and made a sound of effort, as if that was all she'd spoken to him for. "Who moving," he asked, quiet, buried under the scrape of burlap.

Ruth's lips barely moved. "Them two men from over the ridge," she said. "The ones that come with papers sometimes. I heard the mistress say it. She said, 'We'll have them ready after supper.'"

Papers could mean anything. Papers could mean buying. Selling. Borrowing. Papers made decisions look clean. Samuel's mind flicked to her boy near the stable, small enough to be useful and young enough to be wanted.

"Your boy been near there today?" Samuel asked.

Ruth's breath caught and then steadied. "I kept him away," she said. "I told him there was rats."

Samuel nodded once, a movement so small it could have been nothing. "Good," he murmured. "Keep him close tonight."

Ruth kept walking, not waiting for thanks, not risking a pause that would turn her message into a meeting.

Samuel stacked another sack and let his mind arrange the new piece. Two men from over the ridge. Papers. Horses readied. Tonight.

That could mean they were transporting someone. It could mean they were coming to collect someone. It could mean nothing, the usual white movement that didn't require explanation. But Ruth's fear gave it weight. Fear was how most truths announced themselves here.

Later, Joseph limped up carrying a broken harness strap, an excuse to be close. His eyes darted once toward the yard, then dropped. "You hear about Isaiah?" he asked, voice low.

Samuel kept his hands busy with the strap, fingers testing the leather's weakness. "What about him."

Joseph swallowed. "He been asked questions," he said. "Overseer kept him late by the toolshed. Folks say he asking who else been talking river."

Samuel felt the old hollow in his chest, the one that wasn't guilt and still felt like something rotting. He didn't let it reach his face. "Overseer always asking," Samuel replied.

Joseph's mouth tightened. "He asking different," he whispered. "He asking like he got names already."

Samuel's fingers stilled on the leather for a half beat, then resumed. "Who told you that."

Joseph's eyes flicked up, quick. "Mary," he said. "She heard it from the house side."

Mary. Contempt and sharp ears. Samuel filed it away, then handed the harness strap back. "You keep your head down," he told Joseph. "And you keep your ears open."

Joseph hesitated, then leaned closer by a fraction, voice even lower. "You going to do something with it," he said. Not a question. A statement shaped like one.

Samuel met Joseph's gaze for one heartbeat and then looked away. "Depends what it worth," he said.

Joseph's face tightened at the coldness of it. He nodded once and limped off, taking his fear with him.

That was the thing Samuel understood better each day: fear produced information the way pressure produced sweat. People didn't speak because they wanted to gossip. They spoke because they needed something to change, even if only in their own minds. They spoke because holding it alone felt like drowning.

Samuel let them speak, and he decided what their words could buy.

In the afternoon, Mary found him without appearing to.

She was behind the kitchen outbuilding, dumping peelings into a slop bucket, her hands moving with practiced speed. Samuel came by carrying a pail, an ordinary errand that gave him reason to be near. Mary didn't turn her head, but her voice slid out.

"Mr. Boone's boy was over here," she muttered.

Samuel's skin tightened, just a little. The Boone name had been traveling lately, carried on white tongues and guarded mouths. "Which boy," Samuel asked.

Mary made a small sound that could have been a laugh if she'd ever laughed freely. "Not the master's boy," she said. "A different one. White, but not big enough to own anything yet. Came with a message. Talked about fences. Talked about sending that blacksmith again."

Elijah. Samuel kept his grip on the pail steady. "When."

Mary's hands scraped peelings into the bucket. "This morning," she said. "Mr. Carter told him, 'We'll keep watch on our side. You keep watch on yours.' Like they can stitch the river shut with talk."

Samuel let the image sit in his mind: white men stitching, thinking they could sew up water. "Anything else," he asked.

Mary finally glanced at him, eyes hard. "You want it all," she said.

Samuel didn't flinch. "I want what matters."

Mary's mouth tightened. "He said something about dogs," she replied. "About bells. About making it so a body can't move at night without the whole yard hearing it."

Samuel nodded once. The bells rumor had been floating; now it had white confirmation. That made it heavier. "Good to know," he murmured.

Mary spat into the dirt, not at him exactly, but near enough to show what she thought of this exchange. “You trading in sorrow,” she said quietly.

Samuel kept his tone even. “Everybody trading,” he replied. “Some just don’t call it that.”

He walked away before Mary could answer, because the longer you stayed, the more a conversation became a scene. And scenes drew eyes.

By dusk, Samuel had a pocketful of pieces. None of them were a full story. That was fine. Full stories got men killed. Full stories were what runaways carried in their heads when they believed a route was certain, and then they stepped into the woods and heard a whistle ahead of them and realized certainty had been a lie.

Pieces were safer. Pieces could be arranged. Pieces could be withheld.

Samuel sat outside his cabin as night settled, listening to the quarters as if it were a single animal breathing. He watched Thomas across the yard, young face turned serious now, laughter gone. Thomas was speaking to another man, but his eyes kept sliding toward Samuel, checking, measuring, as if he had realized the price of talking too loose.

Thomas's gaze met Samuel's for a fraction and then dropped fast.

Good, Samuel thought. He's learning.

Ruth's boy appeared briefly, small body darting between cabins with a stick in his hand, then Ruth called him back sharp and quick. The boy obeyed, confused but compliant. Samuel watched the way Ruth's hand closed around his wrist, not cruel, protective. Ownership imitated, turned into something else.

Information could do that. It could make a woman act before the harm arrived.

The overseer's presence moved at the edge of the yard, boots audible, voice carrying in short bursts as he spoke to a white man near the stable. Samuel didn't try to get closer. Being seen trying was the same as being caught.

Instead, he waited for the moment the overseer's path bent naturally toward him, the way it often did now.

It happened near full dark, when the yard was settling and white men liked to make one last pass to remind everybody who owned the night.

The overseer stopped a few feet from Samuel, close enough that his shadow cut across Samuel's knees. "You been quiet," the overseer said.

Samuel kept his gaze lowered. "Ain't much to say, sir."

The overseer made a sound of mild disapproval. "Quiet don't mean loyal," he replied.

Samuel lifted his eyes just enough to look obedient. "I understand," he said.

A pause. Then, as if it were nothing, Samuel offered one piece. Not the whole handful. Not Ruth's fear about papers and horses. Not Mary's news of Boone's message. He chose the safer currency, the one that served the overseer's interests clean.

"They talking about dogs," Samuel said softly. "Folks saying you might put bells on them. They already scared of it."

The overseer's eyes narrowed. "Who saying."

Samuel hesitated, letting reluctance show. He did not give a name. Names were expensive. Names bought meat and tobacco and protection, but they also created obligations. "Just talk I heard," he replied. "Running around the quarters."

The overseer studied him for a long moment, then grunted. "They ought to be scared," he said. "Scared keeps them in line."

"Yes, sir," Samuel murmured.

The overseer shifted his weight, satisfied. He leaned in slightly, voice low. "You keep listening," he said. "You bring me what matters. Not foolishness."

Samuel nodded. "Yes, sir."

The overseer walked off, boots fading into the dark.

Samuel stayed seated, face empty. Inside, his mind moved fast.

He had spent a piece and bought himself nothing visible, which was exactly the point. Not every trade paid immediately. Sometimes you spent just enough to keep the door open, to remind the man with the switch that you were still useful.

And sometimes you saved the better pieces for when you needed to buy something larger.

He looked across the yard toward the dark line of trees beyond the fences. Somewhere out there, the river bent. Somewhere, a mark might exist that was real or might be bait set by men like the overseer. Somewhere, Elijah Boone was shaping metal into quiet possibility, and Lila Carter was memorizing a blue cloth folded where it did not belong.

They were gathering their own fragments, trying to assemble a path.

Samuel understood, with the same cold clarity he'd felt when the ladle tipped extra into his bowl, that they were competing in the same market.

They just didn't know the prices yet.

In the night, a dog barked once, then went silent, as if it had heard an instruction it understood without words.

Samuel leaned back against the cabin wall and let the darkness hold him.

Information was currency. The plantation ran on it as much as it ran on labor. The difference was that labor was taken, but information could be offered. That made it feel like choice. That made it feel like power.

Samuel touched the inside of his cheek where the tobacco had once sat and tasted only bitterness, faint and lingering.

He would keep listening. He would keep collecting. And when the moment came that someone needed something badly enough, when fear sharpened into desperation and desperation into movement, Samuel would be ready to decide what their words could buy.

Sometimes protection.

Sometimes punishment.

Sometimes nothing at all, if the lesson needed to be taught for free.

He closed his eyes and listened to the quarters breathe, already counting the interest on what he knew.

Samuel learned where knowledge lived.

It didn't live in the loud mouths. Those got noticed. Those got corrected. It lived in the pauses people didn't know they made, in the way a woman's hands tightened on a bucket handle when a white rider passed, in the way men suddenly found reasons to be indoors when the moon climbed bright.

He walked through the day as if he were only a body doing what bodies were told. But his mind moved differently now. It moved like a hand inside a glove, feeling for seams.

By the second week after Isaiah's beating, the plantation had adjusted around Samuel without anyone announcing it had. The quarter's voices stayed low, yet the low had changed. People no longer whispered only to share hunger or small complaint. They whispered to place weight somewhere else. A fear passed from mouth to mouth like a cup, and Samuel became one of the hands that decided who drank first.

He didn't need to call anyone to him. He had already taught them how to come.

Ruth found him again near the wash area, not looking up, speaking without stopping her work. "They say them men with papers coming back," she murmured, and the sentence carried the tremble of a mother who had already imagined the empty space her boy could become.

Samuel kept his eyes on the ground as if studying a knot in the dirt. "Who say," he asked.

Ruth's mouth barely moved. "Kitchen talk," she said. "Mary heard it from inside."

Mary. Mary heard everything and hated herself for it, which made her sharper.

Samuel nodded once, small. "Keep your boy near women tonight," he told her. "Not men. Men get used for errands."

Ruth swallowed hard. "You sure you can—"

He cut her off, not harsh, just final. "I ain't sure of nothing," he said. "I'm telling you what keeps him from being convenient."

Ruth's hands shook once, then steadied. She went back to scrubbing as if soap could erase the choice she'd made in speaking to him.

Samuel walked away and let the message settle in his mind beside the others.

He did not go to the overseer with it. Not yet.

If he took every fear upward, he would flood the channel and make himself less useful. White men didn't reward panic. They rewarded control. Samuel understood that. His value wasn't in hearing. It was in deciding what mattered.

He had become a filter.

That afternoon, he found Thomas behind the cabins, pretending to carve a piece of wood with a dull knife. Thomas's face still held youth, but it had lost its looseness. The laughter had been burned out of it by watching Isaiah drag himself through work with his back wrong.

Samuel stopped a few feet away, not close enough to seem like a meeting, close enough that Thomas had to acknowledge his presence.

"You quiet now," Samuel said.

Thomas's grip tightened on the knife. "Got nothing to say."

Samuel tilted his head. "You had plenty to say before."

Thomas's eyes flashed, then dropped fast. "Before don't matter."

"It do," Samuel replied. "Before tells me what you likely to do when you think nobody listening."

Thomas's jaw worked. "You always listening."

Samuel let that sit. Truths were heavier when you didn't dress them up. "What you hear lately," he asked, casual.

Thomas hesitated. Samuel watched the hesitation like a man watching a gate latch. Hesitation meant there was something behind it.

"There's a man," Thomas said finally, voice low. "Out by the far field line. Says he know about the river. Says there's a place where reeds grow thick and the bank hides your feet."

Samuel kept his face blank. "Name."

Thomas swallowed. "Caleb. He work cutting wood."

Samuel nodded once, filed it away. "You hear him say north?"

Thomas shook his head fast. "No. He ain't that stupid."

Samuel's mouth tilted, almost. "Stupid don't keep a man alive long," he said. Then, softer: "You think Caleb telling truth?"

Thomas looked down at his wood, knife scraping. "I think he trying to feel like he got something," he muttered. "Folks like that talk just to hear themselves brave."

Samuel considered it. People did that. They built courage out of sound because silence felt like surrender.

"Courage that make noise is easy to find," Samuel said.

Thomas looked up, wary. "What you want me to do."

The question was the point. Samuel had not ordered him. He had positioned him until Thomas asked for instruction.

"Nothing," Samuel answered. "You just keep your ears open. And you keep your own mouth shut."

Thomas stared at him. "Why you always doing this," he whispered, and there was something raw in it. Not anger. Confusion. The need to believe Samuel had reasons beyond cruelty.

Samuel could have lied and given him comfort. He could have said, "Because I'm trying to keep you safe." He had used that language with Ruth because mothers needed a shape they could hold. Thomas didn't need comfort. Thomas needed fear with direction.

"Because I can," Samuel said simply.

Thomas flinched as if struck, then looked away. The knife in his hand stopped moving.

Samuel left him there, carved wood unfinished, the lesson delivered clean.

That was how knowledge worked when you used it right. You didn't have to beat a man. You only had to make him feel the outline of the cage and understand you could tighten it.

By evening, the yard had that restless quiet that meant something was coming. White men moved more than usual. A lantern passed between the stable and the main house twice, bobbing like an impatient eye. The dogs were fed early, and one of them whined the way dogs did when they sensed their own usefulness being sharpened.

Samuel sat outside his cabin and watched without looking like he watched. He kept his posture loose. He let his face go dull.

Joseph limped past and slowed just a fraction. He didn't stop, but his voice drifted out like a leaf falling. "They saying patrol on the river line tonight."

Samuel didn't turn his head. "Who saying," he murmured.

Joseph's breath hitched. "White talk," he said. "Heard it near the stable. They acting like they expecting somebody."

Samuel nodded once, almost invisible. Patrol meant fear. Patrol also meant opportunity. When white men watched one place, they didn't watch another as well. But only if you knew how their attention moved.

That was the difference between rumor and knowledge.

Rumor made men run straight into the woods and pray the trees would hide them.

Knowledge told you which tree had a gap in the fence behind it, which gate didn't catch clean unless you lifted it, which dog was mean and which one only sounded mean because it had been trained to bark on command.

Samuel did not have all of that knowledge. Not the physical kind. Not the kind Elijah Boone made with his hands, filing hinge pins, shaping wire into hooks. But Samuel had something else. He had the map of people's fear.

He knew who would move if given a push.

He knew who would freeze.

He knew who would trade somebody else's name to keep their own child close.

He had built a circle of listening without calling it that. It wasn't loyalty that held it together. It was need. And need was dependable.

When the overseer finally crossed the yard toward him, Samuel didn't straighten. He didn't look eager. He waited as if the overseer's boots were just another sound in the night.

The overseer stopped with his shadow falling across Samuel again, the same posture as before, the same casual ownership.

"You got anything," the overseer asked.

Samuel lifted his gaze just enough. "Folks talking," he said.

The overseer made a small sound, impatient. "They always talking."

Samuel chose his words with care. This was the trade he understood now: not information for food, but information for position. The overseer didn't want a flood. He wanted a lever.

"They talking about the river line," Samuel said quietly. "Not loud. But it's there."

The overseer's eyes narrowed. "Names."

Samuel hesitated, performed reluctance. He could feel the circle he'd built tightening at the mention of names. If he gave too many away too fast, people would stop bringing him things. The channel would dry up.

"I ain't got names I trust," Samuel said. "Not yet."

The overseer's mouth hardened. "You getting soft?"

Samuel kept his tone even, respectful. "I'm getting sure," he replied. "Soft give you wrong names. Wrong names make you look like you whipping air."

The overseer stared at him for a long moment. Samuel held still, letting his calm do its work. Calm suggested loyalty. Calm suggested control.

Finally, the overseer grunted. "You hear anything solid, you bring it," he said.

"Yes, sir," Samuel murmured.

The overseer walked off, and Samuel watched his back without moving.

He had just done something small but important. He had refused a demand without sounding like refusal. He had kept his position as a listener while proving he wasn't careless. White men didn't mind cruelty. They minded being made to look foolish.

Samuel leaned back against his cabin wall and let the night settle again.

Across the quarters, a woman's baby cried once, then was hushed quickly, as if even infants needed to learn that sound could be dangerous. A dog barked near the stable, then another answered, then both were quieted by a white voice sharp as a switch.

Samuel thought about what he held and what he didn't.

He held Thomas's fear and Caleb's name and Ruth's trembling warnings and Mary's bitter scraps of white conversation. He held the knowledge that patrols were tightening, that papers were moving, that eyes were turning toward the river and, because of that, away from other places.

He did not hold the truth of the blue cloth Lila had seen folded in her root cellar. He did not know whether it was a sign meant to help or bait meant to catch. He did not know what tools Elijah Boone had hidden in plain sight or what seams Elijah had already found in the plantation's hinges and locks.

But Samuel didn't need those truths yet.

Control wasn't built from certainty. It was built from managing what other people believed was certain.

He could make a rumor feel true by letting it spread.

He could make a truth feel dangerous by repeating it upward.

He could make a man hesitate at the edge of the woods by letting him hear, from the wrong mouth at the right time, that dogs had bells now, that patrols were waiting, that somebody already knew.

And the best part was this: he didn't have to touch anyone to do it.

Samuel closed his eyes and listened to the plantation breathe, the sound of many bodies trapped under one system, each of them dreaming or not dreaming, each of them carrying questions.

He had learned to answer those questions with silence, or with a name, depending on what he needed.

In the dark, he pictured Elijah Boone's steady hands and Lila Carter's careful face, both of them collecting fragments, both of them trying to assemble a path without stepping into a trap. Samuel didn't know their full plan, not yet.

But he knew the shape of their hope.

And he knew, with a calm that felt like the settling of a lock, that hope was easiest to control when you didn't crush it all at once.

You let it live.

You let it grow teeth.

Then you decided where it bit.

Chapter 8

Seeds of Doubt

The first secret didn't break open with shouting.

It opened the way a jar did when the lid had been loosened just enough: a soft give, then the slow, unstoppable turn.

Elijah noticed it at the forge.

He came in before full daylight, before the yard had filled with bodies and orders, intending to use the quiet minutes the way he always did. Useful men were granted scraps of time, and scraps were all you could build with. The coals from yesterday still held a faint warmth beneath ash; he could coax them back without smoke if he worked careful. He reached for the iron poker he kept beside the hearth.

The poker was gone.

Not moved to a different peg. Not leaned against the wall. Gone the way things went when someone wanted you to feel it.

Elijah stood still long enough to hear his own breath. The forge had its usual smells: old smoke, iron dust, sweat soaked into wood. But something else sat in the air, too, a thin sourness like a room after an argument. He let his gaze travel without looking like he was searching.

The tool rack was in order. The tongs hung where they should. The hammer sat on the stump. Nothing looked disturbed.

That was what made it worse.

He crossed to the corner where he kept scrap, where broken things waited to be made into something else. Beneath a pile of bent nails and dull chain links, he had tucked the coil of wire he'd drawn out and hidden in a hollow handle. Not because it was valuable, but because it was wrong in a way he couldn't explain if anyone asked.

He slid his hand under the scrap and felt nothing but cold metal and grit.

The coil wasn't there.

Elijah didn't move fast. Fast made noise, and noise brought eyes. He stood with his hand still in the scrap pile and let his face stay blank, as if he'd only been checking for a particular piece of iron.

He could rebuild the wire. That wasn't the point. The point was the message in its absence.

Someone had been in here.

Someone had known where to touch.

He straightened and looked toward the doorway. The yard beyond was waking, gray light, a few figures moving with buckets. No one stood watching him openly. No one needed to. Attention didn't always look like a pair of eyes.

He told himself, for the first time in a way that stuck like a nail under skin, that the forge wasn't his at all.

It was only the place they let him work.

By midmorning, the master came down with a white man Elijah didn't recognize, older, broad through the chest, carrying a small leather satchel at his hip like he had papers inside that could cut. The master's voice was too calm.

"Elijah," he said, as if calling a dog.

Elijah set down his hammer and turned. "Yes, sir."

The stranger stepped into the forge without hesitation, glancing around like he was counting shadows. He didn't look at Elijah's face. He looked at the tools. The rack. The bench. The corner where scrap was piled.

"You been keeping busy," the stranger said.

Elijah didn't answer. Answers were traps.

The master lifted the broken chain link Elijah had repaired days ago, holding it between thumb and forefinger as if it might be dirty. "This was good work," he said, and the praise sounded like a threat. "You can fix clean."

"Yes, sir."

The stranger drifted toward the bench. "You ever make anything you ain't been asked to make?" he asked, tone light, like it was a joke.

Elijah let his face stay steady. "I make what I'm told."

The master's eyes narrowed a fraction. "You hear what he asked."

Elijah looked at the master, then back to the stranger. "No, sir," he said. "I don't make nothing I ain't asked."

The stranger smiled a little, but it didn't reach his eyes. He reached toward the tool rack, fingertips brushing along the handles like he was choosing a knife.

"I heard a story," the stranger said. "About a blacksmith once. Not here. Another place. He made a key for a lock he weren't supposed to open. Made it right under their noses. Clever, wasn't he?"

Elijah said nothing.

The master stepped closer, boots loud on the packed dirt. "You don't look like a clever man to me," he said softly. "You look like a man who'd rather keep his skin where it belong."

Elijah held his gaze. "Yes, sir."

The stranger bent near the scrap pile. He didn't dig. He didn't disturb. He only looked, long enough that Elijah felt the old, familiar heat of danger climbing his spine.

Then the stranger straightened and stepped back, as if satisfied by what he hadn't found. "All right," he said. "Just checking."

Checking. Elijah tasted the word like ash.

They left the forge together. The master paused at the doorway and looked back at Elijah one last time, expression mild.

"You keep your work clean," he said again.

Elijah watched them go, then picked up his hammer and struck the anvil hard enough to make the ring carry into the yard. The sound wasn't for work. It was for cover, for the sense that nothing had changed.

But he knew better.

A secret had been touched.

On Carter's plantation, Lila learned it from the other side.

It began with the cellar door.

Two days after she'd seen the folded blue cloth behind the back shelf, the mistress sent her down again with the same kind of list that didn't match the shelves. Lila took the lantern, went down the steps, and kept her breathing even. The air was cool and damp. The shelves waited in their orderly rows.

The corner behind the last shelf was empty.

No cloth.

No sign it had ever been there.

Lila stood with the lantern held high, light trembling. She didn't crouch. She didn't reach into the corner. She didn't touch the dirt to see if it had been recently disturbed. Evidence could cling to your hands.

She backed away, careful, and climbed the steps with her face arranged into nothing.

When she came out, the cook was waiting near the kitchen doorway, hands wiped on her apron too many times.

"You find what she wanted?" the cook asked, voice flat.

Lila nodded once. "Yes," she lied, because the list had never been the point.

The cook's eyes slid over Lila's face as if searching for cracks. "They was down there," she murmured, barely sound. "This morning. Mr. Carter and that boy from Boone's side. Went into the cellar like it was theirs."

Lila's stomach tightened. She kept her voice low. "What they looking for."

The cook shook her head once, sharp. "Looking for trouble," she said. "Looking for proof of talk. Looking for… I don't know."

Lila carried the jars to the kitchen and set them down. Her hands didn't shake until she was alone behind the wash basin, where no one would see her fingers grip the edge hard enough to whiten.

They had removed it.

The blue cloth had been placed to be seen, and then it had been taken away. Or it had been taken away because it had been seen. Either way, it meant what Elijah had said in Boone's back passage was true in a way she hadn't wanted to admit.

Somebody wanted her to notice.

Somebody also wanted her to understand that noticing could be traced.

Later that evening, Samuel found her without appearing to.

He didn't corner her. He didn't step into her path. He stood near the yard's edge where the light fell thin, holding a bucket as if he'd been assigned some meaningless task. Lila passed with laundry folded over her arms, eyes down.

Samuel spoke softly as she came close enough. "They been in the cellar."

Lila didn't stop walking. "Everybody been in the cellar," she said, making her voice dull.

Samuel's pace matched hers for three steps. "Not everybody," he replied. "Mr. Carter. And a man from Boone's place."

Lila's heartbeat shifted. She kept her face empty. "What you telling me for."

Samuel's voice stayed mild, but she heard the satisfaction underneath it, like a man who'd found a loose board and enjoyed the hollow sound when he stepped on it. "Because folks hide things in cellars," he said. "Because they don't like what's been moving between places."

Lila turned her head just enough to glance at him. "What been moving."

Samuel looked ahead, not at her, as if speaking to the air. "Hope," he said.

The word landed cold. Lila kept walking, laundry pressing against her chest like armor that wouldn't stop a blade. "You don't know nothing about hope."

Samuel's mouth tilted. "I know what it cost," he said. "And I know who pay it."

She wanted to spit at him. She wanted to ask how he knew, who had told him, what he had done. Instead she did what survival required.

She made her voice small. "You trying to scare me."

Samuel's eyes flicked to her face then, quick and sharp. "I'm trying to teach you," he murmured. "Secrets don't stay secret. Not here. Not when folks hungry for something to trade."

Lila felt the shape of it then, the exposed edge under his words.

Trade.

He knew. Maybe not about the cloth exactly, but about the kind of thing the cloth meant. About the idea of signs. About the way fragments were being gathered.

She kept her gaze forward. "I ain't got nothing to trade," she said.

Samuel's voice softened, almost kind. "Everybody got something," he replied. "Sometimes it's just a name."

A name. Lila's throat went dry.

Ahead, a white voice called for her, impatient. Lila quickened her steps, and Samuel let her go, the way a man let a hooked fish run a little before pulling the line tight.

That night, after the cabin quieted, Lila lay with her back to the wall and listened to the dark. The plantation never truly slept. It only lowered its voice.

Outside, she heard a dog's collar jingle faintly as it shifted in its chain. Not a bell, not yet, but the small sound made her think of Mary's scraps of talk and the overseer's interest. She imagined the sound multiplied, dogs moving like a choir of warning.

She thought of Elijah's forge and the missing wire coil she didn't know about, and she thought of her cellar corner, suddenly clean as if it had never held a sign.

Somebody was closing the seams.

Or making it look like they were.

In the days that followed, little exposures came like splinters.

A woman in the kitchen was questioned about where she'd been standing when white men talked. She denied listening too quickly, and they noticed the speed of her denial. Her tasks changed after that, moved away from the house, into the yard where ears were less valuable.

A boy in the quarters was found with a length of twine he couldn't explain. He said he'd found it. The overseer said, "Found where," over and over until the boy began to cry and couldn't speak at all.

Elijah heard that on his side through the thin channels that carried pain between plantations. He didn't hear it as a full story. He heard it as the way men looked at one another more carefully now, as if each face might be the one that had caused the question.

The most dangerous thing wasn't the punishments. They were expected, almost. The dangerous thing was the uncertainty that came after.

Who had been caught.

Who had spoken.

What had been taken.

And what else had been seen.

By the end of the week, Elijah stood at his forge with sweat slick on his spine and realized he no longer trusted the quiet minutes he'd once depended on. Quiet could mean safety. Quiet could also mean someone had already been there and left nothing behind but absence.

On Carter's plantation, Lila stopped looking directly at corners where cloth might appear. She memorized them without letting her eyes linger. She learned to store information the way you stored something stolen: deep, where it didn't show in your posture.

And somewhere between them, in the space of shared danger and separated bodies, a new truth took root like a seed in bad soil.

Their secrets were no longer only theirs to hold.

They were being handled.

Turned over.

Priced.

And once a secret had been exposed to air, it changed shape. It stopped being a private thing, a fragile piece of hope hidden in the dark. It became something that could be used against you.

Lila understood that with a clarity that felt like sickness.

Elijah understood it with the steady dread of a craftsman whose tools had been touched by someone else's hands.

And Samuel, standing just outside the circles he'd built, understood it as something else entirely.

A door opening, slow and quiet.

A lock turning.

The beginning of doubt, not planted by accident, but placed carefully, like a folded cloth in a cellar corner, meant to be noticed and meant to disappear the moment it had done its work.

Trust didn't shatter all at once. It thinned.

It thinned the way rope did when it had been rubbed too many times against the same rough post. Still whole if you looked quick. Still holding, if you didn't test it. But every day it held less, and every day it took less to snap.

Elijah stopped leaving anything in the forge that he couldn't explain with his hands on the anvil and a white man watching.

The missing poker came back two mornings later, placed on the peg like it had never been gone. The wire coil did not. Elijah noticed the way it was returned, too neat, too deliberate. A warning disguised as order. Someone wanted him to know they could take and replace, reach into his space and withdraw again without leaving footprints that mattered.

That meant there were only two kinds of men to fear: the ones who didn't care if you noticed, and the ones who wanted you to.

He worked through the day as he always had, steady and exact. But he stopped using the quiet minutes before the yard woke. He stopped taking comfort in empty air. He began to assume there was always another breath in the room with him.

On the third afternoon after the stranger with the satchel visited, a boy brought him a request from the main house. A hinge on the pantry door had started sticking, Mrs. Boone said, and she didn't like to wrestle with a door in her own home.

Elijah took the hinge, turned it in his hands, and saw immediately what had been done. The pin was bent, just slightly. Not enough to break, enough to scrape. Enough to make the door complain.

It was a small problem, the kind that happened all the time in a house built to hold other people's labor. But Elijah could tell the difference between wear and intent. The bend was too clean.

He fixed it anyway. He fixed it with the care he always used, because care was the only shield he had. When he returned the hinge, he didn't ask questions. He didn't make a face. He didn't let any thought reach his eyes.

Still, on his way back to the forge, he passed two field hands leaning close behind a shed, heads bowed. When they saw him, they separated too fast, like startled birds.

Elijah kept walking. He didn't look back.

A week ago, he would have taken it as nothing. Men whispered. Men traded scraps of talk like they traded scraps of food. Now, everything carried an edge. Now, every quick movement meant the knife was already out.

That night, in the quarters, the old man who mended things on his step wasn't outside. His doorway was dark. Elijah stood in the yard a moment, listening. He heard low voices behind a cabin wall, then silence when footsteps shifted nearby.

He realized something that left him colder than fear.

Nobody was sure who was safe to be seen with anymore.

On Carter's plantation, Lila felt the erosion in different places, inside walls that smiled while they tightened.

The mistress began calling her by name more often. Not kindly. Not cruelly, either. Simply often, as if repetition made ownership feel fresh.

Lila's tasks changed without warning. One day she was polishing silver in the front room where talk drifted freely because they believed she was deaf to meaning. The next she was sent to scrub pots in the kitchen where talk was watched by other eyes, where Mary's mouth stayed tight and the cook's hands moved too fast.

Then she was sent outside, out of the house entirely, to shake rugs and beat dust in the yard under open sky, where every movement was visible.

It felt like being repositioned. Like a piece on a board moved without explanation, only so someone else could see where it landed.

The cook whispered to her once, quick and strained, "They think you been listening too much."

Lila didn't answer. Answering was a way to confirm there was something to accuse.

That evening, she carried a bucket to the wash area, and Samuel was there, as if the yard had arranged itself around him.

He didn't greet her. He didn't need to. His presence had become its own kind of greeting, the way a fence greeted you when you walked too close and remembered the last man who'd tried to climb it.

"You been quiet," Samuel said.

Lila kept her eyes on the water. "Ain't much to say."

Samuel made a soft sound that could have been amusement. "That's smart. Quiet don't make you innocent, but it make you harder to prove."

She dipped the bucket and lifted it, arms tightening with the weight. "What you want."

Samuel stepped closer by a fraction, not blocking her path, but narrowing it. "You ever wonder," he murmured, "why they had you run that basket to Boone's?"

Lila's grip held steady. "Because they wanted to show neighborly."

Samuel's eyes sharpened. "Neighborly don't need a slave girl and a white boy to walk behind her like a shadow." He let the sentence settle, then added, almost conversational, "They wanted to see who looked at you too long. Who made room for you. Who found reasons to be near."

Lila felt her stomach tighten, but she kept her face dull. "You think you know everything."

Samuel watched her the way he watched the yard, as if she were a pattern he could learn. "I know enough," he said. "I know you been carrying things you shouldn't. Not in your hands. In your head."

Lila lifted the bucket and turned away from him. She forced her steps to stay even. Inside her, anger rose, but anger was loud. Loud got you marked.

Samuel's voice followed her, low, confident. "You better be careful who you trust with it," he said. "Folks get scared. Scared folks start naming names just to feel like they got control of something."

Lila didn't respond. She didn't look back. But the words went with her, lodging under her ribs where fear already lived.

He was right about one thing. People were scared.

In the cabins, women spoke in murmurs and then broke off mid-sentence if a shadow crossed a doorway. Men who used to share a glance and a nod now kept their eyes forward, as if even recognition could be counted against them. Lila watched a young man she'd known since childhood flinch when his own uncle touched his shoulder.

Fear was becoming suspicious. Suspicion was becoming discipline.

And discipline was what the plantation wanted.

Two days later, Lila found Mary behind the kitchen steps, alone for a moment, hands busy with peelings. Mary's eyes were tired, but they flashed when she saw Lila.

"You stay out my way," Mary muttered without looking up.

Lila stopped anyway, just long enough to make it look accidental. "You heard anything," she asked, barely sound.

Mary's knife paused. "You trying to get me cut up," she said. "You trying to get yourself cut up."

"I ain't trying," Lila whispered. "I'm asking."

Mary's mouth tightened. "Asking is dangerous now."

Lila felt the sharpness of it. "It weren't before."

Mary finally turned her head, eyes hard. "Before, we ain't had a man like Samuel walking around acting like he can buy safety with other folks' pain."

Lila's throat went dry. She kept her voice low. "You think he the one telling."

Mary's expression shifted, the smallest flicker of uncertainty. "I think he telling something," she said. "And I think he ain't the only one. That's what you don't want to see. When things get tight, everybody start thinking about what they can trade."

Lila looked away, because Mary was right and because the truth of it made her feel alone in a crowd full of bodies.

On Boone's plantation, Elijah felt the same truth from the other side of the fence.

A man named Caleb, who cut wood near the far field line, came to the forge near midday with a cracked axe head. He didn't usually come. There were other men who handled tools. Caleb had strong arms and a restless mouth, the kind of man who could turn boredom into talk just to fill the air.

Elijah took the axe head without comment. He set it on the anvil and tested the crack with his thumb.

Caleb lingered in the doorway instead of leaving. "You heard about Isaiah," he said, too casual.

Elijah kept his eyes on the metal. "Everybody heard."

Caleb leaned a little, voice lowering. "You know why it happened."

Elijah's hammer paused mid-lift. He let it hover just long enough to be noticeable. "You tell me," he said, flat.

Caleb's mouth twitched. "Somebody named him. That's why. Somebody close. Somebody who get extra sometimes."

Elijah's stomach tightened. He didn't ask who. Asking would make it a conversation. Conversations turned into stories, and stories turned into rope.

Caleb went on anyway, the way men did when they wanted to feel powerful by holding attention. "Folks saying Samuel," he murmured. "Folks saying he been slipping words up the line."

Elijah struck the axe head harder than necessary, the ring of iron loud enough to swallow his reaction. Samuel's name wasn't new to him, but hearing it spoken like that, in the open air of his forge, felt like a hand reaching into his chest.

Caleb watched him. "You ever talk to Samuel," he asked.

Elijah kept his face empty. "He talked to me," Elijah said. "I ain't asked for it."

Caleb smiled slightly, as if that confirmed something. "Mm," he hummed. "People always saying they ain't asked."

Elijah felt the trap in it then. Not a trap set by white men. A trap set by a man who wanted information and didn't care whose skin paid for it.

Elijah turned his head just enough to look at Caleb. His gaze was steady, unwelcoming. "You get your axe back when it's done," he said. "That's all."

Caleb held his gaze a moment longer, then stepped away, hands raised as if in surrender. "All right," he muttered. "Just talking."

But Elijah knew better. Nothing was just talking anymore.

When Caleb left, Elijah stood at the anvil and listened to his own breathing. He thought of Lila's voice in the narrow passage at Boone's house, her words careful: Samuel been close. He talking like warnings again.

He had believed her. He still did.

What unsettled him now was the widening circle of mouths around Samuel's name. That meant Samuel had become more than a man. He'd become an explanation people could use. A shape to blame. A reason to stop trusting the person beside you.

That was how erosion worked. You didn't need proof. You only needed the sense that proof existed somewhere you couldn't reach.

That night, Elijah tried to picture Lila's face, to hold onto it as something real, something he could check. But even that felt dangerous now. He didn't doubt her. He doubted the space between them.

He didn't know who watched her on Carter's side. He didn't know who listened when she spoke. He didn't know what Samuel had already convinced others to carry upward. And because he didn't know, his mind started doing what the plantation trained every mind to do when it had no certainty to hold.

It started filling the gaps with fear.

Across the boundary, Lila lay on her pallet and stared at the dark rafters. She thought of the cellar corner, clean and empty. She thought of Samuel's voice, calm as a closed door. She thought of Mary's warning: everybody start thinking about what they can trade.

Then, uninvited, another thought came, sharp enough to hurt.

What if Elijah's forge had been searched because of her? What if her errand to Boone's had been used to connect a line that wasn't there before? What if the brief moment in the passage, their shared danger, had become evidence in someone else's hands?

She tried to push it away. She tried to hold onto Elijah's steadiness, his method, his careful words. But the doubt didn't need to be true to do its work.

It only needed to be possible.

And in a place built on punishment, possible was enough to change how you looked at every face in the dark.

Samuel did not need to invent new fears. He only needed to give the old ones a direction.

Division was already in the soil. The plantation planted it every day with its rules, its rewards, its punishments that always carried a second lesson beneath the first: you might suffer, but you might also survive if you stood in the right place when the suffering passed over.

Samuel understood that better than most. He understood that a man did not have to be liked to be obeyed. He only had to be believed.

He started with small pressures, the kind that could be dismissed as coincidence by anyone desperate to keep believing in coincidence.

On Boone's plantation, it was a sentence spoken too loud.

Elijah was at the forge when Caleb returned for his axe head. The repair was clean, the crack sealed and peened flat as if it had never been there. Elijah held it out without ceremony.

Caleb took it, but instead of leaving, he stayed in the doorway where light cut his outline sharp. There were two other men in the yard within earshot, working slow, listening without appearing to.

Caleb smiled like he'd forgotten what fear cost. "I heard something," he said.

Elijah didn't ask what. He turned back to the anvil and began sorting through scrap with the disinterest of a man already done with the exchange.

Caleb's voice rose just enough to travel. "They saying Carter's girl been asking questions," he said, as if it were nothing. "They saying she got people on both sides."

Elijah's hands did not stop moving. But the skin across his shoulders tightened, a subtle lift that told the truth before his mouth ever could.

One of the men in the yard shifted, the sound of his boot scraping dirt loud in the brief pause.

Elijah set a length of chain down and wiped his hands on his rag slowly. "You talk too much," he said, voice flat.

Caleb shrugged, still smiling. "Talking's all we got," he replied. Then he added, softer, not for the men in the yard but not private either, "Just be careful who you building with. People don't always mean to bring trouble, but trouble follow them anyway."

He left then, axe head over his shoulder, moving with the loose confidence of a man who liked being the one carrying rumors rather than wearing them.

Elijah stood in the forge doorway after Caleb disappeared into the yard. He watched the two men who had been working glance at each other, just once, quick as a blink. Then they looked away as if they'd never made contact.

It wasn't proof of anything. It was worse than proof. It was possibility given a mouth.

On Carter's plantation, the pressure came as a kindness.

The mistress called Lila into the front room near dusk, when the light turned honeyed and made everything look gentler than it was. The silver on the sideboard shone with the soft glow of clean polish. Lila stood with her hands folded and her eyes lowered, waiting.

The mistress sat with a small stack of sewing in her lap, needle moving in and out with practiced ease. For a long moment she didn't speak. Silence from a white woman was never empty. It was a tool.

Finally, she said, "You've been running yourself thin."

Lila kept her face blank. "Yes, ma'am."

The mistress's needle paused. "I've asked a lot of you lately," she continued, tone almost reflective. "And with everyone so… restless, it helps to have someone reliable."

Reliable. The word sat strange in Lila's chest. Reliability here meant you were being watched closely enough to be trusted and trusted closely enough to be used.

"Yes, ma'am," Lila said again.

The mistress studied her as if she were deciding which part of Lila belonged most to the house. "I'm going to keep you in closer," she said. "Less running out to the yard. Less back and forth. It isn't safe, and you don't need to be mixing with everyone's talk."

Lila felt the trap immediately. Kept in closer meant kept within reach. It meant fewer chances to hear what drifted in the kitchen, fewer chances to see the edges of patrol lines, fewer chances to be a person in open air.

"Yes, ma'am," she said, because refusal was not an option.

The mistress resumed sewing. "And if anyone comes to you," she added lightly, "anyone trying to fill your head, you tell me. You're a smart girl. You know the difference between help and harm."

Lila's mouth went dry. "Yes, ma'am."

The mistress nodded, satisfied, and dismissed her as if the exchange had been nothing more than domestic care.

Lila walked out with her spine straight and her stomach tight. In the hall she passed Samuel near the side door, carrying something heavy enough to bend his arms. He looked up as she passed, mild as always.

But his eyes held that small, sharp satisfaction she'd begun to recognize.

He had known. Not because he heard the mistress's words, but because he'd built the moment. He was always building moments.

That night, Lila lay on her pallet listening to the cabin breathe and felt the walls of her world inch inward. Kept in closer. Less running. Less mixing. Less talk.

They were trying to separate her from the only thing she had begun to build: fragments, remembered corners, the sense of a path assembled from small checks.

She thought of Elijah then, and the thought hurt because it came with another one close behind.

What if being seen with her had already begun to cost him?

On Boone's side, Elijah stopped speaking to the old man on the step, not because he no longer trusted him, but because he could no longer trust the space around him. He began to feel that every conversation left a residue, something that could be carried to someone else's mouth and turned into a story with teeth.

He noticed it in the smallest things.

A white boy came to the forge with an order that made no sense, asking Elijah to fix a latch that wasn't broken. Elijah went anyway, because saying no was a kind of attention. When he arrived, the latch was fine. The white boy smirked like he'd been told to watch Elijah's face for frustration.

Later, someone left a strip of blue cloth half visible near the base of the forge wall, caught under a stone like it had been dropped. Elijah saw it and felt his pulse tighten. Blue. The same color Lila had described in the root cellar.

He did not touch it. He did not crouch to examine it. He only looked long enough to memorize the placement.

When he returned at dusk, it was gone.

The absence said more than the cloth ever could.

Elijah's mind began to circle the same question again and again, the way tongue worried a sore spot.

Was it meant for him, or meant to make him think of her?

And if it was meant to make him think of her, then someone was already inside the narrow passage where they'd spoken. Someone had taken that private exchange and turned it into a lever.

That was the thing about division. It didn't require lies. It required angles.

Samuel provided the angles.

He never approached Elijah and Lila directly about each other. That would be too blunt. Too obvious. Obvious threats made people cling tighter to whatever they were protecting.

Instead, he let other mouths do the work.

He fed Caleb a suggestion one afternoon while men hauled wood and the overseer's attention drifted elsewhere. Samuel didn't say Lila's name. He didn't need to. He only said, casual, "Carter's house girl been moving around. Been sent over. White folks don't send a body over for nothing."

Caleb, hungry for the sound of being important, carried it like a torch.

On Carter's side, Samuel didn't speak to the mistress. He didn't have to. The mistress already wanted reasons to tighten her hold. Samuel only needed to make sure fear had something to point at. A glance here. A pause there. A whispered word to Mary in the kitchen about "outsiders bringing trouble with them," framed as concern, not accusation.

Mary didn't like Samuel, but Mary was not immune to the way fear turned into self-preservation. She watched Lila differently afterward, and Lila felt it immediately. Not hostility. Worse. Calculation.

Even Ruth, on Carter's plantation, began to keep her distance from Lila, not because she believed Lila had done something wrong, but because proximity itself had become a risk. Ruth had a boy to keep close. Risk was something she could not afford to wear.

So, Lila found herself alone in a crowd, her movements tracked, her access narrowed, her name beginning to travel in quiet places it had no reason to be.

On Boone's plantation, Elijah felt the same tightening but from the opposite direction. Men who had nodded at him before now greeted him with silence. Not punishment silence. Defensive silence. The kind that said, you might be watched, and if you're watched, anyone near you might be watched too.

Elijah tried to see Lila's face in his mind and hold it steady as something real.

But doubt crept in, patient as rot.

If she was being kept in closer, could she still gather what she needed? If she was being moved like a piece, could she avoid being used to draw him out? If she had seen a sign, was it truly a sign, or had it been placed so she would speak of it to him, so their connection could be traced?

And for Lila, lying awake with the mistress's words still pressing on her, doubt took a different shape.

What if Elijah had already been searched because he'd spoken to her? What if her errand to Boone's had been arranged to see whether he would angle his body to make space for her? What if the brief exchange in the narrow passage had been enough to put his forge under new eyes?

They were not doubting each other's intentions. They were doubting the safety of being connected at all.

That was the leverage.

Samuel did not have to break their bond with force. He only had to make the bond feel like a noose.

A week later, a message came to Carter's kitchen by way of a white boy, a careless order tossed like scrap: Lila would be sent to Boone's again soon, another neighborly delivery.

The cook's mouth tightened when she heard. Mary's hands went still for a beat, then resumed peeling as if the peelings were the only thing keeping her from speaking.

Lila felt her stomach drop. Another crossing. Another chance, if it was real. Another trap, if it wasn't. Another opportunity for eyes to count who looked too long.

That evening Samuel stood near the yard's edge again, watching the house like he belonged to its shadow. When Lila passed, he didn't speak at first. He waited until she was almost beyond him, then said softly, "They sending you back over there."

Lila stopped just long enough that anyone watching might see the hesitation, then forced herself to move again. "You hear everything," she said without looking at him.

Samuel's voice stayed calm. "I hear what matters," he replied. "And I know what it do to a man, getting tied to somebody else's risk."

Lila's breath caught. She kept walking. "What you want."

Samuel let the question hang a moment, then answered with the simplest truth dressed like advice. "I want you to live," he said. "Living means you stop reaching for things you can't hold."

She finally glanced at him, and the look she gave him was sharp enough to cut. "You don't get to tell me what I can hold."

Samuel's mouth tilted, barely. "You already holding it," he murmured. "You can feel it, can't you? The way everything get heavier when somebody else name start getting near yours."

Lila turned away, anger burning behind her ribs. But beneath the anger was the sick recognition that he was describing exactly what she felt.

On Boone's side, Elijah stood in his forge that same night and stared at the empty spot beneath his scrap pile where the wire coil had been. He imagined Lila on her pallet, kept in closer, watched harder, her world narrowed because of how her name had been allowed to move.

They were being pushed toward isolation, each of them made to feel that the safest thing they could do was stop reaching across the boundary at all.

Samuel had built his leverage carefully.

Not by proving betrayal.

By making trust feel expensive.

And the most dangerous part was that the plantation didn't have to say a word to help him. The system itself did the persuading, every time someone flinched at a name, every time a task changed without reason, every time a door that had once been only stuck now felt deliberately hard to open.

In the quiet that followed, both Elijah and Lila began to consider the same thought, each alone with it, each ashamed of it.

Maybe it would be safer to move sooner, before the connection became the proof.

And Samuel, listening to the new shape of their silence through other people's mouths, understood that division had done what it always did best.

It made people rush.

It made them choose with less information than they needed.

It made them vulnerable to any path that looked solid enough to step on, even if it had been built to collapse.

Chapter 9

The False Path

Samuel chose his lie the way Elijah chose where to strike hot iron.

Not all at once. Not with a blow that left a mark you could point to. He shaped it from pieces that already existed, because the easiest false thing to believe was the thing that sounded like what you had already heard.

River. Reeds. A bank that hid feet.

Caleb had spoken of reeds before, and Thomas had carried Caleb's name like a small stone in his mouth. Ruth had spoken of horses and papers. Mary had spoken of bells on dogs and white men stitching watch lines. Lila had seen blue cloth placed where it did not belong, then removed as clean as breath. Elijah had found a strip of blue near his forge, half-visible, then gone.

The world was already full of fragments. Samuel's work was only to arrange them into a road.

He did it in the spaces where people's fear made them lean closer.

He did it without calling it a plan.

In the yard, late afternoon, when the sun was low enough to throw long shadows that made even ordinary men look like they were hiding something, Samuel found Caleb near the woodpile. Caleb was splitting logs with too much force, as if he could chop the rumor out of his own head.

Samuel waited until the axe rose and fell twice more. Then he said, casual, "You still talking about that reed bank."

Caleb's shoulders stiffened, but his mouth stayed hungry. "I didn't say nothing to you," he snapped, as if denying would protect him from being heard.

Samuel lifted a hand, not soothing, just slow. "I ain't saying you did," he replied. "I'm saying I heard you like everybody else heard you."

Caleb's eyes narrowed. "And what you want."

There it was, plain. The currency question.

Samuel didn't answer it directly. He nodded toward the far field line where trees thickened and the land began to soften toward the river bend. "You said there's a place reeds grow thick," he said. "A place the bank hides your feet."

Caleb spat to the side. "That's what I heard."

"From who."

Caleb hesitated, and the hesitation was useful. Hesitation meant Caleb wanted to keep something for himself.

Samuel let his voice drop. "You want to keep breathing, you stop hoarding," he murmured. "White folks tightening. You know it."

Caleb's jaw worked. He glanced once toward the yard, as if expecting an overseer to materialize out of dust. "Old man told it," he said finally. "Said his cousin ran once and got as far as the bend. Said there's a tree out there, got a lightning scar down the trunk. Said you go past that tree; you find a low spot where the fence line's weak."

Samuel listened without changing his face, though his mind moved quick. A lightning-scarred tree was a good detail. It felt specific. Specific made men trust. The fence line being weak was believable because fences always weakened where land refused to hold posts straight.

He asked, "He say which fence."

Caleb shrugged like it didn't matter, like he wasn't already tasting the importance of being asked. "The one they patched last spring," he said. "Near the muck. Posts sink."

Samuel nodded slowly. He let the detail sit between them like something shared. Then, as if it were nothing, he added the first twist.

"I heard something too," Samuel said. "From stable side. They been talking about shifting patrol. Not on the bend itself. They thinking folks too scared to go straight at the river after the last branding. They planning to watch the road crossings more."

Caleb's eyes sharpened. "Who told you that."

Samuel shrugged, mild. "Ears," he said. "Same way you got yours."

Caleb looked down at his hands, gripping the axe handle. "So, you saying the bend safer."

Samuel didn't say yes. Yes was too clean.

He said, "I'm saying if a man was stupid enough to try, he wouldn't go where the dogs already know to run. He'd go where the land's soft and the fence don't like to stand. He'd go at moon down, when sound don't carry as far."

He watched Caleb swallow it. Moon down. Soft land. Weak fence. A tree with a scar like a mark. Pieces that could make a picture.

Caleb's mouth moved, then stopped. His eyes flicked up to Samuel's face, searching for the hook. "Why you telling me."

Samuel let a small honesty show, not enough to be trusted, enough to be believed. “Because folks going to do it anyway,” he said. “Somebody going to get desperate. Better they go where it make sense than where it don’t.”

Caleb’s shoulders eased a fraction. Not relief. Permission.

Samuel left him there with the axe and the new shape of certainty settling into him. He didn’t need Caleb’s loyalty. He needed Caleb’s mouth.

That evening, Samuel fed a second piece to Thomas, because young men carried stories faster than old ones and with less caution.

He found Thomas behind the cabins again, knife in hand, carving wood that didn’t need carving. Thomas looked up when Samuel approached and immediately looked away, as if eye contact itself was a trap.

Samuel said, “You heard about that lightning-scarred tree by the bend.”

Thomas’s knife paused. “I don’t know nothing about no tree.”

Samuel crouched as if to pick up a fallen chip, making his posture smaller, less like a man who thought he owned the air. “You don’t got to know," he murmured. "You just got to listen. Caleb been running his mouth again."

Thomas swallowed. The name Caleb traveled like a spark, because Caleb had become one of those men who always seemed one sentence away from getting someone hurt.

"What Caleb say," Thomas asked, and the fear in his voice was tied to curiosity, a dangerous braid.

Samuel said, "He say there's a place the fence don't hold right. Near the muck. Posts sink. He say an old man told it."

Thomas's breath came shallow. "Old men tell a lot."

Samuel nodded. "They do." Then, as if speaking a simple truth about weather, he added, "And I heard patrol's shifting. More eyes on the road crossing now. Less on the bend. White men think branding did the work."

Thomas's eyes lifted fast. "You sure."

Samuel didn't answer the question. He only said, "If you hear somebody talking about trying, you tell them what you heard. Better they go where a body might have a chance than walking straight into dogs."

Thomas stared at him, and for a moment Samuel saw the boy's need to believe in something that wasn't only fear. Then Thomas nodded, small and quick, and Samuel knew it had taken.

Two mouths now held the outline of the path.

Over the next days, Samuel let the story travel as if it were traveling on its own. He didn't carry it into every space. He let it drift in through cracks, the way smoke did.

A whispered mention near the wash area, offered to Ruth as if it were protection. "If you hear anybody talking foolish, you tell them bend side's their best shot. Road crossings watched harder now." Ruth's eyes tightened, and Samuel saw her mind measure whether a foolish man might pull eyes toward her boy. She didn't need to believe the path was safe. She only needed to believe there was a direction danger could be redirected.

A muttered scrap to Joseph, when Joseph came with another broken strap and fear riding him like an extra weight. "If folks get desperate, tell them to avoid the crossing. White men got eyes there." Joseph nodded, his mouth pressing into a line, because men like Joseph lived on the edge of being sold and would trade anything that kept the overseer's attention from turning too long in their direction.

Even Mary heard it, though Samuel did not offer it to her straight. Mary heard everything. She heard the same name and the same details repeated just enough times that repetition began to look like truth.

She cornered Samuel behind the kitchen outbuilding one morning when no white eyes were near. Her knife was in her hand, peelings falling into a bucket like curled dead skin. "You spreading something," she said without preamble.

Samuel kept his face dull. "Everybody spreading something," he replied.

Mary's eyes were hard. "This one got too many details to be accident. Lightning tree. Muck fence. Moon down. That's you."

Samuel didn't deny it. He looked at the ground as if studying dirt. "Folks need a direction," he said.

Mary's mouth tightened. "Folks need truth."

Samuel lifted his gaze to her, steady. "Truth ain't always what keep a body alive," he said. "Sometimes it's what get them killed quicker."

Mary's knife stopped moving. For a moment her contempt wavered into something like dread, because she understood what he was and what he was capable of. "What you trying to do," she whispered.

Samuel leaned in just enough that his words would have to be kept. "I'm trying to make sure whoever runs, runs where I know they'll be found," he said softly. Then he straightened and let the next sentence sound almost kind. "And I'm trying to make sure it ain't your name that gets carried up when it happens."

Mary stared at him, and in her face, he saw the war that lived in everyone here: the desire to spit in his eye and the need to keep breathing. She looked away first, because looking too long at Samuel was like agreeing he was necessary.

Samuel walked off with the calm of a man who had just placed another stone in the road he was building.

On the surface, nothing changed. Work continued. Orders were given. Bodies moved through fields and kitchens and yards the way they always did.

But underneath, the idea began to take shape.

There is a spot where the fence is weak.

There is a tree you can recognize even in dark.

There is a time when patrol is thinner.

There is a way to step without leaving your feet exposed.

It felt like knowledge. It felt checked, because it was made from checked things. Fence posts did sink in muck. Lightning did scar trees. White men did shift their attention in patterns that could be observed.

Samuel's lie did not claim the river would open and carry you north. It only claimed there was a seam.

And seams were what desperate people lived on.

He sat outside his cabin one night with the yard quieting around him and listened to the way the rumor moved, not loud, not even confident, but persistent. A man murmured it to another like passing a tool. A woman hissed at her husband to stop talking and then, unable to help herself, repeated the detail of the lightning-scarred tree as if the detail could anchor them both.

Samuel kept his face empty, but inside him something settled, firm as a lock turning home.

He had not just created a path. He had created a decision people could make without him standing there to push them.

That was the safest kind of trap. The one that felt like choice.

Across the boundary, on Boone's plantation, the same story began to seep in. Not from Samuel's mouth, but from mouths he had guided.

Elijah heard the first mention near the tool shed as two men spoke too close and then broke apart when they saw him. He caught only the tail of it, the words "lightning tree" and "muck fence," and the way the men's eyes slid away as if they had been caught holding contraband.

Elijah didn't ask. Asking was how you showed hunger.

But later, alone in the forge with the fire breathing low, he thought of the strip of blue cloth that had appeared near his wall and vanished. He thought of how signs could be planted. He thought of Samuel in his doorway, looking around like a man memorizing where to reach.

A path was forming out there, constructed from details that sounded too good to be accidental.

Elijah stared into the coals until the orange sank toward red and the shadows thickened.

He could feel the plantation tightening. He could feel Lila being pulled inward on Carter's side, her world narrowed by the mistress's soft-spoken trap. Hc could feel his own forge no longer private, his tools no longer fully his.

And now, like a gift dropped at his feet, a route was being offered.

That was what made his stomach turn.

Gifts here always came with hands attached, even when you couldn't see them.

It started with a missing pair of hands at roll call.

Not an absence announced, not a commotion. Just a space where bodies should have been lined up, shoulders squared toward the overseer's morning gaze. A woman near the end of the row kept shifting her weight like her feet were trying to step into the empty place. Her eyes were too wide, fixed on nothing.

Elijah saw it and felt the forge heat in his skin even though he wasn't near the fire.

The overseer counted slow, enjoying it. Counting was power. Counting told you they knew how many they owned. When he reached the gap, he paused long enough to make the silence turn thick.

"Where's Caleb?" he asked, voice mild.

No one answered. No one could afford to.

The overseer's eyes drifted across the line, touching faces without settling. He didn't look angry yet. Anger was loud. This was something worse. This was interest.

"He sick?" the overseer asked. "He dead?"

Still no answer.

Then one man's mouth opened before his brain could stop it. "He been coughing," the man said quickly, offering a harmless explanation like a scrap of meat thrown to a dog. "Saw him last night, he was coughing hard."

The overseer nodded as if he'd expected that. As if it confirmed something he already knew. "Mm," he hummed. "Coughing make a man wander off into the woods, does it?"

The line went rigid. Elijah kept his face blank; eyes fixed on a point just past the overseer's shoulder. He could feel Samuel's lie in the air even though Samuel wasn't standing there. Lightning-scarred tree. Muck fence. Moon down.

Details that sounded like knowledge.

The overseer looked toward the yard's edge where the dogs lay, restless even in morning. One of them lifted its head, ears pricking, as if it had heard its name spoken in a language made of blood.

"Go on," the overseer said finally, as if dismissing the thought. "Get to work."

Work moved like it always did, forced and heavy. But under it, the plantation shifted. Men glanced too quick toward the tree line. Women's mouths stayed tight. Somebody had made a choice in the dark, and now everybody had to live inside the consequences of it.

Elijah went to the forge with his mind already counting.

Caleb. That wasn't surprising. Caleb had a mouth that liked to run ahead of sense. He'd carried rumor like it was a lantern, proud of its flame. If a man like that heard there was a weak fence and a tree that could be recognized, he would believe it was meant for him.

Elijah tried not to think of Lila, kept in closer on Carter's side, her world narrowed. But the thought came anyway, sharp and unwanted: if people ran now, the plantation's fear would turn into action, and action always spilled across fences.

He was feeding the coals when Thomas appeared in his doorway, breath tight, eyes darting. Thomas held himself like he didn't know whether he should be seen near Elijah at all.

"You heard?" Thomas whispered.

Elijah didn't look up. "He ain't at line," he said.

Thomas swallowed. "He gone," he breathed. "Not just him. Two more. Joseph say he seen them slipping behind the cabins late. Moon was down like it supposed to be."

Like it was supposed to be. As if the night had been instructed to cooperate.

Elijah's jaw set. "Who else," he asked, voice low.

Thomas hesitated, then said, "Isaiah's cousin. That young one. And a woman from the far cabin, I think. She got a baby, but she left the baby with her sister."

A woman with a baby who still chose the woods. That wasn't reckless. That was desperation sharpened into a blade.

Elijah stared into the coals until the orange blurred. "You know where they going," he said, though it wasn't a question.

Thomas nodded fast, too fast. "Caleb said there's a tree out by the bend, got a lightning scar. Said past that tree the fence don't hold right by the muck." His eyes flicked to Elijah's hands, as if waiting for Elijah to confirm it. "He said patrol was shifted. Said road crossings watched more."

Elijah's throat felt tight, as if smoke had gotten inside him. "Who told you that," he asked, though he already knew how the story moved.

Thomas's mouth worked. He didn't want to say Samuel's name. That name had become a mark you didn't want on your tongue.

"Just talk," Thomas finally muttered. "Talk in the yard."

Elijah struck the anvil once, hard, not because he needed to. Because the sound steadied his hands. Because it let him hide the dread in noise.

"Go on," he told Thomas. "Get away from my doorway."

Thomas flinched as if Elijah had hit him. He nodded and disappeared, leaving only his fear behind.

Elijah stood alone with the fire and listened. Outside, the yard kept moving. The master's house sat calm and distant. A bird called once from the tree line and then went quiet.

By late afternoon, the dogs were brought out.

Not all of them. Three, lean and restless, their paws pacing circles in the dirt as white hands checked collars and straps. The overseer's voice carried, sharp with purpose. "They fresh," he said. "Let them take the scent."

Fresh meant they expected to find someone. Expected meant they already knew where to look.

Elijah kept working, because stopping was another kind of confession. But his eyes watched through the forge doorway when he could, catching pieces.

A scrap of cloth held in a white man's hand, brought close to a dog's nose. The dog sneezed, then leaned forward, eager. The rope tightened. The dog strained.

Then they were gone, pulled toward the far field line, toward the place where reeds grew thick, toward the bend.

Toward the lightning-scarred tree that had been named like a promise.

Night fell with a wrong quiet. The quarters didn't settle. People moved in and out of cabins without purpose, as if their bodies could not accept stillness while others were being hunted. A baby cried and was hushed too fast. A woman prayed under her breath, words broken by fear. Men stared into the dark beyond the fence as if their eyes could reach all the way to the river and pull the missing back.

Elijah sat on his cabin step with his hands clasped. He didn't speak to anyone. Speaking would only spread more heat. He listened instead, the way you listened for thunder when the air went heavy.

The first sound came near midnight.

A whistle.

Not the overseer's daytime call. Not the casual signal between white men in the yard. This whistle cut the dark clean, sharp and deliberate, from somewhere out beyond the cabins. It came again, closer, then stopped.

Elijah's stomach went cold. He thought of the story that lived on this land like a ghost: a runaway running under a moon that gave no comfort, dogs fading behind him, then the whistle ahead. The sound that meant you hadn't outrun anything at all.

Minutes later, the dogs began.

Barking first, then a deeper sound beneath it, a baying that rose and fell like a chant. The noise carried across the yard, through the cabins, into every chest. People sat up on their pallets. A man muttered, "Lord," like it was the only word he had left.

Torches appeared near the far fence line, bobbing through the trees. White voices shouted short commands. The dogs' barking grew frantic, then suddenly changed, clustering into one place.

Elijah could picture it without seeing: the bend, the soft land, the fence line near the muck. A body trying to step quiet and finding the ground itself was a betrayer, sucking at ankles, holding tracks the way clay held fingerprints.

The torches stopped moving. The shouting sharpened into triumph.

Then, after a long stretch where the yard held its breath, the barking began to move back toward the plantation.

They came in before dawn.

Not quietly. Quiet was for men who wanted to hide their power. These men wanted it seen.

Elijah stood with the others as they were driven into the open yard, half-dressed, eyes stinging with sleep and fear. The torches threw light onto faces that looked older than they had the night before. On the edge of the crowd, the master stood with his arms folded, calm as if this were a service he attended weekly.

The dogs were brought in first, tongues lolling, eyes bright. Behind them, three figures stumbled.

Caleb was in the middle, his wrists tied, his shirt ripped open at the shoulder. Mud caked his legs up to the knee, dark and drying. His face was swollen on one side, one eye half shut. But what held Elijah's attention was the look on Caleb's mouth.

It was open, like he was still trying to talk his way out of it.

Beside him, Isaiah's cousin dragged one foot, leaving a thin smear of mud. His head hung low, but his eyes were wide, fixed on the ground as if looking up would invite death.

The woman came last. Her hair had come loose, sticking to her cheeks with sweat and dirt. She was shaking so hard her whole body looked like it might come apart. When she stumbled, a white man yanked her rope and she nearly fell. She made a small, broken sound that wasn't a scream yet, just the beginning of one.

The overseer stepped forward, torchlight catching his teeth when he smiled.

"Well," he said, loud enough for every ear. "Looks like we got ourselves some travelers."

No one spoke. No one moved. The crowd stood packed close, forced to witness not just the capture but the way it had been arranged. Because it felt arranged. Too quick. Too clean. Too certain.

Caleb lifted his head suddenly, as if remembering pride. His good eye searched the crowd, wild. "It wasn't supposed to—" he started.

The overseer struck him across the mouth, hard enough to snap his head sideways. Caleb's words turned into blood.

"That's enough," the overseer said lightly, as if correcting a child at table.

Caleb's shoulders sagged. He coughed, and the cough sounded wet.

Elijah felt something shift in the crowd, a ripple of recognition moving through bodies like sickness. They hadn't made it far. They'd been caught at the exact place they'd been told was safe. The bend. The muck. The lightning-scarred tree that had been named like a landmark toward freedom.

Elijah looked at Caleb's mud-caked legs and thought of how mud held what it touched. How it recorded every step. The land itself had been part of the trap.

The master stepped closer and looked at the three captives as if they were damaged goods brought back before they could be lost.

"You see," the master said, voice calm, carrying. He didn't have to shout. The yard leaned toward him anyway. "You see what happens when you chase stories."

He walked a slow circle around them, examining. "Somebody been filling heads," he continued. "Somebody been whispering about bends and fences and trees. Like the woods is a church and the river is a savior."

He stopped behind Caleb and rested a hand on Caleb's shoulder, almost gentle. Caleb flinched like a whipped dog.

The master's voice softened. "The woods don't save you," he said. "They hide you just long enough for dogs to find you."

Behind the master, white men began to pull out rope, arranging it with the casual certainty of men preparing a lesson.

The crowd stiffened. A woman near Elijah made a small sound and pressed her hand to her mouth.

Elijah kept his face blank, but inside him something was turning, slow and heavy.

This was only the first part. The return. The display. The statement that the plantation could reach into the night and pull you back like you were attached to it by an invisible chain.

The next part would come in daylight, when they could make everyone see clearly.

Caleb's good eye lifted again, unfocused, searching for a reason in the faces around him. For someone to blame. For someone to save him. For someone to confirm the story had been real.

No one met his gaze for long.

Because now the story had changed.

Now the rumor of a path wasn't a path at all.

It was bait, and three bodies had proven it.

And somewhere, not in the open yard but in the unseen spaces where power actually moved, Samuel's work settled into the plantation like a nail driven deep.

Hope had been given a shape.

Then it had been made to fail where everyone could watch.

Morning didn't bring relief. It only brought clarity.

They kept the three of them tied near the tool shed as the sun climbed, as if daylight was a kinder witness than torchlight. The captives sat slumped in the dirt, wrists raw where rope had been cinched tight, shoulders trembling from cold and shock and the long pull of being dragged back through brush. White men moved around them with the ease of men moving around livestock. The dogs slept in the shade, bellies full, their earlier hunger already turned to drowsy indifference.

The quarters were ordered into the yard again just after breakfast, as if gathering to watch suffering was another task that needed doing before the day could be used properly. Elijah stood where he was shoved, shoulder to shoulder with men who didn't look at one another. He could feel fear in the line the way you could feel heat off a forge even before the coals showed red.

Caleb lifted his head once when the crowd formed, his good eye searching faces again, still trying to find a door where there wasn't one. His mouth was split. Dried blood painted his chin. He looked like someone had taken his confidence and beaten it until it showed its true softness.

The overseer walked a slow circle in front of them, hands clasped behind his back, smile unhurried. The master stood off to the side beneath the edge of the porch shade, calm as ever, a man watching an investment being protected.

"You see them?" the overseer asked the yard, voice loud and bright. He didn't wait for an answer. He didn't need one. "You see what your stories buy you?"

No one spoke. The quiet felt thick enough to choke on.

The overseer nodded as if they had responded properly. "It's always the same," he continued. "Always somebody thinks they got a map. Always somebody thinks they got a sign. A cloth on a fence, a tree with a scar, a soft patch of land where a foot don't leave prints."

Elijah's jaw tightened. He had never spoken those details out loud. Most hadn't. But the overseer said them with the casual accuracy of a man reading from a page. That was the point. They weren't punishing bodies only. They were punishing the idea that anything could be hidden.

The young man, Isaiah's cousin, made a small sound and lowered his head further, as if he could tuck himself into the dirt and disappear.

The overseer stopped in front of the woman last. She looked like she'd been wrung out. Dirt crusted the hem of her skirt. Her lips moved without sound, prayer or pleading, Elijah couldn't tell. The overseer crouched slightly, bringing his face close to hers like he was listening for a secret.

"Tell them," he said softly enough that only those close could catch it, which meant everyone leaned without moving. "Tell them what you thought you was doing."

The woman's eyes flicked up, wild. Her voice came out broken. "I thought… I thought it was real."

The overseer straightened and laughed, loud and clean. "You hear that?" he called to the yard. "She thought it was real."

He walked away from them and spread his hands, preacher-like. "That's how it gets you," he said. "Hope don't come like a whip. Hope come like a friend. It come with details. It come with landmarks. It come with somebody telling you they know a place where the fence don't hold."

Elijah felt the words land in the crowd like stones. People flinched inward. Hope turned into a thing that could be mocked in public, felt suddenly shameful, like a weakness everyone could smell.

The master stepped forward then, not hurried. He didn't take the overseer's place; he let the overseer be the mouth while he remained the authority behind it.

"I don't mind you working," the master said, voice carrying without effort. "I don't mind you living. I even don't mind you praying, if it keeps you quiet."

He paused, letting the yard hold its breath.

"But I will not have you thinking," he went on, and his calm made it worse. "Thinking you got somewhere to go that I can't reach."

He nodded to one of the white men near the tool shed. The man came forward carrying a coil of rope and something else, long and thin. A switch cut from a green branch, still flexible, still smelling of sap. Fresh. That was deliberate, too. Fresh meant pain that stayed lively.

They pulled Caleb to his feet first.

Caleb tried to plant his heels, but the mud still clung to him and the rope at his wrists made his balance wrong. A white man jerked him forward until he stumbled. Caleb's mouth opened again, the reflex of a man who'd always believed a quick tongue could save him.

"I didn't mean—" he started.

The overseer struck him with the switch, hard, across the ribs. The sound was a wet crack. Caleb folded with a grunt that turned into a choking cough.

"You didn't mean," the overseer repeated pleasantly. He looked at the yard. "He didn't mean."

The laughter that followed from the white men was brief, controlled, like seasoning. Not enough to turn it into entertainment. Enough to remind everyone who got to find humor in this.

They beat Caleb not like a man being punished for running, but like a warning being written large. The switch snapped against his back and arms, leaving dark lines that rose quick. Caleb's knees buckled twice. Each time they hauled him back up.

Elijah stood with his hands at his sides, fingers curled so tight his nails bit into his palms. He forced his face into stillness. Stillness was the only mercy he could give Caleb now. If he showed too much, he'd become part of the lesson.

The woman cried out once when the switch came down again. The sound wasn't only for Caleb. It was her recognizing her own fate waiting a few feet away.

Isaiah's cousin began to shake, his shoulders shivering so violently Elijah thought he might collapse before they even touched him. The overseer saw it and smiled wider.

"That's right," he said, almost approving. "You feel it before it happen. That's the lesson. You feel it before you ever step toward the woods."

They made the yard watch all three, one after the other. They did not rush. They didn't need to. Work could wait. Cotton could wait. The kitchen could wait. There was no task more important than reminding the enslaved that their thoughts belonged to someone else.

Elijah realized then that this wasn't only about stopping escape. It was about poisoning the route itself. If a man thought of the river bend now, he would not think of reeds hiding his feet. He would think of Caleb's body folding under a green switch. If a woman heard someone mention a scarred tree, she would see the woman's face, dirt-streaked and terrified, saying, "I thought it was real."

Hope had been made to carry pain in its mouth.

Later, when they finally dragged the captives away toward the punishment posts for what would come next, the crowd was dismissed in a wave, like cattle being sent back to their work. Bodies moved sluggishly, eyes down, shoulders hunched. People did not speak. Not because they had nothing to say, but because every word felt like it might be overheard by the wrong ear and turned into currency.

Elijah walked back toward the forge with the yard spinning quietly around him. He noticed small things the way he always did, because noticing was his nature and his curse.

A dog collar jingled as a hound shifted in its chain. Not a bell, not yet. But the sound carried anyway.

A white man spoke to another near the stable, and the word "bend" floated out, casual as dust.

Someone had taken the rumor and pinned it to a post where everyone could see it bleeding.

In the forge, Elijah stood over cold coals and didn't light them. The thought of fire made him sick. Fire was supposed to be controlled. Fire was supposed to obey. What had happened in the yard had been controlled too, and that was the problem.

He thought of Lila, kept in closer now on Carter's side, and he felt an ache that wasn't softness. It was urgency tightening.

If the path people had been given was false, then someone had built it. Someone had made sure it led to the exact place dogs and patrols would find them quick. Someone had made sure the capture would look inevitable.

Samuel.

Elijah didn't have proof. Proof wasn't available to men like him. But he had patterns, and he had the memory of Samuel standing in his doorway, calm and measuring, as if the forge was just another place to reach into.

By afternoon, the story had crossed the boundary without anyone carrying it openly.

On Carter's plantation, Lila was shaking rugs in the yard when she heard the cook whisper to another woman near the back steps, words snapped quick and low.

"Boone's place caught three last night. Beat them this morning. They saying it was by the bend."

Lila kept beating the rug, arms moving as if her body belonged to the task. Dust rose in pale clouds and fell back to the ground like ash. Her breath stayed even with practiced discipline.

By the bend.

Her mind flashed to the folded blue cloth in the root cellar corner, how it had appeared like a promise and vanished like it had never been. She thought of Elijah seeing a strip of blue near his forge wall, then gone. She thought of how details could be planted, lifted away, leaving only the memory to do its work.

She heard Samuel's voice in her head, calm as a closed door. "Secrets don't stay secret. Not here."

This wasn't only secrecy breaking. This was secrecy being used.

The mistress called her name from the porch, sharp and impatient, and Lila answered, "Yes, ma'am," without missing a beat. She carried the rug to the line and hung it with careful hands that did not shake.

Inside her, something else shook loose.

The North, she thought. The word that had been kept poisonous and precious. The word that was supposed to be a direction.

They had taken that word and attached it to mud and rope and switches. They had turned it into a trap you could step into just by believing.

And the worst part, the part that made Lila's stomach twist, was understanding that the plantation didn't have to outlaw hope. They could let it exist.

They could even let it spread.

All they had to do was make sure it led to the right place.

That was how you weaponized hope. You didn't crush it. You sharpened it into something that cut the hands that tried to hold it.

As the day dragged on, the sound of hammering carried faintly from somewhere on Boone's side, iron striking iron. Work continuing. A man keeping his face arranged. A man with scarred hands trying to shape a world that refused to be shaped.

Lila listened to that distant ring and felt her own resolve harden into something quieter and more dangerous.

If hope could be used against them, then they would have to learn to hold it differently.

Not as a rumor.

Not as a gift.

But as something tested, checked twice, three times, and never spoken aloud until it was too late for anyone listening to turn it into a leash.

In the evening, when shadows lengthened and the yard settled into a tense hush, a sharp whistle sounded from the direction of the main house on Carter's side. Not the same whistle as the woods story, but close enough to make Lila's skin tighten anyway.

White voices followed, brisk and satisfied.

Lila understood without being told. Boone's punishment had been seen. Now Carter's would tighten too. The lesson would spread, not only through pain, but through preparation.

Somewhere, across fences and fear, the false path lay trampled into the mud, and the people who had tried it would carry marks that would outlive the bruises.

Hope had been given a shape, then dragged through the yard for everyone to memorize.

And in the memorizing, the plantation had done what it did best.

It had made the idea of leaving feel like the first step toward being owned even harder.

Chapter 10

The Branding

They waited until the second morning.

Not because time softened anger, but because time sharpened anticipation. A beating could be dismissed as temper. Branding was something else. Branding belonged to order. It belonged to the kind of cruelty that wore clean hands.

Before daylight had fully settled into the yard, the quarters were pulled from sleep by white voices and the stomp of boots. Doors opened and bodies spilled out half-dressed, eyes swollen, mouths dry. No one asked why. The question had already been answered two days earlier at the bend, in the mud, with dogs pulling at rope as if rope were a promise they could taste.

Elijah stood with the other men from Boone's side, forced into a line that faced the wide space between the tool shed and the porch. The air was cold enough to sting the inside of his nose. The sky held a thin gray light, the kind that made everything look stripped and honest. Torches had been planted anyway, their flames small and steady, not for brightness but for ceremony.

A barrel had been set near the center of the yard, iron braced inside it like a ribcage. Coals glowed deep, fed early. A man tended them with a poker, turning the heat the way Elijah turned a piece of metal when he needed it to take shape evenly. The sound of the coal shifting was soft, almost domestic, and that softness made Elijah's stomach tighten.

Tools had been arranged nearby as if for work.

That was what they called it when they did this: work.

The overseer walked in slow, boots clean, coat buttoned. He was not in a hurry. A man with power never hurried. Behind him came the master, and behind the master came two other white men Elijah did not recognize, men in good hats with hands that looked unaccustomed to labor. One of them carried a small case. The leather looked new.

Elijah watched the case and felt the old dread settle deeper. Cases held instruments. Instruments meant planning.

The captives were brought out last.

Caleb's face was still swollen, but the swelling had settled into bruising now, dark and mottled. His mouth was split and crusted. His arms were pinned behind him by rope that had dug into his wrists so long his skin looked raw around it, as if he'd been trying to worry the rope loose with small movements. He walked like his ribs hurt. He walked like he had learned there was no way to keep his body from being used.

Beside him, Isaiah's cousin moved stiffly, eyes fixed on the ground. The woman they had caught at the bend was between two men, not dragged now, not yet. She was walking on her own feet, which was part of the performance. Her hair had been tied back again, but not neatly. Her cheeks were hollow with fear. She looked smaller than she had before, like the night had taken pieces of her and kept them.

They placed the three in front of the barrel of coals.

The yard held its breath in a single, long silence. Elijah could hear small sounds he did not want to hear: someone's teeth clicking in cold, a baby's thin whimper cut off too fast, the faint jingle of a dog collar as a hound shifted near the stable.

From Carter's side, across the boundary that was nothing more than distance and the permission of white men, other bodies were lined too. Elijah could not see faces clearly, but he felt their presence the way he felt wind. He knew Lila would be there, because punishment was not only for the ones who ran. It was for everyone who might think of running later.

The overseer spoke like a man giving instruction.

"Bring them up," he said.

They moved the three closer to the coals. The man tending the barrel lifted the poker and stirred again, and the coals brightened as if pleased.

The master's voice carried, calm as ever. "This is what happens," he said, "when you borrow a story and call it yours."

No one answered. No one would. The plantation did not require response. It required witness.

One of the men in good hats opened the leather case. Inside, wrapped in cloth, were branding irons. Three of them, their metal ends thick and squared. Elijah could not see the mark on them from where he stood, but he could see the way the white man handled them carefully, like they mattered.

The white man passed one to the man tending the coals.

The iron disappeared into the barrel.

For a moment, nothing changed. Then the metal began to drink heat. A dull red bloom spread across the end, slow at first, then brighter. The air above the barrel wavered. Elijah felt sweat gather at the base of his neck despite the cold morning.

Caleb made a sound, small and involuntary. He wasn't trying to speak. His body had spoken for him.

The overseer walked to stand in front of Caleb. He looked at him the way a man looked at a damaged tool.

"You want to talk now?" the overseer asked, almost conversational. "You been full of words before."

Caleb swallowed. His good eye flicked across the crowd, searching, still, for a face to hold onto. His gaze snagged somewhere near Elijah's line and held for a fraction too long. Elijah did not move. He could not offer comfort. Comfort was a thing that got turned into a weapon here. Even a look could be used later, named later, punished later.

Caleb's voice came out rough. "I didn't…" He stopped. The sentence had nowhere safe to go.

The overseer smiled as if Caleb had amused him. "You didn't what," he prodded. "You didn't mean to run? You didn't mean to believe? You didn't mean to make us chase you into the woods like you was worth the trouble?"

Caleb's shoulders trembled. "I thought it was… I thought—"

"You thought," the overseer echoed, and the yard stiffened. The master's calm sharpened in the air around them. Thinking was the sin they punished hardest, because thinking was the first step toward any door.

The man at the barrel lifted the iron out.

It was orange now, bright at the edges. The heat rolled off it in visible waves. Ash clung to the metal end, then fell away in black flakes.

The smell came before the touch. Hot iron had its own odor, sharp and clean. Elijah knew it from the forge. But this smell carried something else with it, because the iron was not meant for hinge or chain. It was meant for flesh.

The overseer nodded, satisfied. "Hold him," he said.

Two men grabbed Caleb's arms and forced him forward. Caleb tried to pull back, but the rope at his wrists made his balance wrong. His feet slid in the dirt. He made a sound that was half breath, half animal.

"Please," he rasped, and the word startled the yard because it was not aimed at mercy. It was aimed at memory. It was the sound of a man realizing that once this happened, there would be no pretending it hadn't.

The iron touched.

It was not a quick press. It was placed deliberately, flat and certain, against Caleb's shoulder where skin was bared by the torn shirt. The sound was small at first, like fat spitting in a pan. Then it grew into a hiss, steady and horrible, as the heat bit down and held.

Caleb screamed.

The scream did not rise clean. It broke. It split into pieces the way metal splits if you struck it wrong. Elijah felt it in his teeth. He felt it in the bones of his hands. He could taste it like smoke.

A stench rolled out across the yard, thick and sickening. Burned hair. Burned meat. Not the clean scent of a forge, but the rancid truth of what they were doing.

Caleb's knees buckled. The men held him up anyway. The overseer watched Caleb's face with the mild interest of a man watching a lesson take shape properly.

When the iron was finally lifted, the skin beneath it was no longer skin. It was a raw, bubbling mark that already looked like it belonged to someone else.

Caleb's scream fell into a choking sob. He hung in the men's grip, shaking so hard his teeth clicked.

The overseer turned to the yard. "Look at it," he said, voice bright. "Look good. This what a story leaves behind."

No one moved, but Elijah felt bodies flinch inward. Some looked because they were forced. Some looked because the mind, when cornered, watched pain the way it watched fire: with horror and the need to understand how it spread.

The man with the poker slid the iron back into the coals to reheat, as if it were a tool that had cooled too fast.

The overseer nodded toward Isaiah's cousin.

"Next," he said.

The young man made a sound, high and thin. He tried to turn away, but hands grabbed him. They held him with practiced grips, pinning him in place. Elijah watched his shoulders tense, watched his throat work like he was swallowing something that couldn't be swallowed.

From Carter's line across the distance, a small cry rose, quickly smothered. Elijah's chest tightened. He could not see Lila, but he felt the idea of her eyes on this, the same forced witnessing, the same lesson being driven through skin into memory.

The iron came out again, glowing.

Elijah's mind, traitorous, supplied the details he knew too well: how the heat would travel, how the skin would resist for a split second and then give. How the smell would rise again. How the mark would not fade the way bruises faded.

He thought of the word north, whispered like prayer, and understood what the master meant to do.

They were not only marking bodies. They were marking the idea of leaving, stamping it into flesh so that every movement afterward would carry the reminder.

The iron pressed down on the young man's shoulder.

His scream followed, and the yard became a place where sound had no hiding place at all.

The young man's scream did not sound like Caleb's.

Caleb's had been anger breaking into pain, the last of his loudness torn open. Isaiah's cousin screamed the way something small screamed when it understood there was no way to bargain. It came out thin and high, then dropped into a sobbing wail that didn't stop when the iron lifted. It kept going, as if his body didn't know the difference between the moment and what would come after.

The iron was pulled away at last. A white man dipped a rag in a bucket and slapped it against the raw mark, not to soothe but to keep the flesh from sticking to cloth and making the mark unreadable. Steam rose. The young man gagged and folded forward, but hands held him upright until the overseer nodded.

"See," the overseer said, satisfied, voice pitched to carry. "See how quick it takes. Like it was meant for him."

Elijah stood in his line with his jaw locked and his eyes forward. He knew heat. He knew metal. He knew the stubbornness of iron that fought you until you hit it at the right angle. Flesh was different. Flesh surrendered because it had to.

The man tending the barrel pushed the iron back into the coals. The orange faded into red and then brightened again as it drank. The barrel's glow painted the underside of the overseer's chin, turning him into something carved.

The woman was next.

She had been shaking since they brought her out, but now she went still, sudden and terrible. Stillness wasn't acceptance. Stillness was the mind leaving the body for a moment because the body could not hold what was coming.

Two men took her arms. One pinned her shoulders. They did not have to wrestle her at first. They only had to position her like a piece being set for display.

The master stepped closer, not into her face, but near enough that she had to smell him. Clean wool. Tobacco. The calm of a man who never had to imagine his own skin used this way.

He spoke softly, as if offering something reasonable. "You got a name," he said. "You got a place. You got a life right here. You go running into the woods and you think you can turn yourself into something else."

Her lips moved. Elijah couldn't hear the words, but he saw them: prayer, maybe, or a name that belonged to someone who wasn't here. Her eyes were wet and bright, fixed on a point beyond the crowd as if she could look through bodies and fences and find the baby she'd left behind.

The overseer nodded toward the barrel. "Do it," he said.

The iron came out again, glowing hard, the end bright enough to hurt the eye. Heat rolled in waves, bending the air. Elijah smelled it before it touched her: not the clean forge smell, but the waiting stink of what the iron was meant to do.

The woman made a sound before contact, a small, broken whimper that rose out of her without permission. The man holding her shoulders tightened his grip, as if she were an animal that might bolt.

The iron pressed down.

The hiss was immediate. The smell followed, thick and sickening, and then her scream tore through the yard with such force Elijah felt his own body flinch, not outward, but inward, the way you flinched when something struck close to your head.

She fought then, in a sudden burst, feet scrabbling for purchase, head thrown back, mouth open wide enough Elijah could see the dark inside. One of the men holding her cursed and shifted his stance, bracing. The iron stayed planted. The overseer watched, expression mild, as if the struggle only proved the iron's necessity.

When it finally lifted, the woman sagged. Her knees buckled, and for a moment her body hung between the men like laundry on a line. Her scream fell into a choking, ragged breath. Her eyes rolled, then focused again with the startled look of someone dragged back into her own body.

The yard was silent except for the barrel's coals shifting and the woman's wet, shuddering breaths.

"Look," the master said, and the word was an order.

Elijah looked because he was forced to. Not by chains, not by hand on his chin, but by the way the whole system demanded witness. Refusing to look was its own defiance, and defiance earned extra attention.

The mark on her shoulder was already swelling at the edges, raw and shining, the shape pressed into her as clean as a stamp in wax. It was not just damage. It was a sign meant to be read.

Elijah's stomach turned as he understood the deeper cruelty of it. They had not branded them with something random. Not a simple burn. Not an accident. A symbol. A declaration.

A new name.

The overseer turned and let his eyes sweep the crowd, slow. "Now they don't just belong," he said. "Now they show it. Anywhere they go."

Anywhere they go. The words were meant to reach beyond the yard, beyond the fences, beyond the bend in the river. The North. The whisper that people held like a coal in their mouths. The overseer was telling them the truth the masters had always understood: escape didn't end ownership if ownership could travel on skin.

Elijah felt it land as a weight behind his ribs. A mark didn't fade. A mark didn't let you become unknown. A mark turned you into proof.

From across the boundary, he heard a sound, not loud enough to be called a cry, but sharp enough to pierce. A woman's breath catching too hard. Someone trying and failing not to react.

He could not see Lila clearly, but he could picture her face the way it would be right now: eyes wide, mouth pressed tight, every muscle in her holding itself still because stillness was the only control left.

On Carter's side, Lila stood in a line that wasn't a line, bodies arranged by white will so that everyone could see. The morning air tasted like ash even though no one was burning wood. The smell came anyway, carried on the thin wind between properties, and it made her stomach clench.

She watched the iron rise and fall. She watched the woman's body go slack. She watched the men handling the branded as if they were tools taken from a fire and set aside to cool.

And as she watched, she understood the point the way you understood a blade when it finally broke skin.

A beating ended. Even a whipping ended, leaving only the knowledge that it could happen again.

This did not end. This went with you.

If you ran and lived, the mark would stand up on your shoulder and speak for the plantation when you refused to. If you hid in a free city and kept your collarbones tucked under cloth, the mark would still be there, waiting for the wrong moment, waiting for a sleeve to slip, waiting for someone to catch sight and decide what kind of body you were.

Lila felt her own shoulders tighten as if her skin could protect itself by shrinking.

Beside her, Mary stood rigid, face turned toward the yard on Boone's side. Mary's mouth was set hard, but her eyes were wet in a way she would never admit. Not pity. Not softness. Fury with nowhere safe to go.

The cook's hand hovered near her own throat as if holding down sound.

Lila thought of Samuel then, because Samuel was always somewhere nearby when fear turned into policy. She scanned the edges of the crowd, careful not to move too much, and saw him on the fringe where men like him could stand without being placed. He was still, his posture loose, his eyes fixed on the ceremony with the focus of a man studying a mechanism.

He looked almost calm.

And that calm told Lila more than any confession could have. Samuel wasn't watching as if he feared the iron. He was watching as if he recognized the lesson it carried and wanted to know how far it would reach.

On Boone's side, the overseer gestured, and the branded were hauled backward, not released, not allowed to collapse where the crowd could pretend they weren't looking anymore. They were moved like objects. Their ropes were shortened. Their shoulders were turned so the marks would face the yard as long as possible.

"Don't you look away," a white man snapped at someone near the front when a head dipped too low. "You want to run, you look. You want to whisper north, you look."

The master's voice came again, calmer than the snapping. "This isn't for them," he said, as if explaining a kindness. "This is for you."

Elijah heard that and felt his hands curl tighter. The master was right, in the sick way men like him were always right. The branding wasn't about correcting the three who had already tried. It was about rewriting the rest. About turning the entire yard into a memory that would rise up the next time someone thought of a tree line and a river bend.

The woman's head lolled to one side. Caleb was barely standing, his breath coming in shallow, ugly pulls. Isaiah's cousin was weeping without sound, tears tracking down dirt-streaked cheeks, his eyes empty as if the scream had burned them out from the inside.

Elijah's gaze snagged on the marks one more time.

They were not just burns. They were letters, or something shaped like letters, something that could be recognized even by those who pretended not to read. A sign that told any white man who saw it what to do, what to assume, what authority traveled with the scar.

Property.

That was the identity imposed. Not in papers, not in the master's ledger, but in the body itself.

The overseer stepped back as if admiring finished work. "Take them," he said, and his tone carried the satisfaction of completion.

The branded were dragged toward the punishment posts, because the branding was not the end. It was only the part that lasted the longest. The yard watched them go, and Elijah felt the crowd's fear shift into something quieter and more corrosive.

Not just terror of pain.

Terror of being made legible.

Lila stood on Carter's side, the smell still clinging to the air, and understood that the plantation had reached farther than the river ever could.

A mark could cross any boundary.

It could follow you into the North.

It could sit under your best shirt and wait.

And in that waiting was the true message of the iron: you do not get to become someone else, not even in freedom. Not if they can write their claim into your skin and make the whole world learn to read it.

They did not let the yard scatter the way it wanted to.

The branded were dragged toward the posts, and the crowd was made to turn with them, bodies pivoting like a single animal forced to keep its eyes on the knife. The morning light had strengthened, bleaching the dirt a pale brown, making the blood at Caleb's split mouth look darker, more definite. The iron barrel still glowed behind them, coals breathing, tended like a hearth that had done good work.

Elijah felt the pull in his own muscles as men shifted, as women tightened their arms around their own ribs, as if they could hold their insides steady by pressure alone. The plantation was teaching with more than pain. It was teaching with choreography. Look here. Stand here. Watch this. Remember it exactly the way we show it to you.

At the posts, they tied Caleb first. His knees buckled as soon as the rope took his weight, and for a moment it looked like he might fold and never come back up. A white man yanked the rope higher until Caleb's shoulders jerked back, exposing the raw brand again. The flesh was already swelling, the edges raised and angry. It shone wetly in the light.

The woman made a soft sound that might have been her name trying to climb out of her throat and failing. Isaiah's cousin didn't make any sound at all. His face had gone slack in a way that frightened Elijah more than screaming. It was the face of someone who had learned too quickly how to leave his body and let it be used.

The overseer stepped back and looked at them as if checking a fence line.

"All right," he said. "Now they'll heal."

The word heal hit Elijah wrong. Healing was supposed to mean returning to wholeness. Here it meant the wound would close around the mark and keep it safe, keep it readable.

The master's voice came again, calm as a man discussing weather. "You see how it's done," he said to the yard. "That's what order looks like. That's what it costs when you forget what you are."

Forget what you are. As if any of them had ever been allowed to remember anything else.

He gestured with one hand, casual. "Get them water. Keep them breathing. I don't want them dying. Dead men don't carry lessons."

White men moved to obey. A bucket was brought. A tin cup. Water was poured into mouths that didn't want it but took it anyway because thirst was its own whip. Caleb gagged and swallowed. The woman's lips trembled against the cup rim. Isaiah's cousin drank without looking, eyes fixed on nothing.

Elijah understood then another part of it. Mercy was not absence of cruelty. Mercy was maintenance. They would keep the branded alive the way they kept tools oiled and horses fed. Not because life mattered, but because the mark had to last long enough to be seen.

Across the distance, on Carter's side, the line of bodies was still held in place, as if the boundary between plantations was only another part of the yard. Lila stood with her hands clasped, nails pressing crescent moons into her palms. The smell still rode the air, clinging to the back of her throat. She tried to swallow and found the taste stayed.

A white voice snapped on her side, impatient. "Eyes up."

Someone beside her lifted their chin too fast, and Lila saw the panic in it, the reflex to obey even when obedience didn't save you. The system taught that too: move when told, move quickly, move wrong, and the wrongness became proof.

The mistress on Carter's porch did not shout. She didn't have to. Her attention was enough. She stood with her hands folded at her waist and watched the neighboring punishment the way one watched a storm line moving in. Not with pity. With calculation. With the satisfaction of knowing the storm kept everyone indoors.

"Let this settle," Mr. Carter said to the few white men near him, voice low but carrying in the quiet. "We don't need any excitement here."

Excitement. Like pain was a form of entertainment that could be overdone.

Lila felt something in her loosen and tighten at the same time. She had grown up under these voices. She knew their language. The calm words, the softened phrases, the way violence was framed as necessity. This wasn't only Boone's lesson. Carter was taking it into his own house without lifting a hand.

The line on Carter's side was dismissed in stages, not all at once. Women first, then men, then the children, as if the order of release was part of what was being taught. Separation. Sorting. The message that even in a crowd, you were alone.

As Lila turned, she saw Samuel on the fringe where he had been, posture loose, as if nothing in him had been pulled tight by what he'd watched. His eyes followed the branded as they hung at the posts, and there was a focus in him that made Lila's stomach go colder than the morning air.

He did not look away when the woman's knees buckled and a white man yanked her upright again. He didn't flinch at the wet sound of Caleb coughing. He watched like a man memorizing steps.

When Lila passed close enough, he spoke without turning his head. "Now you know," he murmured.

Lila kept walking. Her voice came out low, controlled. "I knew before."

Samuel's mouth tilted slightly, not a smile, something thinner. "Before was stories," he said. "This is how it look when they make it real."

She wanted to spit at him again, the old instinct to reject him like poison. But the yard was full of eyes, and Samuel understood the yard better than most. He stayed just out of reach of accusation and still managed to make his words feel like hands on her shoulders.

"What do you want," she asked, not stopping.

Samuel matched her pace for two steps, then let her pull ahead. "Same thing I always want," he said softly. "For folks to learn."

Lila's throat tightened. She did not answer. She did not give him the pleasure of any sound he could carry elsewhere.

On Boone's side, Elijah was dismissed back to work as if the yard had only been a break in routine, a brief demonstration before the day's labor resumed. Men drifted toward fields. Women turned toward kitchens. Children were shooed away. The branded remained at the posts, not hidden, not moved. They were part of the landscape now, like a sign nailed to a tree.

Elijah walked toward the forge, but his body felt wrong inside itself, as if his bones had shifted under the weight of what he'd seen. He passed the posts at a distance that was still too close. Caleb lifted his head a fraction, and for one moment his good eye found Elijah.

There was no accusation in it. No anger. Only stunned betrayal, as if Caleb was still trying to understand how the bend could have been waiting for him so precisely. As if he still believed the world had rules he could learn and use.

Elijah didn't look away, but he didn't offer comfort either. Comfort would have been a lie. The only honest thing he could give Caleb was witness, and witness was what the master had demanded anyway. Still, Elijah held Caleb's gaze long enough for Caleb to know he had been seen as a man, not only as a lesson.

Then Elijah kept walking.

In the forge, the tools hung in their places. The anvil waited. The cold coals waited. Everything looked ordinary, and that ordinariness felt like another cruelty. Elijah reached for his hammer and found his hand steady, not because he felt steady, but because steadiness was what he had learned to perform.

He struck iron that afternoon and listened to the ring travel out into the yard. It sounded like work. It sounded like compliance. It sounded like the world continuing.

But under the ring, he could hear the system's voice.

It wasn't only in the overseer's speeches. It was in the way the branded were kept visible. In the way water was given to preserve the lesson. In the way the master spoke of thinking as if it were theft. In the way everyone's movement had been rearranged after the iron touched skin.

The system did not simply punish escape. It punished the idea that escape belonged to the enslaved to attempt.

Elijah understood another part by late afternoon, when a white boy came to the forge with an order that made Elijah's stomach knot.

"Master says fix the collar," the boy said, tossing a strip of leather onto the bench. The leather was thick, darkened by use. A brass ring was set into it, and beside the ring were two small holes where something had been attached before.

Elijah picked it up and turned it in his hands. The leather still held a faint animal smell. Sweat. Dog.

"Whose collar," Elijah asked, careful, because questions were dangerous.

The boy shrugged, bored. "Dogs," he said. "Overseer wants it ready by tomorrow. Says they going to make a change."

A change. Elijah's mind flashed to Mary's earlier scraps, bells. The rumor Samuel had fed upward like a test. The overseer's interest.

Elijah nodded once, because nodding was survival. "I'll do it."

When the boy left, Elijah held the collar a moment longer, thumb pressing into the old holes. He could picture it: dogs moving at night with small sounds attached, turning silence into an alarm.

Another lesson. Another tightening.

That was how the system worked. It did not rely on one brutal morning. It built layers. It took what people feared and turned it into policy. It took what people whispered and made it louder, not in their own mouths but in iron and leather and rope.

On Carter's side, Lila learned the same truth by evening when the mistress called her in and spoke as if offering protection.

"I don't want you mixing," the mistress said, voice soft. "Not now. Not after what happened. You stay close to the house where I can see you. You hear me?"

"Yes, ma'am," Lila replied, and felt the word close around her like a cuff.

The mistress studied her a moment, then added, almost kindly, "You keep your mind where it belongs, and you won't have to worry about marks."

Marks. The mistress didn't say brand. She didn't say flesh. She said marks, as if it were ink that could be avoided with good behavior.

Lila lowered her eyes and felt rage move under her ribs like a living thing.

That night, in the quarters, nobody spoke of north. Nobody spoke of reeds or lightning-scarred trees. They spoke of work. They spoke of water. They spoke of weather. But their bodies spoke in other ways. People kept their shoulders slightly turned away from one another, as if hiding the skin there preemptively. Men adjusted their shirts higher at the neckline even in heat. Women pulled cloth tighter around children's arms, as if sleeves could stop memory.

Samuel moved through the spaces between cabins and kitchens and yards and listened to the new quiet. It wasn't only fear now. It was instruction settling in. The plantation had taught what it wanted to teach, and the lesson had taken.

Hope would still exist. It always did. But now hope had to move through a narrower passage. It had to move without sound. It had to survive not only dogs and fences, but the fact that the system had learned how to turn rumor into bait and bait into spectacle.

Elijah lay on his pallet with the dog collar's brass ring glinting in his mind and the brand's raised edges burning behind his eyes. He thought of Lila kept close to the house. He thought of Samuel watching without flinching.

The lesson was not simply that escape would be punished.

The lesson was that the plantation could change the rules whenever it wanted, could make new tools out of old fears, could take even the attempt at freedom and fold it back into control.

In the dark, Elijah held his breath and listened to the night.

No bell yet. No jingling choir of warning.

Just the soft, ordinary sounds of bodies trying to sleep beside a memory that would not let them.

And somewhere between Boone's yard and Carter's house, the system settled deeper, satisfied, like iron cooling into a shape that would be hard to bend again.

Chapter 11

The Proposal

The first time Samuel spoke to her after the branding, he did not choose a moment of chaos.

He chose a moment that looked safe.

The house had gone quiet in that particular way it did after supper, when the white family's voices lowered and the work that remained was the kind they preferred not to see. The kitchen smelled of grease and lye and the last of the cornbread cooling on a rack. Outside, dusk pressed against the windows, turning glass into dark mirrors.

Lila was at the wash basin with her sleeves rolled up, hands sunk in water that had already gone lukewarm. She scrubbed a shirt slowly, letting the rhythm keep her face arranged. Around her, the other women moved carefully, each one guarding her own space as if closeness could be counted against them. Mary worked at the table with a knife, cutting up what was left for tomorrow's stew, her shoulders rigid.

The mistress had said it again before sending them back to the kitchen: stay close, stay where I can see you. Don't mix. Don't wander. Don't give your mind anywhere to go.

As if the mind asked permission.

Samuel appeared in the doorway like he had a right to it. He did not step in. He leaned against the frame, arms loose at his sides, posture relaxed enough to look harmless. He had learned, long ago, that harm announced itself too often. The worst kind did not.

Mary's knife paused for half a breath. Her eyes flicked up, then down again, the message clear even without words: don't.

Lila kept scrubbing. She didn't look at him. Looking invited conversation. Conversation invited misunderstanding. Misunderstanding invited punishment.

Samuel waited until the room's small sounds smoothed again. Water sloshing. A pot lid settling. The soft scrape of Mary's blade on wood.

Then, as if he were speaking about weather, he said, "They going to start keeping dogs closer."

No one answered. No one could afford to answer, not with his voice carrying through an open door. But the words landed anyway. Lila felt her fingers tighten on the wet cloth.

Samuel continued, calm. "They already talking about bells."

Mary's knife stopped again, this time long enough to be dangerous. She forced it to move. She did not look up.

Lila did not lift her head, but she heard the faint metal memory of the collar Elijah had been ordered to fix, the brass ring, the holes where something would be attached. The plantation taking fear and turning it into policy, the way you turned raw iron into a shackle.

Samuel let silence stretch until it became a thing.

Then he said her name. "Lila."

He didn't put heat in it. No demand. No impatience. Just a simple calling, like he was offering her the chance to respond before someone else decided she had to.

Lila kept her voice dull. "What."

Samuel's mouth shifted as if he might smile, then didn't. "Not here," he said. "Not in front of knives."

Mary's blade scraped hard enough to make the sound ugly.

Lila rinsed the shirt, wrung it out, and laid it in the basket with careful hands. She turned as if she had a reason unrelated to him, stepping past the doorway into the narrow side passage that led toward the pantry. She didn't want to be alone with him. But being alone was sometimes safer than being seen.

Samuel followed at a distance that suggested courtesy. He stopped where the passage widened near the back steps, where a little of the outside light bled in. He did not block her. He stood off to the side, leaving her a way to move away if she chose.

That, too, was deliberate. Samuel understood how to make control look like freedom.

Lila faced him with her arms at her sides. She didn't fold them. Folded arms could look like defiance. She kept her shoulders neutral, even though her skin still remembered the sight of the iron rising, remembered the way the marks looked when the light caught them.

Samuel's gaze went to her face, not to her body. He did not let his eyes linger in a way that would give her something clear to name and hate. He kept his expression steady, almost tired.

"I ain't come to trouble you," he said.

Lila heard the lie in it. He was trouble made into a man. She kept her voice even. "Then move on."

He nodded once, as if acknowledging a reasonable request. "I would," he said, "if things was the way they used to be."

Her mouth went tight. She didn't speak.

Samuel went on as if he had all the time in the world, as if the night was not full of listening. "You seen what they did over there," he said softly. "And you seen what it did over here."

Lila stared past him at the yard, where shadows were thickening. Somewhere a dog barked once and then stopped, like it had been corrected.

Samuel followed her gaze. "This place don't like feeling surprised," he said. "When it get surprised, it punish everybody till the surprise is gone."

Lila's voice came out low. "You think I don't know that."

Samuel looked back at her. "I think you know it," he said. "But knowing don't always keep a body safe."

Safety. The word was bait, and they both knew it. Lila didn't let her face change. "What you want, Samuel."

He took a breath, slow. He did not step closer. He spoke like a man offering terms, not like a man begging.

"I want you to stop being the kind of person they can make an example of," he said.

Lila felt something cold move through her belly. "I ain't made myself nothing," she said.

Samuel's eyes narrowed slightly, not with anger, with focus. "You don't get to decide that," he replied. "They decide it. They decide who get watched, who get moved, who get pulled close to the house and called reliable like it's a compliment."

The word reliable struck her, because it was exactly what the mistress had said, the soft trap dressed as care.

Samuel saw the flicker, and he used it.

"You got eyes on you," he said. "More than you used to. Mistress watching. Mary watching. Cook watching. Even the ones who love you watching, because love don't stop fear from making folks measure distance."

Lila's throat tightened. She hated that he could name it so clean. She hated more that he was right.

"And you," she said, letting a little sharpness into it because she couldn't hold it all down, "you watching too."

Samuel accepted that without offense. "Yes," he said simply. "I been watching. Because watching is how you live long."

Lila held his gaze. "You live long by trading."

His eyes did not flinch. "Everybody trading," he said. "Some trade talk. Some trade quiet. Some trade bodies. Some trade their own people and call it necessity. The only question is whether you get to pick what you pay with."

Lila felt the pressure of the moment like a hand closing around her ribs. She didn't answer.

Samuel's voice stayed calm, steady as a closed door. "I can make some of them eyes look away," he said. "Not all. I ain't pretending I'm God. But I can shift things. I can make sure you don't get sent out where mistakes happen. I can make sure your name don't get attached to certain kinds of talk."

Lila's mouth went dry. "How."

Samuel hesitated just long enough to make it seem like he was choosing honesty. "By being the one attached to you," he said.

The words settled between them.

Lila felt her skin try to crawl. "Attached," she repeated, keeping her voice quiet. A single loud word could travel through a wall and become evidence.

Samuel nodded. "People already think I got reach," he said. "They already think I can pull a string. If they see you under my eye, they'll stop thinking you worth the trouble. They'll stop trying to test you. You'll be… settled."

Settled. Like dirt. Like something pressed down until it stopped shifting.

Lila's hands curled into fists at her sides. She kept them low where he couldn't use them as proof of her reaction. "And what do I give you," she asked, though she already knew.

Samuel's gaze held hers, steady. He didn't pretend to misunderstand. He didn't dress it up with tenderness. That was part of what made him dangerous. He could speak plainly without ever sounding emotional, and plainness could feel like truth.

"You give me your yes," he said.

Lila's breath caught. She forced it out slow. "You want me to be yours."

"I want you alive," Samuel replied, and his voice stayed gentle enough that someone listening from a distance might think he was offering a kindness. "I want you not branded. I want you not hanging on a post while folks learn a lesson off your skin."

Lila saw it again, the woman's knees buckling, the white man yanking her upright, so the mark stayed visible. She swallowed hard.

Samuel softened his tone even further, as if lowering it would make it less ugly. "You smart," he said. "You know what's coming. Boone's side got hit, and Carter's side going to tighten now. They going to find somebody else to scare. They always do. It's how they keep the air full of fear, so nobody breathes too deep."

Lila held his eyes and found no heat there, only certainty.

"And Elijah," she said before she could stop herself. The name slipped out, and the moment it left her mouth she felt exposed, like she had opened her own skin for inspection.

Samuel did not smile. He didn't need to. His eyes flicked, just once, a small confirmation that he had been waiting for that name, that it mattered to him as leverage.

"What about him," Samuel asked, voice still calm, still controlled.

Lila's heart beat hard against her ribs. She could feel the risk of saying anything at all. She lifted her chin a fraction, forcing steadiness into her posture the way Elijah forced steadiness into his hands at the anvil.

"You offering protection," she said, careful. "Does it reach across the fence."

Samuel's gaze stayed on her, and for a moment she saw something true beneath the composure, something hard as iron cooling. Possession. Not of her body only, but of the space around her. The right to decide what names could be spoken.

"It could," he said at last. "If you stop reaching for what you can't hold."

There it was again, the same sentence he had used before, reshaped. He wasn't asking her to forget Elijah. He was asking her to accept the plantation's math: one life traded for another, one connection cut so the rest could keep breathing.

Lila felt anger rise, hot and dangerous. She pressed it down until it became something colder.

Samuel watched her do it. He understood restraint. He mistook it for movement.

He spoke again, voice low, almost careful. "I ain't forcing you," he said. "Not tonight. I'm just telling you what's true. The world got smaller after that iron. It's going to keep getting smaller. And when it get small enough, there won't be no corners left to hide hope in."

Lila's mouth tightened at the word hope. Weaponized. Dragged through the yard. Made shameful.

Samuel shifted his weight, still not stepping into her space, still making his calm feel like respect. "Think on it," he said. "You don't got to answer right now. But you should answer before they decide for you who you belong to."

He turned as if to leave, then paused, the final hook delivered softly.

"I can't stop the system," he murmured. "But I can tell it where not to look."

Then he walked away down the passage, back toward the kitchen's light, leaving Lila in the dim with her hands clenched and her skin remembering the smell of burned flesh carried on morning wind.

She stood there long after he was gone, listening to the house settle, listening to her own breath. The calm in his voice had been the worst part. It wasn't the language of lust or rage. It was the language of arrangement.

Like he was offering her a place on a shelf, safe from being knocked to the floor, as long as she accepted being owned twice.

When she finally moved, she did it slowly, smoothing her face into nothing before stepping back into the kitchen where Mary's knife kept working and the other women kept their eyes down.

Lila picked up the next shirt from the basket and put it into the water.

Her hands did not shake.

But inside her, something had begun to tremble in a different way, not with fear alone.

With the understanding that Samuel wasn't only listening anymore.

He was proposing. And proposals, in a place like this, were just another kind of trap that came wrapped in the sound of reason.

Lila did not answer that night.

She went back into the kitchen with her face smoothed into its working shape, the one that said nothing lived behind her eyes but obedience and the next task. She rinsed soap from cloth until her fingers went numb, folded shirts into neat squares, and carried them where she was told. She listened to Mary's knife and the low voices that tried to pretend they were only talking about stew and weather.

But Samuel's words sat in her like a stone that warmed slowly, pulling heat from everything around it.

I can tell it where not to look.

It sounded like mercy. It sounded like power. It sounded like a man offering to stand between her and the iron barrel, between her and the collar with bells they were already talking about. It sounded, too, like the same system with a different mouth.

When the house finally went dark and the kitchen was left with only the banked coals in the hearth, Lila lay on her pallet and stared at the rafters. Sleep came in scraps. Each time she drifted, she saw the iron lifted from the coals again, saw the air wobble above it, saw the woman's shoulders forced forward so everyone could read what had been burned into her. She woke with her jaw clenched and the taste of that morning still caught in her throat.

By the next day, Samuel did not approach her in the open.

He did not need to. He had already placed himself in her path.

The mistress called Lila to the front room before noon, as if the hours of work behind her were nothing but a warm-up. The windows were open. Summer air stirred the curtains with a gentleness that made the room feel like a lie. The mistress sat with her sewing again, needle moving with calm precision.

Lila stood with her hands folded.

The mistress did not look up at first. She let the silence settle, thick enough that Lila could feel it in her shoulders.

“I hear you’ve been restless,” the mistress said at last.

Lila kept her eyes lowered. “No, ma’am.”

The needle paused. “You don’t have to deny it to me. I see what I see.”

Lila didn’t answer, because there was no safe answer. If she said she was restless, it became an admission. If she said she wasn’t, it became a lie the mistress could punish.

The mistress’s voice softened, the way it did when she wanted something to feel like care. “After what happened across the way,” she said, as if speaking of a storm that had passed near the house, “I want quiet here. I want steadiness. I want to know you understand what kind of trouble a mind can make."

"Yes, ma'am," Lila said, and the words were practiced enough to be automatic.

The mistress finally looked at her. Her eyes were pale and direct, the kind of gaze that seemed to weigh you without moving. "Samuel has been helpful," she said, lightly, as if bringing up the name of a tool that worked well. "He has sense. He pays attention. He understands the value of order."

Lila felt her stomach tighten. The mistress's tone made it sound like praise, but Lila heard the meaning beneath it: Samuel had been in her ear, and now he was being placed where he belonged, close to the house and its trust.

"I want you to keep your distance from foolish talk," the mistress continued. "And from foolish people. I don't intend to lose what's mine because someone else wants to make a story out of the woods."

What's mine. Lila kept her face blank. She could feel her own name inside the sentence even if it wasn't spoken.

"Yes, ma'am," she said again.

The mistress nodded once, satisfied, and dismissed her as if the conversation had been a kindness.

By the time Lila returned to the kitchen, Mary had already heard. Mary heard everything, or if she didn't hear it, she read it in the way the house shifted. She didn't ask a question. She only said, without looking up from her work, "She talk his name at you."

It wasn't exactly a question, but it demanded an answer.

Lila kept her voice low. "Yes."

Mary's knife cut through a potato with more force than it needed. "That man," Mary muttered. "He keep finding ways to put himself in rooms he ain't belong."

Lila washed her hands at the basin, slow. Water ran clear, but her skin still felt dirty. "He say he can make eyes look away."

Mary snorted, sharp and humorless. "He can make eyes look wherever he point them."

Lila's throat tightened. "He want my yes."

Mary's knife stopped. The silence that followed was the most dangerous sound in the room, because it meant Mary was choosing words carefully enough to keep them from becoming a weapon.

"You don't say nothing about yes to nobody," Mary said finally, voice flat.

"I didn't," Lila whispered.

Mary resumed cutting. "Good," she said. Then, quieter, "Ain't no yes in a place where you can't say no."

The sentence landed hard, because it was true in a way that made Lila feel both less alone and more trapped. She watched Mary's hands, the sure movements, the way Mary kept control where she could find it, in the slice of a knife, in the order of chopped food.

Lila's mind went to Elijah without asking permission. She thought of him at his forge, hammer steady even when the world was shaking. She thought of the dog collar tossed onto his bench. Of the brass ring, the holes where bells would be fixed. She imagined his hands over leather, doing what he was told so the system wouldn't turn and notice him in a way that would get him marked next.

Samuel's voice returned like a whisper you couldn't cover. It could, if you stop reaching.

Lila understood then what he was offering.

Not protection.

Purchase.

And not only of her body. Of her choices. Of her silence.

That afternoon, Samuel waited until the yard was busy enough to hide conversation inside movement. Women carried baskets. Boys hauled water. White voices drifted from the porch. If anyone looked, it would be easy to pretend Samuel had only asked for a tool or an errand. He met her near the back steps where the passage shadowed, the same place he had chosen before.

He didn't smile. He didn't lean in. He stood to the side again, leaving her space, performing respect like a man wearing a clean shirt over dirty skin.

"You thought on it," he said, as if discussing a practical thing, as if he had offered a trade of corn meal.

Lila set her basket down carefully. She did not look toward the porch. She did not let her eyes dart, because darting eyes were confession. She faced him and let her voice come out steady.

"Yes," she said.

Samuel's gaze sharpened. His mouth didn't move, but something in him rose, the quiet satisfaction of a man watching a gate swing the way he planned.

Lila did not let him fill the silence with his own assumption. She continued, voice calm.

"My answer is no."

The word sat in the air between them, plain as a stone.

Samuel's expression didn't change at first. He blinked once, slowly, as if he hadn't heard correctly.

"You don't understand," he said, and his tone was still calm, still arranged. Calm was his favorite mask.

"I understand," Lila replied.

He tilted his head slightly, the gesture of a man trying to turn refusal into confusion. "You seen what happens," he said softly. "You seen the iron. You seen the marks. And you still want to gamble your skin on somebody else's stories."

Lila felt heat climb behind her ribs. She kept it down. Anger was loud and loud got punished. "This ain't about stories," she said. "This about you wanting to own me with different hands."

Samuel's eyes tightened. For the first time, a thin edge showed through his composure. "I ain't white," he said, the words clipped.

Lila didn't flinch. "You don't have to be," she answered. "You talk like them. You count like them. You think if you stand close enough to power, it'll forget you ain't one of them."

Samuel's jaw worked. He glanced past her shoulder, quick, checking the yard, checking who might be near enough to hear. When his gaze returned, it had hardened.

"You think you brave," he murmured.

"I ain't brave," Lila said. "I'm tired."

The truth of it steadied her more than anger could. She had been tired for years. Tired of moving her body where it was placed. Tired of swallowing words until they rotted. Tired of watching men like Samuel find small ways to survive that required someone else to bleed.

Samuel took a step closer then, small, subtle, still leaving her space if someone looked from a distance. But the step narrowed the air.

"You tell me no," he said quietly, "like no mean something."

Lila met his gaze. Her heart hammered, but her face stayed still.

"It mean something to me," she said. "It mean I ain't giving you what you want. Not willing."

Samuel's mouth twitched, almost a smile, but it was empty. "Willing," he repeated, tasting it. "You think they care about willing. You think the mistress care. You think the master care."

"No," Lila said. "I know they don't."

"Then what you holding onto," Samuel asked, and now the calm carried something sharper beneath it, the sound of patience thinning.

Lila took a slow breath. She thought of Elijah's hands, scarred and careful. She thought of the woman's scream at the posts. She thought of Mary saying there ain't no yes where you can't say no.

She looked Samuel in the eye and let her voice stay low enough not to carry, but firm enough to land.

"I'm holding onto the part of me you can't trade," she said. "Even if it's small. Even if it's all I got."

Samuel stared at her a long moment. The yard noise continued around them. A bucket clanged. A white laugh floated from the porch and died. Life went on like it always did, indifferent to the wars fought inside a single sentence.

"You think you can keep that part," Samuel said at last.

Lila lifted her basket again, hands steady. "I know I can," she said. "Because I'm telling you no, And I'm going to keep telling you no."

Samuel's eyes followed her hands, then her face. Something in his expression shifted, a recalculation done behind stillness. He didn't reach for her. Not here. Not now. He was too careful for that.

"All right," he said, and the words were smooth again, as if the edge had never shown. "You made your choice."

Lila started to turn away.

Samuel's voice followed her, quiet as a thread pulled tight. "Just remember," he said, "choices got consequences. And in this place, consequences don't always pick the person who made them."

Lila did not look back. She walked on with her basket and her spine straight; her refusal held inside her like a hidden blade.

But she felt the air change as she moved away, felt the invisible line draw itself between them.

No was a word that could not be taken back once spoken.

And Samuel, who lived by trading what other people could not afford to lose, had just been denied the one thing he believed he deserved.

Lila carried that knowledge with her into the kitchen's heat and the mistress's watchful quiet.

Her refusal had been absolute.

Now she had to survive what Samuel would do with it.

Samuel watched her walk away until the basket and her straight back disappeared into the kitchen's shadow.

He did not follow. Following would have looked like need, and need was a kind of weakness that made a man careless. He stood where he was, half in light and half in shade, listening to the yard breathe around him. A bucket clanged near the wash line. Somebody laughed on the porch as if laughter could keep the day clean. A dog barked once, bored.

No.

The word didn't strike him like an insult at first. It struck him like a miscalculation.

He had expected fear to do what it always did: make people choose the nearest shelter, even if the shelter was another kind of cage. He had offered her what he believed was shelter. His name, his reach, his ability to turn eyes away, shift tasks, soften attention. He had offered her a life that could be endured.

And she had said no as if endurance was not enough.

Samuel stood still long enough to feel the heat of anger try to climb into his face. He pressed it down before it could show. Anger was loud. Loud drew notice. He had lived too long inside other people's notice to give anyone a new reason to look at him.

He walked away at an unhurried pace, back into the yard, then toward the quarters where men's movements were looser and white eyes drifted past without settling. He kept his posture the way it always was, easy, like his mind had never been challenged by a single syllable.

Inside him, something shifted into a quieter shape.

It was not heartbreak. He did not let himself have that kind of softness. It was not even humiliation, though he felt the bite of it, the way a man felt a thorn he could not pull out in public.

It was refusal, and what refusal meant in a place like this.

She had not only denied him. She had denied what he represented: the idea that survival required agreement, that the safest path was to attach yourself to someone who had learned how to trade.

She had named him, too, in a way no one had named him to his face.

You talk like them. You count like them.

Samuel returned to his cabin and shut the door behind him. The darkness inside smelled of old wood and sweat and the thin, stale sweetness of stolen molasses he kept hidden. He sat on the edge of his pallet and let his hands rest on his knees, palms down, as if he could hold himself in place by pressure.

He heard Lila's voice again, low and steady: "It mean something to me."

Samuel's jaw tightened.

Meaning was dangerous. Meaning was what made men run into woods believing in scarred trees. Meaning was what made women leave babies with sisters and step into mud. Meaning was what got people marked.

He had believed Lila's intelligence would make her practical. He had mistaken her restraint for negotiation. He had watched her tighten her life down to small movements and thought she would accept any offered structure that promised fewer consequences.

But her restraint, he realized now, was not surrender. It was discipline.

That was worse.

A disciplined person could hold to a no even when the whole world punished no. A disciplined person could keep secrets longer. Could wait. Could plan without speaking.

Samuel had not liked that in her. He had wanted it, the way he wanted all useful things. He had wanted to be the one she used.

He had offered her his name as shield, and she had answered as if his name was another brand waiting to be pressed into her skin.

Samuel leaned forward and picked up a small piece of twine from beside his pallet. He turned it between his fingers, slow, feeling its fibers catch. The plantation was full of fibers. Threads. Lines you pulled, and things moved.

No, did not end a proposition here. It only changed its method.

He stood again and stepped outside. Evening had come down thicker. Smoke from kitchen fires drifted low, hugging the ground. The yard looked almost gentle in the dim, the way it always tried to look when you didn't stare too long.

Samuel walked toward the back of the main house, not to the front where white men sat and talked as if their words were law. He went where he belonged, in the side spaces, the in-between passages, the places where servants moved and whites did not look closely unless something had already been pointed out.

He did not seek the mistress. He did not need to. He had already heard her speak his name in Lila's front-room warning. That meant the mistress's ear was open to him now.

All Samuel needed to do was give that ear something to hold.

He found the cook behind the kitchen outbuilding, lifting a pot to pour slop into a bucket. Her shoulders rose when she saw him, a defensive tension that tried to look like annoyance.

"What you want," she asked, voice rough.

Samuel didn't answer the question the way he could have. He didn't threaten. He didn't bargain. He spoke like a man sharing concern.

"You heard Boone's dogs going to get bells," he said.

The cook's mouth tightened. "Everybody heard."

"Everybody don't listen," Samuel replied. He stepped closer by a fraction, keeping his tone low. "They talking about doing it here too."

The cook stared at him. "Who talking."

Samuel shrugged. "White mouths," he said, as if that explained everything. "And some black ones, the ones trying to stay close enough not to get stepped on."

The cook's eyes narrowed. "You one of them."

Samuel let the accusation pass without reacting. Reacting would make it feel true. "I'm trying to keep this place quiet," he said. "Quiet keeps people breathing."

The cook made a small, disgusted sound. "Quiet keeps people owned."

Samuel's gaze held steady. "Owned people still die," he said softly. "And dying loud makes everything worse."

The cook hesitated. Samuel saw the small crack open, the place where fear lived beside pride. He moved carefully into it.

"Mistress don't want trouble," he said. "Not after what happened across the way. She don't want talk in her kitchen. She don't want errands back and forth. She don't want… connections."

The cook's grip tightened on the pot handle. "You talking about Lila."

Samuel didn't say her name. Names were sharp tools. He only said, "I'm talking about what gets people looked at."

The cook stared at him a moment longer, then looked away, jaw working. "You got something you trying to tell mistress," she muttered.

Samuel's voice stayed calm. "I'm trying to tell you," he said, "so you ain't surprised when she starts asking questions. When she starts moving people around. When she starts making examples small, before they become big."

The cook swallowed. Samuel watched the swallow and saw the decision settle.

"Go on," the cook said finally, tone flat. "Say what you got to say."

Samuel leaned in just enough that his next words would have to be kept, would have to be carried quietly. "Lila been holding herself tight," he murmured. "Too tight. You know how it look when a person got something in them they trying not to spill."

The cook's eyes flashed. "She just trying to live."

"So am I," Samuel said. Then, softer, as if he hated to add it: "She been asking after Boone's side."

The cook went still. "She ain't."

Samuel tilted his head, a gesture that could be taken as uncertainty, not accusation. "I didn't say she did it loud," he replied. "I said she been doing it careful. Careful is what scares white folks most, because careful means there's sense behind it."

The cook's lips parted, then shut again. Samuel could see the cook's mind move, measuring loyalty against danger, love against the risk of being pulled into another plantation's punishment.

Samuel gave her one more piece, small and poisonous.

"Samuel Boone's blacksmith," he said. "Elijah. Folks been saying Lila's name near his."

The cook flinched as if struck. Samuel didn't push further. He let the flinch do his work for him.

"That ain't my business," the cook said, too quickly.

Samuel nodded, as if he agreed. "It shouldn't be," he said. "But business changes when white folks start hunting for where hope been hiding."

He stepped back, letting his face soften into something that could pass for sympathy. "Just watch," he murmured. "If she get sent over there again, you keep your eyes open. It could be a test. Could be a trap."

The cook's gaze stayed hard, but Samuel saw the fear sitting behind it, the fear that made even good people do ugly math.

Samuel walked away before she could say more, before she could ask the question he didn't want to answer: why are you telling me this.

He didn't want to admit the truth, even to himself.

Because Lila had said no, and now he needed her world to get smaller until no became a word she couldn't afford.

He moved through the yard, listening. The quarters were quiet in that watchful way they had become since the branding. People spoke about weather, about work, about nothing. But Samuel heard the gaps. He heard the silences that meant someone was thinking.

He found Mary near the water barrel, rinsing her hands. She looked up as he approached, eyes narrowed, ready.

Mary had always been harder than most. Mary didn't like him, and she didn't fear him the way others did. That made her dangerous in a different way.

Samuel stopped at a distance that looked casual. "You keeping your knife close," he said.

Mary's mouth didn't move. "You want something."

Samuel studied her face, searching for the crack he could slide a word into. “Mistress been restless,” he said instead, offering nothing and watching what Mary did with it.

Mary’s hands slowed. “Might be,” she said.

Samuel nodded. “She worried about talk moving,” he murmured. “About folks getting ideas.”

Mary’s gaze sharpened. “Ideas been here since the first chain.”

Samuel let that pass too. He didn’t need agreement. He needed Mary’s attention.

He lowered his voice. “If she start asking,” he said, “you don’t put your mouth in it. You hear me. You don’t let her pull you into naming nobody.”

Mary’s eyes narrowed further. “Why you telling me.”

Samuel’s expression stayed smooth. “Because she’ll ask you,” he said simply. “And when she do, she’ll act like it’s for order. She’ll act like she protecting you. Same way white folks always do when they want your hands dirty.”

Mary stared at him, suspicion and something like reluctant understanding crossing her face. Mary knew that truth already. But hearing it from Samuel made it feel like bait, and Mary was not a woman who took bait without looking for the hook.

"You got a name you trying to keep safe," Mary said quietly.

Samuel held her gaze without blinking. "We all do," he replied.

Mary's eyes flicked away, then back. "Lila," she said, and it wasn't a question.

Samuel didn't answer. He let the silence sit, letting Mary fill it with whatever she feared most.

Mary's mouth tightened. "You stay away from her," she said.

Samuel's voice stayed mild. "I been trying," he replied, and the lie slid out clean.

Mary took a step toward him, just one. "You ain't trying nothing but trouble."

Samuel's eyes remained calm. Calm was his weapon. "Trouble's already here," he said softly. "It just need a place to land."

He walked away then, leaving Mary with her hands dripping water and her suspicion burning bright. He didn't care if Mary hated him. Hate was predictable. What he cared about was that Mary would be careful, and careful people made mistakes when they believed they were being watched.

By the time night settled fully, Samuel had done what he needed.

Not an accusation. Not a report. Just a nudge, a suggestion placed in the right mouths: Lila is too careful. Lila has Boone's side in her head. Lila's name is near Elijah's.

The system didn't require proof. It required scent. Once a scent was laid, white men and women followed it the way dogs followed cloth held to their noses.

Samuel sat outside his cabin and listened to the dark. Somewhere, a chain collar jingled as a dog shifted. He imagined the future sound of bells, small and bright, turning every night step into an announcement.

He thought again of Lila's no, the steadiness of it.

His intent had been simple before. He had wanted her to choose him because it would make her safer and make him feel, for once, chosen rather than merely used.

Now the wanting changed shape.

He would not beg. He would not press her in a passage where she could spit defiance and walk away with her spine straight.

He would arrange the world around her until the straight spine became too costly.

Samuel leaned back against the cabin wall and let his face remain empty, as if he were only a man resting at the end of a day's work.

Inside him, the plan settled, cool and deliberate.

If Lila would not accept protection as an offer, then protection would become a condition.

If she would not choose him freely, then choice itself would be narrowed until it looked like there had never been another path at all.

And somewhere beyond Carter's house, across fences and fear, Elijah Boone's forge rang each day with the sound of iron obeying the hammer.

Samuel listened to that sound in his memory and felt no admiration now, only the hard recognition of a problem that needed solving.

He had tried persuasion.

Now he would try control.

Not with loud force. Not with grabbing hands.

With the quiet tightening of the system, one small turn at a time, until the lock clicked and the door Lila thought she still had inside herself would open only the way Samuel allowed.

Chapter 12

The Trap Tightens

By the third day after Lila's refusal, the plantation stopped pretending it was only reacting to Boone's side.

Carter's yard had always been watched. That was the nature of a place built on ownership. But there were different kinds of watching. The old kind was lazy, habitual, meant to remind you that you were never alone. The new kind had purpose. It pressed in at the edges of ordinary things and made them feel arranged.

It began with small changes that could be explained away if you wanted to keep your mind quiet.

The mistress appeared more often in doorways, her sewing left unattended on a chair, her hands empty as if she'd merely stepped out for air. Her gaze would pass over Lila and the other women with that pale calm that never raised its voice.

When she spoke, she spoke softly, as if softness made her words less sharp.

"You missed a spot," she told Lila once, pointing to a smear of ash on the kitchen tile that Lila would have sworn wasn't there five minutes earlier.

"Yes, ma'am," Lila answered, and scrubbed until her fingers burned.

In the yard, Mr. Carter's men lingered longer near the back line. They leaned on fence posts as if resting. They spoke to each other in low voices and looked out toward the trees as if they were counting how many ways a body could disappear. When Lila carried water, she felt their attention track her path, not openly, but with the slow, steady certainty of eyes that had been given a reason to search.

In the kitchen, the cook's mouth tightened whenever Lila stepped too near the doorway.

"You got work here," the cook said, when Lila drifted toward the passage that led to the back steps with a basket of linens. The words weren't harsh, but they weren't neutral either.

"I'm taking these to the line," Lila replied.

The cook wiped her hands on her apron. “Somebody else can,” she said. “You stay where I can see you.”

It sounded like protection. It felt like a leash.

Mary said nothing at first. Mary had learned that silence could be a knife if you held it right. But Lila saw the way Mary’s eyes moved, taking measure of the room, the door, the windows. Saw the way Mary kept her knife close even when she wasn’t cutting.

That evening, when the kitchen was finally empty enough to risk a sentence, Mary spoke without looking up from the basin.

“They got a reason,” Mary said.

Lila kept her hands in the water. “For what.”

“For watching,” Mary replied. “They don’t watch like this unless somebody gave them a reason to think they might catch something.”

Lila’s throat tightened. She wanted to say Samuel’s name out loud and could not. Names were dangerous. Names were handles.

Mary glanced toward the door, quickly, then back to her work. “You don’t walk nowhere alone,” she said. “Not even to the line. Not even to the privy. You hear me.”

Lila’s voice stayed low. “I ain’t a child.”

Mary's hands stilled on the rag. "No," she said. "You a target. That's worse. A child gets overlooked. A target makes everybody look."

Lila swallowed. The water in the basin had gone cold, but her palms felt hot anyway.

The next morning, the dogs came closer.

They had always been present, part of the plantation's background threat, kept nearer the stable and the far yard line where their barking could be summoned like a bell itself. Now they were brought into the center of Carter's side as if they belonged there, as if their place had always been underfoot.

A white man led them by thick leather collars. The dogs strained and snuffled at the dirt and the air, pulling their handler's arm taut. One of them lifted its head and stared toward the kitchen yard, ears pricked, as if it had heard a whisper under the sound of chores.

Then Lila saw the change.

Small brass bells had been fixed to the collars, not many, just enough to make sound. The bells were bright in the morning light, too clean, too deliberate. They sat against the dogs' throats like jewelry.

When the dogs moved, the bells spoke.

A thin, cheerful sound, wrong in this place. A sound that belonged on a church door or a child's toy, turned into an instrument of warning.

Lila felt her stomach drop. She thought of Boone's side, of the leather strip Elijah had been handed in the forge, the old holes where bells would be attached. The system didn't invent new tools if it could force the enslaved to build them.

The handler walked the dogs past the kitchen yard slowly, making a show of it. The bells chimed with each step. The mistress stood on the porch and watched as if approving a new piece of furniture.

"Better," she said, not to anyone in particular.

The cook made a small sound that might have been disgust and might have been fear.

Lila kept her face arranged and her eyes down, but inside her, something calculated quickly. Bells meant the night had been changed. Bells meant silence no longer belonged to the dark.

All day, the dogs were walked in patterns.

Not random, not wandering. A loop by the back steps. A pass near the quarters. A slow circle toward the tree line and back again. The bells stitched sound into the yard. No one could move without being reminded that the plantation could hear what it couldn't see.

By afternoon, Mr. Carter's overseer began asking questions.

He did not gather people into a line the way Boone's man did. Carter liked his cruelty quieter. The overseer moved through the yard with a clipboard and a pencil, writing as if writing made the world more orderly. When he spoke, he spoke politely enough to make the answers feel like cooperation.

"You seen anything strange?" he asked an older man near the shed. "Anybody walking after dark?"

"No, sir," the man replied, eyes lowered.

The overseer nodded and wrote something anyway.

He asked a woman carrying laundry, "You heard talk from Boone's side? Any names?"

The woman shook her head too fast. "No, sir."

He smiled. "Good," he said, and made another mark on the paper.

When he approached the kitchen yard, the cook's shoulders rose as if bracing. Mary shifted half a step so she was between him and the pantry doorway without making it obvious. Lila kept her hands busy, wiping down the worktable even though it was already clean.

The overseer stopped where he could see them all. His eyes moved across faces the way a man's eyes moved across a row of tools, deciding what he might need.

"Mistress says things been unsettled," he said. "She don't want unsettled."

"Yes, sir," the cook replied.

He looked at Lila longer than he needed to. "You're Lila," he said, not a question.

Lila kept her posture still. "Yes, sir."

"You do good work," he said mildly. The compliment felt like the touch of a hand you hadn't invited. "You been here a while."

"Yes, sir."

His gaze slid to Mary. "And you're Mary."

Mary's face stayed hard. "Yes, sir."

The overseer tapped his pencil once against the clipboard. "You women hear things," he said, voice pleasant. "Kitchen hears everything. Folks talk when they think you ain't listening."

Nobody answered. They didn't know which answer would be punished.

He continued, "Boone's side got trouble because folks got ideas. We don't want ideas over here."

The bells on the dogs chimed somewhere behind him, as if agreeing.

The overseer's eyes returned to Lila. "You been over to Boone's side recently?" he asked.

Lila's throat tightened. She could feel the question trying to hook into her. Recently. Over. Boone's side. It was a net cast with careful words.

"No, sir," she answered.

The overseer nodded slowly, as if weighing whether her no sounded too quick or too practiced. "You got family over there?"

"No, sir."

He wrote something down. Lila couldn't see what. That was part of it, too. The writing made everything feel permanent, like a ledger that could be brought out later to prove she'd lied.

Behind him, the cook's mouth pressed into a line. Mary's hands were still, but her stillness was controlled, not fearful. Lila felt a strange gratitude for Mary's presence. Mary's quiet anger was a kind of shield. It reminded Lila that she wasn't the only one who could see the trap being built.

The overseer closed his clipboard as if satisfied. "All right," he said, still pleasant. "Keep your minds where they belong. If you hear anything, you bring it to me. You understand?"

“Yes, sir,” the cook said.

Mary didn’t speak. The overseer waited a beat, then looked at her.

“Yes, sir,” Mary said finally, the words flat as a stone.

The overseer smiled again, and walked away.

When he was gone, the kitchen yard did not exhale. It stayed tight. The bells chimed again as the dogs passed, their handler leading them along the fence line, deliberate as a metronome.

Lila went back to wiping the table. Her hands moved steadily. That steadiness was her only protection.

Mary leaned close enough to speak without being heard by the yard. “That was a test,” Mary murmured.

Lila kept her eyes on the wood grain. “For what.”

“To see if you’d stumble,” Mary said. “To see if your face would say Boone when your mouth said no.”

Lila swallowed. “I didn’t.”

Mary’s voice lowered further. “You don’t stumble,” she said, and it wasn’t praise. It was warning. "So, they going to tighten it till even a steady person trip."

That night, the quarters were quieter than usual, not because fear had increased, but because fear had been given a schedule. Patrols moved at set times. White voices called to each other from the yard as if announcing their own presence made it righteous.

And the dogs, with their bright bells, walked the edges of the sleeping world.

Lila lay on her pallet with her hands folded at her stomach and listened.

A chime. A pause. Another chime.

The sound was small. It shouldn't have been powerful. But it turned the dark into something measured, broken into pieces that belonged to someone else.

She thought of Elijah, across the boundary, hearing his own version of this tightening. She thought of the forge, the collar on his bench, his hands forced to shape the tools that would hunt them. She thought of Samuel sitting outside his cabin, listening to the night, satisfied by the new quiet he'd helped create.

Lila kept her breathing even. She did not let herself imagine movement, because even imagination felt dangerous under this kind of listening.

In the middle of the night, a dog barked once, then twice, then settled. The bells chimed as it shifted.

A white man's voice carried faintly, calm and annoyed. "Keep 'em moving."

The handler spoke back, "Yes, sir."

Then the yard returned to its new rhythm: the soft chime of bells, the slow sweep of patrol, the sense that every corner had been named and inspected.

Surveillance had always existed here. But now it had sharpened into something intimate.

It did not only watch the woods.

It watched the spaces between people.

It watched who looked too long, who walked too carefully, who held themselves too tight.

It watched for the smallest proof that a mind had gone somewhere it wasn't supposed to go.

And in that watching, the plantation began to do what Samuel had promised it could do.

It started to make the world smaller, one measured step at a time, until the idea of a private moment felt like a rumor you weren't allowed to believe.

Opportunities didn't vanish all at once. They thinned the way breath did when you held it too long, leaving you aware of loss only when your chest began to ache.

The first thing Lila noticed was the errands.

Before the branding, before the false path turned into spectacle, the house still needed things it didn't have. A spool of thread from Boone's side, a slab of soap that Carter's cook claimed was better there, a borrowed pot returned with careful politeness. Those trips were never safe, but they were movement, and movement meant the possibility of a glance that carried more than words.

Now the mistress stopped sending.

When the cook said, "We need more lye," the mistress replied, "Make do."

When Mary muttered that the pantry latch was sticking, the mistress said, "Tell the carpenter. No need for running around."

And when the cook tried to push Lila toward the back gate with a basket and a reason, the mistress's voice came soft and decisive from the porch: "No. Not today. Not any day until things settle."

Things settle. Like dust after a beating. Like a body after it stops fighting.

Lila learned to hear the new meaning underneath ordinary instructions. Settle meant stay. Settle meant be visible. Settle meant let the house keep you where it could put eyes on you without having to admit it was doing so.

Even inside Carter's yard, the patterns changed.

The laundry line used to be a place where women could stand with cloth snapping between their hands and speak in half-sentences, their words lost in wind and work. Now a white boy lingered by the line pretending to mend a bucket handle, his gaze drifting like it wasn't fixed on anything when it was fixed on everything. The well used to be a natural gathering point, a place where buckets knocked and arms strained and someone could say something small without it seeming like a meeting. Now the dogs were walked past the well on purpose, bells chiming, the handler's boots scuffing slow as if he had nowhere else to be.

The kitchen door became a border.

It had always been a threshold between the house's soft cruelty and the yard's open one. Now it felt like a trapdoor that could close at any moment. The cook kept Lila inside more often, inventing work that didn't need doing, keeping her hands busy where the mistress could glance in and see a body doing what it was told.

"You stay here," the cook said more than once, her voice rough with a fear she wouldn't name.

Lila nodded each time, face smooth, and did what she was told. But inside her, she counted what was being taken.

There would be no trip to the smokehouse near the back line where the boundary between plantations ran close enough that a person could see shapes moving on Boone's side.

There would be no late carrying of ash buckets to the far pit where a man from Boone's place sometimes passed on his way to the creek.

There would be no small overlap where an eye could catch an eye and confirm that someone else was still alive, still thinking, still holding something inside themselves that the plantation hadn't managed to brand out.

At Boone's plantation, Elijah felt the same narrowing from a different angle.

The collar had been only the beginning. After the boy brought it, more came.

A hinge from the master's smokehouse that needed tightening, ordered with impatience as if the hinge had chosen to loosen out of spite. A chain for the stable that had to be repaired before nightfall. A length of iron shaped into a new latch for the tool shed, thicker than the last, as if anyone with hands could be assumed to be a thief.

Work that used to come spaced with gaps now came in a steady press, each task delivered by a white mouth that stayed too close to the forge doorway, eyes tracking the room like it was learning it.

Elijah understood the purpose. They weren't only using his skill. They were filling his time so completely that he couldn't find a corner of it to claim as his own. A man couldn't plan if he couldn't breathe. A man couldn't listen for the right rumor if his ears were filled with orders.

And they were changing where he stood.

Before, the forge had been a fixed point. Men came to him. Broken tools, bent nails, handles that needed new rivets. He could see who approached. He could read the yard while his hammer moved. Now the overseer sent him out.

"Take this to the stable," they said, handing him a repaired shackle as if it were nothing.

"Fix the latch in the smokehouse," they ordered, forcing him under the house's side shadow where voices drifted from open windows above.

"Go to the back shed," they commanded, making him cross open ground in full view.

Elijah went where he was told. Refusal was a quick path to the posts. But each step outside the forge felt like a leash tugged. Out there, he was visible in a way that made his skin tighten. Out there, he could be interrupted, questioned, followed.

And the yard itself had learned new habits.

He heard the bells first before he saw them, a faint, bright chime floating in from Carter's side on a thin wind, wrong as laughter at a funeral. A day later the sound came from his own side too, closer, unmistakable. Boone's men had done it. The change he'd been ordered to prepare had been finished, and now the night would have its own language of warning.

Elijah stood in the forge doorway at dusk and watched the dogs pass. Their collars looked newly oiled. Brass bells caught the last light and flashed as they moved, each swing of a throat turning silence into sound.

The handler's face was blank. The dogs' eyes were eager.

Elijah felt the bitter twist of recognition. He had been part of making this. His hands had touched the leather. His skill had been used to tighten the plantation's grip. It wasn't new, that feeling of being forced to build the thing that would hurt you. But seeing the bells on moving bodies made it sharper.

He thought of Lila then, because he always did. He thought of her trapped closer to the house now, watched more carefully, her world narrowed until even standing still could be used as evidence.

The hardest part was that he couldn't even confirm it.

Before, there had been small chances. A gathering between plantations under white supervision where he might be assigned to stand near a wagon and she might be assigned to carry water, their bodies angled so that a brief word could slip out with the sound of horses. A Sunday moment when work eased and people were allowed a controlled loosening, enough to trade a glance and remind themselves they weren't alone.

Now even that was being stolen.

The master announced, almost casually, that there would be no visiting. No shared work between properties until further notice. He said it as if he were protecting his investment.

"We don't need trouble traveling," he said. "We got enough on our own land."

Men nodded because nodding was survival. Elijah kept his face empty and felt the last thin thread of opportunity fray.

On Carter's side, the mistress made her own version of the announcement.

"You'll stay close," she told the kitchen women. "No wandering. No stepping beyond what you're assigned. You'll do your work and you'll do it quiet."

Quiet. Again, that word, dressed like peace.

The quarters changed under it.

People began to move in straight lines, not because straight lines were safer, but because straight lines looked obedient. Men didn't linger by doorways. Women didn't cluster at the well. Any gathering larger than two bodies felt like a risk. Not because it was forbidden in any official way, but because the watching had become so intimate that even proximity could be translated into suspicion.

Lila felt it when Mary tried to speak to her and then stopped, eyes flicking to the window, to the door, to the yard. Mary's caution was new, and that newness scared Lila more than Mary's anger ever could.

One evening, as Lila carried a stack of folded linens toward the pantry, she heard the cook's voice behind her, low and tense. "Don't stand there."

Lila paused. "I'm just—"

"I said don't," the cook snapped, then softened her tone as if remembering who might be listening. "Mistress don't like you in that passage."

The passage. The same narrow side place where Samuel had spoken calm poison to her, where her no had been delivered like a stone.

Lila's fingers tightened on the linens. "Why."

The cook's eyes darted toward the door. "Because it look like you waiting," she whispered. "And waiting look like planning."

Lila swallowed. She turned and went back into the kitchen, the linens pressed hard against her chest like a shield.

Later, when she was alone long enough to risk a breath that wasn't work-shaped, she saw Samuel in the yard.

Not close. He didn't need to be close anymore. He stood near the quarters with two other men, talking softly, their heads inclined toward one another. It could have been nothing. It could have been a complaint about rations. It could have been weather.

But Lila had learned how to read him. She saw the way the other men's bodies angled toward Samuel, the subtle deference, the way information flowed one direction. She saw Samuel's face, calm as ever, and felt the cold certainty settle in her gut.

He wasn't pressing her again with words. He was letting the system press her for him.

He had promised he could tell it where not to look. Now he was telling it where to look until there was nowhere left that felt unobserved.

The next opportunity disappeared in a way so small it almost didn't announce itself at all.

A child dropped a tin cup near the back steps, and it rolled into the dirt. Before, Lila would have stooped, picked it up, handed it back with a quiet word, a human moment that reminded her she could still choose kindness. This time, when she bent, a white voice snapped from the porch, sharp and immediate.

"Leave it."

Lila froze. She straightened slowly, hands empty, heart pounding. The child stared at her with wide eyes, then hurried to retrieve the cup himself, small fingers shaking as the bell-chimed dogs passed too close.

Lila stood still until she was dismissed by silence.

The message wasn't about the cup. It was about motion. Any motion not ordered was suspicious. Any choice not assigned was dangerous.

That night, Lila lay on her pallet listening to the bells as they stitched their bright sound through the dark. She tried to remember what it had felt like to have even a few feet of privacy, even a few seconds of being unseen.

It felt like something she'd imagined.

Across the boundary, Elijah lay with his arms folded over his chest, eyes open in the dark. The forge had been quiet for hours, but his mind still rang with iron and orders and the sound of bells. He thought of the false path and the branding and the way the plantation learned from its own cruelty. He thought of Samuel's name, unspoken but heavy, like a tool left on the bench where it didn't belong.

The trap wasn't only tightening with dogs and patrols.

It was tightening with subtraction.

Removing overlap. Removing wandering. Removing the accidental moments when a person could catch a scrap of truth that hadn't been filtered through someone else's mouth.

And in that subtraction, Elijah felt the pressure building toward a choice he wasn't ready to speak aloud.

Because if you waited for the right opportunity here, the plantation would simply erase the idea of opportunity itself.

And if you moved without one, you were stepping into dark that had been measured, watched, and turned into policy.

In the quiet between bell chimes, Lila understood the same thing.

She had said no. She had kept the part of herself Samuel wanted to trade away.

Now the cost of that no was being collected in pieces, each day smaller than the last, until survival began to look less like living and more like standing still long enough not to be noticed.

And standing still, she knew, was its own kind of death.

Two days after the last errand was refused, Lila realized the house had begun to rearrange her without ever saying her name.

It happened in the smallest humiliations, the kind that could be denied later because no one had put a hand on her throat. The mistress started calling her to the front room at odd hours, not for work that mattered, but for presence. A chair moved. A curtain adjusted. A piece of silver polished twice. Lila's hands were used, but the real task was simpler: keep her where the mistress could see her.

In the kitchen, the cook stopped letting Mary send her anywhere alone. Mary would open her mouth to say, "Lila, take this—" and the cook would cut it off with a look, then with a whisper that didn't sound like command but carried the same weight.

"Not her."

Lila learned to accept it with her face arranged. She learned to keep her eyes down even when anger rose like bile. The cook wasn't cruel for cruelty's sake. The cook was frightened, and fear made people build fences inside the fences that already held them.

Mary, though, did not soften into fear. She sharpened.

One evening, when the mistress had finally gone upstairs and the kitchen had its brief, exhausted lull, Mary worked at the table with her knife and said without looking up, "You can't keep standing still like this."

Lila rinsed a pot slowly, hands in water that had gone cloudy with grease. "I ain't standing still. I'm doing what I'm told."

Mary's knife stopped. The silence that followed was not gentle. "That's standing still," Mary replied. "They telling you where to be every minute. They got bells on dogs, white boys by the line, overseer with his paper. That ain't work, that's a pen."

Lila swallowed. She thought of the passage by the back steps, forbidden now because it looked like waiting. She thought of the snapped order when she bent to pick up the child's cup. Any motion not assigned was suspicion. Any kindness not ordered was a sign you still belonged to yourself.

Mary's voice lowered even more. "You heard from Boone's side at all?"

Lila didn't answer fast. Fast looked guilty.

"No," she said finally. "Not since they stopped the trips."

Mary's mouth tightened. "That's the point."

Lila forced her hands to keep moving. The pot's rim squeaked under the rag. "You asking me what

I'm going to do," she said, careful, "or you telling me what you want me to do."

Mary's eyes flicked to the doorway, then back. "I'm telling you the truth. They tightening. They going to keep tightening. And Samuel…" Mary said his name like she was spitting out a thorn, "Samuel ain't finished."

The name made Lila's stomach clench. She felt, for a moment, the old urge to speak back loudly, to say his name as accusation. But accusation needed ears that cared about justice. Here, accusation only gave the system a shape to grab.

Mary went on. "He done put your name in people's mouths. Now people scared to be near you because being near you might make them seen."

Lila set the pot down. Her arms ached. Her throat ached more. "So, what you want," she whispered.

Mary glanced again toward the door. "I want you to stop waiting for a moment that ain't coming back."

Lila held herself still, as if stillness could keep the world from hearing her next breath. "And what about Elijah," she asked, the name falling out before she could stop it, as if the sound of him was the only thing that proved this was not just a prison but a life she had tried to build inside it.

Mary's knife resumed, slower now. "You think he waiting too?"

Lila didn't answer. She didn't know, and not knowing felt like another kind of punishment.

That night, the bells moved in their usual loops. The sound came and went like a thin, bright needle stitching the dark shut. When the yard finally quieted enough that sleep might have been possible, Lila lay with her hands folded over her stomach and tried to picture Elijah's face. Not the careful, composed one he wore in daylight, but the one she had seen for a second at the gathering, when his attention had landed on her like something warm and dangerous.

She imagined him on Boone's side, stretched on his pallet with his mind still working, his hands still remembering iron and leather. She imagined him hearing the same bells now, his own work turned against him. She imagined the anger in him, not loud, but held tight the way he held a hammer.

She imagined him deciding something without her, because he could not afford to wait for a message that might never come.

The next day, Lila almost missed it.

The kitchen yard was busy. The cook barked orders. A white boy loitered near the well with a bored slouch that fooled no one. The dogs passed close enough for their bells to chime against Lila's nerves. Lila moved through her tasks like water, slipping around obstacles, not drawing attention.

When she carried a basket of linens toward the back room, she saw it: a scrap of blue cloth wedged beneath the pantry shelf, tucked so close to the shadow it could have been nothing. The same color she had seen once in the root cellar corner, the same kind that had appeared and vanished like breath.

Her pulse kicked hard.

She did not bend quickly. Quick looked like hunger. She set the basket down slowly, as if adjusting its weight, and let her fingers brush the floor. The cloth caught her skin like a secret.

She slid it into her palm and stood again, face smooth, breath even. She carried the basket out as if nothing had changed.

In the narrowest moment she could steal, behind a barrel where the cook couldn't see her hands, Lila unfolded the scrap. It was small, frayed, and there was no writing. But tied into it was a single twist of wire, thin as a hair, bent into a shape that wasn't a letter, not quite, but a sign to someone who worked metal. A hook. A question mark without the curve.

Elijah.

Her throat tightened so fast she nearly gagged. The scrap wasn't proof of safety. It wasn't a plan. It was only confirmation that he was still reaching, still trying to touch the edge of her world.

Lila wrapped it back up and hid it inside her sleeve, pressing her arm against her ribs to keep it from slipping.

All day, the cloth warmed against her skin like a coal.

By evening, Mary noticed. Mary noticed everything.

Lila said nothing until the kitchen emptied and the hearth had been banked. Then, with her back to the door, she eased the blue scrap into Mary's hand.

Mary's eyes dropped to it, then lifted. Her face didn't change much, but something in her gaze sharpened into focus.

"Where," Mary whispered.

"Pantry," Lila murmured.

Mary's lips pressed tight. "They letting it happen," she said, and it was not relief. It was recognition. "They want to see who picks it up."

Lila felt her chest go cold. "You think they watching my hands now too."

Mary's fingers closed around the cloth until her knuckles rose. "They been watching," she replied. "The question is what they watching for."

Lila swallowed. "It's from him."

Mary didn't ask who. She didn't need to. "That man," she said quietly, meaning Elijah, and her voice held something like respect buried under fear. "He still trying to make a seam."

Lila leaned in, voice barely sound. "I can't get over there. I can't even get to the line alone."

Mary's eyes flicked to the doorway again. "So you don't," she said. "You let the message move the way rumor move. Through mouths that ain't supposed to be carrying it."

Lila felt anger flare. "That's how we got the false path," she hissed, then immediately hated the heat in her voice. Heat drew notice. Heat was what Samuel fed on.

Mary's gaze held hers, hard. "That's how Samuel built his trap," Mary said, "because he controlled what moved. We don't control nothing. We only choose what risk we take."

Lila's hands curled at her sides. She could feel the friction inside her, the grinding of two needs that refused to fit cleanly together: the need to act and the need to stay alive long enough to act right.

Mary kept her voice low and steady. "Elijah going to push," she murmured. "He been pushed for days now. He going to start thinking waiting is the same as dying."

Lila thought of him being sent out of the forge, made visible. Of his hands forced to tighten collars. Of his time filled until he could not breathe. She could picture the urgency in him, the way it would harden, the way it would demand motion even in a measured dark.

"And I'm supposed to what," Lila whispered. "Catch up."

Mary's jaw tightened. "You supposed to hold him back just enough he don't run into Samuel's hands," she said. "And you supposed to be ready when holding back ain't possible no more."

Lila looked at the blue cloth again, now crumpled in Mary's fist. A piece of color in a world trained toward gray. It was not a promise. It was a signal. It meant Elijah was still aligning himself toward her, toward north, toward something beyond the plantation's math.

But alignment required distance to close, required moments to meet and agree. Those moments were gone. All that remained was guesswork, and guesswork was where traps lived.

On Boone's side, Elijah felt the same friction without knowing the cloth had reached her.

He had sent the blue scrap with a man who hauled firewood between properties under white supervision, a man with a limp and a habit of being overlooked. Elijah had pressed the twist of wire into the cloth himself, fingers working from memory, shaping what he could in the few seconds before someone called his name.

It was a small thing. Too small to be safe. But he could not keep holding everything inside his own chest. Pressure made men crack. Pressure made them speak wrong, move wrong, trust wrong.

All day, Elijah listened for any sign that it had landed. None came.

By late afternoon, a white man brought him another order. Another latch. Another chain. Another piece of iron to fix the master's world so the master could sleep well.

Elijah took it and nodded because nodding was survival. But inside him, something twisted harder.

He thought of Lila, held close to the house. He thought of Samuel's calm eyes on the edge of punishments. He thought of the false path and how quickly hope had been turned into bait.

If he waited too long, the plantation would finish subtracting every gap where a plan could be built.

If he moved too soon, he would be moving through a night full of bells and listening mouths, guided by nothing but urgency and a direction that could be poisoned again.

That was the friction: two people pulled toward the same word, north, but pressed by different weights. Elijah's need to strike while any seam still existed. Lila's need to test every seam twice, because she had watched what happened to people who believed too quickly.

Somewhere between them, Samuel tightened the system like a hand turning a screw, making sure any attempt at alignment would hurt. Making sure urgency and caution would grind against each other until they sparked, until one of them made a mistake that could be turned into proof.

That night, as the bells chimed their measured loops, Lila lay awake and held the thought of

Elijah as carefully as she would have held a lit match in wind.

She did not know if he would wait.

She did not know if she could reach him in time.

But she knew, with a certainty that felt like another kind of mark, that the plantation was no longer only watching for escape.

It was watching for the moment when two people tried to become one plan. And it was building its trap around that attempted joining, using distance and fear to turn love into miscommunication, and miscommunication into capture.

Friction wasn't just between her and Elijah.

It was the sound of the system pressing in on both sides, making alignment itself feel like a risk they might not survive.

Chapter 13

The Break Attempt

Lila stopped trusting the shape of a day.

Morning no longer meant a beginning. It meant the same loops restarting: the dogs with their bright bells, the overseer's clipboard, the mistress appearing in doorways with her quiet, weighing eyes. The hours didn't open into anything. They folded inward, tighter each time, until even sunlight felt like another kind of surveillance.

The blue scrap stayed hidden against her skin for two days, then three, tucked into the lining of her sleeve where sweat could not soak it through. She did not look at it again in daylight. Looking would have made it real, and real things drew attention. She carried it like a coal you could not show in your palm.

Mary carried it differently.

Mary didn't keep it on her. Mary kept it in her mind, turning it over the way she turned over every new tightening of the system. Lila saw it in the way

Mary watched the yard now, not with simple anger, but with a careful hunger for patterns. Mary had always had fury. Now she had strategy layered over it, and it made her more dangerous to anyone trying to control her.

The cook noticed the change too. The cook didn't name it, but her fear shifted shape. She snapped more. She kept Lila closer. She watched the mistress the way a person watched a pot that might boil over.

On the fourth evening, when the kitchen had thinned to shadows and the last of the supper work was done, Mary nudged Lila toward the back room under the pretense of fetching a bucket. It was not privacy, not truly. Nothing in the house was private. But the back room had one advantage: the walls were thicker there, and the mistress's footsteps on the upstairs floor sounded farther away.

Mary waited until the cook's back was turned.

"You been thinking," Mary murmured.

Lila kept her face neutral. "Always."

"No," Mary said. "Different. Like you holding yourself ready."

Lila swallowed. Her throat felt raw in the evenings now, as if every swallowed word left a scratch. "What you want me to say."

Mary's eyes stayed on Lila's face, searching for the smallest tremor of truth. "You want to go," Mary said.

Lila did not answer quickly. Quick answers were traps. But silence could be one too.

"I want to live," she said, finally.

Mary's mouth tightened, a line drawn hard. "Living ain't what we doing," she replied. "Not like this. Not with them watching your hands and calling it care."

From the yard, a bell chimed, thin and cheerful, and Lila felt her stomach clench at the sound. Even inside the house, the bells reached her. They reached everything.

Mary leaned closer, voice lower. "If you go," she said, "you can't go the way you want."

Lila's pulse kicked. She forced her shoulders to stay loose. "Meaning what."

Mary's gaze flicked toward the doorway, then back. "Meaning you can't go with him."

The word him did not need a name. Lila felt it anyway, felt Elijah like a pressure behind her ribs.

She kept her voice small. "You don't know what he planning."

Mary's expression didn't soften. "I know what the system planning," she said. "It want y'all together. Together makes a story. Together makes something folks can point at and say, see. Together is how they make an example that travels."

Lila's mouth went dry. "They can make an example out of one body too."

Mary nodded once, sharp. "Yes," she said. "But two bodies together makes a lesson for everybody. A lesson that says even love ain't a seam you can slip through."

The word love sat between them like contraband. Lila felt heat rise in her face and pressed it down before it could be seen.

Mary's voice stayed steady, almost cold. "They already got bells to catch the night," she continued. "They already got boys loitering by the line. They already got that overseer writing down lies like writing make it true. Samuel been feeding them scent. If two of you move the same direction, same night, they going to feel it. They going to follow it."

Lila's nails dug into her palm, crescent marks she would carry into sleep. "So, what," she whispered. "You saying we supposed to just… go alone and hope."

Mary's eyes sharpened. "I'm saying you supposed to break the shape they expecting," she said. "Don't give them a pair to hunt. Give them a mess."

Lila breathed once, slow, deliberate. A mess. Noise. Confusion. Anything that forced the system to choose where to aim itself.

And then she heard it, underneath Mary's words: the ugliness of it. The trade.

If they chased Elijah, Lila might slip. If they chased Lila, Elijah might slip. The thought made her stomach twist with something close to sickness.

Mary watched her face and didn't pretend to be gentle. "You don't like it," Mary said. "I don't like it neither. But liking ain't what save you. The system been making trades out of bodies since before you was born. All we can do is decide which trade got a chance of breaking its teeth."

Lila's throat tightened. "How do I even get out," she whispered. "I can't get to the line alone. I can't even pick up a child's cup without a white mouth snapping."

Mary exhaled through her nose. “You don’t move like you sneaking,” she said. “You move like you obeying.”

Lila stared at her, not understanding.

Mary’s voice lowered further. “You leave in daylight,” she said, and the words sounded insane until Mary shaped them into something sharper. “Not walking out the gate. But you get yourself placed somewhere that gives you a direction. A chore. A reason. You get yourself close enough to the edge of their sight, then you slip the last inch when it ain’t an inch they thought mattered.”

Lila felt fear curl in her gut. “They’ll hear me,” she said. “Bells. Dogs.”

Mary nodded. “So, you don’t go when the bells quiet,” she replied. “You go when the yard already noisy. When the house busy. When a white man drunk and talking too loud. When the dogs already moving in their loop and folks think the sound belongs to the routine.”

Routine. Use routine as cover. Lila had lived her whole life inside it. She had never been allowed to use it.

Mary reached out and tapped Lila’s sleeve lightly, not where the cloth was hidden, but close enough that Lila felt the meaning. “And he,” Mary murmured, “he go different.”

Lila's chest tightened at the thought of Elijah alone in the woods, alone under a moon that gave no comfort, alone with dogs and men and that thin, deliberate whistle that had cut the dark for the first runner. The plantation had already shown them the shape of the hunt.

"You think he'll do it," Lila asked before she could stop herself.

Mary's eyes hardened. "He already doing it in his mind," she said. "That man been getting pushed out his forge, told to fix collars, told to build locks. They choking him with work and calling it order. He going to choose a moment they don't control, even if it kill him."

Lila's breath shook once. She forced it steady again. She could not afford shaking. Shaking made sound.

Mary's voice softened by a fraction, not into kindness exactly, but into something like acknowledgment. "If you ever get word to him," Mary said, "you tell him this. You tell him you not running away from him. You running so one of you can keep running."

Lila stared at Mary, and for a moment her eyes burned. She blinked hard until the heat retreated. Tears were dangerous. Tears were proof of humanity, and humanity was something the plantation punished.

"I can't send word," Lila whispered.

Mary's gaze flicked toward the front of the house, as if she could see through walls. "Word always move," she said. "Even when it ain't supposed to. The question is who carrying it."

Lila thought of the limp man who hauled firewood between properties under white supervision, overlooked because his body already wore its own excuse. She thought of the cook, frightened into fences. She thought of Samuel, who moved information like a knife.

And she thought of the way the blue scrap had appeared where it could be found and where it could be used as bait. The pantry shelf. The shadow. The test.

Mary read her face. "Don't you put nothing in the open again," Mary warned. "Not where they expect it. If you got to answer him, you answer him in a way that don't look like an answer."

Lila swallowed. "How."

Mary's mouth tightened. "A thing missing," she said. "A tool moved. A knot tied wrong. A piece of thread left in a place only he would notice if he ever got close again."

Only he would notice. But he would not get close again. Not if the system had its way.

From the kitchen, the cook's voice rose, sharp with impatience. "Mary. Lila. Get in here."

Mary straightened first, face sliding back into its working mask. Lila followed, smoothing herself into obedience so quickly it felt like pulling a sheet over a body.

They returned to the kitchen and did what they were told. Lila kept her eyes down and her hands busy while her mind ran in circles she did not let her face reflect.

Separate paths.

The phrase did not have words yet, but it formed anyway, an ugly necessity hardening into plan. Not a plan made of maps and sure directions. A plan made of refusal and subtraction: if they could not meet, they would not wait. If they could not run together, they would run so the system could not catch both with one net.

That night, when the house finally went still, Lila lay on her pallet and listened to the bells. She counted them without meaning to. A loop close. A loop farther. A pause, then another chime as a dog shifted its weight.

In the dark, she touched the inside of her sleeve where the blue cloth hid. The wire inside it was thin and bent, a question held in metal. She pressed her fingers against it and imagined Elijah's hands shaping it quickly, his hammer mind translating feeling into form.

She answered it silently, because silence was all she had.

Not yet. Not together. Not the way they want.

Across the boundary, Elijah lay awake too.

The forge had been silent for hours, but his body still held the day's weight. The orders had not stopped. The latches, the chains, the collar leather. The constant pushing him out of his own corner, making him visible, making his movements legible.

He had tried to reach Lila with the blue scrap, and the lack of reply sat in him like a stone. Not because he doubted her, but because doubt was what the system planted when it wanted people to move wrong.

He stared into the dark and listened to the bells on his side, the bright chime that turned every step into an announcement. He imagined Carter's side sounding the same now, the same wrong cheerfulness stitched into the night.

He thought of the false path. How quickly hope had been fed and punished. How the plantation had turned a direction into bait.

If he moved with Lila, if they moved as a pair, it would be a story too perfect for men like Samuel not to sell upward. Two bodies. Two sets of footprints. Two mouths that could be forced open later.

But one body moving alone could be mistaken for something else. A man sent on an errand. A shadow miscounted. A chase that went the wrong direction long enough for another person to slip away.

The thought made him sick with its own cruelty. It felt like deciding which hand to cut off to keep the rest of you alive.

Elijah turned his head on the pallet and stared at the thin line of moonlight cutting across the floor. His jaw tightened until his teeth ached.

"We ain't getting a clean chance," he whispered to nobody, because nobody could be trusted with words anymore. "So, we do it dirty."

He pictured Lila's face, composed even under watching, eyes steady, mouth firm enough to say no to Samuel's calm poison. He pictured her trapped closer to the house now, rearranged by the mistress without being named.

He could not wait for a message. Waiting was what they were forcing on him. Waiting was the slow death the plantation offered in exchange for obedience.

He would move. But he would not move in a way the system could use once and be done.

In the dark, Elijah made the decision the way he made a bend in iron: slowly, with pressure, knowing once it held shape it would not easily be unmade.

He and Lila would not run side by side.

If freedom existed at all, it would not come as a shared sprint into the woods with their hands clasped. That was a story. Stories got branded.

It would come as two separate disappearances that refused to line up cleanly. Two paths that did not intersect until far beyond the reach of bells and dogs and Samuel's listening mouth.

Elijah exhaled once, careful, as if even breath could carry through walls.

In the distance, a bell chimed again.

The night was measured now. Watched. Patrolled.

But Elijah listened beneath it, for the thin places, the seams Mary had spoken of without ever meeting him. The moments when routine made its own blind spots. The moments when a system that believed it controlled everything grew confident enough to miss something small.

He held onto those moments the way he held onto the word north: not as comfort, but as direction.

Separate paths, he thought.

Not because he wanted distance from her.

Because distance might be the only thing that kept one of them from being dragged back as a warning at dawn.

The first time Elijah saw the man who would try to guide him, it was not in the woods.

It was in the ordinary, where danger liked to hide because everyone was trained to look for it in shadows instead.

A wagon had come up from the river road with sacks of salt and a small crate of lamp oil. White men did the talking. Enslaved men did the lifting. Elijah was sent out of the forge with the rest, made visible in the yard, made to carry weight in straight lines so nobody could claim later that he had wandered.

The driver was white, broad through the shoulders, sunburned at the neck. But it wasn't the driver who caught Elijah's eye. It was the man walking behind the wagon like he belonged to it, like he was part of the cargo the way rope and chain were part of the cargo.

He was Black, older than Elijah by a decade at least, with hair gone gray at the temples and hands that looked like they knew work. He kept his gaze low and his face arranged into nothing, but he moved with a careful steadiness that didn't look like submission. It looked like calculation.

When the wagon stopped near the shed, the driver spat and barked, "Get it down. Don't tear my sacks."

Elijah stepped close, grabbed a sack, and felt salt dust puff faintly into the air. The older man grabbed the other end at the same time.

For a moment they shared the weight.

The man didn't look up. His voice came out quiet, meant for no one beyond the sack between them. "Forge man," he said, as if naming a tool.

Elijah felt his throat tighten. He kept his face blank. "That's what they call me."

The man shifted his grip, fingers strong. "You ever hear folks talk about the long road," he murmured, and the words were plain enough to be nothing, to be dismissed as a story.

Elijah could feel the yard watching, white eyes drifting, black eyes avoiding. He kept his hands steady. "I hear talk I don't repeat."

"Good," the man said, and the slightest edge of approval flickered in his tone before vanishing. "Then you hear this and swallow it like stone. There's a place where water talk louder than dogs. Tonight, when the bells start making folks think they safe, you find the old sycamore by the creek bend. Not the big one. The split one."

Elijah's pulse hit hard. The words were too much to be said in a yard. Too direct. Too shaped like hope.

He almost didn't believe it. The false path had taught him what belief cost. Samuel had taught him that information could be bait, and bait could be shaped to look like salvation.

Elijah didn't respond. He lifted his end of the sack and moved with the routine, making his body obedient while his mind tried to decide whether this was a rope being lowered or a noose.

The older man added, still not looking at him, "If you don't come, you don't come. Don't come halfway. Halfway get you killed."

Then he stepped back as if they had never spoken, as if the only thing between them had been salt and work.

All day Elijah carried that sentence inside him and tested it against everything he saw.

He watched for Samuel. Samuel wasn't on Boone's side often, but Samuel's influence moved where Samuel didn't have to. Elijah watched the white men instead, the way their attention shifted, the way patrol patterns were discussed loud enough for the yard to hear. He listened for laughter that sounded too easy. He listened for the sudden tightening of routine that meant someone was setting a net.

He went back to the forge with a straight back and steady hands. He fixed what he was ordered to fix. He nodded when spoken to. He did not ask for anything that would create a reason to be remembered.

But the day did not pass clean.

Near late afternoon the overseer came to the forge doorway with his boots too polished for the dirt and his eyes too sharp.

"You'll be at the shed after supper," the overseer said. "Driver want his chain checked. Says it's slipping."

Elijah felt his stomach drop. A chain. A wagon. The river road. The timing was wrong in a way that made the hairs along his arms rise.

"Yes, sir," he said.

The overseer's gaze lingered on his hands, then his face. "You hear me," he added, almost casual. "After supper. Not before. Not tomorrow. Tonight."

"Yes, sir," Elijah repeated.

When the overseer left, Elijah stood in the forge and listened to the quiet ring of his own blood. It could have been nothing. It could have been simply another order. They had been filling his time for days. But the order's shape felt like a hook, the kind that caught you by the sleeve right when you tried to slip away.

He thought of Mary, though he had never spoken to her. He thought of Lila held close to the house, her world made smaller on purpose. He thought of the branded bodies at the posts, kept alive so the mark could travel.

Halfway get you killed.

Elijah worked through the rest of the afternoon with a careful emptiness, like he was saving every real thought for later. When supper ended and the yard began to dim, he went to the shed as ordered, checked the wagon chain, tightened the link. He made sure his work was clean. He made sure the driver saw him finish.

Then he returned to his cabin and waited for the bells to start.

Night came measured now. There was no longer a soft falling into darkness. There was the sound of dogs being led into loops, the bright chime of brass announcing each step, turning the yard into a clock you could hear.

Elijah lay on his pallet with his eyes open. He counted bell passes. One close. One farther. A pause that meant the handler had stopped to speak to someone. Then the bells again, moving on.

When the timing felt familiar enough to predict, Elijah sat up and moved.

He did not slip out like a thief. He walked as if sent. He carried a broken bucket handle in one hand, an excuse. If a white man saw him in the dim, he could say he was taking it to the shed for morning repair. A small lie shaped like obedience.

He kept his shoulders loose. Loose shoulders looked unafraid. Unafraid looked innocent.

The ground under his feet was hard, packed by years of bodies made to move in straight lines. Somewhere in the yard a white voice called, low, annoyed. The dogs chimed past near the stable. Elijah waited until the sound moved away, then angled himself toward the creek path that ran behind the far field.

The split sycamore stood where the land dipped, close enough to the creek that the air tasted damp. Elijah had passed that tree a hundred times under supervision, never thinking it could become a point of meaning. Now it looked different. The split in its trunk resembled a mouth held open without sound.

He stopped two paces short and listened.

Water slid over stones, steady. Night insects clicked. Far off, bells chimed and faded, like a warning that kept repeating itself until you stopped trying to imagine silence.

A shape moved near the tree line.

Elijah's muscles tightened. He didn't raise his hands. He didn't back up. Sudden motion could trigger a chase. Stillness could look like waiting, and waiting could be mistaken for trap. He held himself in between, a man standing where he had no right to stand, trying to look like he belonged to an errand.

The older man stepped into the thin light. He was not alone.

A second figure lingered farther back, half-hidden, only the pale of an eye visible. That eye watched Elijah without blinking.

The older man spoke first, voice barely above the creek. “You came.”

Elijah didn’t answer with relief. Relief was what got people killed. “You told me a place,” he said. “You didn’t tell me a name.”

The man’s mouth shifted, not quite a smile. “Names don’t help,” he murmured. “Names get carried. I’ll be called what I need to be called. Tonight I’m just the one asking if you got sense.”

Elijah’s jaw tightened. “Sense is what kept me here this long.”

“Sense is what can get you out too,” the man replied. He lifted his hand slightly, palm out, a calming gesture that still held authority. “You ain’t running tonight.”

Elijah felt anger flare, hot and sharp. It rose out of days of tightening, out of the forge being turned into a leash, out of Lila’s absence becoming a wound. “Then why bring me here.”

“Because I needed to see you,” the man said. “And because you needed to see something else besides your own wanting.”

Elijah’s fist tightened around the broken handle. “Speak plain.”

The man’s gaze held steady. “Plain is dangerous,” he said. “But you asking for it, so here. The road north ain't a line you walk. It's a set of hands you don't see until they decide you worth touching. Some hands will feed you and hide you. Some hands will sell you back because selling pays better than mercy. You understand that?"

Elijah swallowed. He understood too well. "I understand traps."

"Good," the man said softly. "Then you understand me too. I don't trust you yet."

The words landed like a slap and a gift at the same time. Elijah felt the second figure's eye still watching from the dark, measuring.

The older man continued, "I heard there's a man on these lands trading talk for favor. I heard the masters learned how to set bait with rumor. I heard folks got branded because somebody wanted to prove a lesson."

Elijah kept his face still, but his blood turned cold. Samuel's shadow stretched even here.

The man tipped his head slightly, studying Elijah. "So, I'm not going to hand you a map and send you walking like you got God in your pocket. If you move, you move when I say. If you eat, you eat what you're given. If you hide, you hide where you're told. You don't drag nobody else into your hiding place without being asked. You don't speak names. And you don't go looking for stories."

Elijah heard the warning underneath. No hero thinking. No romantic faith. No believing that wanting made you special.

"And if I say no," Elijah asked, testing, because testing was how you survived.

The older man's voice stayed calm. "Then you go back," he said. "And you live with what you live with. But you don't come again. Not to this tree. Not to this water. You don't go sniffing around like a dog that caught a scent. That get all of us killed."

The creek's sound filled the gap.

Elijah's throat burned. He thought of Lila, of her no spoken with a straight spine. He thought of Mary's warning, that the system was watching for the moment two people tried to become one plan. He thought of his own decision to do it dirty, to move without giving the plantation a clean story.

"I ain't asking you for a story," Elijah said. "I'm asking you for a way."

The older man's gaze softened by a fraction, not into kindness, but into recognition. "A way ain't a promise," he said. "It's a series of doors. Some open. Some don't. Some open and there's a man behind it with a gun smiling like he doing God's work."

Elijah's mouth went dry. He nodded once.

The man lifted his chin toward the darker figure behind him. "That one back there," he murmured, "he ain't going to step into your light. He ain't going to talk to you. He just here to make sure I don't bring a snake into the crawlspace."

Elijah felt the weight of that unseen judgment. He understood it. Trust was not a thing you offered because you wanted to believe. Trust was a thing you rationed like food.

The older man stepped closer, still keeping distance enough not to feel like threat. "Here's what you do now," he said. "You go back. You sleep. Tomorrow, you keep your face the same. You don't move different. You don't start acting like a man with secret fire, because secret fire shows through cracks."

Elijah clenched his jaw. "And when."

The man's eyes narrowed, listening toward the yard where bells chimed faintly. "When the hunting starts," he said, and his voice was so quiet it almost sounded like the creek. "Because it always starts. They don't tighten like this for nothing. Somebody going to move. And when somebody move, they'll send dogs. When the dogs go one way, another way might open for a breath."

Elijah's stomach turned. "You talking about using somebody else's chase."

"I'm talking about surviving," the man replied, and there was no apology in it. "The system already decided it'll sacrifice bodies to teach itself. We only deciding whether we'll die polite or live ugly."

Elijah stood in the damp night and felt the world tilt into a colder shape. He thought of Lila again, and his chest ached with the need to tell her: there is a hand here, but it won't hold you unless it decides you're worth saving. He couldn't send that. He couldn't warn her without exposing her.

The older man held Elijah's gaze as if reading the thought anyway. "You got somebody," he said, not a question.

Elijah didn't answer. Silence was the only protection he could offer her from here.

The man nodded once, as if the lack of answer was answer enough. "Then you be smart enough not to turn love into a lantern," he murmured. "Lanterns get shot at. You keep it covered."

A bell chimed closer, then faded again.

The older man stepped back toward the dark. "Go," he said. "And remember. If you see me again, you don't see me because you went looking.

You see me because I came to find you. That's the only way this works."

Elijah held still a heartbeat longer, then turned and walked back the way he had come, bucket handle in his hand, shoulders loose, face empty.

Behind him, the creek kept talking to itself, steady and indifferent.

And in front of him, the plantation waited with its bells and dogs and listening mouths, tightening its grip as if it already knew that somewhere near a split sycamore, a cautious hand had offered something that was not hope, not yet, but the shape of a door that might open only when the system was distracted by its own hunger.

Elijah did not sleep.

He lay on his pallet with his hands folded behind his head, eyes open to the dark, listening to the plantation's new language. The bells stitched their thin chime through the night in measured loops. A handler's boots scuffed and paused and scuffed again. Somewhere a white man muttered, annoyed, and the dogs answered with a low huff that made the bells tremble against brass.

Secret fire shows through cracks, the older man had warned.

Elijah practiced emptiness the way he practiced steady blows with a hammer. He let his breathing settle. He let his body go still without going rigid. He pictured the forge as it looked in daylight, tools hung in their places, nothing out of order, nothing missing that would call attention. He pictured his own face when a white man spoke to him: eyes down enough to look respectful, not so far down it looked sullen; mouth neutral; shoulders loose.

When morning came, it came like it always did now: not as a beginning, but as the same tightening made visible.

He went to work. He took orders. He fixed what was put in his hands. He answered "yes, sir" to voices that did not deserve it and kept his mind quiet behind his eyes. He did not ask after the wagon. He did not look for the older man. He did not linger near the creek path.

But he listened, because listening was how you survived long enough to choose a moment.

By midmorning, the yard carried a different kind of noise. White voices moved in clusters. The overseer crossed open ground with purpose, his coat flaring behind him, and the men near the stable tightened the dogs' leads until leather creaked. A boy ran toward the big house and returned with a paper folded in his fist like it was money.

Elijah's hands were on a length of iron when the first shout carried from the field line.

"He's gone."

The words weren't meant for the enslaved to hear, and that was how Elijah knew they were true. White men spoke differently when they believed their own kind were the only ones listening. The shout had no performance in it. It was sharp with surprise, and surprise was the one thing the plantation hated most.

Another voice barked back, closer. "Who."

A pause, then, "Ben. The one from the lower row."

Elijah kept his hammer moving. He let the ring of iron swallow his attention the way it always did. He did not lift his head. He did not change his rhythm. But inside him, something went cold and precise.

The hunting starts.

Ben. Elijah knew Ben in the way you knew most men here: by the shape of his walk, by the slowness in his left shoulder, by the fact that his eyes were always a little too bright, like he held a story inside his mouth and had to keep it from spilling. Elijah had never spoken to him beyond the necessary. Keeping distance was its own kind of protection. Still, Ben's name landing in the air felt like a stone dropped into water.

White men moved fast now, boots pounding, voices overlapping.

"Get the dogs."

"Which way."

"Check the creek."

"Don't let him double back."

The bells began to chime hard, no longer a routine loop but a quick, jangling music as the dogs strained and lunged, excited by the sudden purpose. The handler cursed. A chain snapped taut. The sound of it was ugly and familiar.

Elijah kept his face empty and worked.

A white man appeared at the forge doorway, breath up, eyes scanning. "You," he snapped, pointing at Elijah like selecting a tool. "You seen Ben this morning."

Elijah's stomach tightened, but his voice stayed flat. "No, sir."

The man's gaze narrowed. "You sure."

"Yes, sir. I been here."

The white man looked past him into the forge as if expecting to find a hiding place inside heat and iron. Then he spat and moved on, already forgetting Elijah because his attention had found a bigger hunger.

Elijah understood another part of it then. The plantation did not only tighten. It also narrowed its own focus when it believed it had a single scent. That was the seam. Not freedom, not safety, but a thin place where the system's eyes went one direction hard enough to miss something else moving in the opposite.

He waited.

Waiting was torture now because it was not passive. It was active restraint, a man holding his own muscles back while the world surged around him. He counted the passing of time by sound: the bells racing away toward the creek; the echo of dogs' barking fading and returning; the sudden hush that fell when white men listened for something they could not see.

By noon, Boone's yard felt like a stirred nest. Men on horseback came through, faces tight. A hound bayed near the far fence and the bells shook against its throat. The master's voice carried from the porch, calm like always, which meant anger was being kept for later.

Elijah kept working until he was dismissed for the midday meal, then he ate quickly, head down, chewing without tasting. He did not look for reactions in the other enslaved faces. Looking was dangerous. Looking could be read as interest, and interest could be translated into suspicion. But he could feel the fear moving through the quarters like heat trapped under a roof. Ben had run. That meant punishment was coming for someone, even if Ben never came back.

And it meant the plantation's attention was anchored to a chase.

That afternoon, the older man found him without appearing to.

Elijah was carrying a repaired hinge toward the smokehouse when he saw a figure near the edge of the yard by a stack of split wood. A wagon hand, head down, shoulders arranged into ordinary labor. For a moment it could have been anyone. Then the man lifted one piece of wood, shifted it, and set it down again in a motion that made no sense for work.

A signal. Not words. Not a name. A small wrongness placed on purpose.

Elijah did not change his pace. He walked past the stack as if he had no choice but to pass it.

The older man's voice came low, threaded through the sound of wood and yard noise. "Tonight," he said, as if speaking about weather. "Not moonrise. Later. When they get tired."

Elijah kept his gaze forward. "Where."

"Same water," the man murmured. "But not the tree. Don't go to the tree. Tree is where they think a man would go if he was looking for a story. You go past the split. You go where the bank drops and the reeds hide your feet."

Elijah's throat went tight. "And if they catch Ben."

"They already caught him," the older man said, and there was no softness in it. Only fact. "They just don't know they did yet."

Elijah felt the blood leave his face and forced his expression to stay neutral. The older man's certainty was a knife. It cut away the last illusion that any runner had a fair chance here.

The older man added, "Don't carry nothing you can't lose. Don't carry no paper. Don't carry no name. Carry hunger and carry quiet. When you hear owls, don't answer. When you hear a man calling like he know you, don't turn. You hear me."

Elijah's jaw tightened. "Yes."

"Good," the older man murmured, and went back to moving wood as if he had never spoken.

Elijah walked on, hinge in his hand, and felt the day tilt into its final shape.

That evening, on Carter's side, Lila felt the same shift without anyone explaining it to her.

The house had been tense for days, the mistress's quiet watching and the cook's fear making every room feel smaller than its walls. But now there was new movement in the air, like news traveling without permission. A white man rode up the drive, spoke quickly to Mr. Carter on the porch, and rode away again without even drinking the water offered to him. The mistress's face tightened, then smoothed. She looked toward the yard as if the yard itself had misbehaved.

Lila stood at the kitchen table with her hands in dough. Mary was cutting vegetables, knife moving with controlled speed. The cook hovered near the door, listening too hard.

A dog's bells chimed close, then farther, then close again. The pattern was wrong, hurried. A handler's voice snapped, "Keep them back. Keep them steady."

Mary's eyes flicked up, then down, and her mouth moved barely at all when she spoke. "Somebody ran," she murmured.

Lila's fingers tightened in the dough. "How you know."

Mary's knife didn't stop. "Because the yard sound like it," she said. "White folks don't move that quick unless they chasing."

The cook made a small sound in her throat and crossed herself without meaning to. Then she caught herself and looked toward the door as if embarrassed by her own humanity.

Lila felt her pulse kick. Fear rose, immediate and sharp, because a chase meant dogs. Dogs meant bells. Bells meant the night would be louder than it already was. And a chase meant the plantation's hunger would be fed, satisfied, and then redirected toward anyone else it wanted to punish.

Mary leaned closer as if reaching for a bowl, her voice low enough that it barely existed. "This your noise," she murmured to Lila. "This the mess. You said you wanted to live."

Lila swallowed. Her throat was dry. "I can't just walk out."

Mary's eyes stayed on the cutting board. "You don't walk out," she whispered. "You get yourself sent."

Lila's mind moved fast now, assembling scraps the way she assembled cloth into clean folds. Sent where. Sent how. The mistress didn't allow errands now. The cook kept her close. The overseer watched the yard. But a chase changed the rules. A chase made white folks improvise, and improvisation created cracks.

The cook turned back into the room, face pinched. "Mistress want the lanterns checked," she said, voice sharp with the need to sound useful. "She say we might have to stay up."

Lanterns. Lila felt the word land with weight. Light meant searching. Searching meant a night full of moving feet and distracted eyes. A night when a woman carrying a lantern toward the back line might not be questioned the way she would be questioned on a quiet night.

Mary glanced at Lila once, fast, and Lila understood. Not a plan drawn on paper. A timed opening.

Lila kept her face smooth and said, "I can do it, cook."

The cook hesitated, eyes darting toward the hallway that led to the front of the house, toward the mistress's quiet presence. Then she nodded once, quick, like she was swatting a fly. "Fine," she said. "But you don't go nowhere you ain't told. You hear me."

"Yes," Lila replied, and did not let her face show what the word meant inside her.

On Boone's side, as dusk came down, Elijah moved through his tasks with the same careful emptiness. He waited until the yard's noise shifted from frantic to tired. The hunt's first hunger had burned itself out into irritation. White men cursed more. They listened less. They began to believe the runner was already caught, or already dead, or already a lesson they could deliver tomorrow.

That was when exhaustion made them sloppy.

When the bells began their evening loop again, Elijah watched the timing the way he watched heat in a forge. Too soon and the metal fought you. Too late and it cooled into stubbornness. You struck when it was ready.

He did not go to the split sycamore.

He went the long way, past the back shed, carrying a small bundle of cloth in his hand that looked like rags for cleaning. Not food. Not tools. Nothing that would mark him as a man leaving. He had a piece of stale cornbread hidden in his mouth like a plug, something to swallow later when he needed to keep from shaking with hunger.

He walked as if sent.

At the far edge of the field, where reeds thickened near the creek bank, he stopped long enough to listen. The water talked low. The night insects clicked. Far behind him, bells chimed in a

steady, bored rhythm now, the sound of men convincing themselves the world was under control again.

A shadow moved near the reeds.

The older man did not step into light. He did not offer a hand. He only murmured, "Now," and the word felt like a door opening just wide enough for a body to slip through.

Elijah stepped into the reeds and let the creek swallow his footsteps.

Behind him, Boone's plantation kept ringing its bells, bright and wrong, measuring a night it believed it owned.

And on Carter's side, Lila lifted a lantern from its hook, felt its weight settle into her hands, and walked toward the back of the house like a woman sent to do what she was told.

Her face was calm. Her spine was straight. Her steps were measured.

It was the only way to move in a world that punished panic.

It was the only way to disappear on time.

Chapter 14

The Hunt

The reeds cut at Elijah's shins as soon as he stepped into them, thin blades slick with creek damp that clung to his trousers and tried to hold him in place. The water smelled like mud and rot and something clean underneath, a cold current that didn't care what men did on either bank. Behind him, Boone's yard still existed as sound: a bell's thin chime somewhere far back, a dog's bored huff, a handler's boots scuffing a familiar loop as if routine could be nailed down and owned.

The older man stayed low, not crouching like a frightened animal but moving with the economy of someone who had learned which motions cost you. He didn't speak again. He didn't have to. His silence wasn't emptiness; it was instruction.

Elijah followed, placing his feet where the reeds grew thickest, letting the creek's wet ground swallow the small betrayals of a step. The water took his weight and gave it back wrong, unsteady, as if even the earth here refused to promise safety.

He kept his shoulders loose. He kept his breath quiet. He tried to keep his mind from racing ahead into pictures of dogs fanning out through these same reeds, bells chiming bright like laughter.

The older man angled them toward the bank's drop, where the creek widened for a stretch and stones broke the surface in hunched, dark backs. They moved into shallower water, cold seeping through Elijah's shoes until his toes went numb. He welcomed the numbness because it gave his body something to focus on besides panic.

A low whistle floated from far off, not the sharp plantation whistle that cut the dark like a blade, but an owl's call bending through the trees. Elijah's muscles tightened anyway. Sound could be anything in the night. Sound could be men pretending to be animals. Sound could be bait.

The older man lifted a hand without turning his head, a brief stop. He listened with a stillness so complete Elijah wondered if his heart had learned to beat quieter too. After a moment, the hand lowered. They kept moving.

Elijah realized then that the unknown was not only the woods. It was the rules. On the plantation, danger had a routine. It had bells. It had patrol loops. It had daylight cruelty and night cruelty, predictable in their own way. Out here, the danger did not announce itself. It waited to be mistaken for wind.

They crossed the creek where the water tugged harder, then climbed a shallow bank into brush that grabbed at Elijah's shirt. Branches snapped softly underfoot and sounded too loud in his own head. He expected, with every small crack, a shout behind him. He expected the sudden swell of dogs surging forward with that eager hatred that was trained into them.

But the night stayed wide.

The older man led him through a stand of trees where the trunks grew close enough to make a corridor. Here, the air changed. It held the bitter scent of pine and the sweeter smell of crushed leaves, and beneath it all the faint, sour trace of smoke carried from someone's distant fire.

Elijah's stomach twisted at the smell. Smoke meant people. People meant doors. Doors meant hands you couldn't see until they decided what you were worth.

The older man finally spoke, barely moving his mouth. "You keep your head down when you see light," he murmured.

Elijah swallowed. His mouth was dry and tasted like cornbread he hadn't swallowed yet. "Where we going."

"Not north yet," the man said, and the bluntness of it landed hard. "Just away."

Away. It wasn't the word that lived in Elijah's chest. North was the word. North was the thing whispered like prayer and rumor, the direction that was supposed to mean a world without brands. But away was truer in the moment. Away was what his body could understand: distance from Boone's yard, distance from the forge, distance from men who could point and say, you, and make his whole life fold into a post at dawn.

They moved until the ground softened into a low hollow. The trees opened slightly, and through them Elijah saw a shape that might have been a shed or might have been a lean-to built with the kind of care that tried not to look like care. It was tucked into the dark as if ashamed to be a structure at all.

A faint light pulsed once, then was covered.

Elijah froze. His breath caught before he could stop it.

The older man did not touch him. He simply murmured, "Don't stare. Staring makes you remembered."

A figure stepped out from the shadows beside the structure, so close to the dark that Elijah couldn't tell where cloth ended and night began.

When the person moved, the outline suggested a woman's skirt, the hem damp with dew.

She didn't greet them. She didn't ask Elijah's name. She didn't ask anything that would make a story.

Her voice came low and tight, as if every word hurt to give away. "You late."

The older man's tone stayed even. "The yard was stirred."

"Yards always stirred," she replied. "They just pretending to notice tonight."

Elijah felt his pulse thudding in his throat. He waited for the older man to offer him up like proof, to say who he was, what plantation he'd come from, what skills he carried. But the older man only said, "He's one. That's enough."

The woman's gaze slid to Elijah. In the dim, her eyes caught the thin light and reflected it back like an animal's. Not fear. Calculation.

"You can't stay," she said.

"I ain't asking to," Elijah managed, his voice rough.

She looked past him into the trees. "You were followed?"

The older man answered before Elijah could. “No.”

“No didn’t mean safe. It meant not yet.

The woman stepped closer, and Elijah caught the faint smell of lard and soap on her, the scent of a life lived close to fire and work. Her hand moved, and he flinched before he could help it, but she wasn’t reaching for him. She lifted a tin cup from beside the door and held it out.

“Drink,” she said. “Small.”

Elijah took the cup with fingers that didn’t feel like his. The water inside tasted like iron and leaves, but it was wet, and wet was mercy. He forced himself to drink slowly, as instructed, as if even thirst could make you reckless.

The woman watched him swallow, then said, “You got a mark on you?”

Elijah’s stomach turned. He thought of the branded backs on Boone’s side, the smell of burned flesh in morning air. He shook his head once.

“Good,” she said, and it didn’t sound like kindness. It sounded like a door clicking into a different position. “Marked men get hunted harder. They want their lesson back.”

A rustle moved in the brush beyond the lean-to. Elijah's shoulders tensed again.

Another figure emerged, this one a man, tall, hat brim low. He stayed just outside the faint light, the way the second watcher by the sycamore had stayed back. Elijah couldn't see his face clearly. That seemed intentional.

The tall man's voice came quietly, with a flatness that made it hard to read. "They took Ben."

Elijah felt something drop in his gut, as if his body had been expecting that sentence and still wasn't ready for it. The older man didn't react outwardly, but his jaw tightened once, quick as a blink.

The woman's mouth pressed into a line. "How you know."

"Dogs turned back," the tall man said. "Men turned mean. That's how."

Elijah pictured Ben's bright eyes. He pictured the moment in the yard when the shout had carried. He had used that chase. He had let it open a seam for him. The knowledge sat ugly in his chest, heavy as a shackle.

The older man leaned slightly toward Elijah, close enough for the words to land and not travel.

"You don't carry that," he murmured. "Not now. It'll slow you."

Elijah wanted to argue. He wanted to say a man should carry what he owes. But arguing was a luxury, and the night was not generous.

The woman glanced at the sky through the trees, measuring time by darkness. "You leave again in a minute," she said. "Not long enough to warm this place with your shape."

Elijah's hands tightened on the cup. "Where do I go."

The tall man spoke this time. "Through," he said, and the word made no sense until he added, "Through what you don't know. That's the only way. You follow what he tells you. You don't make your own path because you think you got sense. Sense gets loud."

Elijah looked at the older man, searching his face for some promise that wasn't there. The older man gave him none. His eyes held only the same truth he'd offered at the creek: doors, not guarantees.

On Carter's side, Lila moved with her lantern held steady, the flame inside it making the glass glow soft and gold. The house behind her was a block of dark with a few lit windows, as if it was watching through eyelids that never fully closed.

The yard felt different tonight, stirred by news carried on white tongues and tightened into commands.

She had been sent to check the lanterns, and that meant she belonged outside for a reason. Belonging was the only cover she could wear.

The dogs' bells chimed too close, then veered away, the handler snapping at them as if they were children. Somewhere near the front, Mr. Carter's voice rose and fell, clipped with irritation.

Lila kept her face calm and her steps measured. She did not hurry. Hurrying was confession.

She walked toward the back line where the outbuildings sat in deeper shadow, the places the mistress didn't like to look at unless something had already gone wrong. The lantern light wobbled with each step, and she forced her hand steadier, knowing that even a trembling flame could draw a glance.

Mary's words pressed in her mind. You get yourself close enough to the edge of their sight, then you slip the last inch when it ain't an inch they thought mattered.

The unknown for Lila was shaped differently than it was for Elijah. It was not miles of woods. It was the space just beyond the familiar: the ditch behind the smokehouse, the gap between fence and tree line, the place where the yard's rules thinned and the night's rules began.

She reached the back corner where a stack of split wood leaned against the side of an outbuilding. The shadow there was thick enough to swallow a body for a moment. She paused as if inspecting a lantern hook, lifting it, letting it clang softly like an honest mistake.

No voice snapped at her.

No white footstep turned sharp in her direction.

The dogs chimed again, farther now.

Lila took one breath, then another, and stepped into the deeper shadow, letting the lantern's light angle away from her face so it didn't betray her eyes. The flame made her hands visible, and she hated that visibility, but she needed the light for one more minute, to walk as if she still belonged to the task.

Then she reached the edge of the outbuilding, and with the smallest shift, she lowered the lantern into the grass behind the woodpile, tucking it where the glow would be hidden.

She stood empty-handed for a heartbeat, feeling the night rush in to replace the light.

Her heart pounded so hard she was certain it must be audible. She pressed a hand to her stomach, not to quiet it, but to remind herself she was still inside her own body.

In the distance, a shout carried from Boone's side, faint but sharp enough to turn her blood cold even across land and fences. Another voice answered. She couldn't make out the words, but the tone was the same as the day the branding happened: the plantation's voice when it felt itself losing something.

The hunt had begun somewhere, and hunts traveled.

Lila stepped forward into the dark beyond the outbuilding, toward the tree line that waited like an open mouth.

Behind her, the house stood with its windows half-lit, and the yard's bells kept chiming their bright, wrong rhythm, as if daring her to believe she could move without being counted.

Ahead of her, there was no bell, no loop, no routine.

Only the unknown, wide and unmeasured.

And somewhere in that same unmeasured dark, Elijah was being pushed from one door to the next, told without comfort and without ceremony that the only way out was through what he couldn't name, through hands that might hold him or hand him back, through a night that did not care about north or hope, only about whether a body could keep moving without turning its fear into sound.

They did not linger long enough for the night to learn their shapes.

The woman took the tin cup from Elijah's hands and set it back where it belonged, as if even objects could be questioned later. She opened the lean-to door only a sliver and looked out into the trees, listening more than seeing. The tall man shifted his weight in the dark and made no sound at all, like he had practiced disappearing while still standing upright.

The older man waited until the bells from the plantation were distant enough to feel like memory.

"Come," he murmured.

Elijah followed, stepping back into brush that grabbed at his sleeves and tried to pull him into stillness. Behind them, the woman's faint light vanished as if the lean-to had swallowed it whole. The night turned black again, thick and close. Elijah kept wanting to look over his shoulder, kept feeling the itch of being counted, but he didn't. Staring made you remembered. Staring made you look like a man carrying something he couldn't afford to lose.

They moved in a broken line, never straight long enough to become a trail you could trust. The older man's feet found places that didn't crack, places where leaves were already disturbed by deer or fox, places where the ground was damp enough to hold sound down. Elijah tried to match him, tried to make his own body small without making it tense. Tension turned into mistakes. Mistakes turned into noise.

After a time, the older man slowed and lifted his hand again. Not a stop this time. A warning.

Elijah listened.

At first there was only the ordinary night. Then he heard it: a second set of footsteps far off, careful but not careful enough. Someone moving with the wrong kind of patience. The older man angled them toward a thicker stand of trees and crouched behind a fallen log. Elijah lowered himself beside him and felt cold rot seep through his trousers.

The footsteps passed at a distance. A pause. Then the faint scrape of a boot turning, as if the person had stopped to taste the air with their whole body.

The older man's mouth stayed close to Elijah's ear. "Don't breathe loud," he whispered.

Elijah held his breath until his chest ached.

The footsteps moved on.

Only when the sound was gone did Elijah let himself exhale, slow through his nose. He expected the older man to say something about patrols, about white men widening their net. But the older man's face was turned toward the direction the footsteps had gone, and his eyes narrowed in a way that felt different than fear.

"That ain't a dog handler," the older man murmured. "That's a man."

Elijah swallowed, throat tight. "One of yours?"

The older man didn't answer right away, which was an answer in itself.

They moved again, faster now, using the night like a cloth pulled up to cover their mouths. Elijah's mind tried to chase the meaning. If there was a man moving out here without bells, without barking, without white voices calling orders, then there was somebody else hunting too. Somebody hunting with intent.

He thought of Samuel, calm as a closed door, telling the system where to look. Samuel wasn't here in body. Samuel didn't need to be. He had turned information into legs that walked.

The older man led them toward a low structure crouched in a shallow dip, half-hidden by brush. It might have been an old smoke shed long abandoned, or a hunter's shelter. It had a roof that sagged in the middle like an old back, and the door hung crooked on its hinges. No light showed inside.

Elijah felt his heartbeat jump. A place like that could be shelter. A place like that could be where people disappeared.

The older man did not go straight to the door. He circled once, slow, and pressed his palm against the wall as if reading a language in the wood. Then he leaned close to the gap by the hinge and listened.

A small sound came from within. Not speech. A shift of weight. The softest cough caught and swallowed.

Elijah's muscles tightened.

The older man spoke, barely louder than thought. "Open."

For a moment nothing happened. Then the door moved, the gap widening just enough to reveal a sliver of face. A man's eye, wide and wet in the dark.

The older man's tone stayed even. "You alone?"

The eye blinked hard. “Yes,” the man whispered.

The older man stepped closer, but not all the way. “You got the bread?”

A pause, then a shaky, “Yes.”

Elijah’s stomach turned. He hadn’t been promised bread. He hadn’t been promised anything. But he’d heard enough to know what this was supposed to be: a handoff, a small mercy, something that kept a body moving.

The door opened wider. The man inside was younger than Elijah, but worn, his cheeks hollowed by hunger and fear. He held a cloth bundle to his chest like a baby.

Elijah tried to read him the way he read metal, watching for weakness, for stress, for the place something might crack. The man’s hands trembled too much. Trembling could be fear. Trembling could be guilt.

The older man took the bundle, loosened it, and checked what was inside with quick fingers. Cornbread, wrapped tight. A small piece of salted pork. A twist of cloth that might have been for binding a cut. No note. No name.

“Good,” the older man murmured.

The younger man's gaze slid to Elijah, then away. He swallowed hard enough for Elijah to hear it. "You moving him far?"

"As far as God allow," the older man said, and the words sounded like routine, but Elijah felt the older man's attention sharpen, waiting for something.

The younger man nodded too fast. "I ain't seen nothing," he whispered. "Ain't heard nothing. I just… I just been waiting like you said."

Waiting looks like planning, Lila had been warned. Elijah's mouth went dry.

The older man's voice didn't change. "You been waiting long?"

The man hesitated. The hesitation was small, but in the dark small things grew teeth. "Not long," he said. "Not… not too long."

The older man tipped his head slightly, studying. "Then why your hands shaking like you ran here."

The younger man's face tightened. His eyes darted to the trees. "Because," he whispered, "because I heard dogs."

"You heard dogs out here?" the older man asked.

The younger man nodded quickly. “Back that way. Not close. But I heard them.”

Elijah felt the older man go still beside him. A man’s body could speak without words. The older man’s stillness said he didn’t believe this.

Elijah’s own mind flashed to the footsteps they had heard. A man, not a handler. A man moving with care. A man who could carry news back to others.

The younger man’s throat worked. “I don’t want trouble,” he whispered. “I don’t want no part of it.”

The older man’s voice stayed low and calm, as if calm could keep the world from hearing. “Then you shouldn’t have opened your door.”

The younger man flinched. “You told me—”

“I told you a lot of things,” the older man interrupted softly. “And you did what you could with them. That’s all it is.”

Elijah’s spine prickled. Something in the older man’s tone had shifted. Not anger. Assessment. Like he was measuring how much time they had left before the night turned on them.

The younger man licked his lips. “I ain’t say nothing,” he insisted, too fast, too desperate.

Elijah felt it then, a quiet certainty settling into his stomach like cold water: the man had said something. Maybe not with his mouth. Maybe with his movement. Running to this shed instead of walking. Leaving a trail of panic. Drawing attention by trying to hide it.

The older man stepped back from the doorway. "Close it," he said.

The younger man hesitated, eyes pleading now, and Elijah saw the truth in that look. Not villainy. Not cruelty. Just the ugliest kind of fear: the kind that made a person choose themselves even when the choice killed someone else.

"You going to leave me?" the younger man whispered.

The older man's voice stayed flat. "You already left yourself," he replied.

The door swung shut with a soft, shaking click.

Elijah stared at the closed door, at the dark seam where light could have leaked and didn't. "He going to bring them," Elijah murmured.

The older man didn't deny it. "Maybe he already did," he said.

Elijah's pulse hammered. "Then why come here."

“Because I had to know,” the older man replied. “Because sometimes the betrayal ain’t the one you can name. Sometimes it’s the one you fed last week. Sometimes it’s the one you told, just wait.”

Elijah tasted bile. Ben’s name surfaced in his mind again, bright eyes, gone body. The system had taught everyone to measure mercy against survival until mercy became a kind of debt nobody could afford.

The older man gripped Elijah’s sleeve and pulled him away from the shed, not rough, but urgent. “Move,” he whispered. “No running.”

They slid back into the trees, keeping their bodies low where brush thickened. Elijah clutched the food bundle against his ribs and felt its weight like proof of how close he was to being seen. Behind them the night stayed quiet for a few breaths, and Elijah almost wondered if he’d misread it, if fear had made a betrayal out of nothing.

Then he heard it.

A sound that didn’t belong to owls or wind.

A single sharp whistle, distant but deliberate, cutting through the dark like a blade.

Elijah’s blood went cold.

The older man froze, eyes lifted, listening.

The whistle came again, answered by something farther off. Not a human voice. A dog, low and eager, then another. The bells were not on them out here, but the dogs' language carried anyway, the baying that meant scent had been offered and taken.

Elijah's stomach turned. "They got a line," he whispered.

The older man's jaw tightened. "They got help," he said, and there was no surprise in it, only bitter recognition.

They moved faster, still not running, because running made noise and noise made direction. The older man led Elijah downhill toward water again, toward the place where sound could be drowned and footprints could be erased. Elijah followed, legs trembling now despite his effort to keep them steady.

In his mind he saw the younger man's shaking hands, the too-fast nod, the eyes darting to the trees. A man trapped in his own fear, choosing the quickest escape from consequence by pushing it onto someone else.

And on Carter's side, Lila moved through her own dark with the same understanding blooming in her chest: the unknown was full of people, and people were the most dangerous part of it.

She had left the lantern behind the woodpile, and the darkness swallowed her so completely she felt for a moment like she had become nothing. She crept along the fence line where weeds grew thick, keeping her hands out in front of her just enough to catch herself if the ground dropped away. Her breath was quiet, but her heart wouldn't stop pounding, as if it was trying to call the dogs itself.

A shadow shifted ahead.

Lila stopped so abruptly her knees almost buckled. She held still until her muscles burned.

The shadow moved again, and a voice came low, female, close enough to make Lila's skin crawl. "Girl," the voice whispered, urgent. "You lost?"

Lila didn't answer. Answering made you real.

The woman stepped closer, just enough for Lila to see the faint edge of her face, the pale of her eyes. "You from Carter's," she murmured. "I know you. I seen you by the house. Come on. You can't be out here. They hunting. They going to blame you for it."

The words sounded like concern. They sounded like a hand offered in the dark.

Lila felt fear rise, but underneath it something colder. The woman had named too much. Carter's.

House. Hunting. Blame. A stranger who knew where Lila belonged also knew where to return her.

Lila took a slow step back. The woman reached out, not grabbing, just reaching like she wanted to guide Lila by the elbow, like it was help.

Lila jerked away.

The woman's voice tightened. "Don't be foolish," she hissed. "You want to live, don't you?"

Lila's throat went dry. The exact words Mary had used. You said you wanted to live.

It could have been coincidence. It could have been common sense. But Lila had learned what a system sounded like when it spoke through someone else's mouth.

She backed deeper into shadow, keeping her face turned down so her fear didn't shine. "Go on," she whispered, making her voice small, harmless. "I'm coming."

The woman paused, suspicion flickering. "Then come."

Lila moved one step, then another, but angled her body wrong on purpose, as if clumsy, as if confused. She let her foot catch on a root and made a soft sound, a little gasp, performing helplessness.

The woman surged forward, impatient now, and in that impatience, Lila heard it: not care, not fear for Lila's safety, but the hungry need to keep control of the moment.

Lila pivoted and slipped sideways through thicker brush, letting branches rake her arms. She didn't run. Not yet. She disappeared the way she'd learned to disappear inside the house: by making herself smaller than what people expected to chase.

Behind her the woman cursed under her breath, not like someone worried, but like someone whose hand had missed its grip.

Then, faint and far, Lila heard it: a whistle, sharp and deliberate, cutting the night open.

The same sound the first runner had heard in the woods under a moon that gave no comfort.

Lila's stomach dropped. She moved faster, finally, no longer caring about the quiet snap of twigs, because she understood now what Elijah was learning too, somewhere beyond fences and fields.

The betrayal didn't always come as a man in a white coat with a gun.

Sometimes it came as a trembling hand opening a door at the wrong time.

Sometimes it came as a familiar voice pretending to offer help.

Sometimes it came as a whisper in the dark that knew your name without earning it.

And once the whistle sounded, the shadows stopped being empty.

They became full of intent.

The whistle did not belong to the woods.

It belonged to men who wanted the woods to behave.

Elijah and the older man dropped low and kept moving, not running, not yet. The older man kept them near water, where mud held footprints poorly and sound didn't carry clean. The creek ran close again, a black strip between banks, and the air above it felt colder, as if the night had a spine here.

Behind them, voices rose and fell in quick bursts, not loud enough to be sure of words, but shaped like orders. A dog bayed and another answered, and the answering wasn't random. It was timed, like someone was calling the sound forward in pieces.

The older man glanced back once, quick as a blink, and Elijah caught the hard set of his jaw.

"They shouldn't be this close," Elijah whispered.

The older man didn't look at him. "They ain't following," he murmured. "They driving."

Elijah's stomach tightened. Driving meant they weren't just chasing a scent. Driving meant men were placed ahead, waiting to turn a runner like you turned cattle with fire and noise. Driving meant somebody knew where a body would try to go when it got scared.

They slipped into the creek again, water up to Elijah's calves, cold biting through cloth. The older man moved upstream a short distance, then angled toward reeds that stood thick as a wall. Elijah followed, clutching the food bundle against his ribs. He could hear his own breath, too loud in his head, too alive.

Another whistle cut the night, closer now. Not the same pitch as the first. A second voice answering the first, as if the men had agreed on a language that didn't need words.

A light bloomed on the far bank, then covered. Another light, farther down, blinked twice in quick succession.

The older man stopped so sharply Elijah nearly bumped him. He lifted his hand, palm out, and held it there as if he could press the night back into place.

Elijah listened.

Footsteps on dry ground, not near enough to see, but near enough to feel. A man clearing his throat. Leather creaking. The soft clink of metal.

Not bells. Not dogs.

Men waiting.

Elijah's mouth went dry. "How they know," he breathed.

The older man's answer was quiet and bitter. "Because somebody told them what a desperate man would do."

Elijah thought of the split sycamore, the earlier instructions, the way the older man had told him not to go to the tree tonight, as if the tree had already become a thought other people might predict. Elijah thought of the shed door closing with its shaking click, the younger man's trembling hands, the fear in his eyes that wasn't cruelty but could still kill.

Fear could sell you without meaning to.

The older man leaned close enough that Elijah could smell creek water and sweat on him. "We not going north," he whispered. "We going nowhere. We going through."

"Through what," Elijah asked, and hated how small his voice sounded.

The older man didn't answer with direction. He answered with a truth that made Elijah's blood cold. "Through them."

The dog bayed again, closer. Then, as if a rope had been jerked, it stopped. Silence fell for half a breath, the kind of silence that meant men were listening to see if fear would make you move wrong.

The older man shifted, gathering himself.

Elijah felt it before he saw it: the precision. The way sound and light and silence were being used like tools, the same way Elijah used heat and pressure and timing at the forge. The night wasn't wild. It was being worked.

The older man angled them toward the reed wall and pushed in, not hard enough to make thrashing noise, but firm, creating a narrow seam. Elijah slid after him, reeds scraping his face and arms. The ground beneath was slick, half mud and half root. Each step tried to take his balance and give it back wrong.

They moved ten paces, maybe twelve, deeper into the reeds until the creek was a hiss behind them. The older man stopped and listened again.

Elijah heard nothing.

That was worse.

The older ma n's shoulders tightened. He turned his head slightly, eyes narrowing at something Elijah couldn't see. "They quieting the dogs," he murmured. "They want you to think you got away so you'll step out."

Elijah's heart hammered. "We stay."

"We can't," the older man said.

And then, without warning, a voice rose from the dark to their left, close enough to make Elijah flinch as if struck.

"Hold."

The word was spoken softly, not shouted, as if the man saying it already knew he'd be obeyed.

Another lantern flared, not behind them, but ahead, revealing a strip of open ground beyond the reeds. The light lasted only a moment, but it was enough to show shapes: two white men standing with rifles held low, not aimed yet, confident. A third man behind them with a coil of rope in his hands. And off to the side, half hidden, a dog handler with two hounds held tight, their bodies vibrating with contained hunger.

The lantern dipped. Darkness returned, but the knowledge didn't leave. The trap had been there already, waiting for the reeds to spit them out.

Elijah's throat tightened. "They already placed."

The older man's mouth flattened. "Yes," he said. "That's what I been telling you."

Another whistle sounded, very close now, and it wasn't answered by dogs. It was answered by a man's low laugh, the kind that carried satisfaction.

Elijah's mind raced. If he went back, there were men behind. If he went forward, there were men ahead. If he stayed, they would close in slowly, let panic do what rifles didn't have to.

The older man turned slightly, scanning the darkness. For the first time Elijah saw something like anger crack through his careful control. Not anger at the white men. Anger at the shape of the trap, at the fact that it had been built with knowledge that should not have been available.

"They got a man inside," Elijah whispered, though he didn't know who he meant. Samuel. The younger man. Somebody in a cabin with power leaned close enough to listen and then leaned closer to speak.

The older man's eyes cut toward him. "You don't say that name out here," he murmured, as if Elijah had spoken Samuel aloud. As if names themselves could be heard.

The reeds behind them rustled.

Not wind.

A body moving carefully, slow enough to be almost silent.

The older man's hand shot out and gripped Elijah's forearm, not to restrain him, but to anchor him. Elijah felt the older man's fingers dig in, hard.

"Don't," the older man whispered. "Don't run."

Elijah's teeth clenched. "If I don't—"

The older man's voice dropped lower, urgent and rough. "If you run, they shoot. They want you whole. They want you back. But a panicked white man do panicked things."

Elijah's breath caught. They want you back. Not dead in the reeds. Alive in the yard. Alive for morning.

The rustle behind them became a step, then another. A man clearing his throat softly, the sound of someone about to speak.

A lantern flared again, this time behind the reeds, lighting the stalks from the wrong side and turning them into a thin fence of shadows.

A white voice spoke, close and conversational, as if addressing a neighbor in daylight.

"Come on out," the man said. "Ain't no sense making it harder."

Another voice joined, farther off, coordinating. "Bring the light around. He's in there."

He's. Not they. Not a guess. A certainty.

Elijah's stomach dropped. The hunt wasn't searching anymore. It was confirming.

The older man's face tightened. Elijah saw the calculation in it, quick and brutal. The older man had brought Elijah into this night. He had opened doors. Now he was trapped too.

"You got to decide," the older man murmured, close enough for the words to vibrate in Elijah's bones. "You want to live long enough to try again, or you want to die proving you can't be held."

Elijah's eyes burned. He thought of Lila, walking out with a lantern like obedience, disappearing into a dark that didn't speak. He thought of her refusal to Samuel, her straight spine. He thought of the forge, and the collar leather, and the bells he had been forced to help make.

He thought of Ben, already taken, used as noise.

And he understood, with a sickness that tasted like metal: this trap had been designed to end with him standing exactly here. Not by chance. By method. By a listening mouth that knew how people moved when they were desperate.

A dog whined softly, a high sound that made Elijah's skin tighten. The handler shushed it, and the dog went quiet again, trained even in its hunger.

The lantern behind the reeds moved closer. Light seeped through, striping Elijah's hands and the older man's face.

"Last chance," the first white voice said, still calm. "You come out, you don't get hurt. You make us pull you, it'll go worse."

The promise was a lie dressed like reason. The system always offered a softer path so it could punish you for not taking it.

Elijah swallowed hard. His jaw ached with restraint.

He shifted his weight and raised his empty hand slightly, fingers spread, showing he held no weapon.

The older man's grip on his arm tightened for a heartbeat, then released.

Elijah stepped forward, pushing through the reeds into the open.

The lantern light hit him full and made him feel naked. The night air felt suddenly thin, as if the world had lost its cover.

The men were closer than he'd thought. Three white men, faces set, and one of them held a shotgun angled down, ready to lift. The rope man moved first, quick and practiced, looping the line around Elijah's wrists with a speed that spoke of repetition. Behind them, the dog handler stood with the hounds held tight, their eyes fixed on Elijah as if he were meat that had learned to walk upright.

Elijah didn't fight. Not because he had surrendered in his spirit, but because fighting here would be used later as justification for worse.

A white man stepped closer and tilted the lantern up to Elijah's face, inspecting him like property recovered.

"Well," the man said, satisfied. "Ain't you Boone's blacksmith."

Elijah's stomach turned. The man knew him. Knew his role. Knew his value.

Not found. Identified.

Elijah's eyes flicked toward the reeds. He caught one last glimpse of the older man's shape slipping backward into darkness, not running, not making noise, vanishing the way survival demanded.

The white man holding the lantern smiled faintly, like he had completed a task neatly.

"Let's take him home," he said.

And as they turned Elijah back toward the direction of Boone's yard, the whistles sounded again, not as calls searching the dark, but as signals of completion. A job finished clean.

Precision.

That was what made Elijah's blood go coldest of all.

They hadn't caught him by luck.

They had caught him the way a man closed a trap he'd already measured, already set, already baited with the exact shape of hope.

Chapter 15

The Choice

Lila ran without meaning to.

Not the wild running of a child chased for sport, but the hard, controlled sprint of a woman who understood exactly what the whistle meant. Her feet struck uneven ground and found purchase anyway. Branches snapped and scraped her arms. A thorn tore the edge of her sleeve and left a hot line of pain she did not have time to acknowledge. Behind her, the darkness did not stay empty. It filled with voices that were careful not to shout, careful not to waste breath on panic.

That was what made her fear go cold.

Men who were panicked yelled. Men who were hunting did not. Hunters spoke like they were already sure.

Another whistle cut through the trees, closer than the last, and Lila felt the sound pass through her ribs. It was not a call searching the woods. It was a signal. Something answered it, faint and farther off. A second signal, a confirmation. The night became a conversation she was not allowed to understand.

She angled toward the low ditch Mary had once pointed out in daylight, the one that ran behind the far outbuilding and dipped toward the boundary where the land turned rougher and less used. If she could get to the ditch, she could drop down and let the earth swallow her shape for a few seconds. A few seconds mattered. A few seconds could be the difference between being seen and being guessed at.

Her foot slipped in mud, and she caught herself with both hands on a fallen log. The bark bit her palms. She pushed off and kept moving.

The dogs' bells chimed behind her.

Not close enough to see, but close enough to hear the wrong cheerfulness of brass. She had thought she'd left the yard's sound behind with the lantern hidden under the woodpile. She had thought the dark beyond the outbuilding belonged to a different kind of silence. But the plantation had followed her, stitching its sound into places it did not belong.

A white voice murmured somewhere to her right. "Hold there."

Another voice, farther back, replied, "She's in the trees. Don't spook her toward the creek."

They were already talking as if her body was a piece on a board.

Lila dropped into the ditch anyway, letting the mud take her knees and the weeds close over her shoulders. The air was damp and smelled like rot. She pressed her cheek to the dirt and listened hard enough that her ears hurt.

Footsteps approached, slowly. Not the heavy, careless steps of a man walking home. Steps placed with intention, spaced to keep from snapping twigs. A lantern light flickered through the weeds above her, then moved away, then came back, searching.

She kept her breath shallow. The blue scrap was still inside her sleeve, warm against her skin, and for an instant she thought of pressing it into the mud like an offering, a thing to hide the part of her that still believed in a seam.

A dog whined softly. The bells trembled.

"Easy," a handler's voice said, low and soothing. "Easy now. She right here."

The weeds above Lila's head rustled. A shadow blocked what little sky the ditch could see. A hand reached down.

Lila did not scream. Screaming was what they wanted. Scream meant fear, and fear made a story. Instead she surged upward and sideways in one motion, trying to slip past the reaching arm, trying to turn her body into a shape too quick to grab.

A rough hand caught her wrist with practiced certainty.

Another hand clamped on her shoulder and shoved her back into the ditch. Her knee struck a buried rock and sent pain shooting up her leg. She bit down on the inside of her cheek hard enough to taste blood and still made no sound.

A face leaned in above her, lantern light throwing it into hard angles. A white man, young enough that his jaw still looked soft, but his eyes held no softness at all. Behind him the dog handler stood with the hound's lead wrapped around his fist, the animal's nose quivering, eager.

"Well," the young white man said quietly, almost pleased. "Mistress said you'd try."

Lila's chest tightened. Mistress. So, this had not been a random sweep of the yards. Her name had been placed in mouths. Her motion had been expected.

She kept her gaze down, then lifted it just enough to look at the man without giving him her fear. "I was checking lanterns," she said, voice rough with mud and swallowed panic. She shaped the lie like obedience. "Cook sent me."

The white man's mouth curved. "With no lantern," he replied, as if discussing a simple mistake. He nodded at the grass behind her where the ditch narrowed. "Where you set it down, girl?"

Lila's stomach dropped. They had already found the lantern. Or they had followed the light until it vanished. Or someone had seen her tuck it away.

She did not answer.

The white man leaned closer, lantern held so that the light washed her face. It felt like being undressed. "You been told to stay close," he said. "You been told there ain't no wandering until things settle."

Things settle. Dust after a beating. A body after it stops fighting.

Lila kept her mouth closed. Any word she gave him could be carried back as proof she'd known more than she should.

The handler shifted, and the dog's bells chimed again, bright and hateful. The hound strained toward Lila, not because it wanted her, but because it had been taught that her fear was a game.

The white man straightened. "Get her up," he told the handler, as if Lila was a sack of grain to be lifted out of a ditch.

Hands hauled her to her feet. Mud clung to her skirt and legs, heavy and cold. Her knee throbbed. Her wrist ached where fingers had pinched. She forced herself not to limp. Limping made weakness visible, and weakness invited extra hands.

They walked her back through trees that no longer felt like unknown. The woods had become a corridor. Lanterns blinked at measured distances now, held low, then lifted, then covered. Whistles signaled positions. Men moved like pieces sliding into place.

When the outbuilding came into view and then the yard, Lila saw the house with its windows half-lit and felt something inside her twist. It looked the same as it always had, calm and sure. A place that could swallow a person and still present itself as orderly.

The mistress stood on the back porch.

She had thrown a shawl over her shoulders, the fabric pale against the night, and she held a small lantern of her own like a decoration. Her face was composed, almost gentle, as if she had simply stepped outside to check on a noise.

The men brought Lila to the edge of the yard and stopped, waiting, as if the mistress's quiet presence was the real command.

The mistress's gaze traveled over Lila's mud-smeared skirt, her torn sleeve, her scraped hands. Then it settled on Lila's face.

"There you are," the mistress said softly.

Lila did not speak.

The mistress tilted her head. "You gave us a fright," she continued, tone still mild. "Running around like that. You know better."

Lila kept her eyes lowered. She could feel Mary somewhere behind the kitchen window, could feel the cook's fear like a hand on the back of her neck, but she did not look. Looking would pull them in. Looking would make them part of her punishment.

"I wasn't running," Lila said carefully. The words came out flat, not pleading, not defiant. "I was working."

The mistress smiled faintly, as if amused by a child's insistence. "Of course," she said. "Always working. Always so useful." Her voice softened further, and the softness made Lila's skin crawl. "That's what makes you valuable."

Valuable. The word landed like a chain.

The mistress's gaze shifted past Lila, toward the men holding her. "You can let go," she said.

The hands on Lila's arms loosened but did not leave. Not yet. They waited to see if she would try again. They waited for a mistake.

The mistress stepped down from the porch slowly. She stopped a few feet from Lila, close enough for Lila to smell lavender on her skin, a clean scent that belonged to a world built on other people's labor.

"Do you know," the mistress said, conversational, "what happens when the master thinks something of his is about to be stolen?"

Lila didn't answer. She knew the answer anyway. She had watched the branding. She had smelled burned flesh in morning air. She had heard screams that carried past fences and into sleep.

The mistress continued as if Lila had asked politely. "He gets frightened," she said. "And frightened men do ugly things. Even men who like to think of themselves as reasonable."

Reasonable. The plantation's favorite mask.

Lila forced her breathing to stay even. Her sleeve pressed against her forearm, and she felt the hidden blue scrap there. She thought of Elijah. She did not know if he was free or caught. The woods did not tell her. The North didn't speak, and neither did the dark. It only returned you or swallowed you, and she did not yet know which had happened to him.

The mistress leaned in slightly. "I don't want Mr. Carter frightened," she murmured, as if confiding. "I don't want him angry. And I certainly don't want him looking for someone to blame."

Lila lifted her eyes just enough to meet the mistress's chin, not her eyes. Meeting eyes was too intimate. Too dangerous.

The mistress's voice stayed gentle. "You understand me."

It wasn't a question. It was a statement meant to make obedience feel like agreement.

A man's voice carried from the front of the house then, sharp and irritated. Mr. Carter. "Where is she."

The mistress did not flinch. She simply raised her voice slightly, still calm. "Here."

Footsteps approached across the yard, heavier, impatient. Mr. Carter came into view with his coat thrown on and his hair disordered from sleep, his face tightened into the kind of anger that liked to be witnessed.

His eyes landed on Lila and did not look away. He didn't need to raise his voice to make her feel small. His attention did that on its own.

"What is this," he demanded, and the words were not for information. They were for ownership.

"She wandered," the mistress said, still soft. "She was found."

Mr. Carter's jaw worked. He looked Lila up and down like he was counting the damage to something he'd paid for. Then his gaze shifted to the men who had brought her in.

"Any sign she met somebody," he asked.

The men shook their heads, quick. "No, sir," one replied. "Just her. Dogs picked her up near the trees."

Mr. Carter's eyes narrowed. "Just her," he repeated, as if he didn't believe in a world where a woman could act alone. His gaze sharpened. "You been talking to Boone's side again?"

Lila kept her mouth closed.

Mr. Carter stepped closer, and the smell of him hit her, sweat and tobacco and anger held in a tight fist. "Answer," he snapped.

The mistress touched his arm lightly, a gesture that looked soothing and was not. "Not here," she murmured, as if reminding him that the yard had ears, that cruelty was best delivered in the right room.

Mr. Carter's nostrils flared. He stared at Lila another beat, then looked past her toward the kitchen window where shadows moved.

"Get her inside," he said. "And keep her where I can see her."

A threat wrapped in instruction.

Hands closed on Lila again, firmer now. As they turned her toward the back steps, she caught a glimpse of Mary's face through the kitchen doorway, half-hidden in shadow. Mary's jaw was clenched so hard it looked like it might crack. Her eyes met Lila's for a fraction of a second.

No comfort. No rescue.

Only warning.

Because the plantation had brought Lila back without a beating. Without a brand. Without the spectacle it liked to use when it wanted to teach everyone else a lesson.

Which meant this return wasn't meant to end in punishment.

It was meant to begin in leverage.

As Lila was guided up the steps and through the kitchen door, the mistress's soft voice followed behind her like a ribbon pulled tight.

"We'll talk tomorrow," the mistress said gently. "When you're clean. When you're calmer. When you're ready to be sensible."

Sensible, Lila thought, as the door shut and the yard's bells continued their bright chiming outside.

Sensible meant compliant.

Sensible meant quiet.

And the way they were holding her now, the way they were saving their anger for daylight, told Lila with a certainty colder than mud that her body was no longer the point.

She was the message they planned to deliver to someone else.

Somewhere beyond Carter's walls and Boone's fields, Elijah was either still moving or already bound, being carried back as property recovered.

Lila did not know which.

But she knew this: they had not dragged her back to end her. They had brought her back to use her.

And whatever threat was coming would not be spoken like a shout.

It would be offered like a choice.

Morning came without release.

Lila had not slept. The house kept shifting around her in small sounds: a board settling, a door opening too softly, the mistress's steps crossing the upstairs floor with deliberate calm. Even when everything went still, it did not feel like permission. It felt like a pause held on purpose.

They kept her in the back room off the kitchen, not tied, not locked in a way that could be spoken about later, but watched. A white boy sat on a stool by the door with a stick across his knees like a toy rifle, eyes half-lidded with boredom that never quite became carelessness. Every time Lila moved, his gaze snapped sharp.

Near dawn the cook brought her a basin and a rag.

"Wash," the cook said, voice flat.

Lila looked at the water. It trembled in the basin as if it, too, had a pulse. "Why."

The cook's eyes flicked to the door, then away. "Because mistress don't like mud in her house," she whispered. "Because they calling you out front."

Calling you out front. Not a beating behind the kitchen. Not a lecture in the passage. Out front meant performance. Out front meant the kind of cruelty that liked witnesses.

Lila stripped the mud from her hands and wrists slowly, rubbing until the skin burned. The water went brown. She washed her face. She rinsed her mouth and spat into the basin. She tried to scrub the taste of blood from where she'd bitten her cheek, but the inside of her mouth still felt bruised.

When she was done, the cook handed her a clean dress. Not her best, not the one reserved for Sundays, but clean enough to make her presentable. Clean enough to pretend this was something other than what it was.

"Put it on," the cook said.

Lila changed without turning her back on the door. She had learned long ago that even modesty could be used against you, that any moment you could not see was a moment someone else could decide what you were.

When she stepped out, the mistress stood in the kitchen doorway, hair neat, face composed, as if she had slept soundly. She held her hands folded at her waist.

"There," the mistress said softly, like approval. "Much better."

Lila kept her eyes lowered. "Yes, ma'am."

The mistress looked her over again, not at Lila's face but at her posture, her steadiness, the way her hands hung at her sides. The mistress seemed almost satisfied.

"You frightened my husband last night," she said, still mild. "Mr. Carter doesn't enjoy being surprised."

Lila said nothing. Words were a rope here. Every sentence could be looped into a noose if someone wanted it.

The mistress stepped aside. "Come," she said.

Outside, the yard looked ordinary enough to make Lila feel as if she were losing her mind. The chickens scratched at dirt. The sun sat pale and thin behind a morning haze. The dogs were tethered near the stable, bells glinting faintly, not chiming now, quiet as if they were asleep. Quiet dogs were never asleep. Quiet dogs were waiting.

A wagon stood by the drive.

Not the river wagon. This one was Carter's, plain and clean. Two white men sat on the bench seat, reins loose in their hands. Another stood by the back, one hand resting on the wagon's side as if he were steadying it against wind.

Mary was nowhere in sight. Lila could feel her absence like a hand pressed against Lila's spine.

The cook stayed by the kitchen door, face turned away, as if not seeing could keep her from being part of it.

Mr. Carter stood on the porch. He did not come down. He watched from height because height mattered to men like him.

Beside him, Samuel stood half a step back.

Lila felt her throat tighten so fast it hurt.

Samuel's face was calm, his posture relaxed. He looked as if he had simply come to receive instructions, as if he were useful. As if he were still the man who offered assistance before it was asked for, positioning himself where he must be acknowledged.

His eyes found Lila, and in them she saw no heat, no anger, no obvious triumph.

Only a steady, patient certainty. The certainty of a man who believed the world would eventually arrange itself into what he wanted.

Mr. Carter spoke first. "Get in," he said.

Lila did not move yet. She kept her gaze on the wagon's boards, on the way the sun lit the grain of the wood. If she looked up, she might catch Samuel's eyes again, and she refused him that.

The mistress's voice floated from behind, close to Lila's ear. "Don't make it harder," she murmured. "You've already had your excitement."

Excitement. Like it had been a childish impulse, not a calculated attempt to save her own life.

Lila climbed into the wagon. The boards were cool under her hands. She sat with her back straight and her hands folded in her lap.

Samuel moved then, stepping down from the porch with a smoothness that made her skin crawl. He climbed into the wagon's back, not sitting beside her, not close enough to touch. He chose a corner where he could watch her face without appearing to.

The wagon rolled forward.

They passed the yard, the kitchen, the quarters, the place where women bent over wash lines and pretended not to watch. The plantation held its breath in a way that felt practiced.

Lila kept her face arranged into nothing.

The road between properties was short. It had always felt long because it was a boundary made of men and rules, but the wagon crossed it in minutes. Trees leaned in on either side. The air smelled damp, as if the night's mud still clung to the world.

Boone's land appeared like a memory she had been forced to live inside. The forge's smoke rose thin from its chimney. The yard moved with early labor. Men and women were already bent into their tasks.

Then the sound reached her.

Not bells. Not dogs.

A single, broken shout. Cut off too quickly to be accidental.

The wagon turned toward a cluster of outbuildings behind the main house. The driver did not slow as he approached. He drove like he had done this before.

They stopped beside a barn.

Two white men stood at the door. One held it open without stepping aside, blocking the entrance with his body as if the doorway were his to own.

Mr. Boone stood nearby, hands behind his back, speaking in a low voice to Carter. Lila could not hear the words at first, only the tone: businesslike. Men arranging another man's suffering like a trade.

Samuel climbed down from the wagon. He offered Lila a hand as if she were a lady stepping from a carriage.

Lila ignored it and climbed down on her own.

Samuel did not react. He simply folded his hands behind his back and waited, composed.

Mr. Carter nodded toward the barn. "Show her," he said, and the words were plain enough to hide their cruelty.

One of the men at the barn door stepped aside.

The smell hit Lila first.

Blood. Sweat. Damp hay. And underneath it, that sour, coppery scent that rose when skin had been broken and kept breaking.

Her stomach turned, but she held herself still and walked into the shadowed space.

Elijah hung near the back.

Not by his neck. Not dead. They wanted him alive. The ropes held his wrists above him, stretched enough to make his shoulders strain. His shirt was torn open. His skin was marked with fresh welts, some still slick, some already darkening. His face was swollen on one side, one eye half shut.

His feet barely touched the ground.

A man stood near him with a bucket and a rag as if tending to livestock. Another man held a strap in his hand, not lifted now, just present. The strap's presence spoke louder than any raised arm.

Elijah's head lifted slowly.

For a moment his gaze didn't seem to find her. His eye looked through the space as if searching for something to hold onto. Then his focus sharpened, and he saw her.

His mouth opened. No sound came out at first. His lips were cracked. When he tried again, his voice came rough and thin.

"Lila," he whispered.

The sound of her name in his mouth felt like a blade sliding between her ribs. She took a step forward before she could stop herself.

A white hand shot out and blocked her path at the barn's threshold. Not striking. Just stopping. A boundary made of flesh.

"Stand there," the man said.

Lila froze. Her hands clenched at her sides. She did not look at the rope. She did not look at the strap. She kept her eyes on Elijah's face because if she looked away she would be admitting something the plantation wanted her to admit: that she could be made to turn from him.

Samuel's voice came from behind her, calm, measured. "You see what happens," he said quietly.

Lila did not answer.

Samuel stepped closer, stopping just behind her shoulder, leaving enough space that it could be called respectful. His voice lowered further, meant for her alone. “This is the part you don’t like,” he murmured, as if he were the one burdened by it. “But it’s the part that’s real.”

Lila swallowed. Her throat felt scraped raw. “You did this,” she said, and the words came out before she could shape them into something safer.

Samuel did not deny it. He didn’t smile either. He simply breathed once, as if accepting an obvious truth.

“I prevented worse,” he replied, and his tone made the lie sound almost reasonable. “You think men like Boone and Carter need much excuse to do this? They don’t. Excuse is just how they sleep at night. I give them one that keeps the rest of us breathing.”

Elijah’s head sagged for a moment, then lifted again with effort. His gaze stayed on Lila, not on Samuel. As if Samuel did not deserve his eyes.

Lila kept her voice low. “Why bring me here.”

Samuel’s answer came gentle, almost tender. “Because you keep choosing a hard road,” he said. “And hard roads cost people you care about.”

Mr. Carter's voice cut in from the barn door behind them, impatient. "Well? Say what you got to say."

Samuel inclined his head as if receiving permission, then looked at Lila again.

"This is simple," he said. "You don't run again. You don't speak to Boone's side again. You stop making yourself a problem."

Lila's breath caught. "And if I do all that."

Samuel's voice stayed level. "Then this stops," he said, nodding toward Elijah without looking at him. "He goes back to work. He heals as much as a man can heal here. He keeps his hands. He keeps his life."

Lila's fingers curled so tight her nails bit skin. "And what do you get," she asked, though she already knew.

Samuel's eyes held hers. His calm did not break.

"I keep you safe," he said. "Here. Under my notice. Under my protection."

Protection. The same word he had offered before, dressed in practicality, hiding its teeth.

"You mean I belong to you," Lila whispered.

Samuel's expression softened by a fraction, like patience. "You already belong to somebody," he replied. "At least with me, you're not alone in it."

Elijah made a sound then, a rough exhale that might have been a laugh if his body could still laugh.

He lifted his head, forcing his swollen eye open a little wider. His voice came out broken but clear enough.

"Don't," he rasped.

Lila's chest tightened so hard she could barely breathe.

Elijah swallowed, grimacing with the movement. "Don't give him you," he whispered, each word dragged from him like metal drawn hot. "They can take… they can take what they want from my body. Don't let them take yours from the inside."

A white man shifted, irritated, and lifted the strap slightly as if to remind Elijah what speaking earned. Samuel raised a hand, small, and the strap stopped. Samuel didn't want noise. He wanted control.

Samuel leaned closer to Lila, voice so low it nearly disappeared. "You hear him," he said.

"He's brave. Brave don't keep you fed. Brave don't keep you unbranded."

Lila's eyes stayed on Elijah's face. She saw the strain in him, the effort it took to keep looking at her. She saw blood dried at the corner of his mouth.

Samuel waited, patient as a trap.

"Choose," he murmured.

The barn seemed to close in around that word. The wood, the hay, the rope, the men's bodies at the edges. The whole world narrowing to a decision shaped by other people.

Lila felt something inside her settle, not into surrender, not into defiance, but into a cold, steady refusal to let Samuel name her choices for her.

She did not nod. She did not shake her head.

She looked at Elijah, and then she looked past him, to the dark behind him where the barn wall met shadow, to the thin seams where daylight leaked through cracks.

She let the silence stretch until it became its own statement.

Samuel's calm tightened. Just slightly. The first sign that patience had limits.

Mr. Carter's voice snapped again from the doorway. "Well, girl."

Lila breathed in. Mud still lived under her nails. The blue cloth still pressed warm against her skin, hidden, a question she had not answered in words.

She kept her voice even when she spoke.

"I hear you," she said, and gave them nothing more.

Not yes.

Not no.

Only the promise of waiting, held like a closed fist.

And in the barn's dim hush, with Elijah hanging and Samuel watching and white men positioned like fence posts around them, Lila understood that refusing to choose could be its own kind of choice.

If she could hold the moment long enough, the system might show its hand.

And once a hand showed itself, it could be bitten.

Samuel did not move for a moment.

The quiet inside the barn had weight now, the way smoke had weight when it sat too long in a room and made your eyes sting. Lila could hear Elijah's breathing, ragged and careful, each inhale sounding like it scraped against something inside him. She could hear the faint drip of water from the bucket near the wall. She could hear a fly circling, trapped by the stink of blood and sweat and fear.

Mr. Carter shifted on his boots at the threshold. Impatience came off him like heat.

"Well?" he snapped again.

Lila kept her hands still at her sides. She could feel the tremble in her fingers and refused to let it become motion. Motion could be taken as panic. Panic could be used as proof that Samuel was right about her needing to be managed.

"I told you," she said evenly, not lifting her voice. "I hear you."

Not yes. Not no. Just air held in place, forcing them to decide what to do with it.

Samuel's calm tightened into something sharper. It was not anger, exactly. It was the discomfort of a man who had built his power on predictable outcomes and had just been reminded that a person could refuse to be an outcome.

He looked past her toward Elijah, then back to Lila again, as if trying to find where her refusal lived. In her eyes? In her mouth? In her posture?

He found nothing that satisfied him.

"Take her back," Samuel said finally, tone mild, as if this were the natural next step. "She's had enough excitement for one morning."

Mr. Carter's nostrils flared. "We ain't done."

Samuel inclined his head slightly. "Not here," he murmured, and the words carried like a leash being tugged. "Not in front of Boone's men. You want this clean."

Clean. They wanted cruelty that didn't leave witnesses with names. They wanted a version of violence that could be explained later as discipline, as necessity, as something Lila had asked for by being difficult.

Mr. Carter stared at Lila as if deciding whether to break the barn's order with his hands. Then his gaze slid to Boone, who stood a little apart, watching with the cold interest of a man observing another man's tools.

Mr. Boone's mouth curved faintly, not amusement, but permission. He didn't need to speak to remind Carter that power was always being measured by other power.

Mr. Carter looked away first.

"Fine," he said, spit-rough. "Get her on."

A hand closed around Lila's upper arm, firm enough to bruise later. Another man moved behind her, close enough that she could feel his breath on the back of her neck. She did not flinch. She let them guide her as if she were an object being repositioned.

At the doorway, she turned her head once, careful, slow, like she was simply glancing at the light outside.

Elijah lifted his head as if the small movement pulled him.

His good eye found her.

She could not speak. Not here. Not with Samuel listening like a door pressed against a wall.

So, she let her face do the only thing it could do without giving the system a word to carry. She held Elijah's gaze and stayed still inside it. A promise with no shape they could punish. A message made of endurance.

Elijah's mouth moved. No sound came out at first. Then, thin as breath, she heard it.

"Wait," he rasped.

The word broke something in her chest and repaired something else.

She didn't nod. She didn't shake her head. She simply looked at him one last second longer, then let the men pull her away.

Outside, the air tasted cleaner than the barn, but it did not feel free. The yard was full of morning work, bodies moving under orders, heads down, hands busy. A world pretending not to notice what it had just been forced to witness.

They put her back in Carter's wagon like cargo.

Samuel climbed into the back again, choosing his corner. Not close enough to touch, close enough to remind.

The wagon rolled.

As Boone's land receded, Lila watched the forge smoke thin into the pale sky. She thought of Elijah's hands, the hands that had shaped iron and leather and been forced to make the plantation's tools sharper. Now those hands hung useless above him, bound and split by rope.

She forced herself not to cry. Tears were not just danger; they were surrender made visible.

Samuel spoke as if continuing a conversation that had never stopped. "You think silence is power," he said calmly.

Lila kept her eyes on the road ahead, the trees sliding past like bars. "Silence is all I got."

Samuel's tone warmed, almost gentle. "No," he said. "You've got choice. You just want a choice that costs you nothing. There isn't one."

Lila felt the urge to spit at him, to turn her mouth into a weapon. But she understood, with a clarity that felt like cold water poured over her head, that he wanted reaction. Reaction was the crack where he could insert himself again as savior, as protector, as the only man who could help her manage the consequences of her own emotions.

So, she gave him nothing.

Samuel watched her for a few beats, then leaned back as if bored. "You'll learn," he said quietly. "Waiting doesn't make the teeth disappear. It just gives them time to settle in."

The wagon wheels creaked. The horses snorted. Somewhere in the distance, on a wind that carried sound wrong, she heard dogs bark. Not the close bells of patrol, but the raw voice of a hunt that had not finished eating.

Back at Carter's house, the mistress was already in position, waiting on the porch as if she had never moved. The same composed face, the same pale hands folded at her waist, the same lantern set aside because daylight did not need pretense.

They guided Lila inside without ceremony and did not return her to the back room this time.

They put her in the front parlor.

It was a room built for comfort and display: heavy curtains, a polished table, a faint smell of lemon oil on wood. A room meant to show visitors that the house was civilized. That nothing ugly happened here unless it was earned.

Two chairs sat near the window. Lila was placed in one.

A white woman she did not know sat in the other chair with embroidery in her lap, needle moving slowly, eyes lifting now and then to rest on Lila as if Lila were a stain being evaluated.

A guard stood by the door. Not a man with a gun. A man with time.

The mistress sat across from her, hands folded, expression serene.

"We will be patient with you," the mistress said softly, as if explaining a lesson to a child. "Mr. Carter is upset. Mr. Boone is upset. Everyone is strained. We don't want to make rash decisions."

Lila stared at the carpet's pattern, letting the words slide over her without catching. Rash decisions meant bruises that showed, brands that smelled, screams that carried. They didn't want that yet. They wanted something quieter. Something that lasted.

The mistress continued, "Samuel has spoken for you," she said, and Lila felt that name tighten around her throat. "He says you are frightened. He says you don't understand what you almost caused."

Almost caused. As if Elijah hanging in Boone's barn was a consequence of Lila's stubbornness, not Samuel's careful feeding of information.

Lila did not respond.

The embroidery needle kept slipping in and out of cloth. The sound was small, but it made time feel counted.

The mistress leaned forward slightly. "You will sit here until you are ready to be sensible," she said. "When you have something to say, you may say it. Until then, you will not be working in the kitchen. You will not be moving about the yard. You will not be near other people. You will not be given a chance to stir anyone's thoughts."

Isolation delivered like politeness.

Lila felt a pulse of fear, then forced it down. Isolation was the system's way of turning a person into their own echo chamber. It made you doubt your memories. It made you bargain with yourself. It made you start to believe that surrender might feel like relief.

She thought of Mary's jaw clenched in the kitchen doorway, the warning in her eyes: they brought you back to use you.

They were using her now, even without touching her. They were making her absence from the kitchen noticeable. They were making the other enslaved people wonder what she had done, what she had said, what she had refused. They were making her into a story without allowing her to speak.

Hours passed in pieces.

The sun moved across the parlor window. Dust floated in the light. The guard shifted his feet. The embroidery woman changed thread colors with a careful neatness that made Lila want to scream.

At midday, the cook appeared at the doorway with a tray. Bread. A cup of water. Not much. Enough to keep Lila's body from collapsing in a way that would demand attention.

The cook's eyes met Lila's for half a second, then dropped.

But as the cook set the tray down on a small table beside Lila's chair, her hand lingered for the smallest moment too long.

Her fingers brushed the table leg.

Once. Twice.

A pattern that didn't belong to serving.

Lila's breath caught. It was not a message in words. It was the kind of message Mary had described. A thing done wrong on purpose, meant for a person who knew to see it.

The cook straightened and left without a glance back.

Lila sat still for another long moment, refusing to move too quickly. Quick movements drew eyes. Eyes drew questions.

Then, when the guard's attention drifted to the window, bored by a world that obeyed him, Lila lowered her hand slowly to the table leg.

There, pressed into the seam where wood met wood, was a tiny knot of blue thread.

Not cloth. Not a scrap that could be held up as proof.

Just a single twist of color, caught where it did not belong, like a drop of sky trapped inside the house's polished order.

Lila's throat tightened.

Mary had found a way. Or the cook had agreed to be used for something other than fear. Either way, it meant Lila was not alone in her waiting.

It also meant waiting was not only a refusal.

It could be a signal. A held breath timed to someone else's held breath.

Lila kept her face blank as she lifted the bread to her mouth and chewed slowly. Inside her sleeve, the blue scrap still pressed warm against her skin, Elijah's wire question mark curled like a hook.

Wait, Elijah had said.

Lila swallowed and let the word settle inside her where Samuel could not reach it.

She would wait.

Not because she believed patience would soften the system.

Because waiting was the only way to watch the system closely enough to see the seam it couldn't hide.

And as the afternoon light thinned and the parlor shadows lengthened, Lila felt something else moving under the quiet: the house's growing irritation, the mistress's polite mask tightening, the sense that Samuel's patience was being tested by a woman who refused to give him the satisfaction of a clean answer.

The plantation could punish a yes.

It could punish a no.

But her silence made them work.

It forced them to decide how to break her without breaking what they needed her to be.

And that, Lila understood, was a kind of leverage.

A thin, dangerous kind.

The sort that could cut both ways.

She sat in the front parlor and held herself still while time dragged forward like a chain, listening for the first sound of the system losing its composure.

Listening for the moment when the trap, built so carefully around her choices, would have to show its hand.

Chapter 16

The North Doesn't Speak

The house did not change when night came.

The lamps were lit. The curtains were drawn. The parlor filled with the soft, even glow of comfort meant to convince anyone who stepped inside that nothing violent could happen in a room so carefully arranged. The embroidery woman kept working, needle in and out, the thread making small sounds that counted time more precisely than any clock.

Lila sat where they had placed her and listened to the house's breathing. It was not the deep, sleeping breath of a place at rest. It was the shallow breath of vigilance: a floorboard settling, a voice murmured in the hall, the guard shifting his stance at the door as if reminding himself he had authority even over stillness.

The knot of blue thread remained hidden against the table leg where her fingers had found it. She did not touch it again. Touching it would be seen. Seeing would become suspicion. Suspicion would become story.

Instead, she held it in her mind like she held the word north: not as comfort, as direction.

The mistress returned near supper time with the same serene face she had worn all day, carrying a small tray herself. A performance, Lila understood. The mistress wanted witnesses to kindness. Kindness was another kind of leash.

"I thought perhaps you'd like something more substantial," the mistress said softly, setting a bowl down on the table beside Lila. Soup, thin but warm. A piece of bread. The sort of food a person could call mercy.

Lila didn't reach for it immediately.

The mistress sat across from her in the other chair, folding her hands in her lap. The embroidery woman did not look up, but her needle slowed slightly, as if listening.

"You're very strong," the mistress said, as if strength were a compliment and not an accusation. "You're also very stubborn."

Lila kept her gaze on the table edge. "Yes, ma'am."

The mistress sighed, a sound practiced to suggest disappointment rather than threat. "My husband is not a patient man," she continued. "Mr. Boone is even less patient. Men of that sort…" She let the sentence hang, implying ugliness without having to speak it. "Samuel has tried to help you."

Lila's stomach tightened at the name. Samuel's help had always come shaped like a trap that wanted to be thanked.

"I didn't ask him," Lila said quietly.

The mistress's voice remained smooth. "No," she replied. "You didn't. That is part of your problem. You behave as if you are alone in this world. You behave as if consequences only touch you."

Lila felt the urge to glance toward the window, toward the dark outside, as if the night might offer her a sign. She refused. The house would read a glance as longing, and longing was a weakness they could use.

The mistress leaned forward a little. "You have until morning," she said. "That is my kindness. By morning you will either be sensible or…" Again, she let the words dissolve into silence, leaving Lila's imagination to supply the rest.

Lila heard Mary's voice in her head, hard and honest: Isolation delivered like politeness.

She nodded once. Not agreement. A motion small enough to pass as obedience.

The mistress seemed satisfied. She stood and smoothed her dress. "Eat," she said. "You'll think more clearly with food in you."

She left the parlor with the guard following her into the hallway for a moment, then returning to his post. The embroidery woman's needle resumed its steady puncturing of cloth.

Lila waited until the soup's surface stopped trembling. She lifted the spoon and ate slowly, tasting salt and heat and the faint metallic tang of a pot scraped too often. She chewed the bread in careful bites. Survival required fuel even when the fuel was offered with strings.

When the bowl was half empty, the embroidery woman finally spoke without looking up.

"You don't touch things twice," she said, voice low, her tone suggesting she was speaking about sewing.

Lila froze with the spoon halfway to her mouth. She kept her face blank and finished the motion, tasting nothing now.

The woman continued, needle moving. "First time is an accident. Second time becomes a habit. Habits get noticed."

Lila lowered the spoon. “Yes, ma’am,” she said, giving her the title because titles were what kept white women comfortable.

The embroidery woman’s mouth tightened faintly. “Don’t call me that,” she murmured. Then, after a pause: “Not in your mouth.”

Lila’s pulse kicked hard, a sudden wildness she forced back down into her chest. She kept her eyes on her lap. “What should I call you.”

“Nothing,” the woman replied. “Nothing is safest.”

Lila swallowed, the motion scraping her throat. “Why are you here.”

The embroidery woman’s needle pricked, drew thread through, pulled it taut. “Because this house likes to present itself as orderly,” she said. “Orderly houses invite visitors. Visitors see what they’re allowed to see.”

Lila felt the air around her shift, a thin seam opening. “Are you a visitor.”

The embroidery woman did not answer directly. “You were meant to be made an example,” she said. “Quietly. Not like a brand in the yard. Something softer. Something that makes other girls watch you and decide obedience tastes better than hope.”

Lila's fingers tightened in her skirt. "They brought me to Boone's," she said, unable to stop the words from slipping out. "They showed me him."

The embroidery woman's needle paused. The smallest pause, but Lila saw it. The woman's hand resumed motion again, slower for a few stitches. "I heard," she said.

Heard. The word carried a world of listening beyond these walls.

Lila tried to keep her voice even. "Then you know what they want."

"I know what they say they want," the woman replied. "I also know what people do when they don't get it."

Lila's mouth went dry. She could feel Samuel's patience tightening in the background of everything, like a wire drawn taut. "If you know all that," she whispered, "why are you talking to me."

The embroidery woman's eyes lifted for the first time and met Lila's face directly. Her gaze was not kind. It was not cruel. It was assessing, the way the older man by the creek had assessed Elijah.

"Because you're still sitting," she said, and there was something like respect in her voice that made Lila's stomach ache. "Most people break themselves trying to prove they haven't been broken."

Lila breathed in slowly through her nose. The guard shifted at the door, bored. The house creaked. Somewhere far off, a dog barked once and fell silent again.

The embroidery woman looked down at her work again, voice barely above the scrape of thread. "When the lamp is turned down for the night, you'll be told to go upstairs," she said. "They'll put you in the small room at the end of the hall. The one with one window and no lock on the inside."

Lila's heart hammered. She kept her face still. "How do you know."

"I've been in that room," the woman replied simply. "Not as you. Not as a prisoner. But I've watched what houses do when they want someone to feel trapped without leaving marks."

Lila's tongue felt too thick in her mouth. "They won't leave me alone."

"They will," the woman said. "Long enough. This house believes it can afford to be careless with you because it believes you can't go anywhere."

The needle dipped. Rose. Dipped again.

"When you're taken upstairs," the woman continued, "you will not cry. You will not plead. You will not act like a girl planning anything. You will act like what they want you to be: tired. Frightened into silence. A body grateful for a bed."

Lila's throat tightened. She could do that. She had been performing obedience since childhood. It tasted bitter, but she could swallow it.

The embroidery woman slid her hand under the hoop for a moment, fingers hidden, then brought her hand back up with thread still running clean. "Under the window," she said, "there's a loose board. Not loose enough to be obvious. Loose enough if you know to press where the nail sits wrong."

Lila did not look up. Looking up would be too much. "And then."

The embroidery woman's voice flattened, practical. "Then you'll find something wrapped in oilcloth. A small bundle. Not much. A strip of bread. A pin. A folded paper with no names, just marks you follow."

Lila's breath caught at the word paper. Paper meant evidence. Paper meant something that could be taken from her and used against someone else. But the woman's tone suggested this paper was not a letter. Not a confession. A map made of symbols only meant to live long enough to be used once.

Lila whispered, "Why would you put it there."

"Because you're already being watched," the woman replied. "If you were caught with a bundle prepared in the kitchen, it would become a story about planning. This way, if you're searched, your hands are empty. Your pockets are empty. Your story is just a girl taken to bed. If they find the board later, it will look like rats. Houses always blame rats."

Lila's mind moved fast now, gathering pieces. The blue knot under the table leg. The cook's fingers tapping twice. This woman's calm voice sliding instruction into ordinary air. An unexpected intervention, quiet enough to hide in plain sight.

The guard at the door cleared his throat, shifting his weight as if reminding them he existed.

The embroidery woman raised her voice slightly, not enough to sound loud, just enough to sound normal. "You should drink the rest," she said, nodding at Lila's bowl.

Lila obeyed, lifting the bowl and finishing what was left. Warmth spread through her belly, and with it a fierce, aching gratitude she did not allow to reach her face.

When she set the bowl down, the embroidery woman spoke again without looking up. "You have someone," she said, tone unchanged.

Lila's fingers went still. She thought of Elijah in the barn, hanging, the rope biting into his wrists. She thought of his rasped word. Wait.

She did not answer. Silence was the only protection she could offer him now.

The embroidery woman gave a faint nod, as if she had expected that. "Then you do not go looking back," she said. "If you get out of this house, you don't turn into a ghost that circles its grave. You keep moving. You keep your head down. You take the hand that finds you next and you do what you're told, even when it doesn't feel like what you want."

The language was the same as the older man's language. Doors. Rules. No stories.

Lila's nails pressed half-moons into her palm. "What hand," she whispered.

The embroidery woman's needle paused again, just for a breath. "Not mine," she said. "Mine is only this room. After this room, you belong to people you won't meet until you're already in their care. That is how it stays alive."

A sound came in the hall: the mistress's steps, composed and unhurried. The embroidery woman's needle began moving faster, the rhythm returning to something mindless and decorative.

The mistress entered the parlor with a small lamp in her hand, turning the wick down. The light dimmed, softening the room into shadow and glow.

"It's time," the mistress said gently. Her gaze slid to Lila's empty bowl. "Good. I'm glad you ate."

Lila stood when told. She kept her shoulders slightly rounded, her eyes lowered, her posture a little smaller than it had been. Not defiance. Not strength. A girl subdued.

The mistress seemed pleased by the shape of her. "See," she murmured, as if to the embroidery woman, as if Lila were not fully human in the room. "She can be sensible."

The guard opened the door. Lila walked out.

As she passed the embroidery woman, the woman's voice slipped out, low and precise, not lifting her head from her work.

"When you press the nail," she said, "don't pry. Push down first. Then lift."

Lila did not react. Reaction would betray the seam.

She followed the mistress up the stairs, each step a careful placement on wood that could betray her with a creak. The hallway upstairs smelled like candle smoke and clean cloth. The small room at the end waited with its single window like an eye that didn't blink.

The mistress opened the door and stood aside. "Sleep," she said. "You'll feel better in the morning."

Lila stepped inside.

The mistress closed the door behind her, not locking it, because the lack of a lock was part of the lie. The lie that a person stayed because they chose to.

Lila stood in the dark room and listened.

Footsteps retreated down the hall. A murmur of voices. Then the hush of a house settling into what it believed was control.

Only when the silence held steady did Lila move to the window. The night outside was black, the yard mostly hidden, but she could make out faint shapes: a fence line, a tree, the suggestion of the outbuilding roofs.

Under the window, her fingers found the floorboard seam. She located the nail the embroidery woman had described by feel alone. The head sat slightly higher than the others, a tiny wrongness.

Her hands shook once. She forced them steady. She pressed down first.

The board gave a fraction, a soft complaint. Then she lifted.

The wood rose enough to slide her fingers under.

Oilcloth, cool and slick.

Lila pulled the bundle out inch by inch, careful not to make a sound. She held it in her lap and did not open it yet. Not until she had listened again, confirming the house still believed she was simply a girl in bed.

The North doesn't speak, she thought, and felt the phrase settle into her bones like truth. It didn't speak here either. Not in the parlor. Not in the hallway. Not in this small room.

But someone had spoken without words, had intervened without making themselves visible as a savior.

A seam had been offered.

Lila held the oilcloth bundle against her stomach and waited one more breath, timing herself the way Elijah had timed heat and strikes at the forge, the way Mary had timed routine and noise, the way the older man had timed doors opening only when the system was distracted by its own hunger.

Then she began to unwrap what had been hidden beneath her window, not like a thief, not like a hero, but like a woman who understood that escape was never a single act.

It was a chain of quiet, careful choices made in rooms where the world insisted you had none.

The oilcloth resisted at first, stiff with grease and careful folding. Lila worked at the corner with the pad of her thumb, not tearing, not rushing, listening for any change in the house's breathing. Somewhere down the hall a floorboard sighed as it cooled. A voice murmured and then stopped. The quiet held.

When the cloth finally opened, the smell rose faint and sharp, lamp oil and tallow, the scent of things made to burn clean. Inside was a small, mean inventory: a strip of bread wrapped in rag, a straight pin, a twist of dark thread, and a folded square of paper pressed flat as if it had been sat on for days to kill its edges.

She did not unfold the paper yet. Paper was loud in the wrong way. It wanted to crackle. It wanted to be seen. She kept it under her palm and touched the other things first, as if her fingers could learn the shape of her chances before her eyes did.

The pin was ordinary. Not a weapon. A tool for cloth, for hair, for a hundred small obedience's. But Lila understood immediately what it could become in the right seam of a lock, in the right knot of a cord, in the right moment when a man's hand came too close.

She slid the pin into the lining of her sleeve, beside the blue scrap and its thin wire question. The sleeve felt crowded now with hidden things but crowded was better than empty. Empty meant you had nothing but your body to bargain with.

The bread she tucked into her pocket, then reconsidered and moved it into her bodice, where it would not fall if she had to run. The thread she wrapped around her finger once, twice, then hid it the same way, leaving no loose end that could snag and betray her.

Only then did she unfold the paper.

There were no words. No names. No north written like a promise. Only marks. A line that bent, a circle, then another circle with a slash through it. Three short strokes in the margin like someone had counted breaths. A tiny drawing that might have been a fence post or might have been a tree. A cross that could have meant church or could have meant don't.

It was not a map meant to be kept. It was a map meant to be remembered and destroyed.

Lila studied it until it felt like it had burned itself into the back of her eyes. Then she folded it again, smaller, and pressed it into the same sleeve seam as the pin. She would carry it only until her mind could carry it without help.

She lay back on the narrow bed without undressing. She arranged her face the way the mistress wanted, slack with exhaustion, mouth slightly open as if sleep had taken her without permission. She practiced breathing slowly. She listened for footsteps in the hall. None came. The house, satisfied with its own story, let time pass.

Minutes went by like hours.

At some point the lamp in the corridor dimmed. The silence thickened. Lila kept her eyes closed and let her mind move while her body stayed still. The marks on the paper replayed themselves: bend, circle, circle, slash, three strokes. Fence or tree. Cross or warning.

A faint sound rose outside the window, almost nothing. Not a voice. Not a whistle. A soft clicking, like a branch tapping twice against wood.

Two taps. A pause. Then one more.

Lila's heart stuttered once and then steadied. It could be wind. It could be a mistake that killed her. It could be the seam.

She waited until the sound came again, the same pattern, controlled enough to feel intentional. She did not move to the window like a girl eager for rescue. Eagerness was dangerous. Instead she slid from the bed slowly, feet searching for the cold plank floor, and crossed the room with her hands kept close to her body.

She lifted the curtain only a finger's width.

Outside, the yard was a black shape, fences and trees turned into shadow against darker sky. But near the edge of the garden, where the house's back wall threw a blind patch, a figure stood still as a post. The figure did not wave. Did not signal. Only stood where someone who knew the house would stand to avoid the windows that watched.

A second tap sounded, closer now, and Lila understood: it was not a branch. It was a small stone against the siding, thrown softly from a careful hand.

Her mouth went dry. She glanced at the door. No lock on the inside, the embroidery woman had said. That meant a lock on the outside, or nothing at all. Nothing at all could be more dangerous because it meant anyone could enter.

Lila approached the door and pressed her ear to it.

No footsteps. No guard's breath. Only the far-off creak of the house settling and the faint night sound of insects outside.

She turned the knob slowly. The latch lifted without complaint. The door opened into the hallway, which was dim with low lamp light. No one stood there. The house still believed in its control.

She stepped into the hall, bare feet silent, and moved down the corridor with the cautious steadiness she'd used for years in kitchens and stairwells, the steadiness of a person taught that any noise could be answered with punishment. At the top of the stairs she paused and listened again.

A man's cough floated up from somewhere downstairs, followed by the soft murmur of a voice. The parlor, maybe. The guard, bored into carelessness, speaking to someone else to stay awake. Lila did not look over the banister long enough to see. Seeing invited being seen.

She turned away from the stairs and moved to the back passage, the servant route she knew by touch. Down the narrow steps, past the kitchen door that she did not open. The kitchen was a trap made of familiar smells. If she walked in there now, the cook might cry out without meaning to. Mary might move wrong. The system would swallow them all.

At the back door, she hesitated with her hand on the bolt.

She thought of Elijah's voice, broken and thin: "Wait."

She thought of him hanging in Boone's barn, rope biting into his wrists, blood dried at the corner of his mouth. Waiting had been his only weapon in that moment, and he had given it to her like a tool, the way he had given her wire shaped into question.

"I'm sorry," she whispered, not to the house, not to the night. To the part of herself that wanted to turn back and trade her own body into Samuel's hands if it meant Elijah could be unbound. The system had built that bargain on purpose. It had tried to make love into a leash.

Lila slid the bolt and opened the door.

Cold air hit her face and made her eyes water. She stepped out and closed the door without letting it click. The yard smelled of damp earth, manure, and the faint sweetness of flowers the mistress planted as if beauty could disinfect what the ground remembered.

She moved along the wall, staying in the blind patch the figure had chosen, and when she reached it she stopped, just out of arm's reach. Close enough to hear, not close enough to be grabbed.

The figure shifted slightly. A woman, not much older than Lila, wrapped in a dark shawl. Her face was mostly hidden, but her eyes caught what little light there was.

"Keep your hands where I can see them," the woman said softly.

Lila lifted her hands, palms angled outward and forced herself not to flinch at the command. It sounded too much like white men. But the voice did not carry ownership. It carried fear sharpened into rules.

"I'm Lila," she whispered before she could stop herself.

The woman's gaze hardened. "Don't," she said. "No names."

Lila swallowed the rest.

The woman tilted her head toward the garden fence. "You can climb," she said.

"Yes."

"Then you climb quiet. When you drop, you don't run. You walk. You understand?"

Lila nodded once.

They moved together, not side by side, but close enough that Lila could feel the woman's presence as an anchor. The fence was low, meant to keep animals out, not people in. Lila put her hands on the top rail and swung one leg over slowly, lowering herself instead of dropping. Her skirt snagged on a splinter, and her heart stopped for a beat, but she freed it with careful fingers and eased down into the soft soil beyond.

On the other side, the woman climbed as easily, like she'd done it before, like fences were just another kind of line you learned to cross without announcing yourself.

They walked through the orchard rather than cutting straight into open field. Trees broke their silhouettes. Fallen apples softened their steps. The night air was colder there, and the smell of fruit gone sweet and rotten clung to the ground.

Only when the house was a darker shape behind them did the woman speak again.

"You got anything on you that can identify you," she asked.

Lila's hand went to her sleeve instinctively and stopped. "No," she said, and the lie felt true enough. There were things on her, but nothing with her name. Nothing that could be held up and declared evidence.

The woman nodded once, satisfied, then led her toward a narrow path that dipped into a shallow ravine. Water ran there, not loud, but constant, a quiet cover for footfalls. Lila thought of Elijah in the reeds, the older man keeping him near the creek because water swallowed sound and footprints.

The world repeated itself in different places.

They followed the ravine until a low structure appeared ahead, a small shed half sunk into the earth as if trying to hide. No lantern burned. No sign marked it as safe. But the woman approached it without hesitation.

She rapped on the wood with her knuckles: three quick taps, then one. The same kind of pattern as before, but not the same. A new language.

A panel shifted. A face appeared in the crack, only an eye at first, then more. An older Black man with gray at his temples, his gaze sharp and tired.

He looked at the woman, then at Lila. His eyes lingered on Lila's hands, on her bare feet, on her face arranged into forced calm.

“How’d you come out,” he asked the woman, voice low.

“Same way,” she replied. “Quiet.”

The older man studied Lila again. “You got a mark,” he asked.

Lila’s stomach clenched at the question. “No.”

“Good,” he said, echoing the woman Elijah had met, as if the same sentence traveled this road again and again. “Marked ones bring dogs like ghosts.”

He opened the panel wider and gestured them in.

Inside, the shed smelled of damp wood, old straw, and something faintly medicinal. A candle burned low in a jar, its light kept small. Two other figures sat on crates in the shadows, faces turned away. One was a boy with knees drawn to his chest, trembling with cold or fear. The other was a woman with a scarf wrapped tight around her hair, her eyes fixed on nothing.

No one spoke. Speaking made stories. Stories got traded.

The older man closed the panel and crouched near Lila, not touching. “You eat,” he said.

Lila pulled the strip of bread from her bodice. It was flattened and warm from her skin. She broke it in half automatically, offering a piece.

He shook his head. "You," he repeated. "You first. If you faint, you slow everybody."

Lila forced herself to chew. The bread tasted like dust and survival. She swallowed with effort and felt her stomach twist, hungry enough to be angry at the smallness of it.

When she finished, the older man spoke again. "You can't go north the way you think," he said, and the sentence struck her like a remembered voice. Elijah's guide had said the same thing in different words: not north yet, just away. Doors, not guarantees.

Lila nodded, her throat too tight for speech.

The older man glanced at the others in the shed. "We move before dawn," he said. "Not together. In pieces. You," he pointed to Lila without using her name, "you go with her."

The woman in the shawl didn't react, only shifted slightly as if accepting weight.

Lila's mind jumped ahead, trying to see the line of miles, the houses, the hands, the risks. She thought of Samuel's voice in the wagon, calm and poisonous: waiting doesn't make the teeth disappear. It just gives them time to settle in.

The older man looked at her with something like grim understanding. "If you keep thinking back," he said, "you'll turn into a hook. Hooks get caught."

Lila's jaw tightened. She stared at the candle flame trapped in the jar, the way it burned without lighting the room enough to expose anyone.

"I'm not thinking back," she lied.

The older man's gaze stayed on her until she felt seen through. "You are," he said, not unkind. "That's normal. But you don't feed it. You don't speak it. You don't let it steer your feet. North is a direction. Not a promise. You understand?"

Lila swallowed. The blue scrap in her sleeve pressed against her skin like a bruise.

"I understand," she whispered.

The shed fell quiet again, the kind of quiet that held people together without asking them to become family. Outside, the night remained wide and indifferent. Somewhere far off, a dog barked once, then fell silent, as if even the animals were being taught what not to say.

Lila drew her knees up to her chest and tried to make herself small enough to fit inside the narrow space the road allowed.

She did not know what had become of Elijah. She did not know whether her leaving would save him or only leave him alone with Boone's barn and Samuel's patient cruelty. The road offered no answers. It only offered movement.

And as she sat in that half-buried shed waiting for the sky to pale, Lila understood what the title meant in her bones.

The North didn't speak.

It didn't call her by name. It didn't promise her a reunion. It didn't tell her she had chosen right.

It only waited, silent and cold, while she learned how to become the kind of person who could reach it without expecting it to be kind in return.

Before dawn, the shed breathed like a buried animal.

Lila sat with her knees tight to her chest, the shawled woman's shoulder a dark line beside her in the cramped space. The candle in the jar had been pinched lower until it barely existed, only a weak orange ember behind glass. In that light, faces became partial truths: a cheekbone, the shine of an eye, the curve of a mouth held closed on purpose.

No one slept deeply. Sleep would have been trust, and trust was a door that opened both ways.

Outside, the ravine's water kept talking to itself. It sounded like distance. It sounded like a place where a person could step and not be counted.

The older man had said they would move in pieces, and Lila understood the reason without needing it explained. Together was a story. Together was a net you could throw once and catch many.

A soft knock came from the panel, three taps and one. The older man lifted his head, listening. He didn't answer with speech. He slid the panel open a finger's width and looked out into the dim.

Then he nodded, quick. "Now," he breathed, and the word was not hope. It was timing.

The shawled woman rose first, joints quiet, body trained to exist without announcing itself. Lila stood and felt blood rush back into her legs with painful pins and needles. Her bare feet found the earth floor. Cold seeped into her bones from below like the ground wanted to claim her again.

The older man held out a ragged pair of shoes. Too big, cracked at the toes, but shoes. Lila hesitated, then slid her feet into them. The leather smelled like someone else's sweat and miles. It made her stomach clench with gratitude and dread at the same time.

"You keep them," the older man murmured. "If you lose them, you don't stop to cry over it."

Lila nodded once.

He glanced at her sleeve, not at the seam where her hidden things pressed against her skin, but at her hands. "You got something on you," he said.

It was not accusation. It was assessment, the same language the creek man had used with Elijah, the same language the embroidery woman had used in the parlor. Doors, rules, no stories.

Lila kept her voice small. "Just what I need."

"Then keep it quiet," he replied. "You walk like a servant sent on an errand. You don't walk like a woman with a secret."

The shawled woman stepped out first, disappearing into the ravine's dark. Lila followed, ducking through the panel, feeling the cool air hit her face like a slap. The sky was not yet light, but it had softened from black to a thin bruised gray.

They walked along the water until the ravine widened into low brush, then climbed a shallow bank where the ground turned firmer. The shawled woman did not speak. She did not look back often. She moved like someone who understood that the most dangerous moment was the one when a person started believing they had already escaped.

As the horizon paled, they reached a narrow road cut through trees. Wagons had worn it down, leaving two tracks with grass in the center. The shawled woman stopped at the edge and listened, head angled slightly like she could hear into the future.

When nothing came, she crossed, stepping on the packed dirt where the prints of hooves and wheels had already torn the earth. Lila followed, heart hammering, expecting a shout, a whistle, bells. But the road stayed empty.

They walked for hours in silence broken only by the sound of their own steps and the occasional sharp call of a bird that made Lila flinch as if it were a signal. Twice they left the road to cut through woods when the shawled woman sensed movement ahead, a distant cart, a man on horseback, shapes that might be ordinary but could also be teeth.

Near midday they reached a farmhouse set back from the road behind a line of trees. White paint, peeling in places. A low barn. Smoke from a chimney. The kind of place that looked harmless because it wanted to.

The shawled woman did not go straight to the door. She circled wide, then approached from the side, where a patch of garden lay untended, weeds allowed to grow too thick for show. She knelt as if to pull a weed and pressed her fingers into the dirt, lifting a small stone and setting it back down.

A signal. A wrongness placed on purpose.

They waited in the weeds until the back door opened.

A white woman stepped out, older, hair pulled tight, apron stained with flour. She did not smile. Her eyes moved over the yard first, then the tree line, then finally the shadows where Lila and the shawled woman crouched. Her gaze held no welcome. Only decision.

"Come," she said, not loud. "Quick."

Inside, the air smelled of bread and soap, and the warmth made Lila's skin prickle. Warmth was dangerous; it made a body want to relax. It made a mind want to believe this was a home and not a threshold.

The white woman shut the door and slid a heavy bolt into place. "Don't stand where you can be seen from the windows," she snapped, not cruel, not gentle. Practical.

They moved into a small pantry behind the kitchen. Shelves of jars. Sacks of grain. A trapdoor set into the floor with a rug thrown over it.

The white woman lifted the rug and flipped the trapdoor open. Cool air rose from below, smelling of earth and potatoes. "Down," she said, and her voice finally softened by a fraction, as if acknowledging their bodies were still bodies. "And don't make noise. There's men on the road today."

Lila climbed down into the root cellar and sat on a crate, shoulders tight, breathing shallow. The shawled woman stayed standing, watchful even in the dark. Above them, the trapdoor closed, and the kitchen noises resumed like nothing had happened: a pot set down, a spoon stirring, footsteps moving in ordinary patterns.

Lila realized then that this was what the road north actually was. Not a single line, not a promised hand. A series of rooms where people pretended you weren't there loudly enough to keep you alive.

She stayed in the cellar until her legs ached and time lost meaning. Once, voices came from the kitchen. Male voices, laughing too easily. Lila's stomach clenched. She held her breath, expecting the trapdoor to rip open, expecting lantern light in her face, expecting someone to say, "Well, there you are."

But the voices drifted away. The laughter thinned. A door opened. Shut.

When the trapdoor finally opened again, the white woman's face appeared above them, drawn tight with fatigue. "Go," she said. "And don't come back this way. Not ever."

They left by a different door, not the one they'd entered. The shawled woman led Lila through a narrow lane between hedges, then into another stand of woods. There were no goodbyes. Gratitude could be spoken, but speaking created threads, and threads could be traced.

Days stacked like that. Walking. Hiding. Being passed from one set of rules to another. Sleeping in a barn loft with hay sticking to her hair and mice scuttling close enough to brush her skirt. Riding in the back of a wagon under a tarp that smelled of mildew and old manure, listening to a driver sing off-key as if the song could cover the sound of her breathing. Waiting in a church basement that smelled of damp hymnals while footsteps crossed overhead and a man's voice recited Scripture with a steadiness that sounded like a warning.

Once, a Black family took her in for a single night, their house small and clean and tense with the careful quiet of people who had learned that freedom was not the same thing as safety. The woman who offered her a bowl of stew did not ask her story. The man who sat by the door with his hands folded did not relax even after the latch clicked.

"You going far?" the woman asked finally, voice low.

Lila hesitated, then answered the only way that felt true. "Far as I can."

The woman nodded once. "Don't expect it to feel like you think," she murmured.

Lila looked up, and the woman's eyes held something that made Lila's throat tighten: not pity, not romance. Recognition.

On a gray morning that smelled of rain, the shawled woman led Lila toward a town where the roads grew busier, and the buildings pressed close together. People moved with purpose, heads down against the weather. Cart wheels rattled over stone. A river ran nearby, wide and restless, carrying debris and branches as if it was always trying to leave too.

They stopped in an alley behind a shop. The shawled woman turned and faced Lila fully for the first time in days, as if distance had finally earned them a moment of directness.

"This is where I leave you," she said.

Lila's stomach dropped. She had not allowed herself to think of abandonment. Thinking of it would have made it real. "Where do I go."

The woman's gaze flicked to the street, to the passersby who did not look at Lila long enough to see her. "You walk like you belong," she replied. "You go to the boarding house on Willow Street. You ask for Mrs. G. You don't say why. You don't say where you came from. If she tells you no, you leave without begging."

Lila's mouth went dry. "And if she says yes."

"Then you listen," the woman said. Her voice tightened slightly, as if the next part cost her. "And you stop trying to make it make sense. You've been living in a world that trains you to look for the whip. Up here, it don't always look like a whip."

Lila swallowed. The blue scrap and pin pressed against her skin like they were part of her now. "Is this the North," she asked, and hated how small the question sounded.

The shawled woman's eyes stayed steady. "It's a piece of it," she replied. Then, after a beat: "Don't speak your name to strangers. Don't look too long at white men. Don't think a free paper means a free day."

Lila's chest tightened. "What about him," she whispered, and did not have to say Elijah's name.

She could taste it anyway, a phantom word behind her teeth.

The shawled woman's jaw hardened. "You don't look back," she said, and the firmness in it was not cruelty. It was a rule carved from what she had seen happen to people who turned into hooks. "If you got breath, you use it moving forward. That's the only honoring you can afford right now."

Lila blinked hard. The street noise sounded too loud suddenly, every cart wheel like a bell loop, every shout like a whistle. She forced her shoulders down, forced her face into calm.

The shawled woman stepped back. "Go," she said.

Lila walked out of the alley and into the street.

No one grabbed her. No hand closed on her wrist. No dog's bells chimed. Men passed her without ordering her aside. A white woman brushed past, skirts swishing, and did not look at Lila's face long enough to decide what it was allowed to be. A boy ran by with a loaf of bread under his arm, laughing, free in a way that made Lila's throat burn.

She kept walking, expecting at any moment to be corrected.

But the correction did not come.

And that absence was its own kind of terror.

On a corner, she stopped because her legs started shaking without permission. She put her hand on a brick wall, feeling its roughness, grounding herself in something solid. The brick did not flinch from her touch. It did not belong to her, but it did not reject her either. It simply existed.

Lila realized then what she had been carrying in her bones all her life: the constant sound of being watched. Even when no one spoke, the plantation had always been talking through bells, through whistles, through footsteps timed to remind you that you were counted.

Here, the air held no such language. People moved, talked, argued, bought and sold, lived. But the system's voice was not loud enough to announce itself in the same way.

The silence did not feel like peace.

It felt like standing in a room after a scream and realizing your ears are still ringing even when no sound remains.

A man across the street laughed, head thrown back, and the sound made Lila flinch as if it were a threat. She forced herself not to run. Running would mark her. Running would turn her into a story.

She walked again, one step at a time, toward Willow Street, toward a boarding house and a woman who might say no.

She passed a posted notice nailed to a wall. Words crowded it, printed ink. Lila could not read them fast enough, but she caught one word and felt cold spread through her stomach as if someone had put a hand inside her.

Runaway.

Her breath caught. Her eyes flicked away, refusing to stare. Staring made you remembered.

In the North, the world did not shout its rules at her with bells and whips. It let the rules sit quiet in ink, in glances, in the way certain doors closed a little faster when she approached, in the way some voices dropped when they spoke of the South as if the South were a sickness that could travel.

She walked through that quiet, and each step felt like learning a new kind of cage. One without iron. One made of uncertainty and the knowledge that men like Samuel did not need to stand beside you to reach you. They could reach you with paper, with money, with a stranger's question asked too casually.

By the time she found Willow Street, her mouth was so dry she could barely swallow. She stood across from the boarding house and watched its front door open and close as people came and went, ordinary as breathing.

Freedom existed. It stood right there, looking like a door no one guarded.

Lila crossed the street slowly, forcing her feet to move as if they belonged to her. She climbed the steps, lifted her hand, and knocked.

The sound was small.

No whip answered it. No bell chimed. No whistle cut the air.

Only the hollow quiet after the knock, waiting to see what kind of world would answer.

And in that quiet, Lila understood with a clarity that felt like grief: the North did not speak.

It did not tell her she was safe.

It did not tell her she had done the right thing.

It did not tell her what had happened to Elijah, or whether her leaving had saved him or only moved the pain into a different room.

It only opened, or it didn't.

The latch turned from inside.

Lila lowered her hand and held her face steady, bracing herself for the voice that would decide whether this silence became shelter or just another kind of hunting ground.

Chapter 17

Epilogue – The Whisper

The latch turned from inside, and for a moment Lila could not tell whether the sound was welcome or warning. The door opened only a hand's breadth, held by a chain. A white woman's eye appeared in the gap, sharp and tired.

"Yes," the woman said, not a question, not an invitation.

Lila kept her shoulders loose and her hands visible. She did not shift her weight the way she would have on Carter's porch. She did not lower her gaze the way she had been trained to. She let her eyes rest on the woman's mouth instead, a safer place than eyes, and spoke the line the shawled woman had given her.

"I'm looking for Mrs. G."

The woman's face did not change, but her gaze flicked to Lila's shoes, the cracked leather that had come from the half-buried shed, then to Lila's hands, empty. The chain stayed in place.

"You got a letter?" Mrs. G asked.

"No," Lila said, and heard how thin her voice sounded in this clean air. She swallowed and made it steadier. "I got sent."

A pause. The woman's breath came out through her nose like she was measuring whether she could afford the risk of one more body in her house. Then the chain slid free. The door opened wider.

"Come on," Mrs. G said. "Don't stand in the doorway like you're waiting to be claimed."

Inside, the boarding house smelled of boiled cloth and old wood and something fried that had soaked into the walls. A narrow hall ran back toward a staircase. Voices came from somewhere above, a woman laughing softly, a man coughing, the sound of life stacked close together.

Mrs. G closed the door behind Lila and turned the lock with a final click that made Lila's skin prick. Not because she thought she was being trapped again, but because locks had meant something else for so long. Locks had always been a promise that someone else controlled what happened next.

Mrs. G looked her over once more, quicker now, as if refusing to linger on the shape of a frightened girl would keep the girl from becoming a story.

"You got a name?" she asked.

Lila hesitated. Names were dangerous. Names were hooks. The shawled woman's voice returned, firm: Don't speak your name to strangers.

She chose the closest thing to truth that did not hand her over. "Lila," she said, and did not offer a second name to make it easier to find her later.

Mrs. G nodded as if that was enough. "You can't stay in the front room," she said. "People look through windows up here same as down there, they just pretend it's manners."

She led Lila up the stairs and into a small room at the back, under the slant of the roof. A narrow bed. A washstand. A single chair with one leg repaired badly. A window that looked out on an alley where wagons passed and did not pause.

"You sleep," Mrs. G said. "You eat when I tell you. You don't talk about where you came from in the hallways. You don't talk about it in the kitchen either, because the kitchen hears everything and repeats it."

Lila's throat tightened. "How much."

Mrs. G's mouth pressed flat. "You got money?"

"No."

"Then you work," she said simply. "You keep your head down. You keep your eyes open. You don't think you're invisible just because you're not in chains."

Lila nodded once. Her hands shook slightly, and she curled them into fists to stop it. The room was small, but it was hers in a way nothing on Carter's land had ever been. The bed looked too soft. The fact of it made her suspicious.

Mrs. G lingered at the door. Her voice lowered. "You got someone looking for you?"

Lila's chest tightened. She saw Boone's barn in her mind, rope and blood and Samuel's calm face watching like it enjoyed being right. She forced herself to keep her voice steady. "I don't know."

Mrs. G's eyes narrowed in a way that suggested she understood more than Lila had said. "Then you act like someone is," she replied. "Because up here, sometimes they are."

When she left, the sound of her steps faded down the hall and into the hum of the house. Lila sat on the edge of the bed without lying down, listening. The boarding house was crowded with breath, but it was not the plantation's breath. It had no bells. No whistles. No dogs trained to announce your fear.

And still, she listened as if the whistle might cut the air anyway.

In the weeks that followed, the North unrolled itself in pieces. Lila scrubbed floors, carried wash water, mended torn hems for boarders who looked through her more often than at her. She learned which streets felt safer at dusk and which ones turned mean when the lamps were lit. She learned that a man could smile and still measure you. She learned that the word "girl" could still carry ownership even when it came wrapped in politeness.

Rumors drifted through the boarding house the way smoke drifted through cracks, unavoidable, clinging. Men argued downstairs over newspapers, their voices sharp, then dropping when someone new entered. Mrs. G did not allow newspapers in the kitchen, but boarders brought their words in anyway, reciting them in fragments between mouthfuls of stew.

"They say the country's splitting," one man said one evening, his tone like he was discussing weather. He was a carpenter with sawdust always in his hair, hands rough but clean. He did not look at Lila as he spoke, as if she were not part of the nation he referenced. "South don't want to let go."

Another man, thin and red-faced, laughed. "Let go of what. Of who. They got themselves a whole economy built on backs, you think they gonna shrug and say, 'Well, fair enough'?"

The word backs hit Lila's spine like a hand.

Mrs. G's ladle clanged against a pot. "Eat," she snapped, as if food could shut a mouth. But even she could not stop the rumor's movement. Information traveled differently than people. It always had.

The next day, a boarder came in with a folded paper tucked under his arm like contraband. He unfolded it on the front table, and men gathered around as if they were about to look at something holy. Lila carried a basket of linens through the room, eyes lowered, and still caught words like they were stones thrown.

"Fort Sumter," someone read aloud. "They fired on the fort. They saying it's war now."

War. The word landed in the room and did not move. For a moment, even the men who liked to laugh went quiet, tasting what war might mean for them.

For Lila, it meant something else entirely. War was distant, but it was the kind of distance that could still reach you. It was a new kind of whistle cutting through a place that had tried to feel like silence.

That night, she lay in her narrow bed under the slanted roof and listened to the boarding house breathe. Her sleeve still held the thin wire Elijah had given her, the question curled tight against her skin. She had kept it hidden through the journey, through the days of work, through Mrs. G's rules. It was the one thing she allowed herself to keep that had no use except memory.

War, she thought. War might mean men marching south with rifles and flags and songs. It might mean blood spilled on fields far away from Carter's porch and Boone's barn. It might mean nothing at all for Elijah, because plantations had always been at war with the bodies they owned and had never needed uniforms to do it.

A week later, a Black man came into the boarding house kitchen at dusk, hat in his hands. Mrs. G stiffened the moment she saw him, then softened a fraction as if recognizing his face.

"You got news?" she asked.

The man glanced at Lila, then away. His voice stayed low. "They recruiting," he said. "Not us yet, not official. But it's coming. And the South's tightening. Folks trying to run before the lines get locked down."

Mrs. G's jaw clenched. "They always tighten when they're scared."

The man nodded. "And there's talk of laws getting used harder up here. Men going door to door in some towns, asking questions. Offering money to anyone who can point at a face and claim it belongs to someone down South."

Bounty hunters. Lila felt her stomach drop. The North did not speak, but it listened, and there were always men willing to translate listening into profit.

Mrs. G's eyes flicked to Lila's hands, then to her face, then away again. She did not ask questions out loud. Questions could be overheard. Questions could become proof that she knew something worth selling.

The man tucked his hat back on. "You tell your people," he said to Mrs. G. "Keep quiet. Keep papers close if they got them. Keep moving if they don't."

When he left, the kitchen felt colder, even with the stove heat breathing steady.

Mrs. G stirred the pot as if her anger could be worked into the stew. "You hear me," she said, not looking at Lila. "You don't go wandering. You don't go standing on corners just to watch the world. You don't go thinking you're safe because nobody's called you property in a while."

Lila's voice came out before she could stop it. "Do you think it'll change anything."

Mrs. G paused with the ladle held above the pot. She looked at Lila then, really looked, her gaze sharp enough to cut cloth.

"I think people love to promise change," she said. "I think promises are cheap. I think a war is just men deciding to kill each other over what kind of country they want to live in. And I think, for us, the question is whether we get dragged into it as reason or as people."

Lila swallowed. The wire in her sleeve seemed to tighten against her skin, as if Elijah's question had heard the word war and wanted an answer.

That night, downstairs, the men argued again. They spoke names of politicians and generals like those names were prayers. They spoke of honor, of union, of rights.

Lila listened from the stairs with a basket of linens on her hip and felt the distance in every word. Distant war. A thing happening somewhere else, spoken about as if it were a story being written by men who did not know what it cost to be the subject of someone else's decisions.

In her room, she pressed her forehead to the cold glass of the window and watched the alley below. A cat moved through the shadows, quick and silent. A wagon rattled past and did not slow. Somewhere farther off, a bell rang from a church tower, marking an hour that belonged to everyone equally, at least in sound.

She tried to picture Elijah hearing about the war. She tried to picture him still alive to hear anything at all. She tried not to turn into a hook, not to circle her grave, but some nights the thought of him was the only thing that kept her from dissolving into the new quiet.

War was distant, but it seeped closer in small ways. Men in uniforms appeared on streets. Prices rose. Mrs. G began locking the front door earlier. The word "runaway" showed up on more notices, nailed higher, printed cleaner, as if ink could do what chains had always done.

One afternoon, as Lila carried wash water up the stairs, she heard a boarder reading from a paper in the front room.

"They say if the South leaves, the country breaks," he said. "They say it's the end of everything."

Lila paused on the landing, the bucket's weight pulling at her arms. She thought of Boone's yard gathered at dawn, the branding iron glowing. She thought of the whistle in the dark, the trap set with precision, the way hope had been weaponized and made into a lesson.

The end of everything, she thought, had been threatened her whole life. The plantation had always promised that if you moved wrong, everything would end. That promise had never belonged to white men alone. It had been written into Black bodies.

She lifted the bucket again and continued upward, step by careful step, her arms burning, her face blank.

The war was distant, but the whisper of it was everywhere now, sliding through cracks, carried by mouths that had never learned the discipline of silence the way she had.

And in the North's quiet, Lila learned a new kind of listening.

Not for bells.

Not for whistles.

For whispers that meant the world was shifting, and that shifting might crush her or might, if she survived long enough, loosen something that had been held tight for generations.

She did not trust it.

But she could not ignore it either.

In her sleeve, Elijah's wire question rested against her skin, and sometimes, in the hours before dawn, she would touch it lightly and let herself imagine that somewhere, in some barn or yard or field far away, he was still breathing too, listening for the same distant war, the same rumor of change, and holding himself together with the same thin, dangerous discipline.

A whisper could be hope.

A whisper could also be a trap.

Up here, Lila was learning, the difference between the two was not in the sound.

It was in what the sound asked you to risk.

The first time Lila heard about the bearded man, she did not hear his name.

She heard him as a shape in someone else's mouth, a rumor pressed thin enough to pass through a room without catching on anything sharp. It came in the boarding house front parlor on a wet evening when the windows sweated and the air smelled of wool coats drying too slowly.

A boarder with ink-stained fingers sat near the lamp, reading aloud from a newspaper as if the words could protect him from what they described. Two others leaned in, hungry for information the way people down South had been hungry for gossip, as if knowing could keep you from being chosen next.

"They say he spoke again," the ink-fingered man said, tapping the paper. "That long one. The one they print and print."

Mrs. G passed through with a basket of folded linens, not stopping, not listening openly. She didn't have to. Sound traveled; it always had. Lila stood in the doorway between hall and parlor with her hands full of mended cloth, head lowered in the posture that kept her from being asked to join a conversation that wasn't meant for her.

But she listened anyway.

"Who," one man asked. "That lawyer fella."

"The tall one," another answered, and laughed as if height were the only thing that mattered. "With that beard like he trying to hide half his face."

The word beard made a small spark in Lila's chest and then went cold. Beards belonged to white men with time. Beards belonged to men who could let hair grow without being told it was dirty or wrong.

"He ain't even president," the first man said, skeptical. "He's just talking."

"Talking's what starts it," the second replied. "Talking gets men killed before the killing even begins."

Lila felt her throat tighten with a memory of other talking, other words that had moved through cracks: north. Underground. A question that formed between Elijah and her and became dangerous simply because it existed. On the plantation, talking was an invitation for punishment. Up here, talking sat on paper and was passed hand to hand like it was harmless.

Mrs. G paused at the parlor threshold, gaze sharp. "If you want to talk yourself into trouble, do it quieter," she said. Her voice carried irritation, but under it was something else: caution.

The men lowered their voices just a fraction.

The ink-fingered man read on. "He says the country can't stand split," he murmured. "He says it'll become one thing or the other. Free or slave."

Free or slave. As if those were clean categories. As if a border made of ink could make a body safe.

A third man, older, his coat patched at the elbows, snorted. "He can say what he likes," he muttered. "He ain't the one with a rope around his wrists. He ain't the one with dogs trained to love your fear."

Lila's hands clenched around the cloth she held, knuckles whitening before she forced them loose. The room tilted for a moment, not from dizziness but from the sudden closeness of Boone's barn. Rope. Elijah's shoulders straining. His voice, broken thin, pressing one word into her like a tool: wait.

Someone said, "They call him Honest Abe."

"Honest," the older man repeated with a laugh that had no joy in it. "That's a fine name for a politician."

Lila shifted her weight, careful not to make the floorboard creak. Politicians were distant men who made laws that traveled south and north like whips made of paper. The Fugitive Slave Law, whispered about in the kitchen like a curse, had proved that. A white man could point at you up here and call you his, and the law would nod as if it recognized your face.

Honest Abe. A tall man with a beard. A man who spoke in sentences that got printed and passed around like bread.

That night, when Lila lay under the slanted roof in her narrow room, she touched the wire hidden in her sleeve and listened to rain tap the window. The sound was steady, a patient drumming that reminded her of the cook's fingers on the table leg back on Carter's property. Once. Twice. A pattern meant to be seen by the right eyes.

In the boarding house below, men argued late. Their voices rose, then fell. Someone laughed. Someone swore. A chair scraped back. The house creaked, adjusting itself around their living.

Lila closed her eyes and tried to picture the bearded man. She did not allow herself to picture him as a savior. The plantation had taught her what happened to people who believed too hard in rescue. Hope got branded. Hope got used as bait. Hope made you run straight into a trap already measured.

Still, she couldn't stop her mind from reaching toward the idea of a white man in power speaking words that named slavery as a thing that could end. The thought was dangerous not because it was impossible, but because it could make her careless. It could make her think the North was listening on her behalf.

The North didn't speak. It didn't promise. It didn't explain.

It only made room for new kinds of threat.

In the following weeks, the bearded man's shadow lengthened without ever entering the room. His name started appearing in fragments at the edges of conversation, always carried by someone else's confidence.

On a market morning, Lila stood behind Mrs. G at a stall where potatoes were piled in muddy heaps. A white man in a fine coat spoke loudly nearby, his voice bright with certainty.

"Lincoln'll fix it," he declared, as if fixing a country was like repairing a wagon wheel. "He's got the spine for it. He ain't afraid to say what needs saying."

Another man answered, "You think a speech stops a bullet?"

"A speech starts an army," the first replied.

Lila kept her eyes down. She listened to the rhythm of voices, the way men made promises with their mouths when their bodies had never been used as proof. She watched hands exchange coins. She watched a farmer's face harden when he spoke about the South, as if the South were a thief that might come north and steal what belonged to him.

She understood then that white men could be afraid of losing things they had never been forced to earn. Their fear traveled differently than hers, but it could still spill over onto her skin.

Back at the boarding house, Mrs. G pushed a pot across the stove with more force than necessary. "Stop saying his name like it's a prayer," she snapped at a boarder one evening when he grew too loud with his opinions.

The boarder bristled. "Who, Lincoln? You got a problem with him?"

Mrs. G's eyes were hard. "I got a problem with folks who think one man can wash blood off the country with words," she said. "I got a problem with anybody making promises when they ain't the one paying."

The boarder opened his mouth, then shut it. He glanced at Lila, and for a moment she saw something in his gaze that made her stomach tighten. Curiosity. Calculation. The same look Samuel had worn when he realized information could become currency. Up here, there were different men, but the habit of measuring what a person was worth hadn't disappeared. It had only learned new manners.

Later, when the boarders had gone out, Mrs. G leaned against the counter and spoke without looking at Lila.

"They'll tell you he's going to set you free," she said, voice low. "They'll tell you everything's changing because a man with a beard says it should."

Lila rinsed a bowl slowly, letting water run over her hands to hide their tremble. "Is he," she asked before she could stop herself.

Mrs. G's mouth tightened. "He's a man," she replied. "Men do what keeps them standing. Sometimes that helps us. Sometimes it don't."

Lila swallowed. "They said he talked about free or slave," she murmured.

Mrs. G gave a humorless huff. "Free is a word that makes white folks feel clean," she said. "It don't tell you where you can sleep. It don't tell you who can grab you in the street and call it law. It don't tell you whether a neighbor will sell your face for twenty dollars."

Lila dried the bowl with a rag, the motion repetitive enough to keep her from falling apart. "Then why do they talk about him."

Mrs. G was quiet for a moment. The stove popped softly as it cooled.

"Because people need a shape to hang their fear on," she said finally. "And sometimes they need a shape to hang their hope on too. A bearded man is easy to picture. Easy to blame. Easy to love. Easier than looking at the whole country and admitting it's rotten in places nobody wants to touch."

Lila's throat tightened. Rotten. She thought of the smell in Boone's barn, blood and damp hay and sweat. She thought of the plantation's rituals, branding irons heated until they glowed, hope turned into lesson. That rot had been visible. It had been smelled. It had been forced into the air until everyone breathed it.

Up here, the rot hid behind curtains and polite voices. It hid behind printed laws. It hid behind people saying "free" as if the word were enough.

That winter, the bearded man became more than rumor. His portrait appeared on a broadside nailed to a post near the market, paper flapping in wind. Lila saw it from the edge of her vision and felt her body tense as if it were a wanted notice.

She forced herself to look.

The drawing was crude, but the shape was unmistakable: a tall white man, deep-set eyes, a beard that framed his jaw. His expression wasn't kind. It wasn't cruel. It was the sort of expression a man wore when he knew other men were watching to see if he'd bend.

Beneath the portrait were words too small for Lila to read quickly. She didn't stand there to try. Staring made you remembered.

A white woman beside her, carrying a basket, paused and said to no one in particular, "He looks tired already."

A man answered, "That's what happens when you take on the whole country."

The whole country. Lila felt something inside her twist. The whole country had been sitting on her back, on Elijah's back, on Ben's back, on Mary's silence, on the cook's fingers tapping a secret pattern under a guard's bored gaze. The whole country had been built in rooms where Black people were told to keep their eyes down and call it sense.

She walked away from the broadside with her pulse thudding. In her sleeve, the wire question pressed against her skin, a small hard truth that had traveled farther than Elijah had been allowed to. She did not know whether he still lived. She did not know if Boone had kept him alive for work or killed him for spite. The North did not speak those answers. It did not send a letter. It did not open its mouth and explain what her leaving had cost.

But the bearded man's face on paper made the distance feel strange. It made the war's whisper feel less like weather and more like a door cracking open somewhere far away.

That night, one of the boarders came in late with his cheeks red from cold and drink. He sat at the table and began talking before his coat was even off.

"They say Lincoln's going to make it official," he slurred. "They say he's going to end it. All of it. Slavery. Like cutting a rope."

Mrs. G's voice was sharp. "Go sleep it off."

The boarder laughed, leaning back. "You don't believe," he said, wagging a finger. "But it's coming. The bearded man's going to do it."

Lila stood in the kitchen doorway, unseen by him, and felt her stomach hollow out. Cutting a rope. The words dragged Boone's barn up through her ribs. Rope cutting meant Elijah dropping, means hands freed, meant a man able to lift his head without pain.

She wanted to believe it so badly it felt like hunger.

Mrs. G looked at Lila then, quick and cutting, as if she'd heard the sound of belief moving in Lila's body.

"Don't," Mrs. G said softly, not to the boarder, to Lila. "Don't take a drunk man's talk and build a bed out of it."

Lila held still. She nodded once, small.

Later, in her room, she sat on the edge of the bed and pressed her fingers to the wire through her sleeve. The question mark shape felt sharper than usual, as if time had honed it.

She tried to imagine Elijah hearing the bearded man's name. She tried to imagine it reaching Boone's land the way the word north had reached them, in fragments and glances. She tried to imagine it meaning something other than another kind of trap, another promise used to keep people waiting until they broke themselves.

Outside her window, snow fell in thin, quiet sheets, softening the alley into a blank page. The city's noises were muffled. Even the church bell sounded distant, swallowed by cold.

In that hush, Lila understood the worst part of rumors. They didn't just travel. They settled. They made a home in you. They rearranged your insides around their possibility.

The bearded man might do something. He might not. He might end one kind of chain and leave another intact. He might speak a proclamation that sounded like freedom and still leave men with papers and guns hunting bodies like hers.

But his name had become a whisper that moved through the North the way north had moved through the South: a direction people pointed to when they couldn't bear to name the cage they were standing in.

Lila lay down without undressing and stared at the ceiling until her eyes burned.

She did not pray to the bearded man.

She did not curse him either.

She held herself in the thin discipline that had kept her alive through Carter's parlor and Boone's barn and the road north that had offered rooms instead of promises.

And she listened, as she always had, for what the whisper asked her to risk.

Because whether it came from a plantation yard or a printed paper in a northern town, the world's voice had always done the same thing.

It tried to make you believe salvation was something someone else could hand you.

Lila knew better.

Salvation, if it came at all, would come quiet. It would come costly. It would come with rules nobody bothered to print.

And even then, the North would not speak it aloud.

Spring didn't arrive like a blessing. It arrived like a loosening, slow and reluctant, as if the city itself didn't trust warmth. Snow melted into gray slush along the alley and ran in thin streams toward the gutters. The air filled with the smell of damp brick and horse manure and the sour breath of the river.

Lila kept working.

She scrubbed stair treads that never stayed clean. She boiled linens until her hands turned raw, then rubbed lard into the cracks at night so the skin wouldn't split open by morning. She carried trays and chamber pots and baskets of coal up narrow steps that made her legs burn. It was labor she chose only in the sense that she was still alive to do it. She told herself that was what freedom looked like: work you did without a hand on your wrist.

But some nights, when the boarders grew loud downstairs, when their laughter rose too suddenly, she would stop with a sheet half-folded in her hands and feel the plantation return in her body like a smell.

The quietest part of the North was not the streets. It was the way people could stand near you and never ask what had been done to you. Down South, cruelty announced itself. It called the yard together at dawn and made sure no one looked away. Here, cruelty had learned to pass for absence. It simply did not mention you, and the not-mentioning became a wall.

Mrs. G ran her house with rules that sounded like scolding and lived like protection.

"Don't talk to men you don't know," she said one morning, tying her apron tight. "Don't let anybody lead you outside with a smile and a question. You keep your eyes forward. You keep your mouth shut unless you got reason."

Lila nodded, as if she were being taught something new.

Mrs. G paused with her hand on a pot lid. "You still hearing them whistles," she said quietly.

It wasn't a question. It was a statement, like the embroidery woman had made statements. Like Samuel had.

Lila kept her face blank. "No," she lied.

Mrs. G didn't push. Pushing was for people who believed they could afford to be wrong. "All right," she said, and turned back to her stove. But a moment later she added, softer: "Don't let the quiet fool you. Quiet just means you got to listen different."

Lila listened different.

On the street, she listened for the rhythm of footsteps that didn't belong. Bounty hunters walked like men with purpose and patience, like they had time to wait for you to make a mistake. She listened for questions asked too casually by strangers: "Where you from?" "Who you belong to?" "You got papers?"

She didn't have papers.

She had a name that could be traded and a face that could be claimed. She had hands that could be described. A scar on her knuckle. A tear in one ear lobe from a childhood accident. A body that could be pointed at, and a law that might nod and accept the pointing.

Freedom meant you could be taken without a shout. Taken politely. Taken by ink.

One afternoon, Mrs. G sent her to the market with a list written in a tight, efficient hand Lila couldn't read. Lila carried it anyway, because carrying it made her look like she had business. People with business belonged places.

The market was crowded with spring. Crates of early greens. Buckets of muddy potatoes. Fish laid on beds of ice that smoked in the sun. Men shouted prices, voices sharp with need.

Lila waited behind Mrs. G at the butcher's stall, eyes lowered, hands folded, posture quiet. She didn't want attention. Attention was a hook.

A man behind them spoke, voice loud enough to be heard over the market's noise. "They say there's rewards went up again."

Mrs. G's shoulders tightened a fraction. Lila felt it without looking.

"Rewards for what," another voice asked, pretending ignorance.

"For property," the first man replied, and laughed as if the word were harmless. "For runaways. Folks down South sending word up. Paying good money for anybody who can identify."

Identify. The word slid into Lila's bones. It carried Boone's barn and Carter's parlor and Samuel's calm stare. It carried the way men had looked at her like she was already a conclusion.

Mrs. G's voice cut in, hard. "Mind your own business."

The man laughed again. "Just talking. Ain't a crime to talk."

It wasn't a crime to talk. It was a crime to be the wrong kind of person when someone else decided to talk about you.

Mrs. G paid the butcher and took the parcel of meat, then stepped close to Lila, mouth near her ear. “We’re leaving,” she murmured. “And you don’t look back. You understand?”

Lila did. Looking back made you remembered.

They moved through the crowd with measured steps. Lila kept her face arranged into calm. Her heart beat too hard for her ribs, but she didn’t let her pace change. Running was a confession.

Behind them, the man’s voice rose again. “They got one posted outside the courthouse,” he said to someone else. “Description and all. Girl, maybe twenty. Scar on her hand. They say she talks soft.”

Lila’s stomach twisted. She had a scar on her hand. So did a thousand other women. She talked soft because loud talking got you punished. The description could be anyone. That was part of the terror. It didn’t have to be her to catch her. It only had to be close enough for someone to decide.

Mrs. G did not turn. She walked as if she owned the street.

Back in the boarding house, she shut the door and slid the lock into place with a click that made Lila flinch.

Mrs. G turned then, eyes sharp. "You got anything that ties you to a place," she asked. "Any piece you been carrying like it's a prayer."

Lila's hand went, without thinking, to her sleeve.

Mrs. G saw it. Her gaze didn't soften, but something in it shifted into understanding. "If they take you," she said, voice low, "they take what you got on you and turn it into proof. You hear me? They'll hold up a scrap of something and say it's evidence you belong to somebody. Evidence don't have to be true. It just has to be useful."

Lila swallowed. Inside her sleeve, the thin wire pressed into her skin. The blue scrap was worn softer now, its edges less sharp from being handled and hidden, but it still held the color of the one thing she refused to let the plantation bleach out of her.

"It ain't proof," Lila whispered.

Mrs. G's mouth tightened. "That's what you think," she replied. "Men don't need truth. They need a story that gets paid."

Lila stood very still. The room seemed to lean in around her: the narrow hallway, the stairwell, the windows that looked out at a street where anyone could walk past and decide to look up.

"What do I do," Lila asked, and hated how the question scraped at her. She had run. She had followed rules. She had survived rooms and roads. She had come this far. And still she could be taken on an ordinary spring afternoon because a man at a market wanted to feel powerful.

Mrs. G looked at her a long moment. "You do what you been doing," she said. "You don't get careless. You don't get loud. And you don't let their talk crawl inside you until you start making mistakes."

That night, Lila lay in her narrow bed and stared at the slanted ceiling until her eyes ached. She listened to the boarding house breathe. A couple argued downstairs. Someone coughed behind a thin wall. A wagon rolled by outside, its wheels rattling over stone like bones.

In the dark, she touched the wire through her sleeve and tried to remember the exact feel of Elijah's hands. Not the rope around his wrists. Not the blood on his mouth. His hands as they had been before: steady, careful, scarred with work but still capable of gentleness. She tried to picture him alive without turning the picture into a knife.

She wondered, as she had a hundred times, if he had been made to watch someone else suffer the way she had been made to watch him. She wondered if Samuel had stood in Boone's yard afterward, calm, receiving his payment in food or favor or simply the satisfaction of being right.

Samuel did not have to be in the North to reach her. That was the new kind of fear that came with distance. On the plantation, Samuel was a body you could avoid by timing your steps. Here, he could become any mouth that asked the wrong question, any notice nailed to a wall, any man who looked too long at her hands.

Freedom meant the system no longer needed to announce itself. It could work through strangers.

Toward dawn, when the house finally quieted, Lila drifted into a shallow sleep and dreamed she was back in Carter's parlor. The embroidery needle went in and out of cloth, steady as rain. The woman's voice said, You don't touch things twice. Then the needle became a branding iron, glowing, and the thread became smoke. Lila woke with her mouth full of the taste of burned metal and sat up so fast her head spun.

There was no smoke. No iron. Only the thin gray light of morning pressing at the window. Only her own breath, loud in her ears.

She swung her feet to the floor and sat with her hands in her lap until her heartbeat slowed. She refused to cry. Tears made noise inside your face. Noise got noticed.

Downstairs, Mrs. G was already moving, pot lids clanging, the day beginning like a command.

Lila washed, dressed, and went down to work because work was a way to keep her body from being swallowed by memory. She scrubbed the back steps, then the front hall. She shook rugs out in the alley where the air was sharp enough to cut.

As she worked, she heard a boarder reading from a paper again in the parlor, voice solemn as a preacher.

"They say the President's going to do something," he read. "They say there's talk of a proclamation."

A proclamation. A word like a door, like a threat, like a promise.

Another man scoffed. "Paper don't stop men from doing what they want."

Lila froze with the rug half-lifted. Her hands tightened on the edge until her fingers hurt. Paper didn't stop men. But paper could change which men felt entitled to hunt. It could change the story that got told when a person disappeared.

Mrs. G's voice floated from the kitchen, sharp. "Lila. Keep moving."

Lila lifted the rug and snapped it again, dust rising. Keep moving. That had been the rule on the road north. Keep moving because stopping let fear catch up and put its teeth in you.

Later, in the quiet between chores, Mrs. G handed Lila a small bundle of folded cloth. "For your sleeve," she said without looking at her. "You can wrap whatever foolishness you're carrying in there so it don't print through. So it don't catch."

Lila's throat tightened. "Thank you," she whispered.

Mrs. G made a sound that might have been annoyance, might have been discomfort with gratitude. "Don't thank me," she said. "Just be alive."

Lila took the cloth upstairs and sat on her bed with her sleeve rolled up. She slid the extra fabric into the lining carefully, making a pocket within the pocket. When she placed the wire and the blue scrap back inside, she felt the smallest shift in her chest, as if she had hidden them deeper not only from other people but from herself.

She didn't know if that was wisdom or cowardice.

She only knew she needed to keep breathing.

In the weeks that followed, the war's whisper grew louder. More uniforms. More flags. More men talking about sacrifice with shiny eyes. And under it, always, the quieter talk: rewards, runaways, laws.

Freedom existed, but it did not speak the way she had once imagined. It did not lift her up and tell her she was safe now. It did not erase the memory of Boone's yard gathered at dawn, the branding iron glowing, the scream that carried into sleep. It did not answer the question of what had happened to Elijah, or whether he had lived long enough to hear about the bearded man, long enough to imagine a different life before the whip cut the imagining out of him.

Sometimes, in the thin hour before morning, Lila would stand at her window and look down at the alley where stray cats moved like shadows with eyes. She would listen to the city's quiet and feel, beneath it, the old plantation language still ringing in her body: bells, whistles, timed footsteps, the sound of men certain they had placed their trap well.

Here, the trap was uncertainty. The trap was the absence of a clear enemy. The trap was the way silence could be mistaken for peace until the wrong knock came at the door.

She understood then that freedom was not the opposite of slavery. Not in the simple way people liked to talk about. Freedom was a place where the chains were not always visible, where the hand reaching for you might wear a glove and speak softly, where the threat could arrive as a notice nailed to a wall or a question asked with a smile.

The North didn't speak.

It didn't tell her when to relax. It didn't tell her what to believe. It didn't tell her which men were safe and which men carried Samuel's patient hunger in a different suit.

It only gave her days, one after another, and demanded she fill them with caution.

And in that long quiet, Lila learned the truest thing she would ever know about survival.

Silence could be shelter.

Silence could also be a warning.

The difference was not in the sound.

It was in what you did with it.

Chapter 18

After the Mark

The first time Lila smelled burned meat in the North, it came from a street cart.

She was carrying a basket of linens down Willow Street, head lowered against a wind that still had winter's bite left in it, when the smell slid under her nose and took hold. Grease, smoke, char. Ordinary hunger-scent for people who had always been allowed to be hungry in public.

Her body did not understand ordinary.

Her stomach clenched hard, and for an instant the street tilted. The cart's thin smoke became a different smoke. Not food. Not comfort. Heated iron. Hair and skin giving up at once. The sweet, sickly smell that had ridden over the plantation yard at dawn and lodged in every throat that had been forced to breathe it.

She stopped walking without meaning to.

People moved around her. A man bumped her shoulder and muttered, "Watch it," without ever seeing her face. A woman stepped wide with a basket of apples, eyes fixed straight ahead. No one asked if she was ill. No one looked long enough to decide she might be.

The North's silence, Lila had learned, was not gentleness. It was a kind of permission to disappear in plain sight.

Her fingers tightened on the basket handle until her knuckles ached. The smell from the cart thickened as she stood there, and her mind supplied what her eyes did not have to see: a man held down, iron brought forward, the overseer saying nothing because silence could be louder than orders.

Hope will be marked, the memory whispered, not as words but as certainty.

Lila forced her feet to move again. Not fast. Not running. She walked as if she had simply forgotten where she meant to go and remembered it now. She passed the cart without looking. She did not let her face change, because faces were read here in different ways. In the South, a face could be punished for showing the wrong feeling. In the North, a face could be remembered.

At the boarding house, Mrs. G took one look at her and set her mouth into a hard line.

"You seen something," Mrs. G said, not a question.

Lila shook her head once. She carried the basket to the back room and set it down with care, as if carefulness could keep her hands from shaking.

Mrs. G followed, wiping her palms on her apron. "You sick," she said.

"No," Lila lied. Then, because lying took effort she could not spare, she added, quieter, "Just smelled something."

Mrs. G's eyes narrowed, sharpening. She did not ask what. She didn't need to. "You can't let your insides run your feet," she said. "Not here."

Lila swallowed. "I know."

Mrs. G leaned close enough that Lila could smell soap and onions and the smoke that lived in the woman's clothes. "Knowing ain't the same as doing," she replied. Then she straightened, brisk again. "Get yourself water. Then you go back out. You don't let one smell decide your whole day."

One smell, Lila thought as she poured water from the pitcher with hands that wanted to betray her. It was never one smell. It was never one sound. It was always a chain, each link pulling the next.

A bell in the distance became dogs' bells. A sharp laugh became a whip crack in the air. A man's quick step behind her on a sidewalk became boots in the yard, coming for someone who had made the wrong kind of eye contact.

Even quiet had a shape that could turn wrong.

That night, after the house settled and the boarders' voices thinned, Lila climbed the narrow stairs to her room and closed the door. She sat on the edge of the bed and rolled her sleeve up with slow, careful fingers.

The extra cloth Mrs. G had given her lay hidden inside, a second lining meant to keep her secrets from showing through. Lila slid two fingers into the seam and pulled out the thin wire and the worn blue scrap. She held them in her palm, the way some people held coins, the way some people held prayer.

The wire still held its curve, a question mark that had traveled farther than it had any right to. Elijah had made it in the forge with hands that knew how to shape stubborn metal. He had handed it to her with a look that carried more meaning than any safe sentence.

Now the wire's chill felt like a live thing against her skin.

The blue cloth was softer at the edges than it had been, dulled by sweat and hiding and the constant press of her body's heat. But the color was still there, a sliver of sky that refused to fade.

Lila pressed the cloth to her nose.

There was no smell left in it that belonged to Carter's kitchen or Boone's yard. Not really. The North's air had washed it, day by day. But memory didn't rely on truth. It relied on the body's willingness to be taken back.

For a moment she could smell damp earth and rot, the ditch where hands had reached down for her. She could hear the bells chiming bright and hateful. She could feel the mistress's lavender breath close to her face, soft words delivered like a chain.

Do you know what happens when the master thinks something of his is about to be stolen?

The question made her jaw tighten. Up here, men spoke of property with different language, but the law still carried the same idea inside it. A notice nailed to a wall could be a brand without fire. A signature could sear.

She let the cloth fall back into her palm and stared at it until her eyes blurred.

"Don't turn into a hook," the older man in the shed had warned her. Hooks get caught.

Mrs. G had said it different. Don't let their talk crawl inside you until you start making mistakes.

But memory was not talk. Memory was what lived in the body without needing permission. It rose at the wrong times. It arrived on smoke. It hid in grease and candle wax and sudden laughter.

Lila folded the blue cloth and wrapped the wire inside it. Then she opened the seam in her sleeve again and tucked them back into the lining. She smoothed the fabric over the hidden bulge until it looked like nothing at all.

Nothing was safest. The embroidery woman had said that in Carter's parlor.

Lila lay down fully dressed and turned her face toward the wall. She closed her eyes and waited for sleep like it was another kind of guard, one that might or might not show mercy.

It came in pieces.

In the first dream, she was back in the barn, but it was not Boone's barn and not Carter's. It was a room built from every dark place she had ever been trapped. The air smelled of hay and lemon oil at the same time. The floorboards were polished like a parlor, but the walls were rough wood with daylight leaking through thin seams.

Elijah hung there, wrists above his head, but the rope was not rope. It was embroidery thread, pulled too tight, cutting into skin with small, precise cruelty. The embroidery woman sat in the corner stitching calmly, needle moving in and out, in and out.

Samuel stood behind Lila, so close she could feel him without seeing him. His voice was in her ear, steady as a lesson.

"Waiting doesn't make the teeth disappear," he said. "It just gives them time to settle in."

In the dream, Lila tried to turn toward him, but her body wouldn't move. Her feet were pinned to the floor by nails that looked like words, each one stamped with ink: runaway, property, reward.

Elijah lifted his head. His mouth moved.

"Wait," he rasped, the same as before, but this time the word didn't sound like endurance. It sounded like a command given by someone who was already gone.

Lila woke with her throat tight and her mouth dry as dust. The room was dark, but the city outside never went fully black. A faint light seeped in through the curtain like the world refusing to close its eyes.

She sat up and listened.

No bells. No whistles. No dogs.

Only the distant rattle of a wagon, a shout too far away to mean anything, the boarding house settling around sleeping bodies. The North's quiet pressed in.

But her ears still rang with the plantation's language, and she understood something that made her stomach go cold with clarity.

The mark was not only on skin.

Some marks were put on you through your eyes, through your nose, through your memory forced to witness what it could not stop. The branding in the yard had been meant to scar flesh, yes. It had also been meant to brand everyone who watched, to press fear into their minds so deep they carried it like a second spine.

They had tried to do it to her in Boone's barn, too. Show her Elijah broken. Offer her a choice shaped like a trap. Make her believe she could end pain by giving herself over.

She had not said yes. She had not said no. She had waited. She had bitten down on silence until it became leverage.

And still, the memory lingered like smoke that wouldn't clear.

Lila swung her feet off the bed and stood, then immediately regretted it. The room felt too small for standing. She moved to the window and pulled the curtain back just enough to look into the alley.

A cat prowled along the brick wall, tail low, slipping through shadows without ever announcing itself. It paused and looked up, eyes catching light, then moved on.

Lila pressed her fingertips to the glass. It was cold enough to sting. She held the sting on purpose, a small, clean pain to anchor her in this room and not the dream.

Downstairs, a floorboard creaked. Lila froze, every muscle tightening.

A man coughed, then another. A murmur of a voice. Someone shifting in sleep.

Nothing else.

Her body loosened slowly, reluctantly, like a fist unclenching.

This was what the North had given her. Not peace, not forgetting. A new landscape where danger did not always announce itself, where her own mind could become the loudest hunting dog.

She lowered the curtain and turned away from the window. In the dim, she saw her reflection in the washstand mirror, pale and hollow-eyed, hair pinned back too tightly, shoulders held as if bracing for hands.

She stared at herself until the urge to look away passed.

"I'm here," she whispered, voice barely a breath.

The words were not comfort. They were instruction.

She lay back down and forced her body into stillness again. She listened to the boarding house breathe. She listened to her own breath match it, slow and careful.

Memory lingered, yes. It lingered like a stain that didn't wash out no matter how hot the water, no matter how hard you scrubbed.

But lingering was not the same as owning.

Lila closed her eyes and held on to that thin distinction as if it were thread, as if she could stitch herself back together one quiet night at a time without letting the needle become an iron.

The next morning came with rain, thin and persistent, tapping the window like fingers that didn't want to be let in.

Lila rose before the boarding house fully woke, not because she had anywhere to go, but because lying still too long let the past sit up beside her. She washed in cold water that smelled faintly of metal and watched her own hands move as if they belonged to someone else: lift the basin, wring the rag, smooth the dress, pin the hair. Ordinary motions that had once meant nothing now served as proof she could still make herself do what was required.

Downstairs, Mrs. G was already awake, the stove breathing heat into the kitchen. She stood with her back to Lila, stirring something that smelled like oats and water. Not enough sweetness to make it comfort.

"You sleep," Mrs. G said without turning.

Lila paused in the doorway, shoulders held wrong, like she expected to be told she'd done something disobedient just by existing in the room. "Some."

Mrs. G's stirring didn't slow. "Dreaming."

It wasn't a question, and Lila didn't answer it like one. She moved to the table and began slicing yesterday's bread into pieces small enough to stretch. The knife was dull. The work was slow. Slow work gave her mind fewer places to run.

Mrs. G set a bowl in front of her. "Eat."

Lila ate because it was an order and because her body needed it. The first spoonful sat heavy in her mouth. The second went down easier. On the third, she realized her hands were shaking again and forced them still by setting the spoon down between bites.

Mrs. G finally turned. She looked at Lila the way she looked at the lock on the front door, the way she looked at a window left open too long: as a point of risk.

"You keep doing that," Mrs. G said.

Lila's throat tightened. "Doing what."

"Trying to swallow it quiet," Mrs. G replied. "Like if it don't come out your mouth, it don't count."

Lila stared into the thin oats. The surface trembled from her breath. "It counts," she said, voice careful. "It's just… I don't know how to say it."

Mrs. G's eyes hardened, not unkindly. "You don't say it," she corrected. "That's different."

Lila felt heat rise behind her eyes. She blinked it back. Tears made you visible.

Mrs. G leaned a hip against the counter, arms folded. She kept her voice low, practical. "Up here, you keep quiet because quiet keeps you from being taken. Down there, you kept quiet because quiet kept you alive. Don't mix them up so bad you choke."

Lila swallowed. The oats tasted like damp cloth now, like the rag she'd wrung out upstairs. "I'm not choking."

Mrs. G made a small sound in her throat, almost a laugh, but it held no humor. "You got marks nobody sees," she said. "Those are the ones that make you run in place."

Lila's fingers went, without permission, toward her sleeve. She caught herself and curled her hand into a fist under the table.

Mrs. G saw the movement anyway. "What is it," she asked, and then added quickly, "Don't tell me if you can't. I ain't asking for stories to pass around. I'm asking so I know what kind of foolishness might fall out of you at the wrong time."

Foolishness. Lila had heard the word used about her before, on Carter's porch, in the mistress's mouth like sugar hiding poison. Here it landed different. Here it meant Mrs. G was trying to keep the world from taking Lila apart in public.

Lila kept her eyes on the bowl. "It's not… it's not a thing you can use," she said.

Mrs. G's gaze stayed fixed. "Most wounds ain't useful," she replied. "They just hurt."

The kitchen was quiet except for the stove and the rain. A boarder's footsteps crossed the hall outside, slow and heavy, then faded. The boarding house kept breathing, crowded with strangers' lives.

Lila took another bite, forced it down. "They showed me him," she said, and felt her voice change on the last word, thin as a thread pulled too tight.

Mrs. G didn't ask who. She didn't need to. Lila saw it in the way the woman's jaw tightened, in the way her eyes shifted away for half a second as if she'd been forced to picture a thing she didn't want to picture.

"They like to do that," Mrs. G said. "Show you somebody you love and call it your fault."

Lila's nails bit into her palm. "He told me to wait."

Mrs. G's face held still, and Lila understood she'd said too much. The name wasn't spoken, but the truth was there: someone behind her, someone she'd left behind.

"You waiting," Mrs. G said.

It wasn't an accusation. It was a diagnosis.

Lila stared at the oats until the surface blurred. "I don't know what waiting means now," she whispered. "Down there, waiting meant timing. It meant not moving wrong. It meant staying quiet until a door cracked open. Up here, waiting feels like… like I'm just sitting in a room and the room ain't got walls."

Mrs. G pushed off the counter and moved closer, not touching Lila, but standing near enough that Lila could feel her presence like a solid thing. "Up here, waiting means you keep your habits," she said. "You keep your head. You don't go chasing answers that'll get you caught."

Lila's throat burned. "I want to know if he's alive."

Mrs. G's eyes sharpened. "Want is expensive," she said. "Want makes you careless."

Lila heard Samuel's voice in her mind, calm and poisonous: Brave don't keep you fed. Brave don't keep you unbranded. She swallowed hard and tried to force the sound out of her head.

Mrs. G's tone softened by a fraction. "You think if you knew, it would settle something," she said. "Like a bowl put down on a table. But it don't always settle. Sometimes it just changes what haunts you."

Lila's hands trembled again, and she hated the weakness of it. She was in a kitchen, in a northern house, with rain tapping the window. She should have been able to breathe. Instead she felt the barn's damp hay in her nose and saw rope cutting into wrists.

"I can't talk about it," Lila admitted, and the confession felt like stepping onto thin ice. "If I say it out loud, it feels like I'm calling it to me."

Mrs. G nodded once, as if she'd been waiting for that exact sentence. "That's how it works," she said. "You keep it stuffed down and it swells. You let it out wrong and it turns into a shout. Either way, it wants your throat."

Lila looked up then, quick, and met Mrs. G's eyes directly. It was a risk. She felt it in her body like heat. But she needed something to hold on to that wasn't memory.

Mrs. G held the gaze. "You don't got to say names," she said. "Names are hooks. But you got to find a way to let the hurt have air that don't kill you."

Lila's lips parted. No sound came out. She didn't know what to offer besides the truth that lived in her bones: she had been made to watch. She had been made to choose. She had been brought back not to be punished but to be used.

Even in the North, she could feel the shape of hands on her wrists that weren't there.

Mrs. G reached past her and lifted the bread knife off the table. Lila flinched before she could stop herself. The flinch was small, but it was real.

Mrs. G paused with the knife in her hand and looked at Lila, face unreadable. Then she set the knife down on the counter, slow, deliberate, and turned back.

"That," Mrs. G said. "That's the mark that don't show."

Lila's throat tightened with shame, hot and immediate. "I'm sorry."

Mrs. G's eyes narrowed. "Don't be sorry," she snapped softly. "Be honest. That flinch is your body telling the truth your mouth ain't ready for."

Lila's stomach turned. She pushed the bowl away, suddenly unable to eat another bite. "What do I do," she asked, and hated how the question sounded like begging.

Mrs. G didn't answer right away. She picked up a cloth and wiped the counter that wasn't dirty, hands moving because stillness made thinking heavier.

Finally she said, "There's a woman two streets over, Miss Lydia. Colored. She takes in girls sometimes. Not for hiding, for fixing. She don't ask for your whole story. She don't push. She just gives you a place to sit where you ain't being watched for what you might do wrong."

Lila's pulse kicked. "Fixing," she repeated, suspicious of the word.

Mrs. G's mouth tightened. "Ain't no fixing like mending a hem," she said. "But there's learning how to live with yourself without jumping every time the world clears its throat."

Lila stared at her hands. The skin was rough, cracked at the knuckles. Work hands. Survival hands. She thought of Elijah's hands, careful and scarred, shaping metal into tools. She thought of them hanging useless above him, and the thought made her chest constrict.

"What if I go," Lila whispered, "and I start talking and I can't stop."

Mrs. G's gaze didn't waver. "Then you stop," she said. "You learn where the edge is. Talking ain't the same as bleeding."

Lila let the words sit in her chest. She didn't know if she believed them. She only knew she was tired of waking with the taste of iron in her mouth and calling it nothing.

"And there's another thing," Mrs. G added.

Lila's eyes lifted.

Mrs. G's voice lowered. "You keep something in that sleeve," she said. "You keep touching it like a tooth you can't leave alone."

Lila's hand went again toward her sleeve, and she stopped it, too late. She felt caught, even here.

Mrs. G sighed. "I ain't asking what it is," she said. "I'm telling you this: if you carry it, you carry it with sense. Wrapped. Hidden. Not for me. For you. Because one day your hand's going to go there in front of the wrong person, and then your private hurt becomes their business."

Lila nodded slowly. The warning wasn't cruel. It was the kind of warning Mary would have given if Mary could have stood in this kitchen in the North.

Mrs. G turned toward the stove and began stirring again, the conversation dismissed in the only way she knew how: by returning to what kept them fed.

But Lila sat still a moment longer, feeling the unspoken wound in her chest shift, not healed, not gone, just disturbed enough to remind her it was alive.

When she finally stood, her knees felt weak. She steadied herself against the table edge, and the motion made her think of the brick wall she'd touched in the street, grounding herself with something solid.

Mrs. G spoke without looking back. "You go see Lydia after supper," she said. "Not alone. You take the long way and you don't look like you're sneaking. You look like you got errands because you do."

"Yes," Lila said.

She moved through the day with the boarding house's rhythm around her: scrubbing, carrying, mending, keeping her face arranged into calm. But under the work, something had shifted. Not hope, not relief. A new kind of dread.

Because to speak even without names meant admitting the mark existed beyond memory. It meant admitting that what had been done to her could live in her body and shape her reactions long after the plantation had been left behind.

In the late afternoon, a boarder came into the front hall shaking rain off his hat and said loudly, "They caught two runaways over by the river. Dragged 'em back south."

Lila's hands went cold. She kept sweeping as if she hadn't heard.

The boarder kept talking, enjoying the sound of his own information. "Sheriff helped. Said it was the law. Folks clapped like it was a show."

Lila's broom paused for half a heartbeat, then resumed.

A show. The plantation had always loved a show. Up here, they called it law and still let people clap.

Lila felt her sleeve press against her forearm, the hidden wire and cloth and extra lining creating a small weight there, like a stone carried in a pocket. She kept sweeping until her shoulders burned.

Unspoken wounds, she realized, were not only the stories you couldn't tell.

They were also the ways you learned to keep moving while the world described your terror as ordinary news.

And when evening came and Mrs. G handed her a shawl and pointed her toward the door as if she were sending her out for flour, Lila stepped into the wet street with her mouth closed and her heart hammering, carrying her silence like a careful, dangerous package.

Not because she believed silence would save her.

Because she was beginning to understand it might be the only thing she could choose that still belonged entirely to her.

Rain slicked the street into a long, dark mirror. Gaslight and windowlight broke on it in thin, trembling pieces that looked like fire trying not to admit it was wet. Lila walked with her head slightly bowed, not in the old posture of forced submission, but in the newer one Mrs. G had taught her: the posture of a woman who did not invite questions.

Her shawl was rough wool and smelled faintly of smoke from the boarding house stove. It scratched at the back of her neck, a steady irritation that kept her anchored in her skin. She held her hands low and empty. She carried no basket. Mrs. G had said errands, and errands did not need props if you walked like you had a destination.

She took the long way, as instructed, through streets that changed character block by block. On one corner, men stood under an awning and argued about the war as if the war were a play they'd paid to see. On another, a woman in a clean bonnet drew her child closer when Lila passed, a small movement so practiced it might have been breathing.

Lila did not look back.

A wagon rolled past, wheels grinding over stone, and the sound came with a wrong edge. For a second she heard it as Boone's yard waking up, the scrape of a metal ring, the drag of a chain over packed earth. She forced her mind to name what it was: a wagon. A city sound. Here.

Still, her body kept its own language. Her shoulders tightened. Her mouth went dry.

At the next corner, a man whistled. Just one sharp note, careless, meant for a horse or a friend. The sound struck Lila so hard she stopped moving for half a heartbeat. She saw, bright and immediate, the dark woods and the ditch and lanternlight cutting through weeds. She felt hands on her wrist.

She made herself walk again, steady, as if she had merely paused to avoid stepping in a puddle. She counted her steps until the tightness in her chest loosened enough to breathe through.

Mrs. G had said quiet just means you got to listen different. Lila listened now not for obvious danger, but for patterns. Too many footsteps behind her. The pause of a stranger's gaze that lingered too long. The feeling of being measured.

The house Mrs. G had directed her to looked like any other narrow city home pressed tight between its neighbors. Brick, stained darker near the base where rainwater had kissed it for years. A single lamp burning in the front window, its light turned low. Curtains drawn, but not all the way.

A place that wanted to appear ordinary.

Lila climbed the steps and lifted her hand. For a moment she hesitated, not because she did not want to go in, but because doors were never only doors. Doors were thresholds where you became something else in someone else's eyes.

She knocked.

The sound was small, swallowed by rain.

Footsteps came from inside, soft and quick. The door opened just enough to show a Black woman's face, older than Lila, her hair wrapped in a scarf patterned with faded flowers. Her eyes were alert, not unkind, but not giving anything away.

"Yes," the woman said, the same flatness Mrs. G had used the first time she'd opened her own door.

"I was told to come," Lila answered, keeping her voice low. "Mrs. G sent me."

The woman's gaze moved once over Lila's face, then down to her shoes, then back up. Not a curious look. A careful one, as if she was confirming Lila was the kind of trouble that could be managed.

The chain on the door did not rattle. There was no chain. The woman opened it wider and stepped back. “Come in and shut it quick,” she said. “You dripping rain all over my floor.”

Lila stepped inside. Warmth wrapped around her immediately, not the clean warmth of comfort, but the lived-in warmth of a stove used hard. The air smelled of herbs and boiled cloth, and underneath it, something sharp like vinegar. A table stood near the back with a basin; clean rags stacked beside it. Shelves held jars, some labeled, some not.

The woman shut the door and slid a bolt into place. The click made Lila’s stomach jump anyway.

The woman turned. “You got a name you answering to,” she said, and it was not asked like friendliness. It was asked like a tool.

Lila kept her hands at her sides. “Lila,” she said, and immediately wished she hadn’t. The name felt too loose in the room, too easy to carry.

The woman’s face did not change. “All right,” she replied. “I’m Lydia.”

Not Miss Lydia. Not ma’am. Just Lydia, said like they were equals in a world that refused to treat them that way.

Lila's throat tightened. "Mrs. G said you… you take in girls sometimes."

Lydia made a sound that might have been humor. "Girls," she repeated, and there was a weary edge to it. "You old enough to work a grown woman's hours, ain't you."

"Yes."

"Then don't come in here trying to be small." Lydia walked past Lila, gesturing toward a chair near the stove. "Sit. Hands where I can see them."

The command again, like the shawled woman on the night Lila left Carter's house. Lila sat, spine straight, palms resting open on her knees. She could feel her sleeve lining press against her forearm; the hidden cloth and wire and pin crowded together like a secret that had learned to bruise.

Lydia pulled another chair close but did not sit. She stood over Lila the way a person stood over a pot waiting for it to boil, attentive without tenderness. "You been having spells," Lydia said.

Lila's mouth went dry. "Mrs. G told you."

"She told me enough," Lydia replied. "She didn't tell me your whole story, and I don't want it. Whole stories are how folks get themselves in trouble. But she told me you flinch at the wrong things, you go quiet too hard, and you walk around like the ground might open and swallow you."

Lila stared at the floorboards, at the gaps between them that held dust. "I'm fine," she said, because it was what she had always said. Fine was a shield word.

Lydia's voice sharpened. "Fine is a lie people tell when they think the truth will get them punished." She paused, then added, lower, "Sometimes it will. In this house, it won't."

Lila swallowed. Her heartbeat was loud in her ears. "I don't know what I'm supposed to do," she admitted.

Lydia finally sat, not across from Lila like an interrogator, but beside her, angled slightly toward the stove as if they were simply two women sharing warmth. "You listen," Lydia said. "Not to me telling you how to feel. To your body telling you what it remembers."

Lila's hands curled slightly on her knees. "My body remembers things that ain't here."

"That's the point," Lydia replied. "Memory don't need the thing to still be present. It needs a sound, a smell, a shadow shaped close enough to the old shape. Then it climbs right up out of you."

Lila's lips parted. She could not find the right word that wasn't a name. Carter. Boone. Samuel. Elijah. Each name felt like a hook.

Lydia watched her struggle and nodded as if she could see the shapes anyway. "You don't have to speak them," Lydia said. "But you do have to stop pretending the North erased them. The North don't erase. It just changes the way the hurt echoes."

Echoes. The word sat in Lila's chest like a stone. She whispered, "It's quieter here."

Lydia's laugh held no joy. "Quieter," she said. "Baby, it's only quieter because folks up here learned to keep their cruelty polite. A man don't have to shout to steal you. He can smile. He can show a paper. He can put a hand on your elbow like he helping you across a street."

Lila's stomach turned. "I saw a notice," she said, and the words came out before she could stop them. "Runaway."

Lydia nodded once. "You going to keep seeing them. And you going to keep hearing folks talk about rewards like it's weather. That's one echo." She leaned forward and reached for a small jar on the table, unscrewing the lid. The smell that rose was sharp and green. "Smell this."

Lila hesitated.

“Smell it,” Lydia repeated, not unkind, but firm.

Lila leaned in and breathed through her nose. The scent stung, clean and biting, like crushed leaves. It made her eyes water.

“What you feel,” Lydia asked.

“My nose burning,” Lila said, voice rough.

“Good,” Lydia replied. “That’s now. That’s present. When your mind goes running back, you give it something that belongs to where your feet are.”

Lila blinked hard, eyes watering, and the sting pulled her out of the tight coil inside her chest for a moment. Her breath came easier.

Lydia capped the jar and set it down. “You got something on you,” she said, and it wasn’t a question this time.

Lila’s hand moved toward her sleeve before she could stop it.

Lydia caught her wrist gently, not gripping, but stopping the motion. The touch made Lila’s muscles lock anyway. Lydia felt it and did not let go, did not tighten. She waited until Lila’s body understood it was not being seized.

“You keep reaching for it,” Lydia said softly. “Like a tooth, like Mrs. G told me. That thing is part comfort and part poison.”

Lila's throat tightened. "It's all I got."

"It might be," Lydia agreed. "But you don't let it own your hands. You don't let it pull you out of yourself in front of strangers."

Lila stared at Lydia's hand on her wrist. The touch was steady, patient. Not Samuel's patience. Not a trap. A different kind.

"I can hear things," Lila whispered. "Sometimes. Bells. Whistles." She swallowed, forcing the next truth through. "Even when they ain't there."

Lydia released her wrist and leaned back. "That's an echo," she said. "Your mind learned a language that kept you alive. You don't just forget a language because the scenery changes. You translate it. That's what we doing."

Lila's breath hitched. "What if it means I'm not right."

Lydia looked at her then, fully. Her gaze was tired but sure. "You right enough," Lydia said. "You here, ain't you. You working. You watching. You still got sense." She paused. "What you got is a mark that didn't get put on your skin. And that mark don't care what state line you crossed."

The stove popped softly, settling. Outside, rain kept tapping the window, thin fingers insisting on being heard.

Lydia stood. “I’m going to make you tea,” she said. “Then we going to talk about how to walk through a street without jumping every time a man clears his throat.”

Lila nodded, throat too tight to speak.

As Lydia moved at the stove, the room filled with the sound of ordinary life: a kettle set down, a cup placed on a table, a spoon stirring. Small, domestic sounds that should have been harmless.

But Lila heard another layer beneath them, a faint rhythm that wasn’t there and still was. Tap tap. Pause. Tap.

A signal remembered.

She closed her eyes for a second and breathed in the sharp green scent still lingering on her skin. Present, she told herself. Now.

When she opened her eyes again, Lydia was watching her over the rim of the kettle, not with suspicion, but with recognition so direct it made Lila’s stomach ache.

“You hear it too, don’t you,” Lydia said quietly.

Lila’s mouth went dry. “Hear what.”

Lydia nodded toward the front of the house, toward the door, toward the street beyond it. "Footsteps that stop when they shouldn't," she said. "A pause outside like somebody deciding whether you worth the trouble."

Lila's blood went cold. She listened hard, and there it was: not loud, not certain, but a shift in the rain's pattern, a presence near the stoop, a stillness that did not belong to weather.

An echo, her mind tried to tell her. A memory.

But Lydia's face had gone still in a way that belonged to now.

Lydia set the kettle down without a sound. She walked to the window and lifted the curtain the smallest amount, barely enough to see. She looked for one breath, then let the curtain fall back.

Her voice, when she spoke, was calm, but it had edges. "You sit still," she said. "And you don't reach for your sleeve."

Lila's hands went flat on her knees again, palms open, as if obedience could make her invisible.

Lydia moved toward the door, steps quiet, and paused with her ear near the wood. The house held its breath.

Then, from outside, came a soft knock.

Not loud. Not insistent.

Polite.

The kind of knock that expected to be answered. The kind of knock that did not belong to someone afraid of being seen.

Lila felt the sound in her bones like a whistle heard through trees. She did not move.

Lydia's hand hovered near the bolt, not lifting it.

"Who is it," Lydia called, her voice steady and ordinary, as if she were answering a neighbor asking for sugar.

A man's voice came back through the door, smooth as oiled hinges. "Evening," he said. "Sorry to trouble you. I'm looking for a girl. Young. Runs with a boarding house down Willow. Heard she might've come this way."

Lila's throat closed. She could taste iron.

Lydia did not look back at her, but her next words were pitched just right, for Lila alone to understand without anyone outside hearing the change in them.

"Echoes," Lydia murmured, almost soundless.

Then, louder, to the door: "You got the wrong house," she said. "We ain't taking visitors."

The man chuckled softly, like the matter amused him. "No harm meant," he replied. "Just doing my job. There's folks offering good money for information."

Good money. Currency. Samuel's language, in a different mouth.

Lila sat frozen, every muscle tight, listening to the rain and the silence between Lydia's breaths, understanding with a clarity that felt like terror made clean: in the North, the hunt could arrive smiling, and the knock could sound like manners.

And behind the polite voice on the other side of the door, the system waited, patient as ever, for someone to make a mistake it could call proof.

To Be Continued

The North Still Watches

www.ingramcontent.com/pod-product-compliance
Lightning Source LLC
LaVergne TN
LVHW050909080826
845145LV00001B/18

* 9 7 8 1 9 6 9 7 7 0 5 1 7 *